Bloody Lessons
A Victorian San Francisco Mystery

By M. Louisa Locke

This book is a work of fiction. Names, characters, places, and incidents are either the product of the author's imagination or are used fictitiously, and any resemblance to actual persons, living or dead, business establishments, events, or locales is entirely coincidental. Chapter quotes, unless otherwise noted, come from the *San Francisco Chronicle*.

"A true teacher is one who, keeping the past alive, is also able to understand the present."
Confucius, *Analects 2.11*

This book is dedicated to all the teachers in my life.

M. Louisa Locke's Victorian San Francisco Series
(in chronological order)

Maids of Misfortune (novel)
Dandy Detects (short story)
Uneasy Spirits (novel)
The Misses Moffet Mend a Marriage (short story)
Bloody Lessons (novel)

Chapter One
Wednesday, late afternoon, January 7, 1880

"It takes double the capacity, ingenuity, patience and experience to teach a child five years old that it does one of ten." —Mr. Slade, Quincey Board of Education speaking at the California State Teacher's Association, *San Francisco Chronicle*, 1880

Laura Dawson surveyed the row of long division problems she had written on the blackboard. Noting the blurring of a number in the third problem, she frowned, took the eraser, and scrubbed away the offending numeral, replacing it with a neatly written seven that could not be misinterpreted as a one. Thank goodness San Francisco's Clement Grammar School was only four years old, so the slate board that filled the entire back of the room didn't have the chips and scratches that marred the board in the Cupertino Creek School, the rural one-room school west of San Jose where she taught this past fall. Picking up a list of words from her desk, she began copying them carefully onto the board. For some reason, words she had known how to spell since she was five came out wrong when she wrote them for all to see, and she wanted to avoid the humiliation she'd felt back at Cupertino Creek when the pert seven-year-old Daisy pointed out her errors to the whole class, accompanied by the snickers of seventeen-year-old Buck Morrison, who slouched insolently in the last row.

Laura hadn't admitted to anyone how badly her first teaching assignment had gone. None of the lectures on pedagogy at the San Jose Normal School had prepared her for how difficult it was to maintain discipline when a one-room school held thirty students, ranging from a five-year-old who couldn't sit still for more than fifteen minutes to a seventeen-year-old with the body of a man and the maturity of a boy half his age.

Then there was the local wildlife that would drop by just as she got everyone settled down to work at their slates. She shuddered at the memory of the mother skunk that had constructed her nest under the floorboards.

The school board examiner had given her a commendation for her pupils' progress, but she thought that this gentleman was mostly impressed she'd stuck out the full term, something the last two teachers failed to do. Perhaps he hoped if he praised her enough she would stay on. Laura felt a twinge of guilt, because that commendation had helped pave the way for her new position, teaching a seventh grade class at the Clement Grammar in San Francisco. However, she was determined to do better with this new job, which was why she was still hard at work preparing for tomorrow's class. This was only the third day of the term, but it was the first time she had sent the students home with an assignment. She hoped they would be ready for the math test she had planned for the beginning of class tomorrow.

"Miss Dawson, are you ready to go? Mother said we should be home before five because it gets dark so early."

Laura started and turned. Smiling at the young boy who grinned at her from the doorway, she said, "Good heavens, Jamie, you are quite right. If we aren't careful, your mother will be home before us. We need to get going. Were you able to finish helping Miss Chesterton with her maps?"

"Yes, Miss, and I finished most of my homework, so I'll have time to play with Dandy in the back yard after dinner." Jamie raised the battered yellow book he was carrying, and Laura recognized the *Third Reader*.

Since Jamie was only in the fifth grade and most of her seventh graders were only beginning this text, she deduced that the nine-year-old was an excellent student, not unexpected since his mother taught English literature and composition at San Francisco's Girls' High. Jamie Hewitt and his mother, Barbara, lived in one of the attic rooms of Mrs. Fuller's O'Farrell Street boarding house where Laura now resided. Because she hadn't had much occasion to get acquainted with Mrs. Hewitt, she had been surprised when Jamie's mother asked her yesterday if she would mind walking home with her son on Wednesdays. Evidently, she was the faculty sponsor of the Literature and Debate society that met after school on that day, keeping her quite late.

"Shouldn't take us but five minutes to get home," Laura remarked as she gathered up the pile of books sitting on the corner of the desk. "Thank goodness it is all downhill; I'm not used to being on my feet all day." Laura slid the books into the leather satchel her parents gave her when she graduated from the Normal School last May. Threading her way through the rows of student desks, she carefully skewered her small curly-brimmed brown hat on her head with a hat pin and then took the matching light-wool cloak from the peg at the back of the room. She shrugged into the cloak as she turned to check that she'd left the classroom in good order. Pulling on her gloves, she left the door open and the lights on as she had been instructed so the janitor, Mr. Ferguson, could clean the room. As she and Jamie walked down the long gas-lit hallway to stairs at the center of the building, she saw that all the other classroom doors on the third floor were shut, which probably meant that Mr. Ferguson was now working on the second floor classrooms. She hoped she hadn't inconvenienced him by staying late.

Once at the school's entrance, she pushed the heavy front door open and stopped, enchanted by the sight of Geary Street transformed by fog. Monday and Tuesday, the first two days of the term, she had noticed that Geary, one of the city's main thoroughfares, was very crowded and noisy at this time of evening. Businessmen headed west on foot and in hansom cabs to their firesides in the Western Addition, while a stream of wagons, carts, and day laborers went in the opposite direction towards downtown. Tonight, the combination of twilight and fog muted the usual rattle of harnesses, clip clop of hooves, and human voices. Instead, on sidewalk and street, ghostly shapes passed each other, with only the flickering shaft of gas light at the corner of Jones Street providing proof of their corporality.

"My stars, Miss, can't see your hand in front of your face!" Jamie exclaimed, as he crammed a cap on his light brown curls. "I hope my mother is already home. She hates fog something awful. Said it reminds her of the blizzards when she was a child."

"Blizzards! I never thought of them being similar. We had lots of fog on the ranch where I grew up east of San Jose. Sometimes you would just have to let the horse find the way home. But snow so thick you couldn't see, that would be frightening. Where about did your mother grow up?" asked Laura.

There was silence, and Laura glanced down at Jamie, puzzled to see his brown eyes slide away from hers, as if he were embarrassed.

"Oh, somewhere back east," he finally replied, shrugging.

They reached Jones Street and turned right, which would take them down the gentle incline towards O'Farrell Street where the boarding house was located. *My new home,* Laura thought, although she wasn't sure why, never having considered the private houses she had lived in while she attended the Normal School as home. Maybe that was because most weekends she usually went back to her parents' ranch, located just over an hour by horseback east of San Jose.

She certainly hadn't considered the series of houses she'd boarded in last fall as home. There were eight families with children in the small Cupertino Creek district, and part of her salary came in the form of room and board from each of them. This meant moving every two weeks to live with a new family. The bed bugs in one house, the unwashed sheets in another, and the uncomfortable sofa that she had been expected to sleep on in one home had been bad enough, but nothing had prepared her for what happened in the last house when…

"Come, Miss, we best hot-foot it across O'Farrell while the road's clear." Jamie grabbed her hand, his sunny nature having reasserted itself. He pulled her swiftly across the street, well clear of the wagon that was materializing out of the fog. "Shall we cross Jones here? I always go down to the alley, so's I can go in the back way. Unless you have a key and want to go in the front?"

Laura shook off the bad memories and smiled, telling Jamie the back way would be fine. She let the boy escort her safely across Jones, and they turned right to go the half block to the alley. Annie Fuller, the young widow who owned the boarding house, had given her a key to the front door, but the thought of going in through the kitchen was appealing. Beatrice O'Rourke, the cook and housekeeper, had been very welcoming on Monday when she arrived home from her first day of teaching. Mrs. O'Rourke, a stout motherly woman with a lyrical Irish brogue, had given Laura a cup of tea while peppering her with questions about her day. Everyone in the boarding house was very friendly. Even the ancient ladies who lived in the attic across from the Hewitts fussed over her at dinner. Well, one of them did; the other just smiled sweetly and nodded. Hard to imagine that only twelve days ago she had been sitting in her parents' kitchen, reading a letter from her friend Hattie that told her there was a teaching position waiting for her up in San Francisco if she wanted it.

She had jumped at the chance! She'd already obtained the highest level California Teaching Certificate, which qualified her to teach in any California school, and Annie Fuller, who was visiting the ranch, had immediately offered to rent her a room. Laura's older brother, Nate, was courting Annie, and he'd brought her to the ranch right after Christmas to meet his family. Laura was delighted with Annie's offer, and Nate solemnly assured his parents that he and Mrs. Fuller would both keep an eye on her. They stressed how close Clement Grammar was to Annie's boarding house and the respectability of the other boarders, including the wealthy businessman Mr. Herman Stein and his wife Esther who occupied the suite of rooms across the hall from where Laura would be staying.

Laura was rather glad Nate hadn't felt the need to mention that Annie supplemented her income from the boarding house by working as a clairvoyant named Madam Sibyl who pretended to draw on supernatural powers when giving investment advice to prominent San Francisco businessmen. Laura's father had been upset enough over his daughter not completing a full year of teaching at the Cupertino Creek School, muttering about obligations. Because Laura had already confided to her mother her unhappiness at Cupertino, Mrs. Dawson quickly supported the move to San Francisco. Her father then capitulated, as he usually did, deferring to her mother.

So, here she was, where she had always hoped to be, living and working in San Francisco. Jamie moved ahead of her now that traffic on the sidewalk had thinned, reaching the alley that ran behind the section of O'Farrell Street where the boarding house was located. When he turned to look back at her, she smiled and made shooing motions, indicating he should run ahead. No doubt the boy was anxious to play with Dandy, his small snub-nosed terrier. As he disappeared around the corner, Laura speculated about why this particular row of houses had gotten an alleyway, which was pretty rare as far as she could determine, at least in this section of San Francisco. Someone of importance must have built here in the fifties, someone with the money to keep their own stables and horses and require a back entrance.

By the time she reached the opening to the alley, Jamie had been swallowed up by the fog, which seemed impenetrable here away from the street lamps. Picking her way slowly down what felt like a country path, hemmed in as it was by the tall back hedges from the houses on either side, Laura wondered if she would have a letter from Hattie today. Hattie Wilks had been her best friend at San Jose Normal School, and Laura always hoped they would end up teaching in the same school. In fact, Hattie's first job was at Clement Grammar, and when Laura heard from Hattie about the mid-year opening in San Francisco, she thought they would now be colleagues. It was only when she arrived at her interview at Clement Grammar that she learned the opening was actually for Hattie's job. Hattie had resigned, recommending that Laura be hired as her replacement. She'd written to Hattie as soon as she got home from the interview, asking her what had happened. That was five days ago. Still no answer from Hattie. *Maybe in today's mail…*

Laura's thoughts scattered as a body slammed into her, knocking her to her knees. *Drat this fog, I must have run into someone.*

Muttering an apology, she was reaching for her fallen satchel when she felt arms around her waist, jerking her up and backwards. Struggling against what felt like a nightmare become real, Laura clawed at the arms holding her. But the man was too strong. Her ribs felt like they were cracking, and she couldn't get away from his filthy words.

"Bitch, you stupid bitch. Did you think I wouldn't find where you lived? You ruined my life, and you'll have to pay."

Chapter Two
Wednesday, evening, January 7, 1880
"120 O'FARRELL—NICE SUNNY Furnished rooms, double and single. —
San Francisco Chronicle, 1880

Annie Fuller was angry. No, she was furious. How could this have happened? How could she ever face Nate's parents? What could she say to explain how their daughter, who they had so reluctantly handed over into her care, had been assaulted, practically at her doorstep? And Nate, what would he do when she told him?

She pulled the shawl more closely around Laura, who sat huddled in the boarding house kitchen rocker by the old cook stove, and the girl curled into herself further, her face hidden by the long strands of dark hair that had escaped from the neatly coiled braid at the back of her head.

Or at least the coil had been neat this morning when Laura left the boarding house on her way to work. Annie had refrained from saying goodbye to her young boarder at that time since she was already costumed as Madam Sibyl, a scarlet shawl over her old black silk, a medusa-like black wig covering her own reddish-blond hair, and white powder hiding the light dusting of freckles that were scattered across her nose. She preferred not to interact with anyone but Sibyl's clients when she was dressed this way. Instead, she'd gone to the window of the small parlor where she met those clients and peeped through the curtains at the younger woman, noting the similarities between Laura and her older brother Nate. Both were tall, straight-backed, and dark-haired, with long-legged strides. Laura's skin was paler, and, thank goodness, she didn't have her brother's nose, which gave him the look of a bird of prey. But they both were graced by the dark brown and slightly oblique eyes and the high cheekbones that recalled their distant Shawnee ancestor.

Watching as Laura walked confidently up the sidewalk, her shoulders thrown back as if she was going into battle, Annie had felt such pride in the young woman. She knew that Laura was going to work early because she was determined to excel at her new teaching position. Yet now the poor girl sat in the kitchen, mud smeared on the lower half of her skirt, her hair in disarray, her confidence gone, and shivering in fear because of some brute. *I could strangle whoever it was with my bare hands!*

Thank heavens her young maid Kathleen had had the good sense to run upstairs and get her as soon as Jamie arrived in the kitchen with Laura in tow. Annie, just changed out of her Madam Sibyl costume after her last client for the day, ran downstairs to find the kitchen in complete chaos. Jamie's high, excited voice was being drowned out by the small terrier's barking and his mother's admonitions to her son to control his dog. The agitated exclamations of Beatrice, her cook and housekeeper, added to the confusion, while Laura stood silently in their midst, wringing her hands.

Annie had taken one look at the scene and gone over to pull the damp cloak off Laura's shoulders, handing it to Beatrice and asking her to fix a pot of strong tea. She then removed Laura's gloves, rubbed her hands, and urgently asked if she had been hurt. Did she need to see a doctor? When Laura whispered no, that she had just been frightened, Annie led her over to the rocking chair, taking the shawl from its back and wrapping it around her young boarder. Next, she'd instructed David Chapman, one of the other boarders who'd followed her into the kitchen, to go out to the alley and check to see if the man who had accosted Laura was gone. Chapman, a tall, awkwardly put together man in his early thirties, had nodded, picked up the lantern that the maid Kathleen held out to him, and gone briskly out the back door.

As Beatrice handed Laura a cup of tea, Annie tried to stifle her anger and turned to Jamie, asking him to tell her exactly what had happened.

The boy took a deep breath. "Oh, Mrs. Fuller, you see, I'd run ahead down the alley. We were on our way home from Clement Grammar. Mother asked me to wait and come home with Miss Dawson. I asked if it would be all right to come the back way since that's the way I usually come, and she said yes. I would have never have done so if I'd known what would happen. I would never have put Miss Dawson in danger. I should have stayed with her the whole way. It's what a gentleman would do. I am ever so sorry."

Annie moved quickly to give the young boy a hug, fearing he was going to dissolve in tears, saying, "Jamie, dear, I am sure Miss Dawson isn't blaming you; just tell me what happened next, there's a good boy."

He visibly pulled himself together and continued. "Miss Dawson waved that I should go on, so I ran down the alley and into the yard through the back gate. Dandy was there waiting for me. I just popped my head in the kitchen, Mrs. O'Rourke and Mother were there, and I told them I was going to walk Dandy back up the alley to meet Miss Dawson. I snapped the lead onto his collar, and we went back out the gate. Couldn't have been but a minute. As we entered the alley, Dandy began to bark. He jerked so hard on the lead he pulled it right out of my hand and ran snarling into the fog. I was afraid there was another dog, and I didn't want Miss Dawson to get frightened, so I ran right behind him, yelling for him to stop. I couldn't see a thing; night had come on so sudden. I think I fell once."

Jamie looked down at the mud on his knees, shaking his head. "Then a light went on in the second story of the Sanderson's house. You know how their house goes almost all the way back to the alley. I could just make out that there was some man who had grabbed Miss Dawson. They were struggling, and Dandy was leaping and snapping at the man, you know how high he can jump. The man kicked at him, but then I heard a shout from the Sanderson's, and the man just turned, ran back down the alley, and disappeared. Maybe I should'a gone after him, but I went to Miss Dawson. She was crouched down and holding Dandy to her. He was licking her face. I put him back on the lead and brought Miss Dawson home."

"Oh, Jamie, it looks like you and Dandy saved the day once more." Annie smiled warmly at him. "You did just right. Beatrice, do get down a treat for Dandy. He certainly deserves it, and maybe he will settle down."

The small black and white dog, who Jamie said was a Boston terrier, had been barking and leaping, as if to illustrate his prodigious ability to spring up four times his diminutive height. When Beatrice pulled out the jerky she kept in a jar on the windowsill, Dandy trotted over, his tiny crooked tail whirling, and sat down at her feet, his wide mouth open in a doggy smile.

Now that the kitchen was finally quiet, the only sound the bubbling of the celery soup on the stove, Annie turned back to Laura and said, "Do you know who the man was? Did you recognize him?"

Laura shook her head in the negative and whispered, "I never saw his face. It all happened so quickly."

Annie turned to Jamie, whose mother had pulled him close to where she was sitting at the old, scarred kitchen table, and said, "Could you tell anything about him? How tall he was, anything?"

"He was taller than Miss Dawson but not by much. He had on a hat, pulled low, and I think he was wearing a scarf, so's you couldn't see but a bit of his face."

"What about his clothes? Did he seem to be some sort of street tough?" asked his mother.

Annie nodded at this astute question. The young hoodlums of San Francisco, with their short dark jackets and tight, light-colored pants, had a style as distinct as that of the city's prosperous gentlemen. When Jamie shrugged, she turned back to Laura. "Did you have any impression of him at all? Young, old, well-dressed?"

Laura shifted away from her and said, "No, no, I can't think. He was strong. I couldn't move. I didn't see anything. Then Jamie yelled, and Dandy came running up, and the man was gone."

"Did he say anything? Do you think he was trying to rob you?" Annie asked.

"Yes, no, he was saying something…low, filthy words. I don't remember. I don't know what he meant." Laura then sat up straight and began to rise, saying, "Oh! My satchel, it fell to the ground. All my school books were in it. Whatever will I do if it is gone? I must look for it."

As if on cue, the back kitchen door opened, letting in cold, mist-laden air. David Chapman entered, holding the lantern in one hand, and in the other he shook a leather satchel in triumph. "Miss Dawson, look what I found, kicked under the bushes behind the house three doors down."

The entrance of Chapman with her satchel seemed to galvanize Laura. She stood up, took the satchel from Chapman, moved over to the kitchen table, and rapidly pulled out four books, stacking them in a pile. She upended the satchel, and a small notebook and some sort of official record book fell out, followed by a small beaded purse. She opened up the purse, seemed satisfied with its contents, and sighed, clearly relieved.

Annie came over to her and quietly said, "Is everything there?"

"Yes, everything seems fine. I don't know why I was so worried. I only had a few coins, and who would want a bunch of grammar school books?"

Kathleen interrupted, her blue eyes bright with concern and her dark curls bouncing round her ears, saying, "But Miss, the man wouldn't know that. It must've been some good-for-nothing hooligan. Thought you might be carrying something valuable. I think we should send for Patrick, don't you, Mrs. O'Rourke?"

Patrick McGee was Beatrice O'Rourke's nephew and a member of San Francisco's police force, as Beatrice's departed husband had been. He was also Kathleen's devoted beau, and Annie wasn't surprised at her suggestion.

"Isn't he stationed past Van Ness?" Annie responded. "I don't sus-pect his superiors would be pleased he left his post. But I do think that we should tell Mr. Stanley, our own patrolman, what happened. Mr. Chapman, could we impose on you again and ask that you go out on O'Farrell and look for him?"

"Oh, Mrs. Fuller, is that necessary?" Laura agitatedly pushed the books and notebooks back into her satchel and held it to her chest as if it were a shield. "There is so little I have to tell him. I just want to forget about it."

Annie was torn. She sympathized with Laura's desire to put the incident behind her, which was exactly how she would have responded if something similar—when something similar—happened to her, but she also felt that the younger woman wasn't being completely forthcoming. She didn't know Nate's younger sister that well, having met her less than two weeks ago. But from the way that Nate had always described Laura, Annie would have expected her to be more angry than frightened, at least once the first shock was over. Her behavior made Annie feel uneasy. *If only Nate were here.* This thought prompted her to look at the kitchen clock. It was a little before six. Nate should be here by eight at the latest. Annie no longer scheduled clients for Wednesday evenings, since this was the one night Nate could routinely get away early enough from the law offices to see her during the week.

She made a swift decision. "Laura, you don't have to speak to Mr. Stanley. I will. In fact, why don't you go on up to your room, and Kathleen will prepare a bath for you."

Laura visibly relaxed and smiled at her. "Oh, a bath sounds lovely. But I know it's near dinnertime. I don't want to be a bother."

Beatrice came up to her and patted her on the shoulder. "Now dearie, don't you worry. There's plenty of hot water in the stove's reservoir; it won't take a moment for Kathleen to fill the hip bath. Mercy me, half of the boarders who are home are standing right here in the kitchen, so's none of them are going to fuss about dinner being a tad bit late. Besides, all I have left to do is the chops, and that won't take but a moment. Now Jamie, my boy, why don't you let your ma take you up to change out of those muddy pants, and you can tell Miss Minnie and Miss Millie dinner will be at quarter past. Dandy, our hero, can stay down here with me."

Annie's heart warmed as she watched the older woman take command. Beatrice had first been a parlor maid in the home of Annie's aunt and uncle, back when Annie was a young girl. Then she left service and became the respectable wife of a San Francisco police captain. When her husband was killed in the line of duty, she again returned to the O'Farrell Street house, this time as the housekeeper and cook, a position she retained when Annie inherited the house two years ago. She was in her late fifties, short of stature, excitable, opinionated, cheerful, and of unwavering good sense, and Annie loved her.

Chapman, hearing the voice of authority, nodded to Mrs. O'Rourke and politely permitted Barbara Hewitt and Jamie to precede him up the back stairs. Kathleen went into the laundry room to get the tin hip bath, and Annie went over to Laura and put her arm around her. "You will feel more yourself once you have a bath and get warm. After you are done, you can join me in my room for a light supper. Before you know it, your brother will be here. I am sure you will feel better then."

"Oh, no. I can't see Nate, not tonight. I don't feel strong enough… he'd see…" Laura stopped speaking and gave a little shake, pushing her hair back from her face. She began to speak more calmly. "Please, would you tell him what happened? Tell him that I am perfectly well but that I retired early. I know how upset he will be, and I don't feel strong enough to deal with reassuring him that I am all right. And I am; I'm perfectly all right."

Annie said she understood, which she did, having had her own difficulties telling Nate things she knew would upset him. But as she watched Laura leave the kitchen to go to her room, Annie couldn't help but feel that Nate's sister was anything but all right.

Chapter Three
Wednesday, late evening, January 7, 1880

"Mrs. Upham Hendee, Business Medium, 207 Kearny street. Circles Tuesday and Friday evenings, Sittings daily." —*San Francisco Chronicle*, 1880

"What the hell? Why would anyone…was she hurt?" Nate stopped, feeling like he had been punched in the gut. His little sister, attacked. He couldn't breathe.

Annie slid closer to him on the parlor settee and squeezed his hand, saying, "She's fine. She will probably have a few bruises, but Kathleen who attended her at her bath reported that she didn't see any cuts or swelling."

He put his other hand over hers, its warmth providing a small comfort. He took a deep breath and said, "Good, good. And this happened in the back alley? When?"

"Yes, Nate. I told you. Laura and Jamie were coming back from school a little before five."

Nate thought about the thick fog he had waded through this evening on his way from his law offices to Annie's house. How dark it had seemed walking the half a block up from where he got off the horsecar at Taylor. The alley would have been pitch black. He imagined how frightening it would be for his sister to have a man lunge out of the darkness at her.

He felt a new spurt of anger. "It would have been dark by then; why the devil did they come the back way?"

"Since he doesn't have a front door key, Jamie is used to going that way when he comes home. Honestly, I would never have considered the alley dangerous before. Kathleen takes that route all the time when she leaves the house, and I do when I am planning on going south to Market

Street."

"In the dark?" Nate realized how sharp he sounded, and he tempered his tone. "I mean, what kind of lighting is back there?" He knew questioning Annie's judgment on safety issues would just get him into trouble, given their past history. But hang it all, this was his precious little sister!

Annie stirred and pulled her hands away, fiddling with the small brooch at her neck. "The houses on each side of the alley do provide some illumination. However, I see your point. With night coming on, in the fog, I would probably not have chosen to go that way, and Kathleen is usually being escorted by Patrick when she comes home that way at night."

Nate sighed. "I suppose Laura wouldn't have thought anything about going down a dark alley, since that is the condition of most country roads. Even San Jose isn't that well lit, not like San Francisco."

"Jamie was very upset. Not just that it was his idea to go that way but that he ran ahead to the house, leaving Laura alone in the alley for a moment. He felt he'd failed to act the 'gentleman!' Sweet boy. Frankly, if he hadn't gone right back to the alley, and Dandy hadn't made a racket attacking the man, I am not sure the outcome would have been as benign."

The memory of Annie struggling last fall with an unknown assailant filled Nate's mind, and he blurted out, "Do you think this had anything to do with the Framptons and what happened in October? Could the man have been after you?"

Annie shook her head slowly. "I hadn't thought of that. I don't see why it would. Laura is taller than I am, and her hair is much darker, although in the fog that might not be obvious. Oh Nate, I would feel awful if she had a fright because of me! What are we going to tell your parents? I promised so faithfully she would be safe with me!"

Nate pulled her into his arms and said, "Now, Annie. We don't know that you were the target. I just can't think why Laura would be. It was probably just some ruffian looking for a few coins. I imagine Laura is going to have something to say about whether we can tell my parents about this. She didn't have any idea who the man was?"

"No, she said she couldn't see him because he grabbed her from behind, so she had no idea what he looked like or who he was. But…"

Nate looked down at Annie, who was fingering one of his lapels, a mannerism he had come to associate with her when she was worried. When she didn't go on, he said sharply, "What is it? Do you think she knew who he was?"

Annie shrugged. "I don't think so. I just felt there was something odd about her reaction. Of course she was shaken up, but I expected her to be more outraged. I guess I had built up this image from all you had told me about her, that she was fearless…"

Nate chuckled softly, pulling her tighter. "Annie, my love, just because you are capable of facing down murderers and assailants with aplomb doesn't mean every woman is as brave or as foolhardy as you are."

Annie laughed, turned further into his arms, and rested her head on his shoulder. As they sat entwined, Nate breathed in her distinctive spicy scent, rubbed his chin against the silk of her hair, and welcomed the comfort of having the woman he loved in his arms. He had met Annie Fuller last August, less than six months ago, when the death of one of his law firm's clients brought them together. At first, he'd been confused by how attracted he was to a woman who flouted societal norms left and right. Annie was independent to a fault and an assertive advocate of women's rights. She had even been educated in the masculine world of high finance by her father, a famous stock broker. Yet none of this had protected her from the financial ruin and death of her husband that had left her an impoverished widow, dependent on her in-laws back east.

Two years ago, Annie had inherited this house in San Francisco, turned it into a boarding house, and created the role of Madam Sibyl, clairvoyant. She'd explained to him that, while she didn't believe in the palmistry and star charts she used with clients as Madam Sibyl, this was the only way men would take a woman's business advice seriously, and she needed the money to supplement the income she got from the boarding house. He pictured how she had looked as she defended herself, her cheeks flushed, her delicate chin thrust up, her brown eyes darkening with defiance.

Nate had come to admit that some of the very characteristics that made him uncomfortable also made Annie more attractive to him. They were some of the very same characteristics she had in common with his sister, whom he teasingly called his little Susan B. Anthony. Annie was correct; he would have assumed that Laura would respond to a threat, particularly one by a man, by getting angry. But he wasn't sure he still understood her; she'd seemed different over the holidays, more subdued than usual. That was, until she got the letter about coming to San Francisco. Then the old Laura had reappeared.

He said, "Annie, do you think that Laura is hiding something? She didn't write to me very often last fall. Normally, when we are apart, she writes about once a week, letters filled with all her doings and little enthusiasms."

"Oh Nate, from some of the things she has said to me this week, she didn't feel her first teaching assignment went at all well. She might have been embarrassed to admit this to her big brother. At her age, you often think you are invincible, that you can do anything. Then you hit your first obstacle. It can knock the stuffing out of you."

Nate smiled, thinking of his first trial. What a disaster. Thank goodness his Uncle Frank had finally brought a new partner into the firm. Able Cranston was a first-rate defense attorney, and Nate had already had the opportunity to second him in two trials. He was learning a good deal that only practical experience, not law books, could teach him.

Annie continued. "I felt like she was just getting her confidence back. Last night she told me all about her students and new assignments she had planned. Then tonight, I saw her standing in the kitchen, huddled like a small scared animal. Well, I could wring the neck of that man, whoever he was, for doing that to her."

This image of Laura rekindled Nate's anger. He pulled back from

Annie and started to rise, saying, "Look, I need to see her. Make sure she is really all right. Maybe she will tell me more than she told you…maybe she has remembered something. Can I go on up to her room?"

Annie stood up and put out a restraining hand. "Nate, no. She is probably already asleep. She needs her rest to be ready for school tomorrow. Don't worry, I will look in on her before I retire."

"But what if the attack wasn't random? I need to know what to do to keep her safe."

Annie squeezed his arm. "There isn't anything you can do tonight. I have already spoken to Mr. Stanley, our local patrolman. He promised to start making the alley part of his beat, and Kathleen is going to get Patrick to find out if any other women have been assaulted recently in the area. And of course, none of us are going to use the alley at night anymore."

"But even if she stays away from the alley…"

"I know. But we can't keep her in the house like a prisoner. We don't even know if she was the particular target of the man. Barbara Hewitt has already volunteered to make sure that she and Jamie always accompany Laura to and from Clement Grammar. Barbara usually walks with Jamie since it is on the way to Girls' High, so it won't be a bother. I am sure I can convince Laura that it is best for none of them to walk home unescorted once it is dark, and David Chapman has offered to walk with them on Wednesday nights when Barbara has to stay late."

"David who? Oh, that's right," Nate said, as he remembered. "Chapman. I've met him in the hall a few times. One of your boarders. Tall, thin scarecrow of a fellow. What's he got to do with this?"

Annie told him about how Chapman had come down to the kitchen after work and then gone out and found Laura's satchel. "He works for Mitcherson's as a purchasing agent, makes a decent salary," Annie continued. "From what Kathleen says, he is quite smitten by Jamie's mother, Barbara, although there is no indication that she returns the sentiment."

"Ah, hence the offer to escort everyone home on Wednesday nights!

Well, as long as he's not after Laura. Mother is determined she meet and marry a doctor or lawyer. I think this is the main reason she agreed to Laura moving up to San Francisco," Nate said.

He looked down at Annie and watched the play of emotions across her face. He knew she would be upset by the idea that Laura's primary motivation for coming to teach in the city should be to catch a husband. However, since Annie was being courted by Nate, a lawyer, she couldn't really say anything about this without sounding insulting. He kept quiet and watched her struggle with how to respond. He had learned his lesson last fall, when his too-ready tongue had gotten him in real trouble. He had almost lost any chance he had with Annie. The past few months, they had slowly been moving towards a better understanding, and he didn't want to do anything to disturb this new equilibrium. *There it is, that smile.* One of Annie's most endearing qualities was her sense of humor.

"Nate, you are teasing me! I can't imagine your mother plotting any such thing. You've always told me how important it was to her for Laura to get an education and a profession of her own," Annie said, laughing. "Besides, Laura just turned nineteen, much too early to be thinking about husbands."

Nate saw Annie's smile disappear, and he wondered if she was remembering that she had been Laura's age when she'd married. He didn't know many details about her marriage, besides the fact that her husband had lost all of Annie's fortune in the panic and stock market crash of 1873 and then committed suicide. Mrs. Stein, one of Annie's boarders, had intimated to him that the marriage itself had not been a happy one. He wished Annie would be more forthcoming about her past, even though it made him jealous even to think of another man putting his arms around her or kissing her.

Nate dismissed that thought and drew the now somber Annie back into his arms, saying, "You know, my dearest, I would be very glad to encourage her to think about anything, including being courted by some young doctor, if it would take her mind off of what happened this evening."

Laura heard the quiet knock on the bedroom door, and she hastily blew out the candle and scrunched under the covers. She could sense the door open as the light from the hallway hit her eyes, which she squeezed shut. Annie softly said her name, and then Laura heard the whisper of clothing and the door close, extinguishing the light. Annie had been true to her word and had gone down to see Nate without her. He was probably gone now, and she was safe.

She'd been so afraid that if she saw her big brother, she'd spill out all her fears to him.

Instead, she was here, alone in the dark, with those fears. Her fear she wouldn't be able to sleep and would make a mess of her teaching tomorrow. Her fear that her parents would insist that she come home if they heard what happened. And the worst fear of all, that she might know who the man was who attacked her and that she might be responsible, in small part, for his rage.

Chapter Four
Friday afternoon, January 9, 1880
"Miss Mayo, Medium. 327 O'Farrell—Sittings daily, 10 to 9 P.M." —*San Francisco Chronicle*, 1880

Annie sat in the small back room that had been her Uncle Timothy's private study on the first floor. She had taken off the wig of massed black ringlets, and she was massaging her temples. Closing her eyes, she breathed deeply, savoring the faint apple scent of her uncle's pipe tobacco that still clung to the thick velvet curtains and carpet. She remembered him as a big bear of a man, with warm hugs and a cache of peppermint candies he hid in his desk, especially for his young niece. His desk was now stacked with the newspapers, almanacs, and correspondence that she, as Madam Sibyl, consulted in order to give advice to her clients.

The last time she had seen her Uncle Timothy was fifteen years ago, when the telegram arrived telling of her mother's death. He'd been the one to take her to the train heading south to her home outside of Los Angeles, and she never forgot the comfort of his arms. She had no premonition she would never see him or her aunt again, that her father would flee from his grief, dragging his twelve-year-old daughter with him all the way around Cape Horn to New York City. It was during that long ship voyage that her father introduced her to the mysteries of high finance, an education that continued even after she started attending the snobbish Ladies Academy in their new home. Every night for the next five years, they sat together, poring over year-end financial statements, local farm reports, weather forecasts, and transportation bills before Congress as he taught her how to use these disparate bits of information to predict the future prices of stocks and bonds.

Then she had married John Fuller, a troubled young man who viewed her unusual talents as unwomanly and refused to take her advice. To make matters worse, when her father suddenly died, she'd discovered he had left all her assets in the hands of her husband, forcing her to watch helplessly as John gambled away her fortune and her future happiness, leaving her at the mercy of in-laws who blamed her for his subsequent suicide.

Annie grimaced, impatient with such thoughts. At least her aunt and uncle had never forgotten their little niece, leaving this house to her when they died. In the past two years, she had been able to turn this legacy and the business aptitude her father had fostered into two separate sources of income, the boarding house and Madam Sibyl, earning enough so she would never have to be dependent on anyone ever again.

Annie stood up and went to look at her reflection in the washstand mirror, chastising herself for once more going down the dead-end path of anger and resentment. As she carefully wiped the red off her lips and removed as much of the white powder from her face as she could, she repeated to herself that she had her house, her dear friends, and a man courting her who, miracle of miracles, respected her, despite her unconventional occupation and independent ways. She was happy now, and she needed to let the past be the past.

Besides, this autumn she had discovered that being too independent could be equally dangerous to her well-being, a lesson that Nate's little sister might need to learn. Annie was glad to see that Laura had looked rested this morning when Annie caught her in the hall before the younger woman left for work. Laura had skillfully avoided every attempt Annie made, last evening and this morning, to talk further about the attack on her.

The clock in the study chimed the quarter hour, and Annie carefully pulled off the net she wore under her wig and re-pinned the strands of hair that had escaped from the coiled braid at the top of her head. Two years ago, when she first started her business as a clairvoyant, she had rather liked putting on the wig and makeup and speaking in a faintly foreign accent. She'd felt like an actress in a play, not a charlatan fooling people into believing she had gotten her ideas from reading their palms or casting their horoscopes. Then, about six months ago, she'd begun to feel uncomfortable with the artifice.

Today, for the first time, she would meet with a client, Ruthann Hazelton, without assuming the role of Madam Sybil, using the excuse that the wig frightened Ruthann's four-month-old daughter, Lillian. Last week, as Lillian squalled, Annie asked Ruthann if she could try not being "in costume" during their next meeting.

The young woman had laughed and said, "Oh, what a good idea. Anyway, I don't expect how you look has anything to do with the quality of your advice, and we both know that advice doesn't come from the stars!"

Annie gave her hair a last pat and turned to go into the adjoining parlor, wondering if other clients would be equally sanguine if she told them that clairvoyance or palmistry or their horoscopes had nothing to do with her advice, either. *Well, one step at a time.*

"I am so frustrated, Madam Sibyl. I thought Mother Hazelton wanted me to take over the management of the house, including the ordering of the food and planning meals, but all she has done is complain. No matter what I do, it's wrong."

Ruthann Hazelton was a tall, spare woman in her early thirties, with thick, wavy hair the color of deep mahogany, smiling brown eyes that were huge behind her steel-rimmed glasses, and a mobile mouth that was currently turned down. Her rosy-cheeked daughter gurgled and made a grab for her mother's spectacles, immediately turning that frowning mouth into a smile.

They were sitting in the small front parlor where Madam Sibyl met her clients. This room was Annie's pride and joy, with its dark green curtains open to let in the pale winter light, wood-paneled cabinets filled with curios from a sea-faring ancestor, and small lace-covered tables holding bowls of fresh-cut flowers delivered daily by a local flower peddler. She spent most of her days here, meeting businessmen in the morning and late afternoons, offering them brandy from Uncle Timothy's old crystal decanters while guiding them skillfully to financial success. From mid-morning to early afternoon, it was tea and some of Mrs. O'Rourke's pastries that were offered to women like Ruthann, who had their own set of domestic concerns. This morning, a wood fire burned with a satisfying snap and crackle, and for once, Annie felt comfortable turning up the flames on the oil lamps scattered around the room. Today she didn't need shadows to add to Madam Sibyl's mystery. Ruthann sat in a comfortable armchair across from Annie, a round velvet-covered table in between them.

Annie leaned across the table to wave her fingers at the child. She noted with pleasure when the small olive brown eyes shifted and focused first on Annie's waving fingers and then on her face. This time, the result wasn't a startled expression followed by tears. Annie, without wig, was clearly a more acceptable vision to the young Lillian.

She sat back and said, "Ruthann, do call me Annie. That is my real name, Mrs. Annie Fuller. If we are going to banish Madam Sibyl's wig, let's get rid of her completely!"

When Ruthann smiled, Annie said, "First of all, do you want to take over managing the kitchen with all it entails? Or were you doing it just to please your mother-in-law?"

"Well, you know that Bertram and I lived in a boarding house until right before Lillian was born. Since I have boarded out my entire life, first at school in Colorado and then when I came to San Francisco to teach, I confess I've never had to take care of a whole house, much less direct servants or order groceries."

"Yes, but you haven't answered my question. Is this something you are anxious to learn how to do now while Lillian takes up so much of your time? Did your mother-in-law even ask you to do more?" Having been over Ruthann's relationship with her mother-in-law before, Annie suspected the answer would be in the negative.

"I guess not in so many words." Ruthann let Lillian encircle her index finger with her chubby hand. "But she's started complaining about how tired she is. She made me feel guilty. And now that Lillian is sleeping through most of the nights and I am getting my energy back, I thought I ought to make an effort. I am going to have to learn how to keep house eventually."

"But is this something you would like to learn from your mother-in-law?"

Ruthann responded with a chuckle. "Heavens above, no! I would much rather learn later, after she's gone, when I won't have to suffer her constant criticism. Bertram doesn't care two hoots about a few late meals or if there aren't enough meat courses or if the dessert cake falls flat. And *you* won't mind, will you my sweet angel?" Ruthann kissed the wispy curls on the top of Lillian's head.

Annie leaned forward to stroke the baby's tiny hand. Ruthann had come to see Madam Sibyl in the fall of '78, full of despair after her second miscarriage. She was past thirty when she met and married her husband, Bertram Hazelton, an engineer employed by the San Francisco Gas Light Company, and she had wanted Madam Sibyl to forecast whether she would ever have a successful pregnancy.

She'd said to Annie, "I just need to know. Before I met Bertram, I'd resigned myself to being an old-maid school teacher, never being loved by a man, never holding a child of my own. If I have to accept that my fate is to be childless, so be it. I've so much to be thankful for already. But it isn't fair to my dear husband to keep putting him through this. He frets so over my health."

Of course, Annie hadn't been able to give Ruthann the answer she wanted since Madam Sibyl wasn't really clairvoyant. What she could do was give her sympathy and some simple advice. First, she had used her examination of the lines in Ruthann's hands as an excuse to ask her questions about her past, her present, and her hopes for the future. As Annie had discovered with others, Ruthann found a level of peace just from being able to spend an hour every week talking to someone else about her problems.

Concluding that Ruthann was bored, which gave her too much time to worry, Annie encouraged the former elementary school teacher to get involved with some charitable enterprise. Ruthann went on to help with the children living temporarily in the home run by the Ladies Protection and Relief Society. Later, when Ruthann again became pregnant, Annie suggested she not tell her husband until she had felt the baby quicken, since her previous miscarriages had occurred before the fourth month. This way, he wouldn't drive her to distraction with his fears.

Whether it was a coincidence or not, after following Madam Sibyl's advice, Ruthann successfully carried the baby to term, and now she swore the $2 weekly fee she paid for Madam Sibyl's advice was the best investment she'd ever made. In turn, Annie had become quite fond of Ruthann and was glad that the arrival of little Lillian hadn't ended her visits. Until her experiences this past fall with the mysterious Maybelle, Annie hadn't spent much time with children, yet she found herself distinctly drawn to the young mother and her child.

Annie watched Ruthann jiggling Lillian on her lap and brought her attention back to the matter at hand, saying, "Again, if you don't really want to take over running the house now and your mother-in-law didn't ask you to do so, what is it you really want?"

"I want her to leave," Ruthann stated with such vehemence that Lillian's little face scrunched up, and she gave a tiny cry. Deftly distracting her child by shaking a small rattle, Ruthann went on. "Oh, Madam… Annie, that sounds so selfish. I do appreciate that Mother Hazelton's help permitted me to devote myself to this sweet little bundle these first months. But my own mother, God rest her soul, always said, 'You should go along as you want to get along,' and I want to be responsible for my household as well as my child."

"When she was invited, was there a definite time set for her to leave?"

"Invited! We didn't invite her. She invited herself, and Bertram didn't feel he could say no. Although I don't think he had any idea she would stay on so long."

"They had a close relationship?" Annie asked.

"Mother Hazelton *says* they did. And I guess since he still lived with his parents in Chicago well into his early thirties, she has a reason for thinking so. She has two older daughters, but they married years ago and moved away from Chicago; one is in New York, the other Atlanta."

"Bertram's father is deceased?"

"Yes, he died about two years ago. Bertram *does* say he was close to his father, who was also a mechanical engineer."

Lillian began to fret, and Annie found herself rising and holding out her arms for the restless child. Ruthann handed her over willingly. As Annie took Lillian, she was amazed at how sturdy the young child felt, despite her small size. Lillian leaned back as if to check out this new giant was who was holding her, and Annie instinctively put her right hand behind the baby's head, which still tended to wobble, tightening her grip with her left arm. Lillian blew a bubble and then jerked forward to nestle her head against Annie's shoulder. Carefully pulling the baby blanket around the child and breathing Lillian's sweet milky scent, Annie felt a fierce ache fill her chest.

Until very recently, she'd never experienced a strong desire to be a mother, even during her own failed pregnancy. But what if her own miscarriage hadn't been caused by the shock of her father's death? What if she had inherited some essential barrenness from her mother who had only conceived one child? Did she dare tell Nate of her fears? Would that change the way he saw her? Annie began to rock Lillian side-to-side, as much to comfort herself as to comfort the child.

Ruthann began to speak again. "I don't want to give you the wrong impression about my mother-in-law. When Bertram and I married, she sent a lovely letter telling me how pleased she was her 'darling boy' had found his life's companion. And she couldn't have been more delighted when Bertram wrote to her about the impending birth of her newest grandchild. When she first arrived, even though we hadn't invited her, everything was fine. She was an enormous help in the weeks before and immediately after Lillian was born. It's only been these last few weeks that she has become so critical."

"Can you think of what may have precipitated her change in attitude?" Annie asked.

"No. I have wracked my brains over the change. Did I say or do something wrong? Did Bertram?"

Annie rubbed her chin over Lillian's soft curls and said, "Have you asked your mother-in-law how long she is intending to stay?"

"Not directly. Bertram has hinted. He asked her if she isn't missing her friends back in Chicago. She was very active in her church, and she doesn't seem at all pleased with the Lutheran minister at St. Mark's."

"Is it possible she is just tired? How old is she?"

"She is in her early seventies, although she seems in remarkable health. But if she is tired of helping out, why doesn't she go back home? She has plenty of servants. She brought her own lady's maid but left a butler and a housekeeper back in Chicago."

Annie was reminded of one of Madam Sibyl's other clients, Mrs. Crenshaw, whose daughter and grandson were visiting from Iowa, glad to escape the cold and snow of the Midwest in winter. Maybe the answer was that simple.

Annie walked back over and sat down, continuing to cradle a now-quiet Lillian against her shoulder. "Could Bertram's mother not want to go back to Chicago yet because it is the dead of winter? Maybe she is afraid that if you do take over all the housekeeping chores, there will be no excuse for her to stay."

Ruthann's expressive face turned pensive, then she frowned. "She has said a number of times how the warmth of the mid-day sun has eased her arthritis. She won't even hear any complaints from Bertram about the fog. Says his blood has gotten thin. Now that I think about it, I expect she might be finding running our house, with only the cook, one maid-of-all work, and a part-time laundress, pretty exhausting. I just feel churlish. If that really is the explanation, of course she can stay as long as she likes."

Annie thought for a moment then shifted into the decisive tone she recognized as Madam Sibyl's, saying, "I would advise you, after consulting with your husband, to ask your mother-in-law if she would please agree to stay until the end of March. This gives you a definite end to her visit, but she will feel good that you want her."

"Yes, I can do that. I know Bertram will agree. He really does love his mother, but he could see I was becoming unhappy."

Annie continued. "Since she has sufficient income to travel, tell her she is welcome to visit again, next summer, to escape the extreme heat and humidity of that season. It will be easier for her to part with her precious grandchild if she knows she is going to be able to see her at regular intervals. Finally, tell her that you have discovered you just aren't up to running the whole house by yourself and ask her if she could continue to help out with the meal planning. You can then take up some of the other household tasks if you wish or talk to your husband about getting some temporary help."

As Ruthann exclaimed over Annie's advice, exploring different ways to broach the subject with her husband and her mother-in-law, Annie saw that Lillian's eyes were closed fast, the impossibly long dark brown lashes etched against her cheeks. *Surely it would be worth the risk of another loss if it means the possibility of holding my own child in my arms someday?*

Chapter Five
Saturday morning, January 10, 1880

"MONTGOMERY'S TEMPERANCE HOTEL, 227 and 229 Second street; six meal tickets, $1: board and lodging per day, 75c to $1; by the week, $4 to $5: lodging per week, 75c to $2; nice single rooms, $1 25; baggage free." —*San Francisco Chronicle*, 1880

Laura relished the feel of the sun on her face as she and Barbara and Jamie turned northeast onto Market Street. She had already learned that the unexpected gusts of wind that funneled down the city streets could be bitingly cold at this time of year, so she welcomed the wool scarf Mrs. Fuller had pressed on her as she left the house. The quiet concern she'd seen in Annie's eyes had almost undone her resolve to keep her suspicions about the attack to herself, but she needed to talk to Hattie first. In just a few minutes, they would be at Second Street, where they would turn south a block to Mission Street and Hattie's boarding house. Her companions would continue on to the Ferry Building to watch the ship traffic in the Bay, evidently one of Jamie's favorite pastimes. The Grand Hotel on their left, with its four stories of ornate arched windows and cupolas, looked small and old-fashioned compared to the Palace Hotel across the street, which was taller, longer, and more streamlined in its proportions. Laura marveled at the sheer magnitude of traffic on Market. Hansom cabs, carriages, and men on horseback wove around heavily loaded wagons, and pedestrians darted past moving vehicles to make it to the center of the street where the Market Street Railway horsecars plodded along their tracks. Even on a Saturday morning, the bustle of commerce rang in her ears, and the sheer energy of the city began to lift Laura's spirits.

Thursday had been awful. A sleepless night anxiously going over every detail of the assault, looking for evidence to refute her suspicions, left her tired and irritable. Her class of over forty students required enormous energy to keep quiet and attentive, but she had learned the hard way that if she didn't find the right balance between discipline and encouragement, she would spend the rest of the term making up for the mistakes she made in this first week. She had handled the incident when one of the boys "accidentally" dropped a bag of marbles all over the classroom floor and given a stern reprimand to the students who hadn't done their assigned work. But she had also ended the day with the students laughing at her spirited reading of Carroll's poem, "You Are Old, Father William." Not surprisingly, she was completely wrung out by the time she got home.

Friday had gone more smoothly. She slept better, and walking to work with Barbara and Jamie began to feel routine. She was able to recall all the students' names, which obviously pleased them, and every-one had their homework assignments completed. Even the weather had improved and was sunny and warm at noon when Laura nipped across the street to Foster's Drugstore for a few necessities. She'd barely made it back to school in time, entranced as she had been by the array of choices Foster's offered in tooth powders, hand soaps, and headache remedies. One of the advantages of living and working in San Francisco was going to be its shopping opportunities, and Laura knew that she would have to be careful not to spend all her earnings. At least she had been able to save money this fall, since the pokey country store near her school contained nothing to tempt her.

She hoped she would get Hattie to come out with her today to shop in the City of Paris dry goods store. Just a block north of Market on Montgomery, it would be an easy walk from Hattie's boarding house. As soon as she saw how smart and fine most of the teachers at Clement dressed, she'd promised herself she would have a new dress made. Besides the brown wool suit she had worn all week and the royal blue polonaise she was wearing today, she didn't have any dresses fit for public wear. She certainly had no desire to be seen by her students or fellow teachers as some country mouse. Miss Minnie and Miss Millie Moffet, the odd, elderly seamstresses, had offered to sew something up for her if she got the material. Annie's maid, Kathleen, seeing Laura's hesitation in accepting their offer, whispered that they were much in demand and they had made the beautiful navy outfit Annie Fuller wore when she visited the ranch after Christmas. Yes, shopping with Hattie seemed just the thing to take Laura's mind off of her worries.

"Have you gotten to know any of the other teachers yet?" Barbara Hewitt asked, breaking into her thoughts.

"Jamie's teacher, Miss Chesterton, was quite nice about introducing me around the teachers' room and showing me where the supplies are kept. I gather that she transferred to Clement this fall but that she has been teaching in the San Francisco schools for over twelve years. She speaks highly of Jamie. You must be proud of him."

Barbara laughed. "He does know how to ingratiate himself with his elders. I've had to caution Mrs. O'Rourke and Mrs. Stein not to spoil him too much. But he is a good boy."

Jamie wandered down the sidewalk in front of them, looking into the store front windows, oblivious to their conversation.

After a moment, Laura said, "I wondered what you could tell me about Miss Della Thorndike who teaches the normal teacher training classes at Girl's High. I got a note from her yesterday that said she wanted to meet with me on Monday to discuss having a student do her practice teaching work in my classroom."

"Miss Thorndike has taken over the normal class this year while Mrs. Kincaid is back east. Usually, she shares the duties with me for English literature and composition. Everyone speaks very highly of her. She has a long career as a teacher in all the grades. Before she came to San Francisco and started teaching at Girls' High, she taught briefly at the New York Freedonia Normal School. I assume that explains why she was chosen by Principal Swett to take over the normal class. Jamie had one of these practice teachers last year. Since Clement Grammar is only four blocks from Girls' High and it has all seven grades, it has been designated the main teaching school."

"Yes, that makes sense. I guess I rather hoped to postpone having anyone come into my classroom until I had firmly established a routine. The students are just getting adjusted to me, and I...you probably think I am foolish."

Barbara looked over at her and smiled. "Oh, no, Laura. I know just what you mean. Establishing the right rapport with your students takes time and is a very delicate process."

Encouraged, Laura said, "Perhaps Miss Thorndike will understand if I ask her to find another class for her student, at least until later in the term. Do you think so?"

"Well...I can't really say. Miss Thorndike can be a very forceful personality, but her students seem to adore her, and they profess that she is very sympathetic. Oh, here is where we should cross. Jamie, please come hold my hand. It always makes me nervous when I have to cross Market."

Laura's heart lurched as a man pushed by her, hurrying to catch up to the horsecar that was approaching. She was being silly. She couldn't jump every time a man passed her on the street. He wasn't even tall enough to be her assailant. And he didn't look a bit like Seth. But that was what was worrying her to death. Could the man in the alley really have been Seth Timmons? Even before the attack, Laura kept thinking she saw him, despite the fact he was supposed to be in San Jose, finishing up his course of studies at the State Normal School.

The first time she thought she saw him was when she had just arrived in San Francisco eleven days ago. As the cab she and Nate were riding in pulled away from the railway station, she could have sworn she saw Seth standing in the crowd, his battered Stetson pulled down so low that it shadowed his flint-grey eyes, the full black mustache framing a mouth that was tight-lipped but could quirk up in a surprised smile, and the square jaw and broad shoulders straining a rusty black coat. At the time, she told herself she was imagining things. But a day later, she'd glimpsed that hat and broad shoulders in a man walking up the steep incline of

Taylor towards Nob Hill, and the next afternoon, she noticed the hazy profile of a man that looked like him sitting in the depths of a restaurant. Then Friday, when she went to City Hall to register her state teaching certificate, she thought she heard Seth's voice, deep and raspy, behind a closed door.

No wonder she had flashed on the possibility that it was Seth in the alley. Like Seth, that man had been tall, wore a hat, and smelled of Bull Durham tobacco. But that could describe thousands of men in San Francisco. Surely the man couldn't be Seth, a man who was kind and gentle—or had been until his altercation with her student Buck Morrison. Then she'd seen a side of Seth that had frightened her out of her wits.

"Miss Dawson, come quick before the next horsecar comes." Jamie took Laura's left hand and escorted both her and his mother into the street.

Laura pulled her skirts up with her free hand, watching carefully for any dried dung. As they reached the other side of the street, she looked northeast down Market, seeing the stubby clock tower of the Ferry House dominating the skyline. According to Hattie's letter, her boarding house was two doors down from the corner of Second and Mission. Ordinarily, she would have left her companions here, just a block away from her destination. But with thoughts of Seth and the alleyway in her mind, she realized she was glad that Barbara had insisted that she and Jamie accompany her to the doorstep. Laura had also promised Annie that she would get a hansom cab home, despite the expense, and that she would be home well before dark.

"Did you know Miss Wilks prior to attending San Jose Normal School?" Barbara asked politely once they had made it across Market safely.

"No, but we had become fast friends by the end of the first week of our first term there. Hattie came from Santa Barbara, and we shared the fact that we both felt like hicks compared to most of the students who were from San Francisco, or the teachers, who came from even bigger cities back east."

They had also shared a fierce desire to make their first jobs as teachers serve as a means to an end. They made a solemn pact that they would save their money so they both could attend the State University over in Oakland, a plan Laura hadn't revealed to anyone else.

Barbara said, "Jamie told me he'd heard some of the older children in her class say she was a first rate teacher. Do you know why she left?"

"No, I don't. I can't imagine what happened. Just one of the reasons I am anxious to see her today."

She also hoped her friend would lay to rest her fears about Seth. Hattie had tutored Seth in science and math last year and probably got closer to him than anyone. He hadn't started with their class at the normal school, but he had arrived in the Fall of '78, during their last year. He was older than most of the students, but she always suspected that the flecks of white in his otherwise jet black hair, and his reserve, made him seem older than he really was. She did know he had been attending Kansas State Normal School but had to leave when the state took away all its funding. As a result, he needed to make up quite a few of the classes required for the highest grade certificate in California. This was why he didn't graduate with their class and was supposed to stay on in San Jose this fall. He'd told her he was to finish his classes this spring, so why would he be in San Francisco?

"You did say Miss Wilks lived at 225 Mission?" Barbara's words broke into Laura's thoughts as they turned the corner.

"Yes, this must be it." Laura looked doubtfully at the tall, dilapidated four-story residence squeezed between two squat commercial buildings, one housing the Mission Temperance Hotel, the other, ironically, Sullivan's Saloon.

"Do you want us to come up with you? Make sure you have the right address?" Barbara asked.

"No, I am sure that won't be necessary. If for some reason she isn't at this address, I promise I will go right next door to the Temperance Hotel, and I am sure they will be glad to get me a cab." Laura reached out her hand to Barbara, saying, "Thank you so much for offering to walk with me today. I know that Annie put you up to it, and I really appreciate the fact that you didn't make me feel like it was an imposition."

"Well, it wasn't an imposition at all, and I have learned this past year to respect Annie's advice. She does seem to have an uncanny ability to ferret out trouble. If she thinks it's better for you not to travel alone around the city, I would take her concerns seriously. But don't think about any of this right now; just have a lovely time with your friend."

As Laura went up to the short flight of stone stairs that led to an open vestibule, she sent up a prayer that Hattie would be able to put her mind at rest about why she had left her teaching job, about the effect this would have on their plans for the future, and about Laura's fears concerning Seth Timmons.

Chapter Six
Saturday noon, January 10, 1880
"It practically says that these ladies who propose to teach in our public schools must devote themselves to a life of celibacy…" *San Francisco Chronicle*, 1879

"So how are you liking my seventh grade students? Are they behaving for you?" Hattie aksed as she urged Laura to sit on the ancient armchair under the room's one window.

Laura looked around as she gingerly sat down, hoping the wire spring she had seen poking through the cushion wouldn't end up snagging the twisted satin drapery at the back of her best dress. The green stripes of the chair would have clashed terribly with the blue floral print of the window's draperies if they both weren't so badly faded. At least they seemed clean, as did the chenille bedspread covering the narrow bed on which Hattie perched, there being no other place to sit in the tiny room. Laura wondered why Hattie had moved from the boarding house she had been living in when she moved to San Francisco this fall. Her letters had described a large airy room, complete with bookshelves and a desk, just a few blocks from Clement Grammar. Not this cramped fourth floor room reached by a set of uncarpeted stairs so narrow that Laura felt like she was Christian climbing up Difficulty Hill in *Pilgrim's Progress*. Of course, since Hattie was no longer working, she wouldn't have been able to afford the room and board where she had been staying, but how was she affording any room at all, now that she was unemployed?

And was she ill? Hattie, as befitted a farm girl of Iowa heritage, was usually round of cheek and hip, her sky blue eyes sparkling with good health, and her light brown hair shiny and neat. Today, while the curves were still there, her cheeks had thinned, there were dark circles under those blue eyes, and the general disorder of her hair suggested she had been lying down when Laura knocked at her door. Did she quit teaching for health reasons? If so, why hadn't she returned home to let her parents nurse her, and why hadn't she said anything to Laura?

Laura mentally postponed asking these and all the rest of her questions, thinking that she just needed to give her friend time. Taking Hattie's lead, she replied, "The students are such a wonderful change after the Cupertino Creek School. They actually sit in their seats, well, all except John Jenkins. Do tell me you discovered some way to keep him from wandering over to look out the window right in the middle of recitations."

"Oh my, John. He really is a bright boy, particularly good with math, but I swear he is a perfect example of what Miss Frobisher called the 'ants in the pants' malady. Do you remember?" Hattie laughed. "I found that if I assigned him the task of helping some of the other boys who were having difficulty with their sums, it helped keep him occupied, at least for awhile. Now tell me, did Frank Spencer, the small snub-nosed boy who sits at the back, drop his marbles yet?"

Laura spent the next hour delightedly sharing notes on the boys and girls in her class. Hattie confirmed many of Laura's first impressions, and she was thankful to learn which of the pedagogical strategies they had been taught at school worked and didn't work with this group of students. The information was invaluable, and Hattie, who had always been a superb mimic, had her in stitches as she described some of the students' little idiosyncrasies. Laura was also glad to hear from Hattie that she shouldn't be worried about accepting Miss Thorndike's request to place one of the practice teachers in her class.

"Della Thorndike is really a very experienced teacher," she'd said. "I had quite a few conversations with her at lunch time when she dropped by to check on one of her students, and she gave me a good number of useful suggestions on how to exert better discipline."

Laura, thankful that she'd reintroduced the subject of discipline, started to tell her of her own difficulties with teaching in the fall and how miserable she'd been, but Hattie immediately changed the subject. Hurt, she thought, *Why won't she let me talk about this? Doesn't she care?*

In September, Laura had written several letters to her friend about how insecure she felt managing the littlest children, and Hattie had been quite sympathetic in her replies. Then in October, Hattie's letters had changed, were less frequent, and stuck to mostly safe topics like the weather and mundane classroom activities. By that time, Laura had begun to worry that the local postmistress in Cupertino Creek, a terrible gossip, wasn't to be trusted, so she'd shifted to neutral topics in her letters as well. She certainly wasn't going to write about some of the awful secrets she had discovered about the families she boarded with or tell her about the bullying she'd been subjected to by Buck Morrison or report on Seth's unexpected visits each weekend. But she had hoped once she was face-to-face with her friend that she would be able to unburden herself. She had missed her so. Missed getting her wise counsel. Missed her ability to turn the petty problems of a day into a humorous story.

Hattie's voice sharpened, and Laura realized she hadn't been paying close enough attention to what her friend was saying. Hattie repeated her question about what Laura thought of Andrew Russell, the Vice Principal at Clement Grammar. Laura replied that he seemed nice enough, but she could tell that Hattie was miffed. She knew her friend's face as well as her own, and that little knot that appeared between her brows meant she was upset. Realizing that many of Hattie's stories of the classroom had been interspersed with references to what Mr. Russell had said or thought about this and that, Laura leaned forward and said, "I gather that you think very highly of Vice Principal Russell?"

"Oh yes, he was so helpful to me when I started teaching. I don't know what I would have done without his support during those first months of the term. I'm confident you will love and respect him as I do when you get to know him as well."

"What do you mean, love him?" Laura was taken aback by Hattie's statement. Then, trying to soften her reaction, she continued on in a teasing way, saying, "Hattie Wilks. I am surprised at you. Taken in by a handsome face!"

Hattie lifted her chin, a flush covering her cheeks, and snapped, "This isn't a joking matter. Andrew is the most intelligent man I have ever met."

"Don't get angry with me," Laura replied, startled by her friend's reaction. "I am sure he is a very capable man. I just haven't had a chance to do more than say hello to him yet. I was just startled to hear you say you love him. I know how careful you are to avoid using that sort of over-blown sentimental language."

At San Jose Normal School, watching as other classmates lost interest in their studies or even dropped out because they had "fallen in love," they had sworn to each other they wouldn't let romantic impulses interfere with their dreams. Laura couldn't believe her friend would have changed that much in such a short time. This must be just an infatuation on her part. With growing unease she watched as Hattie remained silent, eyes downcast.

"Hattie, talk to me. What is going on? This isn't why you resigned your position, is it? You haven't thrown away your future because a man has paid you compliments. I won't believe my dear, sensible Hattie would do such a thing."

Hattie cried out, "Laura, you don't understand. It isn't like that. Andrew loves me and I love him, and I have pledged to spend my life with him."

"What about the pledge we made to each other?" Laura stood up, her hands clenched. "You promised me! We were to teach and save our earnings so we could afford to start taking classes together at the University. Are you saying you have given this all up for some starched-collar bureaucrat?" Laura turned her head sharply to the side, fighting off tears.

When she turned back to look at Hattie, her friend looked ashen, her lips visibly trembling. Laura's anger drained away, and she moved to sit beside her on the bed, saying, "Oh, dearest, I am sorry. I didn't mean to berate you. I am just so confused. You gave no hint of this in your letters. Now do tell me exactly what has happened. Help me understand."

She put her arm around Hattie's shoulders.

"I know I should have written to you about Andrew and me, but I wasn't sure you would understand," Hattie said haltingly. "We never meant it to happen. He offers a small class in the evening in Greek and Latin for seniors at Girls' High and those in the Normal class who want to go on to the University, and when I could, I joined them." Her voice grew stronger, and she continued. "One evening, when the others left, I stayed on. We talked about, oh, everything. His mind is so superior and elevated compared to most of the boys we knew at San Jose. Laura, he is a follower of Auguste Comte and John Stuart Mill, a true altruist."

"Well I can see how attractive that might be, but how does Mr. Russell feel about your plans to go to the University, eventually medical school? He must recognize how brilliant you are." Laura's impatience returned. "Doesn't he realize what a travesty it would be if you didn't have a chance to fulfill your dreams? Did you tell him what Professor Norton said about you having the finest grasp of scientific principles of any student he had taught, male or female?"

"Laura, you are wrong. He isn't the kind of man to see a woman as just another pretty face, good for nothing but home and hearth. He respects me and wants the best for me."

"Then why did you quit teaching?"

"I had to quit. There were…reasons. For one, as my Vice Principal, he could be accused of favoritism if our relationship became public while I taught under him."

"Couldn't you have simply asked to be transferred to another school? How will you support yourself? How are you even affording this place?"

Laura stopped. Hattie had gotten up and walked over to the window, her back to her. After a moment of silence, she saw her friend's shoulders pull back and recognized that Hattie was screwing up her courage. *To say what?*

"Hattie, what is it?"

Hattie turned around, her voice tremulous. "I had hoped that I would be able to tell you this after you had gotten to know Andrew. Then it wouldn't seem so strange to you at all, but…you see, I quit because Andrew asked me to be his wife. We are to be married as soon as my parents can arrange to come up to San Francisco to attend." Hattie reached out to her, pleading, "Laura, my dearest friend, please just be happy for me!"

Laura's heart melted, and she ran over to pull Hattie into her arms, her friend breaking into sobs.

"Hush, now," she said. When she felt the sobs subside, she drew away and took Hattie's handkerchief, using it to wipe the tears from her friend's face. "What is all this? You silly goose. How am I supposed to be happy for you if you are in tears?"

Hattie smiled a watery smile. "Oh, I have missed you, Laura. I can't tell you how wonderful it is to have you here, to know my darling students are in your good hands. And now you can help me get prepared for my wedding. We aren't planning more than a small civil ceremony. But I want you to be my maid of honor."

There were so many questions Laura wanted to ask. Even if Andrew Russell turned out to be the paragon that Hattie thought him, she still wouldn't understand why her friend was rushing into this marriage. But she loved Hattie, and so she gave her friend another warm hug and kept her mouth shut. For now.

Chapter Seven
Sunday afternoon, January 11, 1880

"A FORENSIC FEMALE: 'I have associated with me for the defense Mrs. Laura DeForce Gordon. The announcement was listened to with interest as the appearance of a female lawyer in a murder case was a novel sight." —*San Francisco Chronicle,* 1880

"I just can't fathom it, Nate. It's as if this Andrew Russell has bewitched her," Laura said. "We had just begun to get comfortable with each other again when he was knocking at her door. Came right in like he owned the place. I was shocked!"

Nate smiled at his little sister's outraged outburst, looking over at her fondly for a moment before returning his attention to driving the hired carriage up Fell Street towards the entrance of Golden Gate Park. At least this was the Laura he knew and loved, fierce and opinionated, not the falsely cheerful girl he had seen on Friday when he stopped by the boarding house. At Annie's urging, his sister had come down to the parlor, just for awhile, and assured him that she was completely recovered from the assault in the alley. Then she had chatted gaily about her first week of teaching. But Nate agreed with Annie's later assessment that there had been something manufactured about Laura's good spirits.

He reminded himself that his sister never liked admitting that she was scared about anything. There was the summer she was thirteen and snuck out early and saddled up Ajax, her father's stallion. Their brother Billy had told her she was just a little girl and couldn't handle him, so of course she was determined to prove him wrong. When she came back after breakfast, her skirts muddy from the stream Ajax had dumped her in, she'd turned the whole escapade into a humorous story. But Nate could tell that she'd gotten a severe fright and simply didn't want to worry her parents. Or admit to Billy, for that matter, that he had been right.

Nate intended to get to the bottom of why she was pretending the assault didn't bother her, so he invited her to come with him to see the Conservatory of Flowers today. She would have a hard time refusing him since botany was one of her favorite subjects, and this magnificent glass structure, with its exotic plants, hadn't been built the last time she visited him in San Francisco.

Despite the ten years difference in their ages, or maybe because of it, he'd always been close to Laura. She was only four when he first moved up to San Francisco to go to high school and seven when he went back east to Western Reserve College. Yet every summer when he came home, she shadowed him day and night. Nate may have complained about how much of a nuisance his little sister was, but he knew it was Laura's hero-worship that gave him a sense of place in the family each time he returned. Laura, bright, energetic, and curious, needed him in ways that his busy mother, and his father who had Billy to depend on, didn't. He worked with her on her letters and numbers, taught her the Latin names for plants when they tramped in the foothills to the east of the ranch, listened to her girlish secrets, and read her to sleep every night with the poetry of Longfellow, Browning, and Tennyson. One of his fondest memories of these years was her head snuggled down on her pillow, a jumbled nest of dark brown curls, her snubbed nose burned from the sun, and her lashes dark against her cheeks.

Then, in '71, he had gone to Harvard to get his law degree, and he didn't make it home for three years, at which point he joined his Uncle Frank's law firm in San Francisco. Laura's newsy letters had kept him from feeling completely cut off, but he had been shaken when he returned and found that the ten year-old little girl he left behind had turned into a young woman.

"Nate, you aren't listening to me! I can always tell." Laura jostled his elbow.

"Yes I was. Your friend Hattie has decided to marry, and for some reason you feel she has betrayed you," Nate said, looking over with another smile.

"This isn't amusing." Laura frowned. "She has betrayed herself. Our science professor said she was one of the brightest students he'd ever taught and that there wasn't anything she couldn't do if she put her mind to it. She *was* going to be a doctor. We had it all planned out. Teaching would support us while we attended the University of California. You know they opened up the medical department to women six years ago and..."

"We? Laura, you aren't telling me you are planning on becoming a doctor, as well," Nate blurted out.

"No."

Nate looked over and saw his sister was biting her lower lip, which usually meant she was about to say something he would find outrageous.

She turned her head towards him and smiled slyly, saying, "Well...if you must know, I have decided to follow in *your* footsteps. You were the one who told me that women can attend Hastings Law now that Mrs. Foltz has won her case before the state Supreme Court. Wouldn't it be a treat when Uncle Frank retires for us to be partners? Dawson and Dawson has a nice ring to it, doesn't it?"

Nate laughed. "I don't think you should pin your hopes on Uncle Frank retiring any time soon."

Laura replied, "Oh, that's all right. Close as I can figure, it's going to be at least ten years before I can practice law, and surely he will have retired before then. I will need to teach full time for at least three more years to have saved up enough to go to the University full-time, and then there are the four years to get my B.A. and another two years for the law degree, which might take longer if I have to work during that time. I was hoping that Uncle might employ me in the firm as a law clerk while I was at Hastings."

Hell fire, she's serious! Nate tugged at the reins, and the horses turned left to take the short jog to the entrance of the park. He didn't know whether to be proud that she wanted to emulate him or appalled that she wanted to pursue such a difficult path. There weren't any women at Harvard Law when he'd been there; in fact, there had been an uproar his first year when a woman had petitioned for admittance and been promptly rejected. His heart constricted when he thought of Laura as the object of the kind of nasty comments his fellow students had made about that woman. But if his relationship with Annie Fuller had taught him anything, it was to be very careful about how he responded to Laura's news.

"Yes, I see," Nate said. "I guess since Uncle Frank once talked to Mrs. Foltz and Mrs. DeForce about sharing offices with us, it would be a bit hypocritical if he objected. Have you discussed these plans with Mother and Father yet?"

He doubted very much if she had. He hadn't been entirely joking with Annie the other day when he had mentioned that his mother's hopes that her lovely daughter would meet and marry a doctor or lawyer now that she was living in San Francisco. His mother had been very support-ive of Laura's plans to become a teacher, but only because she thought it was a good job for a single woman to hold while waiting to marry.

"No, I haven't. There just hasn't been the right time. You know how much Violet has monopolized Mother ever since Billy married her. And this Christmas, with the new baby, I barely got a second alone with her. And don't you dare tell them. I want to do it in my own way in my own time. Promise!"

Nate sympathized with Laura, thinking about his own irritation with his brother's young wife, who had a tendency to cling like some burr to her new mother-in-law's side. The birth of her first child at the end of November just made things worse. No wonder Laura had been out of sorts during her visit over the holidays. Their mother was completely wrapped up in her first grandchild, and then he arrived with Annie in tow, so he had had little time for her. Well, he would give her the time and attention she needed now.

Nate pulled the team to a stop, letting a young dare-devil with a four-in-hand pass in front of them. He grinned at her and said, "I promise." *By her own reckoning, law school is a good seven years in the future. No reason to get in a fuss at this point*, he thought. "I can understand your disappointment with your friend Hattie. Did she say she had definitely given up on her plans?"

"That's just it. I don't know. She went on and on about how supportive her *beloved Andrew* was, but when I asked her directly if he would have any objections to her attending the University after they were married, she changed the subject. Which pretty much tells the tale, doesn't it? All she could talk about was Russell, where he had gone to school, what a good teacher he was, what he had said on this and that occasion. This is just the reason we had agreed that neither of us would permit any romantic entanglements; a woman's rational capabilities go right out the window when a man gets involved."

"Now Laura, you know that isn't true. Just look at Mother, or Annie Fuller, for that matter."

"I am not sure that it says much for Annie's rationality that she appears to have a sweet spot for you, Nate Dawson," Laura crowed. Then she continued more seriously. "Much as I love and respect Mother, you know very well that most of what she does day-to-day doesn't require a tenth of her intelligence. And you told me how frustrating it is for Annie to have to pretend to be a fortune-teller in order for the men she advises to take seriously her business expertise. What will become of Hattie's talents if she marries? How will she use those talents in a life spent planning meals, managing servants, and burping babies? That life might be good enough for silly widgeons like Violet, but not for me or Hattie or Annie."

Nate felt the sting of Laura's words, remembering Annie's response a few months ago when he made the terrible mistake of assuming that she would welcome the chance to end her career as Madam Sibyl to become his wife. As he urged the horses through the park gates and then gave them the signal to break into a trot, he looked over at Laura, who was pulling a brown scarf tighter around her neck. The bit of sun from this morning was long gone, and the gray clouds were beginning to deliver a cold drizzle, so he was glad he'd hired a closed carriage and chosen the well-heated Conservatory as their destination.

"Are you warm enough?" he asked. "We will be there in less than five minutes. The North Ridge Road won't be that crowded on a day like today. I took Annie here for a picnic in November, and all the drives were packed with horses and carriages. We only had time to go through about a third of the Conservatory. Didn't even get a chance to look at the famous Victoria Regis lily. I just hope it isn't too crowded now that the Geary Street railroad goes all the way to the entrance near this side of the park."

"I'm fine," Laura said, pulling the carriage's lap robe up higher, making sure it was covering both of them. "Nate, just what are your intentions towards Annie? You seemed so at ease with her at Christmas. I confess I expected any moment that the two of you would announce an engagement. Mother even asked me if I knew exactly how things stood. I don't mean to pry, but living in her house as I do, I don't want to put my foot in it."

"I wish I knew," Nate said, then instantly regretted his honesty, knowing he couldn't leave it there. "Listen Laura, my intentions are straight-forward. I want more than anything to be Annie's husband. But I played my hand badly in the fall and almost lost any chance of winning her."

"Yet she still lets you call on her and was willing to meet your family. I don't understand."

"It is hard to explain. I sincerely believe that our affection is mutual. Nevertheless, with much better reason than you have, she is equally apprehensive about marriage. From what I can tell, she married in haste, and her first husband turned out to be a grave disappointment. So she has asked me for time so we can become better acquainted. I am willing to wait as long as it takes."

Nate didn't know if Annie believed him when he said that he had changed, that he was willing to accept a life together with her on her own terms, whatever those terms. But what if it meant that, like Laura, she never wanted to get married? Or if they married and she continued to run the boarding house and meet clients as Madam Sibyl, how would that be possible when they had children? *What if Annie doesn't want to have children?*

Nate pushed these thoughts away. Thank goodness, with Cranston as their new law partner, his role in his uncle's firm was now keeping him so busy it was hard to even imagine taking on the additional responsibilities of marriage and children. Better to go slowly and enjoy the growing depth of their friendship.

After a short silence, Laura interrupted his thoughts with a question that appeared out of nowhere. "Did Charlie or Frank ever fight with any Pennsylvania regiments in the war?"

Nate experienced the usual stab of pain at the mention of their two older brothers. Frank, the younger of the two, had died at Shiloh, and Charles died a year later at Chickamauga. He didn't really know the answer to her question, although it was his impression that those Civil War battles had been fought mainly by the Ohio troops his brothers had belonged to. "I don't think so, but I'm not sure. Father would probably know. He followed the newspaper reports of the battles pretty closely, but I don't know that I would ask Father. He doesn't like to talk about it. Why do you want to know?"

"Oh, I wouldn't ever ask him or Mother. I wondered because a professor at San Jose mentioned that one of my classmates who fought in the war was a 'Plymouth Pilgrim.' At first I thought this meant he was from Massachusetts, but then Professor Childs said that this group of soldiers were mainly from Pennsylvania. Seemed odd to me."

Nate pulled the team to a stop at one of the hitching posts at the back of the Conservatory and turned to search Laura's face, alerted by the deliberately light tone she was using that this was more than a casual question.

"If I remember correctly, the Plymouth Pilgrims was the name given to the Union troops captured in the Battle of Plymouth, North

Carolina, a year before the war was over. They ended up in the infamous Andersonville Prison. God rest their souls. Even as a boy, I heard rumors about what happened. There was corruption, torture, and most of the prisoners died. If your friend lived through that hell-hole, I suspect he doesn't much want to talk about it."

"He isn't my friend," Laura said sharply, then seemed to reconsider, speaking so quietly that Nate wasn't sure he heard her correctly. "At least not anymore."

Chapter Eight
Sunday evening, January 11, 1880

"THE INCOMPETENT TEACHERS: Not only influential politicians, but prominent churches and benevolent societies had insisted, he said, that their favorites and protégés should be provided for in the School Department, irrespective of their Qualifications." —*San Francisco Chronicle*, 1879

"She never would talk to me about the man in the alley. She got upset when I brought it up, so I let the subject drop." Nate stood in front of the parlor fireplace, the heat releasing the scent of wet wool.

When Annie saw how soaked Nate and his sister's coats were when they returned from their outing, she sent Laura straight up to her room under the care of Kathleen, with instructions to get her into dry clothes in time to go down to the light supper that was served Sunday evenings. She began to pour out cups of tea for Nate and herself from the large pot sitting on the table next to the settee where she was sitting. This parlor was more elegant and much larger than the one across the hall where she met Madam Sibyl's clients. In addition to the silk brocade-covered settee, and the two matching wing-backed chairs on either side of the fireplace, there was an old up-right piano and enough chairs and small tables scattered around the room to accommodate everyone on the occasional evening when all nine boarders migrated to this room after dinner.

"Nate, come get this tea while it is hot. Mrs. O'Rourke has out-done herself once again. There are turkey sandwiches, some fresh horseradish, and I believe that the cookies are your favorite oatmeal. I also promised I would bring you down to the kitchen before you left. I think she has made up another package of food to take home with you. After I told her about how wretched your boarding house cook was, she seems determined to supplement your fare as often as she can."

"I will be glad to pay her my compliments in person. You can tease me all you want, but her little packages are a godsend." Nate came over and sat down next to her on the settee and took the cup of tea in one hand, grabbing a sandwich with the other.

Annie let him eat in peace while she sipped her tea. She'd attended the Sunday dinner just a few hours earlier, the only meal she routinely took with her boarders, and she didn't have room for one more bite. She loved the routine of Sundays. She got up late and had breakfast in her room while she read the stack of papers from other cities that had made their way to San Francisco during the week. She was searching for the bits and pieces of news that would help her decide what advice to give Madam Sibyl's business clients. Sometimes she would accompany Barbara Hewitt and Jamie to church. Lately, having noticed that her boarder, the love-smitten David Chapman, was tagging along, she had begged off going out of sympathy for the poor man. Usually, Nate came to visit sometime after three, when dinner was done, and took her for a walk or occasionally for a ride. Then back they would come to their cozy chats by the fireside. Even though the door to the hallway was open, as was proper, she loved the sense of intimacy she got when she sat next to him, talking.

When she saw that Nate's eating had slowed, she said, "Laura seemed genuine when she thanked you for the outing."

"Yes, I was pleased to see some of her old enthusiasm return while we went around the Conservatory. I was impressed at her knowledge of botany. She certainly got a good education at San Jose. It turns out, however, she isn't content with what she learned there, and I think she is afraid my parents won't be pleased."

Nate then told her about Laura's plans to attend the University of California with the ultimate goal of becoming a lawyer and her unhappiness with her friend's unexpected decision to marry. He concluded by saying, "You would be proud of me. I didn't say a word in opposition to her plans."

"I would hope not," Annie replied tartly. She leaned over and took his hand in hers. "Do you really believe that your parents would object?"

"I honestly don't know. Father was reluctant at first to even let her move to San Jose to get her teacher's certificate. Mother was adamant that she go, but I think she primarily wanted her to have a chance to meet and marry someone besides one of the local ranchers. Laura and I have talked about this before. While Mother never complains about her life, there is a kind of wistfulness in her voice when she speaks about her two years at a finishing school and the one short year she spent teaching before she married."

Annie patted his hand and said, "I think your mother and mine might have had a lot in common. My mother taught for a few years before marriage as well. Father always told me that if she hadn't married him and had been in better health, he was sure she would have done something extraordinary, like found a school." As usual, memories of her departed parents saddened her.

Nate put an arm around her shoulders and took her right hand and brought it up to his lips, kissing it, and Annie felt comforted. They sat together in companionable silence for awhile until the sound of voices in the hallway, no doubt the boarders coming down to supper, reminded them both of the proprieties. Nate moved away slightly, although he continued to hold her right hand in his, now safely covered by the material in her skirts.

Annie cleared her throat and said, "If I understood you correctly, Laura was particularly upset because she felt that her friend Miss Wilks had failed her in some fashion."

"Yes, she was quite incensed. According to Laura, she and Miss Wilks had made some sort of pledge that they would support each other in their future career paths, Laura as a lawyer, Miss Wilks as a doctor. Laura seems to feel her friend's decision to marry is a kind of betrayal. I think Miss Wilks was Laura's first true female friend. I met her two or three times when Laura brought her home with her on holidays. Her own family lives down the coast near Santa Barbara. She seemed nice enough and quite fond of Laura."

Thinking of some of the passionate friendships she had witnessed at the academy she attended before her marriage, Annie remarked, "Oh dear, how hurt she must feel. Laura told me how excited she was to visit Hattie on Friday. I had hoped that she might be more forthcoming with her friend about the assault than she has been with us. Do you know if she had a chance to tell Hattie about what happened?"

"No, from what she said, Miss Wilks had no sooner dropped the bombshell that she was going to get married when the groom-to-be showed up. Laura sounded scandalized that he just knocked at the door to Miss Wilks' room and came on in. Who would have thought my little sister was such a prude?"

Annie blushed, remembering a few of the occasions when she and Nate got to spend precious time alone together. Recently, he was careful to meet with her only in public. Not that he wasn't affectionate. Whether they were in a carriage or walking along the pathways at Woodward's Gardens or just sitting together in the parlor, he always made her feel like she was the only person alive in the world. Yet she sometimes wished he wasn't as restrained and protective of her reputation. What would he think if she threw herself into his arms and told him how she couldn't stop dreaming of what it would be like to create a child with him, to…

Nate broke the silence, saying, "Laura indicated she'd hoped for a chance to talk to her friend about something that was bothering her. I do think she might open up to you if you pushed a little. I know she respects you."

"I would be glad to if you don't think she will mind," Annie said, hoping he didn't notice the blush she felt staining her cheeks.

"I would be particularly interested if she tells you anything about a male classmate she alluded to. She didn't mention his name, but he evidently was a Union soldier. She was very emphatic that he was *not* a friend."

"Oh, ho! Well, I will look into that, but I won't promise I will tell you everything she tells me. Sometimes there are things an older brother shouldn't know, for his own sake."

Nate looked slightly startled and then smiled at her. "I will rely on your excellent judgment. But speaking of your judgment, I wondered if I could ask for your advice about something that came up today at the firm."

"Of course. Is it the new trial Mr. Cranston has you working on?"

"No, this is actually my case. Do you remember the big scandal last October when some of the city school board members were accused of taking bribes in exchange for placing women in certain teaching positions?"

"Oh yes, but I thought there wasn't anything to it, just part of the general acrimony over this last election. Does this have anything to do with the uproar over the new school board's decision to lower teaching salaries?"

"Quite possibly. Mr. Emory, one of the newly elected board members, came to see me today. Evidently, the scandal last fall was started by an anonymous letter sent to the Board of Education office, and last week another letter arrived. This one accused him and the Girls' High Vice Principal of using their influence to get a position for a Mrs. Anderson. Emory said Mrs. Anderson is a family friend, recently widowed with a small son, and she was given a part-time job teaching at Girls' High this fall. I believe she teaches the classes in art, music, and drama."

"Had she been teaching prior to this year?"

"Not recently," Nate said. "According to Emory, before her marriage she did teach but in the primary grades. The letter stated that she didn't have the necessary certificate that teachers at the high school level are supposed to have."

"Ah, yes." Annie nodded. "Given the recent reduction in primary school teachers' salaries, I would imagine if an unqualified teacher was given a plum position teaching at Girls' High, this would cause some bitterness and perhaps an anonymous letter of complaint. Did Mr. Emory admit to playing a role in getting this family friend hired?"

"He was adamant that he hadn't done any such thing. Yet he then went on to say there was precedent for teachers being hired for the higher grade levels without the higher certificates if they were employed in a part-time position. Made me wonder if he was being completely truthful. He asked me to look into what recourse he had to fight this 'defamation' of his character. Since the letter was anonymous, there isn't a lot he can do. However, if this results in any kind of formal investigation, I would, of course, be glad to represent him."

Annie frowned, trying to remember the facts from a series of newspaper articles she'd read right before Christmas about the Board's actions. "I don't believe I have heard of Mr. Emory, and I know the names of most of the prominent businessmen in the city. Who is he?"

"He owns the City of Hills Distillery. He was the only Democrat elected to the school board this fall. The rest were Republicans or members of the Workingmen's Party."

Annie thought for a moment. Then she said, "If that is true, it does suggest a political motivation. Emory must be pretty popular to have won any position, what with the Workingmen's Party syphoning off votes from the Democrats the way it did."

"Emory said he knew he might be in for some trouble when he sided with the teachers last month during their protests against the reduction in salaries. He spoke at that rally they held."

"My, my," Annie laughed. "I can't imagine that went over well with the Republicans on the school board. Does he think that the anonymous letters came from another board member, not a disaffected teacher?"

"He was too politic to say, but I think this is why he is taking the anonymous letter seriously."

"What of Mrs. Anderson? It seems that she has more to lose in terms of her reputation, as well as her livelihood, if this became a public fight."

Annie well knew the anxiety of being a widowed woman maneuvering through the shoals of polite society. It was one of the reasons she had worked to keep her own identity and that of Madam Sibyl separate and one of the reasons she hoped to get rid of the fiction that she was clairvoyant in the near future. On the other hand, it wouldn't be surprising if it turned out that Mr. Emory had used his personal influence to help a young, and possibly very attractive, woman.

She continued. "Do you know if Mr. Emory is married?"

"Yes he is, although I can see that we are thinking along the same path." Nate chuckled, then turned serious. "I did ask him if he could bring Mrs. Anderson into the office so I could ask about her hiring, make sure there aren't any surprises. I will represent him in any case, but it would make me feel better if I thought I had all the facts. That's why I wanted to ask you if you thought Jamie's mother would be willing to talk to me about Mrs. Anderson since she also teaches at Girls' High. See if she has heard any rumors about her and her teaching appointment."

Annie hesitated. Barbara Hewitt was such a reserved woman. It had taken months, and a rather disturbing event last fall, to get her to the point where she was comfortable enough to call Annie by her first name. Annie thought that Barbara's marriage might have been as unhappy as her own since she never mentioned Jamie's father. But she could be wrong. Unremitting grief over the loss of that husband could explain her reticence. In any event, she didn't know how Barbara Hewitt would feel about gossiping about one of her fellow teachers.

"I will ask her. But I'll also make it very clear that if she feels the least uncomfortable, she need not talk to you. She's been very helpful, taking your sister under her wing. I don't want to do anything to upset their growing friendship. Did you know it was Barbara and Jamie who accompanied her to Hattie Wilks' boarding house this Friday? Maybe I should ask Laura if she has heard anything about any teachers still being upset about the reduction in teachers' salaries. Then I could steer the conversation to other subjects, like what was bothering her so much about her first teaching experience this fall or male classmates who were *not* her friends."

"Sounds like a good strategy." Nate looked out the door to the empty hallway, then put his arm around her again. "Now, before any of the boarders come out of the dining room, I have something of greater importance to discuss. Have I told you yet tonight how beautiful you are?"

And before Annie could answer, Nate kissed her.

Chapter Nine
Monday afternoon, January 12, 1880

"Superintendent Taylor moved that a Committee be appointed to consider the advisability of granting diplomas to the young ladies of the Normal class who are to graduate in May next:" —*San Francisco Chronicle*, 1880

"Miss Dawson, I want to say again how much I appreciate your willingness to let Miss Blaine assist in your classroom this term. I've told her how fortunate she is to get the chance to work with someone who has just graduated from the state Normal School. Such a superior education." Della Thorndike, the Girls' High normal class teacher, smiled warmly at Laura. Pulling the shy Miss Blaine forward, she said, "Kitty, my dear, do tell Miss Dawson how pleased you are."

The young woman, a redhead whose heart-shaped face was marred by a distinct look of annoyance, murmured, "Yes miss, so pleased."

Laura had been annoyed herself when she arrived in the teachers' room of Clement Grammar for her meeting with Miss Thorndike and discovered she had brought along the student teacher she wanted to place in Laura's class. But Hattie's positive description of Miss Thorndike had reassured her, so she didn't object. In fact, by the time Miss Thorndike finished telling her about the well-ordered sequence of training she had developed for the students engaged in practice teaching, Laura felt quite pleased about agreeing to the whole enterprise.

Since Miss Blaine had her pedagogy classes in the morning, she would be at Clement Grammar only in the afternoons between noon and four. The first two weeks, she would be observing Laura's teaching. Then, under Laura's supervision, she would work with small groups of students on their math or reading, followed by four weeks where Miss

Blaine would lead the class for an hour each day. Once a week, Laura would meet with Miss Thorndike to review the progress the student teacher was making. The culmination of her training would come when the young woman would lead the class entirely by herself for a week, under the observation of both Laura and Miss Thorndike. If Hattie wasn't going to have any time for her, then Laura looked forward to being able to discuss her classes in detail with Miss Thorndike.

"Kitty must leave us now. Her father's carriage will be waiting for her, won't it, dear?" Miss Thorndike nodded to Miss Blaine, whose alabaster cheeks turned bright red. "I, however, would like to stay a bit longer, Miss Dawson, if it is convenient, to make sure you don't have any additional questions."

Laura watched with some sartorial envy as Miss Blaine pulled on a pair of expensive kid gloves that were dyed a sky blue to match her fashionably tight-fitting, cuirass-styled suit. After she left, Laura offered to make tea for Miss Thorndike, who had begged her to call her Della, using the kettle that stayed at the boil on the oil stove in the teachers' room. Della Thorndike, obviously well known by the other Clement teachers, chatted with three women stopping by to check their mail boxes before leaving for the day.

While waiting for the pot to steep, Laura covertly examined Della, who was one of those silver blondes with soft, creamy skin that looked ageless. Laura would have judged her to be still in her late twenties if she hadn't mentioned that she was fifteen when she'd started teaching nearly twenty years earlier. She was dressed in an elegant ensemble, a dark green satin underskirt with matching plaid wool overskirt, black ribbon trimming, and a delicate black lace ruff, starched to frame her long pale neck and her jet black earrings, which glinted in the room's gas light. Laura wondered if the Misses Moffet would be able to produce anything that beautiful for her, then added to her list of grievances that Andrew Russell's appearance on Saturday had squelched any chance of Hattie going shopping with her that day.

As Laura listened to Della's easy conversation with the other teachers, the bereft feeling she'd been fighting all weekend returned. How was she ever going to find a friendship as dear to her as the one she'd had with Hattie? Laura had never told any of her family how frightened she'd been her first week at San Jose Normal School. At only sixteen, she had never been away from home before, and because she'd been taught at home by her mother, this was also her first extended experience with people her own age. She'd found her classmates mystifying, as if they were talking to each other in a coded language. Then she'd met Hattie, who lived in her boarding house, and everything changed.

Every room Laura entered became welcoming as long as she was pulled along in Hattie's wake. Hattie turned every missed exam question, muffed recitation, or awkward social encounter into a funny story they would share at night over their hot cocoa. Hattie always made her feel special, cherished, and even brave. Brave enough to go off to her first teaching assignment at Cupertino Creek. Even though she'd made a mess of that job, she had survived by telling herself that once she was reunited with Hattie, everything would be all right. Now it turned out Hattie had pledged herself to another, and nothing would ever be the same again.

Della turned to Laura and drew her into the small group of other teachers, saying, "Dear Laura, you must come here this minute. Miss Beale is longing to ask if you are familiar with a certain Ned Goodwin, her fiancé, who is currently at San Jose Normal School."

"Oh, yes," Laura said, shaking Miss Beale's hand. "Ned was in the class behind me, but we took botany together with Miss Norton. A very lively mind and well-liked by his classmates," she continued, guessing that the quiet Miss Beale wouldn't want to hear how entrancing her female classmates had found Ned's blue eyes, luxuriant mustache, and cheerful smile. As far as she knew, he had not succumbed to any of their blandishments, so maybe it was this shy, soft-spoken young brunette that was keeping him faithful. She wondered if there was a diplomatic way of getting Miss Beale to find out from Ned whether Seth Timmons was still at San Jose finishing up his studies. *Yes, a better acquaintance with Celia*

Beale might be very illuminating.

After a little more conversation, the rest of the teachers left, and Della Thorndike sat down to expand on Laura's supervisory responsibilities with Kitty Blaine. When they got to the plan to have Kitty work on her own with the slower readers, Della said, "I don't know how Kitty is going to respond if they aren't completely cooperative. You might need to intervene if you see things getting out of hand. She is a bright young woman who excels in all her subjects, but as you may have observed, she can be a bit socially ill-at-ease. Her father, you know, is quite wealthy, nothing but the best for his little Kitty."

Laura wondered why being cosseted by a loving parent would make a young girl socially awkward.

As if to answer her unspoken question, Della went on, saying, "Her mother died shortly after her birth, and Kitty was brought up entirely by English governesses. She was educated at home until two years ago when she entered the middle year at Girls' High."

Sighing, she leaned towards Laura and, in a confiding tone, said, "Kitty has had some trouble fitting in with the other girls. We have students from the best families in the city, so I don't know exactly what the problem is. She seems most comfortable with her male instructors, who are dazzled by her erudition. She is fluent in Greek and Latin. Quite impressive. But I have decided this semester to take the poor thing under my wing. Mother her a little. I hope you will do so as well."

Aware that she was only a year or two older than Kitty, Laura wasn't sure that the young woman would take at all kindly to being mothered by her. In fact, it was her distinct impression that Kitty wasn't that enthusiastic about being Miss Thorndike's special protégé. But, since Kitty knew Greek and Latin, the two subjects Laura needed to master if she wanted to pass the entrance exam for the University, it seemed sensible to cultivate her friendship.

Della continued to tell her about her plans for Kitty, getting up to freshen their tea, obviously very at home in the Clement Grammar teachers' room. As she chattered on, Laura's thoughts drifted back to

Hattie. She was frustrated that she hadn't gotten the chance to tell her friend about her oldest Cupertino Creek student, Buck Morrison, and how Seth had intervened. And then there was the alley attack last week that she'd been anxious to talk to her about. The more Laura went over what happened, the less sure she was that it had been Seth. She really could have used some reassurance from Hattie on Saturday, but just when Laura was about to bring up Seth, the dratted Andrew Russell had interrupted them.

She couldn't understand why Hattie found Russell so attractive. He was only of medium build, with regular, unremarkable features. His chiseled jaw and his dark amber-colored eyes, magnified by gold-rimmed glasses, did give him an air of strength, but Laura found his habit of running his hands through his hair both irritating and immature. No doubt Hattie found it *endearing*. After Hattie had whispered into his ear, he had told Laura how pleased he was that she had agreed to attend "his sweet girl" at the wedding ceremony.

Laura hadn't been sure she would be able to stay civil if she had to listen to his fake attempts at try ing to flatter her, so she manufactured a prior engagement requiring her immediate return to the O'Farrell Street boarding house. Mr. Russell had offered to get her a cab, but in her desperation to get away, she'd refused his offer and was down the stairs and halfway home before she remembered her promise to Annie to go nowhere unaccompanied. Fortunately, no one saw her come into the house, so no one was the wiser. At least Hattie had agreed to visit her at the O'Farrell Street house this coming Saturday morning. They could have a longer talk then, without Andrew Russell.

"Miss Thorndike, Miss Dawson, how good to see you two have met."

The tea cups clattered, and Laura was startled to see Russell at the door to the teachers' room. Since he was the Vice Principal of Clement Grammar, she shouldn't have been surprised, but she felt somehow hounded by his presence. Here she was having a nice cozy talk with a potential new friend, and once again he was interfering.

"Mr. Russell, you will be pleased to learn that Miss Dawson has agreed to take Kitty Blaine on this term for her practice teaching," Della Thorndike said, putting a warm hand on Laura's shoulder.

"Wonderful. I am sure Miss Blaine will benefit from the experience." Russell came into the room. "I do hope you are getting settled in with your seventh grade class, Miss Dawson. Miss Wilks was quite fond of her students, I know."

Della responded before Laura could, saying, "I understand that you are distressed that Miss Wilks decided to quit so precipitously, Mr. Russell, but I am very confident that Miss Dawson will have no difficulty filling her shoes." She then gave Laura's shoulder a little squeeze.

Laura, sensing some undercurrent she couldn't define, nodded pleasantly to Russell, hoping if she didn't encourage him, he would just go away.

There was a brief silence while Russell fiddled with his watch fob and ineffectually brushed back the thick shock of mud brown hair that had fallen over one eye. Then he bowed slightly to both of them and said, "Well, well, I won't keep you; I can tell you have business to complete. Miss Thorndike, it was a pleasure to see you. Miss Dawson, do feel free to come to me if you have any questions. I was sorry that our time together on Saturday was cut short, but I am confident that we will have many other opportunities in the future. Once again, let me tell you how pleased I am that you are teaching for us." He left, closing the door behind him.

Della moved back to the tea table and brought the cups over and placed one in front of Laura. "So kind of him to stop by; he is so busy. I don't know what Clement's Principal DuBois would do without Mr. Russell. She is quite capable in terms of academic issues, but the Vice Principal is in charge of school discipline, and I think that it is advisable to have a male in that position of authority. Of course, he also has excellent academic credentials. You may have heard that in addition to his duties here at Clement he also teaches Greek and Latin and tutors students in German at Girls' High. He studied the classical curriculum at the University of Rochester, and he was in the first graduating class of the California State Normal school when it moved to San Jose."

Laura again nodded but said nothing, feeling irritated to find another Andrew Russell admirer. Perhaps Della Thorndike wished to mother him the way she mothered Kitty Blaine.

Della went on. "I was surprised to hear he had time to meet with you on a Saturday, given how busy he is."

"Oh, no, you misunderstood," Laura said. "I was visiting Miss Wilks. We are very old friends, and Mr. Russell happened to stop by."

"Oh, I hadn't realized. Of course that makes sense, since you are both recent graduates of the Normal School. How convenient that you were able to take her place when she had to leave so precipitously. Some health issues, I believe I heard. I hope she is doing well."

Laura, reminded of her own suspicion that Hattie might be ill, wondered if there was something more behind Hattie's decision to leave teaching besides her concern about the proprieties and her decision to marry. Interested in hearing what Della thought, she said, "She did mention in her last letter to me before Thanksgiving that a nasty influenza was going around among the students and teachers. Was Hattie hit particularly hard?"

When Della didn't immediately respond, Laura continued. "I ask only because I know from experience that she tends to downplay her illnesses. I can't count the times at school I had to put my foot down and insist she go to the school nurse, not just soldier on when she was sick. I worry that she is over-taxing herself, planning for her wedding with Mr. Russell in such a short period of time."

"Yes, yes, her wedding." Della leaned closer and said, "I wasn't sure if a date had been set."

"I believe it depends on when her parents can arrange to come," Laura said, wondering what they thought of their daughter's sudden decision.

"It will be in San Francisco, then." Della sounded surprised. "Perhaps the two of us can arrange a nice little wedding breakfast for after the event. Yes, that sounds like a splendid idea. I will visit her and feel her out on the subject. I am sure that the other Clement teachers would be very glad to help out."

A knock at the door to the teachers' room gave Laura a chance to think of a response. Knowing that Hattie might not welcome Della's well-meant offer, she said, "A lovely idea, but I'm not sure there will be time." She opened the door to see Jamie Hewitt standing there, and she said, "Oh my, is it four already? Tell your mother I will be right out."

Laura turned to Della and shook her hand, saying with warmth, "Thank you so much for the time you have given me today, but I must go. Of course you know Barbara Hewitt since you both teach at Girls' High. That was her little boy, Jamie. Because we all live at the same boarding house on O'Farrell, we walk home together."

As she gathered up her coat and satchel and exchanged the last set of pleasantries with Della, Laura felt a definite improvement in her mood. She had the promise of a stimulating working relationship with a colleague, the challenge of guiding Kitty's training while perfecting her own skills, and the welcome knowledge of the boarding house and the friendships waiting for her when she got home. *If Hattie wants to devote herself to Andrew Russell and give up the life we had planned together, well, that is her problem, not mine.*

Chapter Ten
Wednesday evening, January 14, 1880

"Some mothers think they are overburdened with three or four young children to take care of. What might they think if they had half a hundred?" — *San Francisco Chronicle*, 1879

"Mrs. Anderson, the teacher who was mentioned in the anonymous letter, accompanied Mr. Emory to our law offices yesterday afternoon. I had asked to meet with her, but I rather hoped I might see her without Emory," Nate said, sitting down beside Annie in the formal parlor.

Annie was delighted to see him, because even though she kept Wednesday free, he wasn't always able to get away. Now that the law firm had the much-sought-after Able Cranston as a partner, he was working long hours, and sometimes Sunday was the only time they both had free. Nate was good about writing every day, telling her about the cases he was working on, and she looked forward each night to sitting in the privacy of her bedroom, reading his words and hearing his voice in her head. She would write to him in return, imagining his laugh when she told him about how Mrs. O'Rourke had scolded her nephew Patrick McGee for stopping by when he went off patrol and distracting Kathleen from her duties or Dandy's latest exploit as the best rat-catching Boston terrier west of the Mississippi.

She leaned close and gave him a swift kiss on the cheek, thankful once again that he was willing to go against male fashion dictates and forgo a mustache and beard. She wondered if his Shawnee heritage explained why her lips felt no prickly stubble, even at this time of night, or if he had shaved again before coming to visit her. If so, it was one more example of how thoughtful Nate was compared to her deceased husband, John.

"What was that for? Not that I mind." Nate slipped his arm around her. "But I want to know what I did to deserve that welcome so I can do it again."

"Oh, I am just glad to see you," Annie replied. "Last Sunday seems an eternity ago. Go on and tell me about your visit with Mrs. Anderson. Do you still suspect that Mr. Emory hasn't been entirely forthcoming about his relationship to her?"

"I don't know. He certainly is very solicitous. Evidently, her father was his best friend. I suppose it's possible he really sees himself as a sort of paternal figure. Doesn't mean he didn't intervene on her behalf, but I really don't see this as causing much of a scandal."

"What is Mrs. Anderson like?"

"Young, tearful. Pretty enough, if you like the clinging vine sort of female." Nate smiled and tightened his arm around her. Annie leaned away from him and playfully boxed his ear.

He laughed. "She brought her son with her. Jack, a fine fellow of four. Came right up to me and shook my hand like a little man. Mrs. Anderson's mother takes care of him while she is at work, and I must say he seemed very comfortable with Emory. Climbed right up in his lap while we were talking. Not that this necessarily means anything."

"Did Mrs. Anderson tell you about her hiring? Isn't that what you wanted to find out?"

"Yes, and I wanted to see what kind of witness she would make if this came to a formal hearing or even a trial. She was very vague. Couldn't quite remember who had told her there was an opening. She did say she wrote Mr. Swett, the Girls' High Principal, about her interest in the job. I understand it was Mr. Hoffmann, the Vice Principal, plus the senior English instructor, Miss Thorndike, who were responsible for the decision to hire her. When I asked if they had mentioned her lack of the appropriate teaching certificate, she said she couldn't remember."

"Did she have any idea of who might have written the anonymous letter?"

"She says not. Says she can't imagine anybody being 'so mean.' That's why I hope to talk to Mrs. Hewitt, see if she has a different perspective."

Annie nodded. "I caught her before she went into dinner and asked her to come to us in the parlor when she was finished, and she didn't demur."

Annie had spoken with Barbara on Monday evening about Nate's case and his wish to speak with her. At first, Jamie's mother had visibly recoiled, her hands flying up defensively, and she responded that she wouldn't feel comfortable talking about her fellow teachers. Annie understood this attitude, particularly if one were the kind of person who valued one's own privacy, and Barbara Hewitt was an intensely private person. She never talked about her past, where she grew up, her marriage, or what happened to her husband. Annie respected that reticence since she seldom spoke about the painful aspects of her own personal history to anyone. Especially not about the disaster of her marriage to John or the miscarriage. She had never told a single soul about that, not even her closest friends, not even Nate.

However, as Madam Sibyl, Annie had learned to read a person's thoughts from their physical reactions, and, in her opinion, Barbara Hewitt wasn't just uncomfortable with the idea of "gossiping" about her colleagues; she was frightened by Nate's request, and Annie wondered why. Then Barbara Hewitt changed her mind and said she would be willing to speak with Nate. She explained that she had been thinking about how she would feel if she found herself in Mrs. Anderson's position. Annie wondered what information she would be able to contribute but was glad she felt comfortable enough to talk.

Nate shifted and removed his arm from around her, and she realized there were sounds coming from the hallway. Supper must be over. She stood up and went over to the open door and saw Miss Minnie and Miss Millie being ushered out of the dining room by Herman Stein, Annie's most distinguished boarder and a successful west coast merchant. He nodded to her in passing but continued to shepherd the two elderly seamstresses up the stairs, Miss Minnie talking steadily, her sister silent as usual.

Next came Esther Stein, the older boarder who was Annie's closest confidante. She was listening to an animated Jamie, and they turned towards the back stairs that went down to the kitchen. Annie silently blessed Esther, a woman with numerous grandchildren of her own, for taking the boy under her wing after supper. Barbara may have asked the older woman to accompany her son down to the kitchen so he could let Dandy out.

Esther and Jamie were closely followed by Laura and Mr. Harvey, the quiet dry goods clerk who shared a room with David Chapman. Finally came Barbara, who was looking distracted by Chapman's usual attentiveness. When Laura and Barbara saw Annie standing in the hallway, they both broke away from their escorts and came towards her. Nate, standing in the parlor doorway, stepped forward, bowed politely to Mrs. Hewitt, and shook her hand.

Annie had already ascertained that Barbara would prefer to speak to Nate alone, so her responsibility was to make sure they weren't disturbed. Seeing Laura approach, she said, "Could you keep me company for a spell? Your brother has some business with Mrs. Hewitt, and I would like to give them some privacy. Can you spare a minute to sit with me in the hall? I don't know how long they will be, so I would like to stay close at hand." Annie pointed to the bench next to the hall coat stand.

"What does Nate need with Barbara?" Laura asked as they sat down. "I hope he isn't being an annoying older brother, checking up on me?"

"Good heavens, no!" Annie laughed. "It is about a case he is working on. He might want to talk to you about it as well, since it seems that someone is sending anonymous letters spreading malicious rumors about teachers. Have you heard anything of this nature at Clement?"

"I haven't heard a thing like that. How disturbing." Laura frowned. "On the other hand, that doesn't mean anything. Truth is, I haven't had a chance to talk much with the other teachers beyond greet-ings when we meet in the hallways. Last week, Jamie's teacher was kind enough to sit and talk with me at lunch, but I confess we mostly talked about Jamie! And this week, after I agreed to supervise Kitty Blaine, the Normal class student I told you about, I spent my lunch hour with her, talking about my lesson plan for the day."

"Oh yes, how is that going?" Annie asked.

"I really don't know. Miss Blaine is very quiet, and I'm not sure what to make of her. It's just been two days. The only time I have gotten her to say more than a few words was when I asked her about her lan-guage studies. Apparently, she is learning German from Hattie's intended, Mr. Russell. She got very excited for a moment when talking about that. Since she is only observing my class this week and next, she sits quietly in the back of the room. I guess if you are a student at Clement Grammar you are used to having practice teachers, because none of the students batted an eye when I introduced her. I am the one who feels self-conscious."

"I would hate having someone observe me when I work as Madam Sibyl, potentially criticizing my every move," said Annie, "but you probably went through it when you did your practice teaching at San Jose, right?"

"Yes, and I was very nervous then as well. We rotated through all the different grades, from first to eight. Miss Titus, one of my pedagogy professors, was very kind and gave me good marks, but I never felt comfortable, with the younger children in particular."

Annie nodded encouragingly and said, "Did you have many very young children in your school at Cupertino Creek?"

Laura gave a little shudder. "Five of them under the age of seven. It was awful! Only one of them knew the alphabet, and none of them could sit still for more than ten minutes at a time. I would just get one settled, copying letters and numbers on a slate, and another one would have gotten up and wandered away. I finally figured out I had to pair each of them with an older student whose job was to keep them at their tasks. When the weather was nice, I would send one of the more proficient readers outdoors with the group of them to read aloud. That worked better."

Annie chuckled. "Oh my, I don't know how you did it."

"I am not sure how I did it either. Not well, I can assure you. That was one of the reasons I jumped at the offer to teach at Clement. I was certainly more successful with the children at Cupertino Creek who were in the middle grades, and I am starting to enjoy my seventh graders."

"It is interesting to hear your perspective. You weren't here in December, but the newly elected Board of Education voted to lower the primary school teachers' salaries a great deal. There was quite a public outcry, teachers writing letters to the editor, holding a large protest meeting, saying that they would have to leave teaching rather than take these 'starvation wages.' Did your friend Hattie tell you about it?"

"No, but that explains one of the comments that Mrs. DuBois, Clement's principal, made when she was interviewing me. She said that she was glad I had been able to step into Hattie's position at the last minute because there had been a terrible scramble to get all the positions filled in the lower grades in the week before Christmas."

"That would make sense," Annie replied. "I just looked it up in my back copies of the *Chronicle*. Prior to the Board vote, a teacher with the highest level certificate and ten years experience was making $70 a month in the primary grades. Now they can make no more than half that amount. I wouldn't be surprised if many of them looked for jobs outside the city that paid better."

"What could the Board be thinking?" Laura exclaimed. "You couldn't pay me enough to teach a whole class of five-or six-year-olds! Hot sticky fingers pulling at you, unexplained fits of giggles, endless fights over who touched whom first, and tears when you try to give them the least discipline." Laura shuddered again and continued, sounding defensive to Annie. "I know that sounds terrible since taking care of small children is something that a woman is supposed to do naturally."

Annie laughed and said, "I never understood that attitude, but it's very common. The newspaper said that one of the Board members justified lower salaries for the primary grades because taking care of the youngest children didn't require any special training or experience to do well."

"Poppycock!" Laura ducked her head and whispered, "Don't tell Nate I used that term. I know it isn't ladylike. But, since I learned it from him, he will feel all guilty and give me a scold." She then laughed.

Annie promised not to tell Nate but pondered what Laura had said about taking care of young children. She'd had very little exposure to children in her life. She had no siblings, and her mother taught her at home until she was twelve and her mother died. Then her father tutored her on shipboard as they traveled back east. Her first experience with school was at age fourteen when she started the Academy, but that was with girls her own age. Lately, however, Annie found herself thinking more and more about what it would be like to be a mother. What *she* would be like as a mother.

Laura looked at her quizzically, and Annie realized she had been silent too long. Thinking she might learn more about what had upset Laura last fall, she said, "So you didn't like the babies in your class. What about the older students? I always wondered how hard it would be to teach someone who wasn't that much younger than you are. Did you…"

The front bell pealed, followed by a loud pounding on the door. Annie stood up and spontaneously put her arm around Laura, who had given a startled cry. Kathleen was probably down in the kitchen starting on the dishes, so as another thunderous series of raps rattled the front door, Annie wavered. Should she open it? She didn't want to leave Laura, whose nerves were obviously still in a state. Nate appeared, Barbara right behind him, and he said, "Shall I?"

"Yes, do. I don't know who it could be at this hour." Annie retreated with Laura a bit further back down the hall.

Nate undid the bolt and opened the door on a man, a stranger to Annie. He looked to be in his fifties with a small gray mustache. He was neatly dressed in a subdued brown wool suit, but his cheeks were red, and he was clearly out of breath. He immediately took off his derby when he saw there were ladies present and bobbed his head politely, saying, "Please sir, ladies. I am sorry t'bother you, but it's a matter of some urgency. Is there a Miss Laura Dawson residing here? My name is McNaughton, and I have a message for her."

Nate looked back at Laura. When she shook her head in bewilderment, he turned to the man and said, "Sir, I'm Miss Dawson's brother. You may convey your message to me."

"Yes, sir, I understand. It is Miss Hattie Wilks, sir, that boards with me and the missus. We've never had such a thing happen, respectable house we run. Miss Hattie fell some time this evening, dunno when. It were something terrible to see her all broken on the landing, blood everywhere. Hector, my son, got a cab, and he and my missus took her off to St. Mary's. But before they left, the lassie roused a little. She grabbed my hand and told me to get a message to Miss Laura Dawson at Mrs. Fuller's boarding house on O'Farrell Street. The local copper directed me here. Now, sir, I think if your sister wants to see her, she'd best come straight away. I saw too much death in the war, and the poor girl had that look they get, you know. When they are about to meet their maker."

Chapter Eleven
Later Wednesday evening, January 14, 1880
"The new chapel on First Street, in the rear of St. Mary's Hospital, erected by the Sisters of Mercy connected with the Hospital, was dedicated at 3 o'clock yesterday afternoon." —*San Francisco Hospital*, 1879

Hattie looked so small lying on the hospital bed. And so pale. Laura leaned over and stroked her cheek, cold and smooth as marble.

"Sister, shouldn't she have more blankets?" Laura looked at the Sister of Mercy who stood quietly in the corner, wimple and collar glowing white against the black garments that could be barely distinguished from the dark shadows at the edges of the room.

"I am sorry, Miss. The attending physician said that because of her broken bones we should limit the weight of her coverings in order to lessen her pain," the Sister replied quietly, her hands folded into the wide sleeves of her habit.

Laura had noticed the splint on Hattie's right arm when she first came into the room, but now she saw that the contours of the light blanket laying over her suggested there was some sort of splint over both of her legs. She sat down, pulling the chair closer so she could take Hattie's left hand in her own, rubbing it to try to create some warmth. She had been forced to leave Nate and Annie in the hallway, the sister insisting that only one person could be in the room with the patient at a time.

"Poor darling," she whispered. "You took a bad tumble, but the good doctors have patched you up." Hattie didn't open her eyes, and Laura saw that every breath her friend took was slow and labored.

A cry rent the silence from somewhere down the hall, and Laura glanced towards the door, seeing the swift passage of another nun, black veil and skirts making a soft swishing noise. She shivered. She'd never been in a hospital before, and every story she'd read about them as houses of death came flooding back. She barely remembered the ride across the city, but from the moment that Nate and Annie led her through the front doors of the imposing St. Mary's Hospital, she had felt oppressed.

The rows of gas fixtures throughout the building vestibule and corridors filled the air with their distinctive odor and soft hiss yet failed to illuminate the high ceilings or the three flights of wide stairs they trudged up to reach Hattie's floor. The sister had escorted them down a corridor that seemed to stretch for miles. They passed room after room, where Laura caught glimpses of other black-robed nuns leaning over beds, doing goodness knows what. And the smells. Even in this room, the familiar odor of gas lighting, mixed with a strong astringent scent, failed to mask a smell more associated with butcher shops. Laura felt in the grip of some gothic nightmare as she listened to the sound of Hattie's breathing in counterpoint to the click, click, click of the sister's rosary.

Hattie moaned, and her eyes fluttered open and then shut.

Laura leaned closer, squeezing her friend's hand, and whispered, "Hattie dear, it's me, Laura. How are you feeling? Is there anything I can do for you?"

Hattie continued to breathe slowly and with increased difficulty.

Laura turned and said, "Sister, what is wrong? Why isn't she conscious?" She pointed to a small brown glass bottle sitting on the bedside table. "Has she been given some medicine for pain; is that why she doesn't wake up?" Laura recalled the deep sleepiness she'd felt when her mother gave her laudanum the time she broke her arm, but she didn't remember having any difficulty breathing.

When the sister didn't respond, the words of McNaughton, the boarding house owner, crept into her head. She said more sharply, "Sister, please answer me. She's going to be all right, isn't she? There isn't anything wrong besides the broken bones, is there? The man who found her told us there was blood. Did she cut herself?" She reached over and ran her hand over Hattie's hair, searching for a sign of a bandage, vaguely remembering that scalp wounds bled freely. Finding nothing, she went back to stroking Hattie's cheek, saying through her tears, "Dearest, can you hear me? I am right beside you. I won't let anything happen to you. But can't you give me a sign? Let me know you are all right."

The sister stepped forward and put her hand on Laura's shoulder in a calming gesture. "Miss, Miss, you will frighten her. She needs peace now. Be comforted. Your friend is in God's hands, and He will not forsake her."

"Nate, I wish we could be in there with her. Do you think that man was correct, that Laura's friend is dying?" Annie paced in a tight circle. They stood in a little alcove two doors down from Hattie's room, where the Sister of Mercy had directed them. The alcove had a painted and gilded plaster Madonna and Child in a niche high up on the wall and a hard wooden bench that looked like it was designed more for penance than comfort. Nate gathered her into his arms, and for a brief moment she felt calm.

"Let's give Laura some time with Hattie." Nate pulled out his pocket watch to check the time, keeping his other arm around Annie. "If she doesn't come out in the next fifteen minutes, I will go and poke my head in. See what's going on."

She leaned her head on his shoulder, but she found her growing anxiety impossible to ignore. She pulled away and moved out into the hall, looking up and down the long corridor, saying, "I just remembered. Mrs. O'Malley, Tilly's aunt and Biddy's mother, works at St. Mary's. I wonder if she is here now?"

Biddy O'Malley was a good friend of Annie's maid Kathleen, and she had recommended her fresh-off-the boat cousin Tilly to help out last fall when Kathleen spent so much time helping Annie on her investigations into a couple of fraudulent mediums. Annie had kept Tilly on when the investigation was over, and both Beatrice and Kathleen were determined to turn the shy Colleen into a first rate domestic.

"Would Mrs. O'Malley be working at this time of night? Doesn't she need to be home with her children?" Nate said.

"Maybe. But no. Wednesday nights, Tilly needs to be home by four to take care of the little ones. Biddy's factory job doesn't let out until six, and her mother's shift starts at five. Let's ask one of the sisters if Mrs. O'Malley is working nearby." Annie began to walk down the hall towards the two Sisters of Mercy who were standing at the large windows at the end of the corridor.

She felt a tug at her shoulder and heard Nate say, "Annie, wait a minute. By all means, let's ask if we can speak to a doctor, find out more about Miss Wilks' condition. But I don't see why you want to get Mrs. O'Malley involved."

"Have you ever tried to get a doctor to reveal anything definite about a patient? Back in New York, one of the ways I kept a roof over my head was to volunteer to sit at the bedsides of any of my in-laws who were ill. I can tell you it made me furious to see the way the attending doctors answered every question with medical twaddle and polite hemming and hawing that conveyed nothing. Anyone with eyes in their heads could tell when a patient was in a bad way, but the doctor always pretended all was well, until it wasn't. Then it was anybody else's fault but their own. And you heard the sister who brought us here. We should put our faith in God. I doubt very much if either the doctors or the sisters will give us any details, at least not to someone who isn't a relative."

"But what can Mrs. O'Malley tell us?"

"I don't know. But we can at least ask her if she has heard anything about Hattie, and I bet she will know which doctor is the most competent, so we can make sure she is getting the best care."

When Annie asked the two sisters if Mrs. O'Malley was working nearby, they told her that she was just up the corridor that connected the three wings of the hospital. Annie, motioning to Nate to follow her, went quickly past the nuns and turned the corner. There, as promised, was a woman scrubbing at a spot on the tiled wall. She was dressed in dark gray, with a white apron that went almost down to the bottom of her skirt, and a bucket of soapy water sat at her feet. She straightened and turned as Annie approached, letting the sponge drop into the bucket. The white cap, which completely covered her hair, framed a thin, tired, and lined face. But when Annie reached out her hand, introducing herself, Mrs. O'Malley's blue eyes sparkled, and she broke into a wide grin as she wiped her hands on her apron so she could enthusiastically pump Annie's hand.

"Glory be, Mrs. Fuller, I'm ever so glad to meet you and thank you for all you've done for our Tilly. When she arrived at our doorstep this summer, we couldn't get two words out of her, scared little thing. Never been off her da's farm back in Ireland; mucking out the pigs and baby tending's all she knew. But now when she comes home from your place, she's chattering about the proper way to set a table, how she ironed her first shirt, and she amuses the children with her stories about tricks the little dog is up to. It's a marvel the change you've made in the girl."

Annie smiled and said, "Don't thank me. It's Mrs. O'Rourke, my cook and housekeeper, and Kathleen Hennessey you should thank. They have taken her under their wings. But your niece is a fine girl, and you should be proud of her."

Having come up behind Annie, Nate bowed and shook Mrs. O'Malley's hand, introducing himself.

"Oh, Mrs. Fuller, I was that surprised to see you I didn't ask. Is it one of your friends or family that's brought you here?" Mrs. O'Malley asked.

"A young friend of Mr. Dawson's sister was brought into St. Mary's this evening after a bad fall," Annie replied. "A Miss Hattie Wilks. She is in a private room down the next hallway. I believe the room number is twelve. We haven't been able to find out anything about her condition and wondered if you might have heard anything?"

"Oh, my. Room Twelve, you say? The poor girl with all the broken bones?"

"Yes, yes, that is her. She evidently fell down some steps at her boarding house earlier this evening. What have you heard?" Annie asked, frightened by the way that Mrs. O'Malley was wringing her hands.

The older woman came closer and said quietly, "Mrs. Fuller, would you mind if we stepped away and spoke privately? I am not sure I feel comfortable talking in front of the gentleman, you understand."

Annie didn't understand but nodded in agreement anyway. Holding up her hand to Nate to indicate he should stay put, she walked with Mrs. O'Malley a little way further down the hallway.

Looking up and down the hall to make sure there wasn't anyone else to overhear, Mrs. O'Malley whispered, "The good sisters don't think she'll make it through the night. God rest her soul. The poor thing lost so much blood even before she got here, you see, and the sisters haven't been able to stop the flow. Just terrible. And her little babe didn't stand a chance."

Laura's head throbbed, and she realized she had been breathing in the same halting, shallow rhythm as Hattie. She inhaled deeply as if this would fill her friend's lungs, and she said again, "Hattie. What can I do? I'm here. I won't leave you. I promise."

Hattie's hand twitched in her own, then grabbed hold tightly. Her friend's eyes were now wide open, and her lips were moving silently. Leaning so close she could feel a faint stir of breath on her own cheek, she pleaded, "Hattie, what is it? Tell me. Do you need some water?"

As she began to pull away to reach for the glass on the bedside table, Hattie rasped out, "No...Laura. No...time. Sorry...never meant to...must tell...."

"Tell me what? Hattie, never say you're sorry. It's me who should apologize for being such a cross patch about your plans. We are going to get you well, and then you will have a beautiful wedding, and everything is going to be wonderful."

Hattie shook her head sharply side-to-side and struggled out a few more words. "Accident...No...not...tell Andrew...I didn't..."

"Oh, Hattie, don't fret. Of course it was an accident. No one blames you. I am sure he will come as soon as he hears what happened. You can tell him yourself."

Hattie grimaced and tugged on Laura's hand weakly, her eyes again shutting and her chest heaving. Laura stroked her hair with trembling hands, saying, "Hattie don't try to talk; you are too weak."

"Miss, let her speak," the sister said quietly, startling Laura, who had forgotten she was there. "She needs to unburden herself before she meets our Lord. It will bring her peace."

"Don't you dare say that. She's going to be fine. She just needs to rest and heal. If you want to help, go get a doctor. She needs medical attention, not prayer."

When she turned back to Hattie, she could see that her lips were tinged with blue. Panicking, she slid her arms under her friend's shoulders, cradling her to her chest, saying, "Hattie, my love. Don't go. Don't leave me."

She felt Hattie stir in her arms and heard her say in the thinnest of whispers, "Tell him...not his fault...tell him...he needs to know... pushed...pushed..." Then she exhaled in a long sigh and breathed no more.

Chapter Twelve
Late Wednesday evening, January 14, 1880
"The sudden death of Minnie Williams better known as Minnie C. Baldwin, on Monday last...received but little attention. Since then, however, certain matters connected with the death have been elicited which tend to throw a shade of suspicion over the matter." —*San Francisco Chronicle*, 1880

"Kathleen, please tell Mr. Dawson that I won't be coming back down. He should go home because there is nothing more he can do here. You can inform him I will be staying in Laura's room tonight so she won't be alone. Then off to bed with you and make sure Mrs. O'Rourke has retired."

Annie stood just outside the door to Laura's room on the second floor of the boarding house. It was nearly midnight, and she knew Kathleen would need to get up in about four hours to start the kitchen stove in preparation for breakfast for the early risers among the other boarders.

"Yes, ma'am. Can I bring you more tea first?" Kathleen asked. When Annie shook her head no, the young maid moved swiftly to the back stairs on her way to the first floor parlor where Nate would be waiting impatiently for news.

Annie noted that even in the midst of this crisis, Kathleen didn't even think of taking the more direct route down the front stairs. *Such foolishness.* Yet having once been a domestic herself, if only for a short time, she knew how ingrained it was for a maid to use the back way.

Esther Stein, who occupied the suite of rooms across the hallway with her husband, sat with Laura while Annie went next door to her own room to change into her dressing gown and slippers. She didn't expect she would sleep, but she knew from experience how wretched she would feel sitting up all night, fully dressed, with her corset stays becoming increasingly unbearable.

When Annie returned to Laura's room, Esther whispered, "I will be glad to stay with her if you want, since you have to get up and meet your clients in a few hours."

"You are kind, Esther, but no. I promised I would stay close. My heart just breaks for her. Her mother is who she really needs right now. I hope she will let us send word, but…that can wait until tomorrow. No, you go on back to bed."

She gave the older woman a quick hug and closed the door behind her. Kathleen had undressed Laura and gotten her into bed, but she was sitting up, her arms clasped around her raised knees, her long dark hair hiding her face. Annie noticed that Queenie, the old black kitchen cat, had snuck in and was curled up beside Laura.

She stood for a moment to see if Laura would raise her head. When Nate's sister didn't acknowledge her presence, Annie walked over to the rocking chair that sat by the fire. She lowered the flame of the oil lamp on a nearby table and sat down. There was an active fire going in the fireplace, and Annie found the heat oppressive. Nevertheless, she knew that Laura needed the warmth to counter her shock and exhaustion. She sat and rocked and thought back over what had happened earlier in the evening after Mrs. O'Malley had shared the startling information about Hattie's pregnancy and predicted she would not live through the night.

Annie hadn't had time to tell Nate what Mrs. O'Malley said before they'd heard Laura's screams. When they got to the hospital room, the Sister of Mercy was trying to pull the sobbing girl back from where Hattie lay. Annie had sat by enough deathbeds to know what that waxen stillness meant. Nate rushed past her and grabbed Laura from the nun, folding her in a tight embrace. This seemed to quiet her for a moment, but then she tore herself away from her brother and threw herself back on the bed, crying and pleading for Hattie not to go.

Annie had just moved forward to see if she could do anything to calm Laura when a harsh male cry arrested her attention. A man who she guessed must be Hattie's fiancé, Andrew Russell, stood in the doorway. Out of breath, brown hair standing up in clumps, eyes hidden behind thick glasses, he held out a soft slouch hat in his extended hands, as if in supplication. Before either Nate or Annie were able to act, Laura scrambled up and launched herself at Russell, hitting him in the chest and screaming that Hattie was dead and that it was all his fault. It had been an appalling scene, with Russell feebly pushing Laura away as he struggled to get to Hattie's bedside. Finally, Nate had to pick up his hysterical sister from off the ground in order to move her out of the room. The Sister of Mercy had stood in shocked silence.

Out in the hall, Laura continued to sob uncontrollably, scarcely able to take a breath. Annie finally told her sharply that if she didn't settle down, they would have to take her home immediately, and she wouldn't be able to say a proper farewell to her friend. This got through to Laura, and she gradually stopped crying. While Nate continued to hold her tightly, Annie went back in to the room, where Russell was now sitting in the chair next to Hattie, holding her hand and whispering endearments. Apologizing to both Russell and the sister for Laura's outburst, Annie asked if Laura could come back in for a minute. Russell had been most kind, assuring Annie that this would be acceptable, and he went and stood in one of the dark corners of the room. Nate had led his sister back in and she sat in the chair that Russell had just vacated. She took up Hattie's hand and silently stroked her hair.

Annie went over to Russell to tell him how sorry she was for his loss and ask if he would be able to inform Hattie's parents of her death. He'd said he would take care of this, then took off his glasses to wipe the tears from his eyes, looking like a lost boy. Haltingly, he explained that he had arrived at Hattie's boarding house earlier that evening to learn that she had fallen and been taken to St. Mary's. Then he asked Annie if she knew exactly what had happened. Annie told him that she understood that there had been internal bleeding, but he should ask the Sister of Mercy for more details. She didn't feel it was her place to break it to him

that he had lost both future wife and a child at the same time. Maybe he
didn't even know Hattie had been pregnant. Annie hadn't told her own
husband about her pregnancy, and John had died never knowing about
the miscarriage.

About this time, Laura had begun to cry again, and Nate gently
informed her that they needed to leave. She had kissed Hattie's forehead
and let herself be led away. She continued weeping until they were
nearly home. Nate carried her up to her room, where Kathleen brought
her a cup of sweetened tea. After Laura gulped down two cups, she
listlessly accepted Kathleen's offer to get her ready for bed. That was
when Annie had sent Nate back downstairs and Esther had come out of
her room, exhibiting her clear disapproval that Nate had been up on the
second floor.

Annie, who was thinking about how her older friend had shifted so
rapidly from stern guardian of Annie's reputation to sympathetic friend
once she learned the true state of affairs, heard movement from the bed.
She said quietly, "Laura, can I get anything for you? Do you feel able to
lie down and try to go to sleep?"

Laura looked up and pushed her hair away from her face. Her eyes
were red-rimmed, her nose and lips raw from the extremity of her grief.
Annie got up and fetched a towel and wash cloth from the washstand.
She dipped the cloth in the cooling water in the basin, wrung the cloth
out, and then gently bathed and dried Laura's face. Noticing a brush and
ribbon on the bedside table, she said, "Would you like me to brush and
braid your hair for you? Would that help?"

Laura nodded and lowered her knees into a cross-legged position,
turning slightly so Annie could sit down on the bed behind her. Queenie
got up in a huff, walked majestically down to the end of the bed and
back, and climbed into Laura's lap, deigning to permit the girl to stroke
her back. For some time, there were no other sounds in the room besides
the purr of the cat, the pop of the wood fire, and the brush sliding
through Laura's dark brunette waves.

"Annie," the girl whispered. "I'm sorry for all the trouble."

"Shush, now. Never you fret about it. No one blames you. You've had a terrible shock." Annie began to braid the hair in one long plait.

"Nate told me your mother died when you were young. I can't imagine how awful that would have been."

"Yes, but I was here visiting my aunt and uncle at the time, so I don't know what it is like to actually be with someone I loved when they died. And Hattie was so young and her death unexpected. That makes it worse. I do think that in time you will be glad you got to say goodbye. I have always regretted that I wasn't present for either of my parents' deaths."

Laura didn't respond, and Annie worried that she'd gone too far. Laura, seven years her junior, seemed very young and inexperienced. Yet when Annie was just a year older than Laura, she'd already lost her mother, her father, her unborn child, her fortune, and her husband. And she'd no one to confide in, no one's shoulder to cry on. No one at all. She hoped that the younger girl would make it through this terrible tragedy with fewer scars than she herself had accumulated.

A few minutes passed, and then Laura said plaintively, "I feel like I have been living in a nightmare, ever since this autumn when Hattie got the job in San Francisco and we had to part. Cupertino Creek School was the beginning of the nightmare. Not just the teaching. I did get better at that over time. But it was so dreadful living with the students' families, and there was this boy in the school, Buck. He wouldn't let me alone. For a while, things improved when Seth, Seth Timmons, a classmate from San Jose, started coming over from San Jose on weekends. But then Seth and Buck...well, never mind, the important point is that the term ended and I got the offer to teach here. I thought the nightmare was finally over. I would come up to San Francisco and be with Hattie, as we had planned, and everything would go back to normal. But it wasn't over. First the man in the alley and then Hattie turning her back on all our plans...then tonight..." Laura's voice trailed off.

Annie, wishing to divert Laura from where her thoughts were taking her, said quickly, "Who was Buck and what did he do?"

Laura took a deep breath. "Buck Morrison. He was the oldest boy in the Cupertino Creek School. Seventeen, obnoxious, conceited, spoiled, and not very smart. It was bad enough he disrupted class, challenging my authority. Our professors at San Jose told us to expect that from older students. But he kept following me around, being too familiar. I tried to protect myself, tried to make sure that I went to and from the school with the children in whose home I was boarding that week."

"But that didn't always work?"

"No, sometimes the children would be sick and I had to go by myself, and there he would be, waiting outside the school house in the morning. He would pretend it was because he wanted to help get the wood in to start the fire, or he would offer to clean the board. On the surface, perfectly innocuous. But he was always brushing up against me, saying...things. I would tell him to stop, and he would just laugh. After a few weeks, he even started showing up outside the homes where I was staying. If I tried to leave, go for a walk or something, Buck would suddenly appear, acting like I should be delighted at his company."

"Couldn't you speak to his parents or someone on the school board?" Annie asked, her skin crawling at the thought of what Laura had endured.

"I wasn't sure anyone would believe me. You see, it wasn't so much what he said but how he said it. And his father is the wealthiest man in the district and a member of the school board. When I tried to speak to Buck's father, well, you might say he demonstrated graphically where Buck had gotten his notions of how to treat a woman."

"Oh, Laura, I am sorry you had to deal with this. Did you tell your parents what was happening?"

"I was going to, but after the first few weeks, Seth, Mr. Timmons, started showing up at the end of the school day on Fridays. He'd rented a buggy, and he would drive me to wherever I was boarding that weekend. He said he was camping in the hills to the west because he didn't like being cooped up all the time in a city. But it meant he could take me out for rides on Saturdays and take me to church on Sundays. As a result, I didn't feel so much like I was in a prison. Twice, he even drove me to and from San Jose where my father would meet me and bring me on home to the ranch. That was wonderful. Buck still gave me a hard time at school, but it was easier to take."

Laura stopped and after a moment continued. "But I never really understood why Seth was being so helpful...it wasn't as if we were friends before. He just started attending San Jose last year, and he was sort of stand-offish with the other students. He is older. He was a Union soldier in the war, and I always felt he thought the rest of us were just children. Except Hattie. He was friends with Hattie. Everyone was...and when I got to San Francisco, I wanted to talk to her about him, have her assure me that it couldn't have been him in the alley...but now, now..."

Laura began to weep, and Annie drew her into her arms and rocked her back and forth, saying, "Oh my dear, I know it hurts, and it doesn't do any good for me to tell you it will get better. But it will. Look, you have gotten Queenie all upset. Ruffled her dignity." Annie pointed at the old cat, who had again stalked to the end of the bed and was licking her back with ferocious concentration. Laura gave a tearful chuckle.

Annie turned serious. "Tell me why you thought it might have been this Seth who accosted you."

"I didn't think so right at first. Only later that night I realized the man was about the same height, and I recognized the smell of the tobacco on him. Silly, I know, as if that isn't a description of half the men in the city. But something happened the last time I saw him, and...well... I'm not sure I really know what he is capable of. But now that doesn't matter. Because after tonight, I see I was completely wrong." Laura pulled back, her tears forgotten as she continued. "I think the man who attacked me might have been Andrew Russell. He must have known how much I would be against their marriage. What if the attack was his way of frightening me into leaving town? He is the Vice Principal at Clement. It would have been easy for him to learn where I lived and follow me home that day."

Annie, shocked at Laura's accusation, said, "I don't understand. What makes you think that he would do such a thing?"

"I think it is possible he pressured Hattie into quitting her job and agreeing to marry him. I can't believe that Hattie could change her mind about her future, our future, otherwise. She kept apologizing to me on Saturday when I visited her, saying that I couldn't understand...that there were reasons for her decision that I didn't know about. I've been think-ing and thinking about it, and I feel sure she would have told him about me and our plans to go to the University together, pursue our careers. Maybe she even told him that if I was totally against the idea, she wouldn't marry him. When his attack didn't scare me away, he then made sure I wouldn't have any time alone with her to change her mind."

"Laura darling, what do you mean, made sure..."

"Hattie was obviously feeling conflicted," Laura continued rapidly, ignoring Annie's question. "She seemed positively ill when I saw her. And she was supposed to come and see me this Friday. What if he..."

Annie, frightened by how agitated Laura was becoming, tried to stop the tumble of words by putting her hand gently on the girl's mouth and saying, "Slow down now, dearest. Catch your breath."

Laura snatched Annie's hand away and raised her voice to say, "You don't understand. Hattie told me with her dying words that he had pushed her into marrying her. That is the only explanation for why she would agree to something that would destroy all our plans. I think he hounded her to her death, undermining her will to live. Why else would she have died from some broken bones?"

Annie, heartsick that she would have to add to Laura's pain but unsure how else to stop her wild speculations, said, "Listen to me. There is something I need to tell you. Something I learned at the hospital. The reason Hattie would have wanted to marry so quickly was that she was with child. And tragically, the fall caused her to miscarry. That is why she died. The doctors couldn't stop the hemorrhaging, so she bled to death."

Chapter Thirteen
Thursday morning, January 15, 1880
"Various Cases disposed of at the Morgue...In the case of the woman the cause of death was also ascribed to hemorrhage..." —*San Francisco Chronicle*, 1880

"Laura said what? She thinks Russell may have attacked her and caused Hattie's death? That can't be what she meant." Nate thought he must have misheard Annie. They were standing in the doorway to the kitchen pantry, out of the way of Mrs. O'Rourke and Kathleen, who were busy washing up the breakfast dishes.

He had gone directly to the back kitchen entrance this morning, not wanting to put Kathleen to the trouble of coming to the front door to let him in. He'd hoped he would catch Annie before her first Madam Sibyl client, but he mostly wanted some word on how the night had gone for Laura, fully expecting that she would still be fast asleep.

The first shock came at the kitchen door when Kathleen told him he had just missed Laura, who had risen in time to go off to work, accompanied as usual by Mrs. Hewitt and Jamie. The second shock came when Annie started to tell him about her conversation with Laura the night before.

Annie frowned at his raised voice and, looking over at Beatrice bent over the sink under the high kitchen window, she replied very quietly, "You must understand how upset she is. She is trying desperately to make sense of what has happened. To have Hattie die for no reason, a stupid accident, must feel unsupportable."

"What exactly did she say that Hattie said?"

"Laura admitted that it was very difficult to make out her words; Hattie was very weak. But according to her, Hattie apologized to her and said something about telling Russell it wasn't his fault. But at the very end, she repeated several times the words 'tell,' 'no,' and 'accident.' And evidently the last words she uttered were, 'pushed, pushed.'"

Nate repeated the words over in his mind. Then he said, "You know, depending on the order, Hattie could have just as well been saying that she wanted Laura to tell Russell that what had happened was an accident, rather than that it wasn't an accident. It certainly wouldn't hold up in a court of law."

"I know. If Hattie loved Russell—something Laura is having trouble accepting—she may very well have wanted to put his mind at ease that the fall was an accident. But Laura is convinced that Russell forced Hattie into abandoning her job and agreeing to marry him, controlling her like some evil mesmerist. At least that is how she is interpreting Hattie's last words. But we can't even be sure Hattie said 'pushed.' Maybe she was saying hush, hush or something."

Nate thought about how upset Laura had been last evening. The violence of her reaction to her friend's death, her wild sobs. He'd felt helpless and a little frightened by her behavior; it seemed so out of character. He blurted out, "If anyone was exhibiting undue influence, it seems to be Hattie Wilks over Laura. I just don't understand why my sister has acted in such an extreme manner from the moment she found out about her friend's marriage. What is so terrible about a young woman falling in love and wanting to get married?"

Annie cocked her head at him, and he stopped, thinking how easy it was for him to get in trouble with her when he brought up the topic of marriage. He rushed on. "I am not saying that there is anything wrong with Laura's plans to go on to the University, get a profession, even forgo marriage, if that is her wish. I'm just asking why must this be true for her friend. Maybe Hattie wanted both a profession and marriage."

"I think the feelings Laura had for Hattie went beyond simple friendship," Annie told him. "From what she's said, Laura never had a strong connection with anyone beyond her family before she met Hattie. Surely you saw the kind of deep friendships that formed between some students during your college years?"

Nate flashed on Stubbs and Potter, two Ohio farm boys who became closer than brothers at Western Reserve. They studied, drank, even whored together, practically joined at the hip. Thinking of Laura and Hattie like that made him feel distinctly uncomfortable.

Annie continued. "If Laura was the follower in that relationship, and a couple of the things she said suggests that was true, she might doubt her ability to achieve her goals without Hattie's support."

"You're saying it was partly fear for her own future that made her so angry at Hattie when she found out she had quit teaching to marry?" Nate remembered the times in his life when his self-doubts got the better of him.

"Fear and jealousy," Annie replied. "Your sister was bound to feel very hurt if she believed Hattie had transferred her affections to Russell. Rather than blame her friend, it's easier for her to blame Russell, particularly now that Hattie is dead."

"But why did it have to be one or the other? Hattie invited her to be her maid of honor; she obviously didn't want to lose Laura's friendship. If we...well, I wouldn't expect that...I mean Mrs. Stein or Mrs. O'Rourke don't feel..."

Annie chuckled and said, "Yes, Nate Dawson, perhaps it's possible to have friends and a husband both, provided the man isn't the overly possessive type." She smiled and reached up and kissed him swiftly on his cheek.

Nate looked over her head to see if either Mrs. O'Rourke or Kathleen had noticed, but they had their heads together looking at some pot on the stove. Sometimes, it was all he could do to stop from pulling Annie to him and covering her face with kisses. *Hang it all, how can she expect me to take it slowly if she acts this way!*

As if she felt his frustration, Annie stepped back, saying more seriously, "What concerns me more is Laura's thoughts about who might have attacked her in the alley."

"You don't really think that Russell was responsible, do you? He just didn't strike me that way, and the motive doesn't make any sense to me." Nate pictured the scholarly looking Vice Principal he'd seen at the hospital and couldn't imagine him lurking in the shadows to jump out at his sister.

"No, but what about this classmate of hers? The former soldier Seth. Many men came out of the war damaged in mind as well as body. If he was one of the Andersonville prisoners, one of those Plymouth Pilgrims we talked about, who knows how that could have twisted his mind? And then there is Buck, the boy who gave her such a hard time when she was teaching at Cupertino Creek. I wonder if we can find out if either of them have visited San Francisco in the past few weeks."

"You mentioned something about a falling out, and it had to do with Buck and Seth?" Nate just couldn't understand why Laura hadn't told him about her troubles. Even Annie had seemed evasive when she recounted what Laura had said about his sister's experience teaching at Cupertino Creek. He was sure there were details she was withholding. *At Laura's request?*

"Look, we need to talk about this more," he said as he took out his watch. "But I need to go; I have a ten o'clock meeting. Then I have to be in court this afternoon and all day tomorrow. Cranston has asked me to sit in on the Jack Purdy trial I was telling you about. The one where Cranston is challenging the gag law the city passed during the sandlot riots. I am sorry, but this probably means I will be tied up both evenings since he likes to go to dinner and dissect the day in court and give me a bunch of research to do afterwards. Do you have clients Saturday morning?"

"Yes, but I will write to you tonight and tell you how Laura is holding up. Do you think you will be able to get away Saturday evening? I…well there is one more thing I need to tell you about. I…but you go. We can talk about it later."

Nate's heart rate sped up, and he reached out and cupped Annie's chin, forcing her to look him in the eye. "No, tell me right this minute. No secrets. If there is something else I need to know, tell me now. You and Laura are more important than any meeting."

Annie put her hands up and took his hand in hers. She said, "Well, last night I didn't get to tell you what Mrs. O'Malley reported to me. I didn't plan on telling Laura, at least not now, but she was getting so worked up, questioning why Hattie had died of simple broken bones, that I felt I had to tell her the whole truth."

Annie went on to tell him about Hattie's miscarriage, leaving Nate momentarily speechless. Then he started to think about the ramifications, and he said, "No wonder Hattie had to quit teaching. Do you think Russell knew she was with child? Well, of course he did. That would explain why they were rushing into marriage. But the scandal. What did…Annie, what's the matter?"

Nate gathered a weeping Annie into his arms. *Hang propriety.*

She put her arms around him and gave him a hug, but then she moved away and pulled out a handkerchief, wiped her eyes, and said, "Nate, I'm fine. I was just overwhelmed for a moment by how sad it all is. And poor Laura. She was completely overcome. I'm still not sure I was right to tell her, but I didn't know what else to do. But you go. I need to consult with Mrs. O'Rourke about dinner and then get ready for Madam Sibyl's first client anyway." And with that, she turned around and raised her voice. "Kathleen, would you see Mr. Dawson out the front?"

Turning back to him, Annie said, "I promise I will write tonight." She then walked over to where Beatrice O'Rourke stood next to the stove, leaving him no polite alternative but to follow Kathleen up the back stairs.

Chapter Fourteen
Thursday afternoon, January 15, 1880

"There has been a good deal of talk about daughters of wealthy citizens occupying places in the School Department simply for the sake of receiving additions to their pocket money. Of my sixteen teachers I know that fifteen are in absolute need of working for their support." —*San Francisco Chronicle*, 1880

Somehow, Laura made it through the school day without falling apart. Maybe her exhaustion actually helped, creating a feeling of detachment as she went through the day's lessons with her students. She had no idea what time it was when she finally had fallen asleep last night, curled around the warmth of the dear old cat, but she had woken numerous times in the hours before sunrise. However, every time she gained consciousness, she'd felt Annie's warm hand stroking her hair, and she had fallen back asleep. Finally, a sound, probably another boarder's voice, jerked her fully awake. Annie had leaned over and told her to try to go back to sleep; she would be in her room next door getting dressed. But Laura knew that she needed to be up and doing something, anything, to keep the tears at bay. *Keep her fears at bay*. Staying under the covers, letting fear overwhelm her, had never been an acceptable option. Not when she had been a child, afraid of riding a full-grown stallion, or a student, afraid she would fail her chemistry exams, or a teacher, afraid she wouldn't be able to exert enough authority over the older students. As soon as Annie had left, Laura rose and got ready to go to work, knowing she must conquer her greatest fear, that she wouldn't be able to go on without Hattie.

Now that it was three in the afternoon and the school day had ended, all she needed to do was meet briefly with Della Thorndike, then join Jamie on the front steps of the school to wait for his mother, and they would head home. Home to figure out how to survive the next hours until she could return to work, where for whole minutes at a time she didn't think about anything but the tasks at hand. Didn't think about what it meant that Hattie had been pregnant and that a miscarriage caused her death. Didn't think of her friend lying on a dark cold landing, bleeding to death, all alone.

"Miss Dawson, do you have any particular instructions for grading the map assignment?" Kitty Blaine asked.

Laura found herself staring at the young redheaded practice teacher, having forgotten momentarily that she wasn't alone in the classroom. Kitty had been standing at the door to the hall, making sure that the students remembered all their scarves and caps as they jostled their way to freedom.

She summoned forth a smile. "Not really, Miss Blaine. Since there are fifty questions, give them each two points. If you judge that they have gotten a partial answer correct, give them one point. I will go over the papers tomorrow and record the grades, and if there are any problems, we can discuss them then."

"Thank you, Miss. I hope I won't disappoint," Kitty said softly. "Do you need anything else of me before I go?"

Handing over the pile of map tests, Laura said, "I am sure you will do just fine. I can't think of anything we didn't go over at noon. I see no reason you can't leave now, unless you think you should attend my meeting with Miss Thorndike."

"Oh, no," Kitty said quickly. "I mean, I spoke to her this morning before I came over to Clement. *She* didn't say anything about seeing me this afternoon."

Laura noted the odd defensiveness behind this last statement, and she responded firmly, "Then I assume she won't expect you to be there. I will see you tomorrow, Miss Blaine. Have a pleasant evening."

As she watched Kitty move quickly to the back of the room to fetch an expensive dark green cashmere cloak from one of the hooks, Laura puzzled over what to make of the young woman. All week, Kitty had been extremely deferential when she talked to Laura, barely speaking above a whisper, keeping her emerald green eyes cast down and her hands clasped firmly in her lap, making it easy to believe Della's description of her as shy and socially awkward. But she appeared entirely confident and quite at ease when she interacted with the boys and girls in the class, already a clear favorite with them after only four days. Laura wondered if the shyness and deference was an act. Hattie always said…

All the dark thoughts she had been holding off came crowding in, and Laura felt the tears rise, ready to spill over. *No. Not here. Not now.* She took a deep breath and stood up, gathering the last of her books and papers into her satchel and getting her own cloak and hat, not intending to come back to the room after her meeting with Della. The weather had turned nasty this morning, and most of the day, rain drops had splattered against the classroom windows. Nevertheless, she could see that the sun shone weakly on the southwestern side of the houses across from the school, so they probably wouldn't need the umbrella that Barbara Hewitt had brought with her this morning.

As she walked down the hall, she nodded at the janitor, Mr. Ferguson, a wiry older man who was vigorously scrubbing at a spot on the wall that some boy's grubby hand had created. She then stopped and stuck her head into Miss Chesterton's fifth grade classroom, where, as usual, Jamie was helping clean the board. She said, "Good afternoon, Miss Chesterton. Jamie, I will be about twenty minutes; I have a meeting in the teachers' room. When you are done helping Miss Chesterton, wait for me by the front door. If your mother gets there before I do, come get me, won't you?"

When she got to the first floor, she saw Della Thorndike standing with Kitty just inside the building's entrance. The tableau, the tall stately Miss Thorndike speaking animatedly to the petite Kitty, who was staring down at her feet, looked for all the world like a mother scolding a sullen child. Della noticed Laura and stepped back from Kitty, who hurriedly made her way out of the building, no doubt for her waiting carriage. *No walking or taking the local horsecar home for Miss Kitty.*

"Laura, I am so glad to see you. I hope that Kitty has been behaving herself." Della warmly shook Laura's hand. "Do let's have a cup of tea and tell me how your first week of supervising one of my students has gone," she continued, taking Laura's arm and walking her quickly to the teachers' room.

When Laura indicated that she didn't have much time before she would have to leave, Della got right down to business, taking her over to two chairs in the corner of the room where they wouldn't be disturbed by the other teachers coming in and out. Laura spent a few minutes recounting the main outlines of the lessons she had covered during the week and her decision to let Kitty grade the short map test she had given today.

Della praised her warmly for how clearly she had organized the progression of subjects, and Laura felt comfortable enough to ask her opinion on how to handle one of the girls whose spelling remained very erratic. "She seems quite bright. The essays she writes are well-organized and her grammar is correct. Yet she keeps switching letters, sometimes so badly it takes awhile for me to realize what word she intended to write. When I point out the errors to her, she becomes visibly upset. Hattie said she had tried…"

Laura's throat closed, and she stopped speaking.

Della stared at her and was just starting to say something when Andrew Russell appeared suddenly in front of them. Standing there, wearing a black armband around his left sleeve, his eyes red-rimmed behind his glasses, he destroyed the fragile equilibrium Laura had worked to maintain all day. He bowed to Della, who had stood up at his approach, and said, "Miss Thorndike, could you please spare a moment for me to speak with Miss Dawson privately?"

Before Laura could object, Della nodded and went across the room to chat with one of the teachers who was checking her mailbox. Laura stood up, her heart beating rapidly enough that she could feel the blood surging through her temples. *What did he want with her? Did he really want to speak to her in this public place?* Whatever his plans, she would not give him the satisfaction of losing her composure as she had at the hospital.

"Miss Dawson," Russell said stiffly. "Hattie's…Miss Wilks' parents arrived in town this afternoon. They asked me to tell you that they will be taking their daughter…taking Hattie…" Here his voice broke, and Laura found herself throwing up her hands as if she could stop him from continuing, stop him from uttering Hattie's name.

Russell began to speak more quickly. "They are taking her back home with them tomorrow morning. They asked if you would be willing to go to her boarding house. Pack up her trunk. Have it shipped home. They would consider it a great favor if you would do this."

Laura had never met Hattie's parents. Hattie had loved them, but they didn't understand why she wasn't content to stay in Santa Barbara and marry one of the local farmers she'd grown up with. Hattie had laughed and said they were afraid something would happen to her if she went off to the big city. *But something bad had happened. Something terrible.*

"Please, Miss Dawson," Russell went on, his voice stronger. "I have a personal request as well. I know that Hattie kept my letters, and I would appreciate it greatly if you could return them to me. While there isn't anything in them that I am ashamed of, I believe she would prefer that her parents not…"

"Not know how you took her innocence and ruined her life?" Laura spat at him, her anger overpowering her resolve to say nothing to this man who had ruined her life as well.

Russell stepped back as if she had physically struck him. Before he could respond, Della Thorndike hurried over. Placing her hand on his shoulder, she said, "Andrew, Mr. Russell, whatever is the matter?" Not getting an answer, she then turned to Laura. "Please, tell me. Why is poor Mr. Russell wearing mourning? Who has died?"

Laura, feeling she couldn't bear to hear Della's cries of sympathy directed at *poor Mr. Russell,* muttered an excuse and fled into the hall-way, never more glad to see Jamie and his mother standing in the vestibule waiting for her.

Chapter Fifteen
Saturday afternoon, January 17, 1880
"MOST WONDERFUL CLAIRVOYANT—Tells everything without question." —*San Francisco Chronicle*, 1880

Annie's morning wasn't progressing well. The sleep she'd lost the past three nights was finally catching up with her. Not only had she stayed awake all Wednesday night watching over Laura but she found herself unable to go to sleep the next two nights until well after midnight. This was when the squeak of bedsprings from the next room told her Nate's sister had finally retired to bed. Consequently, her morning's work as Madam Sibyl had suffered. Despite the preparation she did before seeing each client—one of the reasons for Madam Sibyl's "by appoint- ment only" policy—she often had to make snap judgments about whether or not to dissuade her male clients from acting on the latest "tip" they got from their barber, brother-in-law, or bar-room buddy. Usually, her financial expertise and experience helped her respond quickly and confidently, but today her brain felt like it was filled with over-cooked oatmeal. She feared she may have steered Mr. Hackett in the wrong direction when he asked about the new stock offerings by the California Electric Light Company, and Mr. Watkins had gotten very huffy when she said his astrological reading indicated that he should invest in the new Inglenook winery that Captain Neibaum was starting up the valley. She had forgotten Watkins was an abstainer from all things alcohol.

Removing her wig, she told herself that the waiting list of people who were anxious to pay the two dollars she charged for an appointment meant that if these mistakes cost her some business, she would still be all right. Yet the years she had spent without a cent to her name, dependent on the not-very-kind charity of her former in-laws, had ingrained in her a level of anxiety that never quite went away. It kept her from moving forward in her plans to shed the Madam Sibyl charade and see if she could still support herself as plain, non-clairvoyant Mrs. Annie Fuller, financial advisor.

Looking at the dark circles that appeared under her eyes as she removed the powder from her face, she wondered if she could find time for a short rest this afternoon. She didn't want to look quite so wrung out if Nate was able to make it this evening. He tended to get protective when he thought she was overdoing, and her tears Thursday morning had already produced a worried note from him in the mail yesterday.

Ever since Hattie's death, she hadn't been able to stop thinking about her own miscarriage. Something she had avoided doing for years. Last year, when she was giving advice to Ruthann Hazelton, she'd never thought to connect that woman's troubles with her own past. But a strange little girl she'd encountered this past fall and the recent experience of holding Ruthann's baby, Lillian, in her arms had started her thinking about that past and her lost chance at motherhood.

She wondered if Hattie had kept her condition secret from her fiancé, Russell, the way Annie had from John. What if Laura was completely wrong? What if Hattie had been upset, not because she didn't really want to marry Russell but because she was terrified he wouldn't marry her, leaving her to raise a child on her own, her reputation ruined? If so, might she have flung herself down the stairs in a desperate attempt to end the pregnancy? Once, early in her own pregnancy, Annie had contemplated doing something similar when her husband had been particularly brutal. Only for a moment. But she'd never completely let go of the guilty fear that her own miscarriage had happened because she hadn't fully wanted the child.

Burying her head in her hands, Annie whispered to herself, "What if that was my last chance to be a mother, and I threw it away?"

"Ma'am, are you all right? You're not coming down sick, are you?" Her maid Kathleen stood frowning in the doorway between the small study and Madam Sibyl's parlor.

Annie sat up and gave her face an unnecessary scrub with the towel so she could regain her composure. She then said, "Yes, Kathleen, I am quite well. I am just feeling tired. I have promised myself a nap once I have eaten. Are the plans still on for the excursion to Woodward's Gardens?"

As she had intended, this change in subject diverted Kathleen, who moved into the room, her voice lowering into a confidential whisper. "Yes, ma'am. This morning I asked Miss Dawson if she would be willing to come with me and Patrick this afternoon."

"And she agreed to go?"

"Well, I hinted that she would be doing me a great favor. Told her about how we'd promised Jamie and Ian we'd take them along but how I was worried that watching after two such lively lads could put a crimp in me and Patrick's time together."

Annie chuckled, knowing very well that Kathleen often invited her youngest brother, Ian, to come with her on those afternoons off with her beau, Patrick McGee, just so she could keep him at arm's length. Patrick, with his freckles and unruly copper hair, always struck Annie as a boy himself, but she knew he was also good-hearted, dependable, and very much in love with Kathleen, who had confessed last week that she was afraid Patrick was working himself up to "pop the question." At the time, Kathleen had told her, "Not that I'm not partial to him. But I gotta think about Ian. I say yes to Patrick, and before you know it he'd be nagging at me to set the date, we'd be hitched, and I'd have a passel of my own young'uns. On what, a beat cop's wages? No. I'm going to make sure Ian stays in school, makes something of himself. Then's the time I can start thinking on having my own family."

This memory had the distressing potential to drag Annie back to her dark thoughts, so she stood up briskly and asked, "How did Miss Laura seem this morning?"

"I'm sorry to say she didn't look like she got much rest. Sorta like yourself, if you don't mind me saying so, ma'am. I think the fresh air will do her good, put some roses in those cheeks. Sure you don't want to come with us?" Kathleen picked up the shawl Annie had carelessly dropped on the floor and removed all signs of powder from it before draping it neatly back over the chair.

"Oh Kathleen, you completely undermine my confidence. Mr. Dawson is coming this evening, and now you tell me I look like a hag!"

"Now ma'am, he'd not notice if you grew warts on your nose and hairs on your chin, he's that smitten with you."

Annie smiled, marveling over how this wise young girl could always lift her spirits.

Following Kathleen down into the kitchen, Annie surveyed the room with pleasure. The kitchen, the heart of the house, was of ample size. Its southern-facing windows over the sink got the full force of the winter sun, and today those windows were open because the rain of yesterday had cleared the skies of the usual grey clouds and fog. What a lovely reminder that the San Francisco peninsula, wedged between the Pacific and the Bay, could produce such warm, spring-like days in late January. A perfect day to ramble around the grounds of Woodward's Gardens. She was sorely tempted to change her mind and go with the group.

Then she noticed Laura standing near the back door with Barbara, Jamie, and Kathleen's youngest brother, Ian, while they tried to get Dandy to stand up on his hind legs. Ian, already ten and in the sixth grade, was small-boned like Kathleen, with black untidy hair and a twinkle of mischief in his dark blue eyes. Jamie was sturdier, with light-brown hair and brown eyes, and although he was a year younger than Ian, he had recently gone through a growth spurt. As a result, when he draped his arm around the other boy's shoulders, Annie could see they were of nearly identical height. The two boys had met at the boarding house Halloween party last fall and had become fast friends, much to the mutual delight of Kathleen and Jamie's mother.

When she saw Laura smile as the black-and-white terrier did his little dance, trying to stay on his back legs, she knew it would be best if she didn't go to the Gardens. Laura would find it easier to forget recent events, if only for a little time, if Annie didn't tag along. She cared more deeply about what was best for the young woman than she'd ever thought possible. In the past, when Nate would tell her stories about Laura, she had blithely imagined what it would be like to have her as a sister-in-law. They would trade secrets, conspire against Nate, teasing him unmercifully, and Annie would provide Laura the advice that was always easier to get from someone other than your parents. What she never expected was the way her heart had expanded and embraced the young woman as she watched over her on Wednesday night.

"Kathleen, dearie, you'll be late if you don't get moving," Beatrice O'Rourke said, rapidly filling up a basket with sandwiches, apples, and what looked to Annie like a whole chocolate cake. "Lovely day like today, the cars to the Gardens will be terrible crowded."

With a shout, the boys announced Patrick's arrival at the back door. Barbara Hewitt leaned down and scooped up Dandy, who was adding excited yips to the boys' welcome of the young policeman. Patrick good-naturedly withstood a pummeling by Ian and Jamie, then came into the kitchen and bowed first to Laura and then to Annie. Next, he went over to his aunt and simultaneously kissed her on the cheek and snagged the food basket from her, following Kathleen and Laura as they shooed the boys out the kitchen door.

When the door shut behind them, it was as if all the sunlight and warmth of the day was snuffed out. A profound exhaustion settled over Annie.

Beatrice O'Rourke came up to her and took her face in her plump but calloused hands and said kindly, "Annie, dear, sit yourself down in the old rocker for a bit of peace and quiet while I fix you a plate. Then I want you to tell me just exactly what happened to Miss Laura's friend and why's it got you so riled up." She gave Annie a gentle pat on her cheek. "And don't go pretending you don't know what I'm talking about. Weeping into Mr. Dawson's shoulder t'other day and circles under your eyes so dark you'd think someone gave you a round-house punch.

Somethin's wrong, and you're not leaving my kitchen until you've confessed all."

Chapter Sixteen
Saturday afternoon, January 17, 1880
"The genial weather and extensive programme drew a crowd to Woodward's Gardens yesterday." —*San Francisco Chronicle*, 1880

"Please, Sis, can we go ride the camels?" Ian dragged at Kathleen's hand.

"No you can't. Nasty, dirty animals. I heard they spit on you if you get too close," his sister said. "Oh, Patrick, do you see that peacock there? How untidy he looks dragging all those great long feathers behind in the dust." Patrick McGee just smiled down at the diminutive maid, and Laura could tell he was more interested in gazing at Kathleen Hennessey than he was in seeing the sights around him.

The trip on the horsecar to Mission and 14th Street had been crowded, as Mrs. O'Rourke had predicted, and it had taken them nearly twenty minutes to make it through the entrance gate at Woodward's Gardens, at which point the boys asked if they could go straight through the 14th Street tunnel to the zoo. Laura had visited the extensive grounds created out of the Woodward estate several times before with Nate, but, as befitted a respectable, mature young lady, she had strolled sedately arm-in-arm with her brother through the flower conservatory and art museum housed in the main building. Seeing the animals in the zoological gardens sounded like a lot more fun, so she had gladly seconded the boys' choice.

Holding determinedly on to Jamie's hand, Laura now stared in astonishment at the three camels being led around their pen, small children and adult men and women clinging to their backs. She had seen illustrations of camels all her life, a staple in illustrated Bible stories and in her geography textbooks. In fact, she had just taken her seventh-graders through a discussion of the differences between the Arabian camel, or dromedary, with its single hump, and the rarer Bactrian camels with their distinctive two humps. But to see them this close up was extraordinary. For some reason, she had thought them much taller than a horse, but at least these specimens, definitely dromedaries, looked to be less than sixteen hands high. Their eyes, however, were very different from a horse. They seemed huge, with long lashes that looked like they had been lined with kohl. And the smell! There was a distinctive astringent odor that was more overpowering than the usual manure and urine aroma she associated with livestock. As one of the laden camels was led over to the section of the fence where Jamie and she were standing, it opened its mobile mouth wide, revealing a formidable set of crooked teeth, and she pulled Jamie back a few steps, remembering Kathleen's comments about spitting.

"Miss Laura, did you see how long its tongue is?" Jamie exclaimed. "I heard they can spit green slime near four feet. What's that noise they're making?"

Laura cocked her head and tried to distinguish the sound he was referring to from the assorted noises made by the crowds milling around them. Finally, she pinpointed a low rumble that seemed to be coming from the camels.

"Why Jamie," she said, laughing, "they appear to be grumbling like some old curmudgeons. I suppose that walking around and around in a circle with a bunch of squealing humans on their backs might be beneath their dignity. Hattie always…"

The sadness slammed into her, taking her breath away. Laura had never realized how often she thought or said the words, "Hattie always." Now, each time she did, she was reminded that she would never hear Hattie say anything, ever again, and her grief overwhelmed her. She'd gone over and over her conversation with Hattie when she'd visited her at the Mission Street boarding house and Hattie's last words at the hospital, looking for clues to her friend's state of mind, trying to make sense of everything.

At least she now understood why Hattie had looked ill last Saturday, and her pregnancy explained why she was marrying so precipitously, giving up her plans for a future career. A child would change everything. But what Laura couldn't decide was whether Hattie had been happy. She'd said she was. She'd seemed genuinely excited about her plans to marry, but maybe she was just putting on a brave face. Oh, why hadn't she confided in Laura about the pregnancy? Had she been too ashamed? If only that dratted man hadn't come and interrupted them. *Russell*...how she hated him. He had ruined everything, ruined Hattie.

"Miss Laura, what's wrong? Do you want to move further back?" Jamie's brown eyes were looking up at her worriedly, and Laura realized she had been squeezing his hand too tightly.

"I'm fine, but look, Ian is moving on to the next pen." Laura pointed down the path. "Go ahead and catch up to him."

Laura followed slowly behind on the path as Jamie wove deftly around a group of three fashionably dressed young women. She knew it was kindness that had motivated Kathleen to invite her to come with them today, probably prompted by Annie, but she wished she had refused. It felt sacrilegious to be gadding about in company just three days after Hattie's death. Hattie's parents were probably already on the train back to Santa Barbara with their daughter's body. She hadn't known where they'd stayed last night, so she wasn't able to give them her condolences in person.

My goodness! Laura's thoughts were diverted when the three young women in front of her scattered, squealing, as an ostrich strode majestically across their path. The bird was huge, its long neck towering over the girls, but its head and beak looked absurdly tiny in comparison to the large, round, feathered body. The eyes, and the sinuous neck, reminded her of the camels she had just been staring at, and she wondered if there was something about the desert geography that would account for these similarities. A good question to ask her students. *Maybe I can take the whole class to the Gardens. I wonder how much that would cost?*

She turned and watched as the odd bird walked slowly down a path with a sign pointing to the reptile house. Seeing that Kathleen and Patrick and the two boys were looking into the monkey cage some ways away, she began to walk more quickly. She had promised to give Kathleen and Patrick a little time alone, and she thought she would offer to take the boys over to one of the lemonade vendors she could see up ahead. Get her mind back on more pleasant things...she was sure that had been everyone's intent in having her come.

Annie told her that first night that, over time, her grief would become less acute. That she would even be able to be happy, and that was all right, that Hattie would have wanted that for her. She knew rationally this was true. But when she found momentary relief, in teaching, or today watching the boys having fun, she felt worse, if that were possible. She'd also found herself avoiding Annie, retiring to her own bedroom right after supper, hustling out the front door in the mornings to wait for Barbara and Jamie on the front porch. With everyone else, she was able to keep up the role she had decided to play...the brave but cheerful girl soldiering on in the face of her sadness. But when she saw the concern in Annie's expression, all her control began to unravel, and she wanted to throw herself into her arms and howl. No, Annie was too dangerous to her equanimity. She had to be avoided until Laura knew what she needed to do next...until she needed Annie's help in exposing Russell for the seducer he was.

Laura paused when she reached the path the ostrich had taken. The cross-flow of people was too dense to move through easily. The sun was directly hitting her face, her hat's up-curled brim doing nothing to shade her eyes, and she wished she hadn't worn her brown wool cloak and her winter-weight undergarments. She should welcome the warmth after days of rain and drizzle, but her head ached and her heavy jean corset was creating a band of fire around her waist that was making breathing difficult.

"Miss Dawson, excuse me, but..."

Laura let out a small cry and stepped hastily back from the man who'd stepped in front of her. Not just any man, but Seth Timmons, her former classmate.

"Mr. Timmons, how did you...I mean, whatever are you doing here?"

Laura's heart was beating so fast she thought she might faint. All her suspicions that he might be the man who grabbed her in the alley came back at the sight of him. She'd told herself he was safely miles away finishing up his classes at San Jose Normal School, but here he stood in front of her, blocking out the sun with his imposing height and wide shoulders. Tall, taller even than Nate, he wore the long, narrow frock coat that always struck her as funereal, and his white shirt was the only part of his outfit that wasn't black, producing an over-all somber impression. Even in winter, his complexion was the color of tanned leather, as if he spent all of his days outdoors, and the double curve of his dark mustache was echoed by deep creases in his cheeks. But it was his deep-set grey eyes that always disconcerted her the most.

He took off his Stetson, smoothed back his black hair peppered with white, and said politely, "Miss Dawson, I apologize. I didn't mean to startle you. I read a short notice in the paper this morning that a Miss Wilks had passed, and I just had to...I was sure you'd know. Was it our Miss Wilks?"

"Yes, yes it was. She fell down the steps in her boarding house on Wednesday. She died later that night at St. Mary's."

Laura stopped speaking, knowing she sounded cold-hearted, but she just didn't know what else to say, and the "*our* Miss Wilks" had angered her. What did he mean, claiming Hattie that way? Recognizing the note of anguish in Seth Timmons' deep voice, she wondered, not for the first time, just what Hattie had been to him besides his math and science tutor. When he had started coming out to visit Laura last fall, she had thought he might be doing so because he hoped she would have news of Hattie. Yet, as the months went on and the news she had from Hattie grew less detailed, he didn't stop visiting. Now she didn't know what to think.

He turned his hat in his hands and shifted restlessly, saying, "Miss Dawson, you have my sincerest condolences. How did it happen? Did you get a chance to see her before…she…"

"Yes. Yes, I was with her when she died. Look, Mr. Timmons, I am here with friends. I really can't talk to you right now." Laura was finding it very difficult to maintain her composure and desperately needed to get away from his penetrating stare. She started to move to go around him.

"No, please don't go yet." He stepped sideways, blocking her passage. "I know this must be terrible for you, but I…"

Laura snapped, "I don't need your condolences. Why are you even here in San Francisco? Shouldn't you be finishing up your classes?"

"I left. I needed to start making some money. I got a position at the last minute at Pine and Larkin Primary. But that is beside the point. I needed to speak to you about Hat…Miss Wilks."

"But how did you find me?" she interrupted. "Did you follow me here?"

Seth looked startled and said, "I came here because I hoped to speak with you. When I read the notice in the paper, I went to your boarding house. I had just gotten there when I saw you leave with your friends, so I followed you, looking for a chance…"

"How did you know where I lived, Mr. Timmons, and why have you been following me? I keep seeing you everywhere I go. Was it you who grabbed me in the alley? No, I don't even want to know. Just go. I never want to see you again."

Laura realized that her voice had risen nearly to the level of a shout and that people around her had started to stare, so she again tried to push past Seth, who reached out and detained her by grasping her arm above her elbow.

"What do you mean grabbed you?" Seth's voice was so quiet she could barely make out his words. "What are you talking about? Someone *attacked* you? When?"

He had pulled her close, and Laura looked down at where his bare hand wrapped around her arm. She said, her voice shaking with anger, "Take your hands off of me before I scream. Then you can explain to Patrolman McGee, one of my companions over there by the monkey cage, just why you are assaulting me."

Laura saw Seth's square jaw clench, his eyes darken. Then he backed away from her, his hands raised palm out. He said, "Miss Dawson, my apologies. I have no excuse for my behavior, beyond my distress over the tragic news about Miss Wilks. I have not been following you. In fact, it was Miss Wilks herself who informed me of your address. I'm sorry to hear that someone has tried to do you harm. I can only assure you it wasn't me. However, I will respect your wishes and not impose upon you further."

With a tip of his hat, Seth Timmons strode away and was almost instantly swallowed up by the crowd, leaving Laura all alone.

Chapter Seventeen
Saturday evening, January 17, 1880

"The Plymouth Pilgrims - We learn that the 2500 Yankee prisoners, captured by General Hoke's forces at Plymouth, left Wilmington last night, and may be expected to pass through Charleston this evening, on their way to the Prison Depot at Americus, Ga." —*Charleston Mercury,* April 26, 1864

When Kathleen opened the door, she gave him her usual smile, then whispered, "Mr. Dawson, if you would step into the small parlor, Miss Laura and Mrs. Fuller are expecting you. Miss Minnie and Miss Millie, you see, are currently using the formal parlor."

Nate, taking off his hat and gloves and handing them over to her, said equally quietly, "Thank you, Miss Kathleen. How thoughtful."

He was finding it easier to withstand the double assault of Miss Minnie's loquaciousness and Miss Millie's odd silence when they decided to chaperone his visits with Annie, but tonight he would have found an hour of being polite to the elderly seamstresses quite trying. He went quickly through the door to the room where Annie, as Madam Sibyl, saw her clients. His sister and Annie were sitting side by side in two chairs that had been drawn next to the fireplace. He was struck by the contrasts between the two of them. Annie, with the red tints glinting in her blonde hair and her pale skin and soft curves, shared only the brown of her eyes with his tall, lean, dark-haired sister.

But, damn, they both look so beautiful in the firelight. Beautiful but tired. He dragged a third chair over and said, "I am glad to find you both together. Laura, I hope Annie explained I would have come earlier, but I am in the middle of a case that is taking up my every spare minute." He wanted to gather her into his arms the way he did when she was a little girl, but instead he reached out and took her hands between his.

"Of course, I am glad you are finally getting some trial work," she replied, giving his hands a squeeze, then pulling away to wrap her arms around her waist as if cold. "Annie has been taking excellent care of me. Everyone has. I know you were worried, and I am sorry I made such a fuss."

"And I have assured her that she has nothing to apologize for," said Annie. "But she has had a bit of excitement today. Do tell your brother what happened this afternoon."

Laura started off describing how she had been persuaded to go with Kathleen, Patrick McGee, and the two boys to Woodward's Gardens, and he could tell she was stalling when she started describing the camels they had seen, but he let her take her time. At least she wasn't weeping, although her eyes seemed sunken in her face, and he knew their mother would be worried if she saw how thin her daughter had become. Now that he thought about it, she had already lost some weight when he saw her at Christmas.

"...then Seth Timmons appeared out of nowhere. Remember when I asked you about those Union soldiers who were called Plymouth Pilgrims?" asked Laura, her voice rising, a sign to Nate that she was getting to the point of her story. "The ones who ended up in Andersonville prison?"

"Yes, Annie mentioned that Mr. Timmons was a classmate of yours at San Jose and that he visited you a few times when you were teaching at Cupertino Creek school," he answered.

"It was more than a few times. It was almost every weekend. I thought at first it was because my school was conveniently located on the road he took to get into the Santa Cruz foothills to the west. Hattie always...well, she had mentioned that he often went camping there. I thought he did this to get away from the rest of us. I think he felt more at ease with the male professors who were also veterans."

"But now you think there was more to his visits with you?"

Laura took a deep breath and looked at Annie, as if for courage, and then she said, "I started to wonder if maybe he was...sweet on me or something. I didn't know why he would be. I never encouraged him. When we met outside of classes, well, he made me feel uncomfortable. He was…is…so intense. I never knew what to say to him, and anyway, I thought it was Hattie that he…well, it was clear he respected her greatly. Me, he just sort of ignored. I don't think he said two words to me before this September."

"But this changed?" Nate asked, trying to keep his voice as neutral as possible.

"Well, he didn't suddenly become talkative. Beyond offering to take me home on Friday afternoons or asking if I would like to take a ride the next day, he didn't say much. I did most of the talking, usually about my students or commenting on the landscape. He must have been bored silly. But I was glad to escape from the homes I was staying in and to avoid Buck Morrison, so I kept going on buggy rides with him. Annie told you about Buck?"

"The young man in your school who made…unwanted overtures?" Nate winced at how stilted he sounded. This was not a conversation he wanted to have with his little sister.

"He was a bully, plain and simple, Nate. I don't think he cared a bit for me. He just liked making me squirm."

"And you told Annie that Mr. Timmons and Buck had some sort of altercation?"

"Yes. Buck was clever at looking as good as gold as soon as there was someone else around, but Mr. Timmons must have picked up that there was something wrong. When he asked if Buck was bothering me, I told him I could handle my students. But he started coming a little earlier on Fridays so that he was waiting for me when I dismissed the rest of the students, including Buck. Buck asked me once if Mr. Timmons was my beau, and I'm afraid I didn't disabuse him of the notion. While he didn't stop pestering me during the week, he was more circumspect after Mr. Timmons started stopping by. He seemed intimidated by him."

"Then what happened?" Nate asked, noticing that Laura was uneasy with his question, hugging herself tighter.

"It was in the last part of the term, after Thanksgiving, and I was scheduled to board at Buck's home for those last two weeks. I had been dreading it."

Annie interjected, "Oh my, Laura, I am sure you were. Nate, Laura told me that earlier in the term, she had tried to speak to Buck's father about his behavior, but he had been as disrespectful as his son. You didn't tell me you had to board with him."

"I was able to get out of it. The only family that had been decent to me the whole term was the Spears. They aren't well off, but they are a lovely, hard-working couple, and their twin boys were two of my best pupils. I'd saved most of my earnings, and I asked if I could pay them room and board in order to live with them for those last two weeks. I knew they could use the extra money, and I would be saved from goodness knows what aggravation."

Nate asked, "Did they agree?"

"Yes." Laura leaned forward. "But Buck was enraged that I had slipped from his fingers by boarding elsewhere. He became impossible. He was defiant in class, refused to cooperate at all. Then he must have noticed on Friday afternoon that Mr. Timmons didn't arrive to pick me up. Seth had told me he wasn't going to be coming up that weekend because it was final exam week at San Jose. Well, on Sunday afternoon, Buck showed up and cornered me behind the Spears' barn. I had stayed in all weekend, but when Mrs. Spear asked me to go and feed the chickens, I..." Laura shivered, and Annie leaned over and put her arm around her shoulders.

"What happened, Laura? Did he hurt you?" Nate felt sick. How could all of this have been going on without any of the family knowing?

"He didn't get a chance. Mr. Timmons must have changed his mind about coming. Afterwards, Mrs. Spears told me that he'd driven up to the house and asked if I was available for a ride, and she sent him out to find me. He found Buck...trying to...kiss me."

Annie cried out, "Oh, Laura, I am so sorry, but Mr. Timmons rescued you?"

"Yes, he pulled Buck off of me and they fought." Laura paused. "It was terrible. It isn't as if I have never seen two men fight before; you and Billy seemed to get into a least one scrap every summer, but this was different. They're about evenly matched in height, although Buck is heavier. Nevertheless, Seth just ignored Buck's punches and kept hitting him, over and over. It's as if he'd turned into someone else, and I thought for a moment he was going to kill Buck."

"What happened?" Annie asked.

"All of a sudden, Seth stopped and just backed away. Buck sort of fell to the ground. His nose was bleeding. There was blood everywhere, mixed with Buck's tears because he was crying. When he saw that Seth wasn't going to fight him anymore, he got up and ran away, shouting that his father would make Seth pay for what he did."

Nate flashed on a night last summer when he'd confronted someone who had harassed Annie at a charity ball, and he found himself clenching his fists, saying, "I can't believe you didn't tell me about any of this. Do Billy or Father know?"

Laura shook her head. "What good would it have done to tell any of you? It was over. Buck didn't come back to school the last week, and it was already arranged that Father would come and to fetch me and my trunk on the last Friday of the term, so I never saw Buck again. I was worried that since Buck's father is on the school board I might lose my position. Then Hattie wrote to me about the job at Clement Grammar, the answer to all my prayers."

"But what about this Timmons? Am I to understand that you thought maybe he was the man who assaulted you in the alley? That doesn't make sense," Nate said.

Laura looked down, where she was now picking at the buttons that ran down the front of her jacket. She said, "You see, after Buck ran away, I kind of lost my temper, said such awful things to Mr. Timmons. He'd been so ferocious, he'd scared me. I was mad at both of them, men in general, I guess. And after what Buck shouted, I was also worried that Seth would get in trouble over the fight. Buck's father is very wealthy and powerful, and I was afraid that he might get Seth expelled from the Normal School."

Nate, feeling more and more confused said, "I still don't know why you thought he was the one in the alley."

"The man was a similar height to Seth, and I thought I had been seeing him around town. Frankly, I couldn't think of who else it might be, because the attack didn't feel random. I got the impression the man knew *me*, was angry at *me*."

"Just exactly what did the man say?" Nate asked.

"It all happened so fast. He called me...a bad word. And said something about me being stupid to think he wouldn't find where I lived and that I had ruined his life. I thought maybe Mr. Timmons had been expelled, ending his chance to become a teacher, and he blamed me for it."

"Is that what he said when he saw you today?"

"No, he said he had quit because he needed to make money. But I don't know that I believe him. He *said* he had read a notice of Hattie's death this morning in the paper and was coming here to see if I could give him more information. He *said* he then followed me to Woodward's Gardens so he could talk to me in private."

"What else did he say?" Nate asked.

"Not much. I was flustered by him appearing like that, out of the blue. I'm afraid I lost my temper again and told him to go away, which he did. But don't you see, this means he knows where I live and that he really could have been the man in the alley!"

Chapter Eighteen
Later Saturday evening, January 17, 1880
"MINNA AGAINST WADHAM - Progress of her Suit for Damages for
Seduction." —*San Francisco Chronicle*, 1879

"Are you sure you are warm enough? We can go inside if you wish." Nate pushed open the back gate that led from the alley to Annie's back yard.

Light spilled from the windows on this side of the house and from the upper stories of the adjacent houses as they walked on the path between the garden on their right, all prepped for spring planting, and the empty clotheslines on the left. With the sunset, the unusually warm temperatures of the day had cooled, but the sky was still clear of clouds or even a wisp of fog. The steady breeze from the west had even cleared out some of the perpetual haze of smoke that came from every house chimney. Consequently, the sliver of new moon was visible, the stars twinkled, and the leaves of the apricot tree shimmered.

"No, I'm fine, and I'm not ready to go in." She tucked her arm through his and said, "We have so little opportunities to be by ourselves nowadays. I'm not ready to share you with Bea or Kathleen, who I can see are still in the kitchen. Let's go sit under the tree." She suspected that Beatrice and Esther were in the kitchen busy discussing their favorite topic, which was Annie, Nate, and why they weren't married yet, and she wanted to spare both Nate and herself the inevitable effect of all that loving concern.

When they got to the bench, Nate leaned down and used his gloves to sweep off the seat. Annie tried to be as graceful as possible as she sat, tucking in her skirts so he wouldn't sit on them. She'd been pleased when he suggested they take a walk around the block, knowing how he would worry about damaging her reputation if they'd stayed alone in the small parlor once Laura retired for the night.

She wasn't surprised, either, when he immediately brought up the circumstances surrounding Buck Morrison's behavior this fall. Nate said, "I'm not condoning what that young man, Buck, did. In fact, I would like to horsewhip him. But what if he saw Laura's buggy rides with Timmons as making her fair game for his attentions?"

"Nate, you know better," Annie snapped. "From what Laura told me, he tried to make her life a misery from the first day she started teaching, and he kept at it when she didn't give him what he wanted. Any proper gentleman would see how innocent Laura is from the moment of meeting her."

"You're right. I just worry. And what about Timmons? Do you think she might be right, that Timmons was the man who attacked her?"

"I suppose he could be. Her description of how violent he got suggests there might be some degree of instability in him," Annie replied. "The man I am most concerned about is Buck. Maybe he got her address through his father. I wouldn't be surprised if the principal of Clement Grammar didn't write her former employers for a reference when she applied for the job."

"But what would Buck be doing in San Francisco?"

"Just because *you* didn't see fit to come visit me this autumn when you were staying at your parents' ranch down the peninsula, it doesn't mean that Buck couldn't take the train up to San Francisco from Cupertino." Annie looked up at him, and she could just make out his sudden smile. She did love to tease him.

"At his age, he could have even left home, be living in San Francisco," she continued.

"I know. It's just that I had started to relax, thinking the attacker was just some ruffian who wanted her money. But now? I really think I should track down Timmons to see what he has to say for himself."

"He shouldn't be too hard to find. He told Laura he was teaching at the Lark and Pine Street School. But do be careful. If he is innocent of doing anything more than protecting your sister, you don't want your inquiries to jeopardize his teaching position or her reputation. And Laura is so ambivalent about him, she might not welcome your interference."

"I must say, the idea that it might be Buck makes a lot more sense than her theory that Miss Wilks' fiancé, Russell, attacked her."

"I agree," Annie said. "Besides the fact that Russell doesn't seem at all the same physical type as the man in the alley, I just don't know why he would see Laura as such a threat to his coming nuptials. I think she just looking for a reason to justify how angry she is with Russell and how she treated him the night Hattie died."

"If she needs a reason to be angry at him, isn't the fact that he got her friend pregnant enough?" Nate's voice rose.

Annie put her hand out and stroked his arm. Her words came out haltingly as she again tried to explain what she thought motivated his sister. "I think Laura has to make Russell into some evil and powerful man so that no blame for that pregnancy will fall on Hattie. If she accepts that he is an ordinary man who got carried away but then planned to do the honorable thing then she has to accept Hattie's role in what happened. Who knows, maybe her deathbed words were an admission of her own sense of guilt. Maybe the pregnancy was 'no accident' and Hattie was saying she was sorry because it was she who had 'pushed' them into that kind of relationship."

"But...I can't imagine that a woman like Miss Wilks would...you aren't saying that she was the seducer?" Nate shifted beside her as if the thought made him physically uncomfortable. "I know that there are women who...well, who lead some men astray."

"But not well-bred women like your sister or her friend? Or me?" Annie interrupted, charmed by the innocence of his reaction.

"Exactly," Nate said. "I mean, I can understand how a woman, in her naiveté, might give the wrong impression. Which is what I was saying about Laura and her buggy rides with Timmons, but to actively... no...I don't believe it."

"Well, obviously Laura feels the same way, or wants to. She has to make Russell the villain, not someone who has lost the love of his life."

"I must say," Nate burst out, "I am not sure my sister thinks very highly of any man."

"Except her father and brothers." Annie leaned into him and touched his cheek. He captured her hand in his and brought it to his lips to kiss.

She basked in the comfort of his arms around her. But then she thought about his last comment, and she said, "I think that living with her students' families was a very rude awakening. From what she told me, she was exposed for the first time to marriages with no mutual respect, marriages where any love that had existed was destroyed by drink or poverty or simply too many children. In time, she will remember there are good men in the world—and good marriages."

Just as you reminded me of that truth. Annie pulled his face to hers, gently initiating a kiss.

Chapter Nineteen
Sunday afternoon, January 18, 1880
"MISSION STREET - THREE NICELY FURNISHED front rooms, with board, very reasonable, references." —*San Francisco Chronicle*, 1880

"I got the poor lassie's trunk down from the attic. It's in her room," said Mr. McNaughton, the boarding house keeper, solemnly shaking Annie's hand and then Laura's. "We've instructions from her parents where to ship the trunk; don't you worry yourselves about that. I just want to say again how sorry I am for what happened. If there is anything I can do to help, please let me know."

Annie assured the man that they appreciated his help. Then she encouraged Laura to follow him as he led the way up the narrow flight of stairs, holding up a lamp. The lovely weather of the day before had been chased away by a storm from the northwest, and the windows on each landing did very little to illuminate the stairs. Annie clung to the banister with one hand and held up her skirts, damp from the rain, with the other. When they got to the third-floor landing and she saw how Laura stared at the large spot where the dark stained floorboard had been scrubbed to a distinctly lighter shade, she was doubly glad she had insisted in accompanying her on this mournful task. *How Hattie must have bled.* She put her arm around Laura's shoulders and urged her onwards, whispering, "These stairs are very steep, and without any carpeting or proper lighting, I can easily imagine that Hattie's fall was nothing more than an accident."

Laura shook her head but continued up the stairs. Once in Hattie's room, Mr. McNaughton placed the lamp on the top of the dresser and left them, closing the door behind him. Annie went over and opened the curtains, a dreary pattern of faded morning glories, and then looked around at the very small room. As a boarding house keeper herself, she appreciated the difficulties in balancing the costs of furnishing rooms with keeping room rent low enough to attract boarders, but this room was depressing, with its mismatched colors, threadbare bedspread, rickety and scarred furniture. And, with no fireplace, it was also cold. She doubted it ever got warm, except in summer, when it would probably be stifling since it was at the top of the house. At least everything was neat and clean, and, unlike Nate's boarding house, there were no unpleasant odors.

"Where do you want to start, Laura?" she asked, taking off her cloak and hanging it on the hook on the back of the door. She also took off her hat and gloves and placed them on the bedside table.

"I don't really know." Laura's voice quivered. She then continued, sounding more decisive. "Her parents, in the note I got from them last evening, said that I could take anything I wanted as mementos. Perhaps I should start by going through the dresser and wardrobe, deciding what I want to keep. You could start folding everything else to put in the trunk." Laura took off her own cloak, hat, and gloves, and, laying them on the back of the chair, she went over and opened up the doors to the narrow wardrobe and started to sort through the garments hanging there.

Annie watched as Nate's sister took up a dark blue wool shawl and held it to her face, breathing in deeply, and it was all she could do not to cry in sympathy for the sharpness of the girl's grief. Instead, she went up and gently took the shawl from Laura and placed it around her shoulders, saying, "Such a lovely color and warm. Why don't you keep it around you? This room is freezing. Shall I fold up the rest of these things?"

Laura straightened her shoulders, pulling the shawl around her tighter. "Yes," she said, "Hattie was a good six inches shorter than me, nothing here or in the dresser would even fit. Oh, how odd. Here is her cloak and purse. I guess I just assumed she had fallen coming in or leaving the boarding house. But then why would they be hanging up here?"

"Well, I suppose Mr. McNaughton or his 'missus' might have...

no, that doesn't make sense. Maybe she was coming down for dinner; the timing would be right." Annie began to take the skirts, underskirts, and jackets from the wardrobe, piling them over her left arm. Everything was well-made and in the newer Basque style, some in good cashmere and others of silk faille and satin.

Laura, who had been looking in the purse, exclaimed, "Oh, look, she has my latest letter here. I imagine the rest are in the dresser. And here are her keys. I remember, the large one is for her trunk, and the other is for the wooden box she kept letters in." Going over to the dresser, she pulled out the first drawer, and, after digging through the undergarments, she lifted out a box and climbed up on the bed. Sitting cross-legged, her skirts bunched under her, she stared at the box as if it might bite.

Annie refrained from telling her to mind her clothes, knowing that Kathleen was more than capable of handling any creases. Instead, she worried about what Laura would find when she opened the box. Last night, she had told them about Russell's request to have his letters returned and her plan to read all of them before she did so. She was convinced that they would reveal once and for all his black nature. Annie worried that whatever she discovered, she would find reading Hattie's correspondence difficult.

Annie put Hattie's cloak, shoes, and hats into the trunk, which was a sturdy, iron-bound wooden one that had probably gone with her to San Jose Normal School. As she laid down the next layer of clothing, the folded suits, blouses, and the long bustle that collapsed into concentric rings, she tried not to think about how the girl's parents would feel when the trunk arrived. Then she went to the tiny two-drawer dresser and began to pack the embroidered cambric chemises, skirts, and drawers, the two corsets with their multiple corset covers, some low-necked ones with lace, others with high necks of lace and embroidery. The night-gowns were of equally fine quality, thin muslin with lace at the neck and cuffs, heavier cambric gowns, and one soft flannel that was probably her favorite. *She must have spent every penny of her fall salary on clothes.*

No wonder she had to move to this wretched boarding house when her employment ended—she had no savings.

In the bottom drawer, she found a long, thin, velvet-covered box that probably held Hattie's jewelry. Picking it up, she turned to give it to Laura, pausing when she saw that the young woman was silently weeping, holding a bundle of letters to her breast.

"Oh my dear, I am so sorry." She moved over to sit on the bed next to Laura, giving her a hug. "Can I do anything to make this process less painful? Maybe we should just bring the box with her letters home. You can sort through them more slowly and send them as a separate package. I am sure her parents won't mind."

"No, it won't get any easier if I put it off." Laura pulled away from Annie. "But I will definitely keep my own letters to her. Do you mind if I put them in your purse?"

"No, not at all." Annie picked up a stack of letters tied with a red ribbon. She said, "What about these? They seem to be from her parents."

"Just make sure that there aren't any other letters in that group, from me for instance, and then put them in the trunk. Oh, that is Hattie's jewelry box." Laura took the box from Annie and opened it. "Look, here is the locket I gave her for her last birthday. I will definitely keep that. But these garnet earrings and the matching brooch were her grandmother's and should go back home. I will just keep the locket and this pair of silver earrings she bought to celebrate her graduation. I bought a stick pin of the same design…I know she would want me to have it."

More tears flowed. Finally, Laura shook herself like a puppy coming out of a rain shower, and she jumped up from the bed, saying, "I will not moon over a bunch of trinkets. Annie, could you put the jewelry box in the trunk and then sort the rest of the letters in piles based on who they are from? It makes more sense for me to go through the books and papers in that valise by the window." Without waiting for a reply, she went over and knelt down by a large leather suitcase and began to pick through what looked like a jumble of school texts and novels.

Annie, curious, leaned over the box of letters and began to take out the stacks of envelopes of various sizes, each tied neatly by a different colored ribbon. There was a fairly large group of letters from someone named Eugenia Wilks, evidently one of Hattie's cousins. They could go into the trunk. She went through a number of greeting and Christmas cards, taking out those that came from Laura. Then she took out a packet that had a good many different-sized objects in it, running from business-sized envelopes, ticket stubs, handbills, and a thick stack of small envelopes that turned out to be from Andrew Russell.

Annie looked over at Laura, who had created two different piles of books and was now looking through some papers. She said, "I've found Russell's correspondence and what looks like keepsakes from him. What do you want me to do with them?"

"If you don't mind, put them with my letters," Laura said flatly. "I will give them to Mr. Russell but not before I have read them. I know that you and Nate feel that I am judging him too harshly, but if he is not the blackguard I think him, let him prove himself with his own words. I need to understand why she would have taken up with him, be willing to give up her plans, our plans."

"I know, dear," Annie replied. "But what if you don't find what you are looking for? What if it is as simple as they loved each other, and they decided to get married right away when they discovered she was pregnant? Then, after a tragic accident, she died."

"But how could she have gotten pregnant! That's what I can't understand, Annie," Laura cried out. "Not the Hattie I knew. While marriage wasn't in her plans, she thought that women like Victoria Woodhull who talked about 'free love' and having relations outside of the bonds of marriage were either addlebrained romantics or just making up an excuse for fornication. How could she have changed that much?"

Annie paused, trying to find words that might help, wishing that Laura's mother were here to comfort and guide her daughter. "Laura, I don't know how much your mother has talked about…marital relations…"

"Marital relations? Isn't that just the point? This was sexual intercourse, *not* marital relations," Laura said. "I'm sorry to be so unladylike. It is difficult enough for me to believe that she 'fell in love' so quickly, but I just can't understand why she would risk everything, for what? I think he must have pressured her into having relations with him. That's the proof I am looking for in those letters."

"I don't know what happened between Hattie and Russell; we may never know," Annie said. "But I have learned through painful experience that when it comes to relationships between a man and a woman, only the people involved really know the full story."

She paused, then continued. "Before we married, John was a perfect gentleman. He courted me with flowers and sweet words. Never even tried to kiss me. But it turned out he was a brute, who, after marriage, had no respect for me or my person. Our marital relations were never...loving." Annie closed her eyes, overwhelmed momentarily by the terrible memories.

She then felt a tentative touch by Laura, who had moved over to sit on the bed beside her and was staring at her with concern.

"Annie, I am so sorry. Does Nate know?"

"No. He knows I was unhappy but not the details, and I hope never to have to tell him. What good would it do? John's dead; he can't hurt me anymore." Annie reached over and clasped Laura's hand. "But you see, I know in my bones that your brother is different. He would never force me to do something I didn't want to do. Perhaps even more importantly, he won't let me do something that I might later regret. You see how careful he is of my reputation."

Laura looked surprised and said, "Won't let you? What do you mean?"

Annie felt that she had gone beyond her depth but also felt she had to try to explain because it might help Laura make peace with Hattie's pregnancy. "I guess that is the point I was trying to make about Hattie and Andrew Russell," she said. "It has only been recently, with your brother, that I have discovered how intoxicating falling in love can be, how it can sweep away rules of propriety, if only momentarily."

Shaking her head, Laura's voice was tinged with disapproval when she said, "Well, I don't understand why the two of you aren't planning on getting married if you both feel that way."

"Well, he hasn't asked me again," Annie said, defensively.

"Again? Annie, you aren't telling me he proposed to you and you turned him down?" Laura was clearly shocked.

"He did this fall, and we had an awful row. He made the mistake of saying he wanted to marry me to take care of me, so that I could sell the boarding house and never have to work as Madam Sibyl again."

"Oh stupid, stupid Nate. I can just hear him." Laura shook her head. "Don't you hate it when he gets paternalistic, tries to sound like my father? I just laugh at him."

"Well I am afraid I shouted at him, but later we agreed to take our time, get to know each other better." Annie's discomfort over the direction this conversation had taken increased, so she said, "Promise me you won't speak of this…or anything else I have said today…to Nate. I really shouldn't have confided in you; it puts you, as his sister, in an awkward position."

"Annie, I feel honored that you have been honest with me," Laura said. "But I promise; I won't say a word. I don't know what I would have done, would do, without your support. But I won't promise not to ring his neck if he doesn't succeed in making you my sister-in-law sometime in the near future."

Annie gave her another quick hug. She then said, "We need to finish up here. I don't know about you, but my feet are beginning to turn into blocks of ice. Are you almost done with the valise?"

"Yes I…Annie, what was that?" Laura stood up quickly and went over to the door. She leaned her head against it and listened. Then she opened up the door and took a step into the corridor. "No one there," she said, coming back into the room. "It must have been just one of the other boarders coming or going. It's been as quiet as a tomb; I had forgotten anyone else lived here."

Annie felt a sudden sense of urgency to complete their sad task and leave. She said, "It's getting late. Let's finish up as quickly as we can. I would like to be heading home well before it gets dark."

Laura went over to the chair by the window where she had stacked some books and papers. "This shouldn't take long. There are a few textbooks and novels of hers that I don't own, so I will want to keep them. I wonder if it would be all right if I kept the valise. We need some way of carrying everything home."

Annie nodded. "That seems a good idea. You can always send it back to her parents later if they want it. I am almost done with the box. There seems to be a thick envelope at the bottom with no address on it."

Opening up the flap on the business-sized envelope, Annie removed several smaller pieces of lined composition paper. When she unfolded the first, she was surprised to see it held nothing but a few lines written in large black capital letters. Assuming that this was some keepsake from one of the children Hattie had taught, she was about to hand it over to Laura when she suddenly took in the meaning of the words.

The note read:
DEAR MISS WILKS
YOU WHORE
YOU DONT DESERVE TO TEACH CHILDREN
A CONCERNED CITIZEN

*****

When Annie and Laura got home from Hattie's boarding house, Nate was waiting for them. He didn't usually come to visit her twice in a weekend, but he'd felt he needed to check in to see how Laura was doing after her trip to pack up her friend's things. Once again, she and Nate and Laura were meeting in Madam Sibyl's small parlor in order for them to have some privacy.

"See, there are three of them," Annie said to Nate, showing him the anonymous notes she'd found in Hattie's box of correspondence. "All saying pretty much the same thing, although this last one is more explicit, indicating that if Hattie didn't quit teaching, something bad would happen. See this phrase, 'Go back to where you came from or else.' What they don't do is mention Russell, at all, but we must assume that it was her relationship with him that prompted the writer's accusations."

As Nate looked at the notes, Annie asked, "Does this sound at all like it might have come from the same person that wrote the accusatory letters to the school board about Mr. Emory and his friend, Mrs. Anderson?"

"Well, the suggestion of impropriety is similar, but, from Emory's description, the letters sent to the school board were very businesslike. These look as if they came from a child, not the words, of course, but the handwriting."

"I wonder how they were delivered to her? There didn't seem to be any envelopes. Could they have been put in her mailbox at Clement Grammar? How difficult would that be, Laura?"

"It wouldn't be hard at all for another teacher, and the door isn't locked so it wouldn't be impossible for a student to slip in," said Laura, who had been pacing up and down in front of the fireplace. "A student could always say they had been sent to put a note in one of the teacher's boxes; I've seen that happen. But I can't imagine a student, or a teacher, writing anything so awful."

"Seems to me that if the letter to the school board and Hattie are by the same person, he or she was being very clever," Annie said. "The school board might dismiss crude notes like this as the product of a diseased mind, but they would take seriously something more professionally written. Yet if you were Hattie and received this note, the very crudeness of it would be frightening. I can testify that the purpose of an anonymous note like this is to ignite fear in the recipient." Annie looked at Nate, who nodded his understanding.

"Poor Hattie, how upsetting this must have been," said Laura.

"Why would anyone do such a thing to her? I mean, I understand that the purpose was to get her to quit teaching, but why? Unless this was part of Russell's plan to hound her into marrying him." Laura picked up the poker beside the fireplace and thrust it at the logs, causing them to collapse in a shower of sparks.

Annie looked over at Nate and shrugged, not knowing what to say about Laura's continued determination to blame everything on Russell. Finally, she said, "It seems too coincidental that two different people would be trying to disparage the morals of city school teachers, despite the difference in the letters' styles. I can't help but wonder if anyone else has received a similar note."

Nate, agreeing, said, "I will definitely make sure that Emory, or Mrs. Anderson, hasn't been withholding any information. They both told me they hadn't received anything directly, but I can imagine that if Mrs. Anderson got something along these lines, she might not admit it."

He then walked over to Laura and put his hand on her shoulder, forcing her to look at him before he went on. "I can only imagine how difficult all this is. But it is possible that your friend was the victim of a political or personal campaign to smear certain administrators in the school system. Russell is, after all, a Vice Principal. The letter Emory showed me accused the Vice Principal of Girls' High of hiring Mrs. Anderson out of favoritism. Didn't you tell us that Hattie suggested that she quit teaching at Clement Grammar because she didn't want Russell to be accused of the same thing?"

Laura frowned, then sighed. "I guess so. I just wish she had confided the truth to me. I need to look at all this more objectively. Hattie always said...*Hattie always said* that I needed to be careful not to try to fit my facts to prove my point but let the facts lead me to my conclusions. She had such a scientific mind."

Annie interjected, "Well, I think it is much too soon to come to any conclusions." She then turned to Nate and said, "Laura has granted me permission to read Russell's letters first. You can be sure I will be looking for any evidence that he knew about these poisonous notes or

Hattie's pregnancy."

"I'm not entirely comfortable with the idea of you reading the man's letters," Nate responded. "But given the circumstances, I suppose someone must. I would be interested in the timing. If he refers to when Hattie received the notes or if the letters reveal when in the term Miss Wilks decided to quit, we might be able to see if it corresponds at all with the anonymous letters that were sent to the board this fall. I will also get Emory to investigate if any other people in authority got similar letters. It is possible, for example, that the Clement Grammar Principal got a letter making an accusation about Hattie and Russell but simply ignored it."

"Oh, my heavens," Laura said, her voice rising. "If these notes aren't from Russell but some sort of broader attack against teachers or administrators, then it is possible that the person who wrote these letters continued to pressure Hattie in some fashion. That last note suggested something bad would happen if Hattie didn't 'go away.' Hattie quit teaching, but she certainly didn't go away…and then she died."

Chapter Twenty
Wednesday afternoon, January 21, 1880

"With other members of the Committee on Salaries, I consider that a reduction of 30 per cent on the salaries of primary teachers would tend to destroy the usefulness of the School Department. Take away our good teachers and replace them by inexperienced ones, and the interior towns will reap the benefit of it, and their gain will be our loss" —San Francisco School Board Director McDonnell, *San Francisco Chronicle*, 1879

"Miss Dawson, Johnny is jiggling in his seat so I can't do my essay properly," Betsy Clarke complained, looking smug. Since her desk, like most school desks, was attached to the seat in front of her, occupied by the fidgety John Jenkins, this had become a constant refrain.

"Mr. Jenkins, would you please get up and move to the chair next to Miss Blaine; take your paper and pen with you. And, Miss Clarke, I will expect that the second half of your essay will show extraordinary improvement in both content and form. Now class, back to work."

Laura smiled at Kitty Blaine, who got Johnny settled and back to work in short order. There were now forty-two students in her seventh grade class, down from the fifty who were enrolled in the fall, and this meant that she had been able to ask the janitor, Mr. Ferguson, to remove the entire back row of desks. This left just two extra desks by the window at the back, where more often than not Johnny Jenkins sat under the watchful eye of her practice teacher. At first, Laura had made the mistake of being sympathetic to Betsy Clarke's complaints; now she realized they were based primarily on the petite blonde's desire to be the center of attention.

As the students returned to their work, she looked out over their bowed heads and realized that the more she got to know their distinct personalities, the more affection she had for them. The challenge was to figure out a way to reward their good qualities and not reinforce the less-than-admirable ones. She'd found, for example, the less fuss she made when Betsy complained, the better. On the other hand, the girl's need for attention could be directed into getting her to work harder on perfecting her handwriting, which was often sloppy, whether Johnny was jiggling or not. And then there was Zachary Martin, who had grown so tall that he could barely contort his legs enough to fit under the rigid desk. He handled his embarrassment over how clumsy he'd become by acting the class clown. Annie had discovered, by accident, that the more she asked him to use his height to help her by opening up the top windows or taking down the globe from the top of the supply cabinet, the less he engaged in any tomfoolery. He was also very gentle with the smaller children, not at all a bully, so she had put him in charge of taking up the rear when they all walked to assembly.

The topic of bullies made her think of Buck, and this of course led to Seth Timmons. She was forced to reassess her opinion of him, once again, when she discovered letters from him among the correspondence she had brought home. She had left Russell's letters and the anonymous nasty notes to Annie, but she read the six letters from Seth that she found when she went through the letters to Hattie. Two of the letters were written last summer, revealing that he had been working on a cattle ranch down near Los Angeles. These letters were very short, primarily asking after Hattie's health, telling her about his success in solving a math problem that she had given him to work on, and commenting on the second volume of Martineau's translation of the Frenchman Comte's work on positivism, which he was reading in the evenings. Laura wasn't sure whether she was more nonplussed to discover he was reading such a difficult work or that he seemed to agree with Comte's views about human society. She couldn't imagine how the men who worked with him would have reacted to a ranch hand who read Enlightenment philosophers.

The greatest shock, however, came when she read the third letter, written the second week of September, right after Seth's first visit with

Laura in Cupertino. From what he said, it was clear that Hattie had asked him to check up on her. Each of his subsequent letters reported on his visits to Laura, where they went each weekend—*up the trail into the Santa Cruz Mountains, a picnic along the Cupertino River, a drive to San Jose*, her health—*she looks tired, she doesn't appear to be eating enough, she has a cold, the fresh air seemed to do her good*, and her state of mind—*she is anxious, she is having trouble with some of her students, she appears much happier after her visit home, and she won't confide in me what is worrying her.*

Laura didn't know whether to be touched that Hattie had been concerned about her or furious that she had enlisted Seth to spy on her. Mostly, she was embarrassed to think of the way she had treated him last Sunday. Reading these letters, which she'd done several times in the past few days, hearing in her mind his calm and unemotional voice, she wondered how she could have ever thought that he had been the one to attack her. The idea now seemed absurd. His attention to her last fall had simply come from his desire to do Hattie a favor.

Probably, if he hadn't figured out that she was being harassed by Buck, he wouldn't have come as often. He certainly wasn't personally interested in her, given the unflattering nature of his comments. *How boring it must have been for him to drive around such an anxious, scrawny, sickly, incompetent woman every weekend.* All he had gotten for his pains was Laura's public abuse when he tried to find out about Hattie's death.

The least she could do was apologize. To that end, she had sent him a short note, addressed to the Pine and Larkin School where he was teaching, asking if he would be willing to meet with her. She would have preferred to simply write an apology and leave it at that. However, since Seth's letters made it plain that he was responding to letters he had gotten from Hattie, she needed to know what Hattie had written to him about Russell and her reasons for quitting teaching. It now seemed possible that Hattie might have confided details to Seth that she hadn't been able or willing to confide in Laura.

Noting the time on her pocket watch, she brought her thoughts back to her job. She stood and announced that the students needed to put down their pens and pass their papers to the front. As usual, this spurred a flurry of last-minute scribblings by some of the students and the rise of noise in the classroom as others opened their desktops to put their pens away.

Laura raised her voice. "Please, everyone be still until Miss Blaine has collected all of your papers. I want to remind you that there will be a spelling test first thing tomorrow. All of you using the *Fourth Reader*, make sure to bring your books to school because Miss Blaine is going to lead you in your discussion. I want you to show her how prepared you are."

After Kitty walked over and placed the pile of collected essays on the desk, Laura turned back to the students and announced, "Dismissed." Pandemonium ensued, but she was pleased at how cheerful everyone sounded as they chattered to their neighbors while they got out the books they needed for doing their homework and made their way to the back of the room to get their coats. Hattie always…yes, she wouldn't shy away from the memory…Hattie always said that a classroom that was too quiet was a classroom where the students were too frightened to learn.

"Is there anything else you would like me to do, Miss Dawson?" said Kitty in her usual deferential manner, so at odds with her ease with the students. "I could erase the board before I go."

Trying not to sound irritated, Laura replied, "No need, thank you. I will see you tomorrow then." Since she would be waiting for Barbara, who had her weekly meeting of the Literature and Debate Society at Girls' High, Laura had plenty of time to clean the board and set it up for the next day. She would write the spelling words for their test, then cover it by hanging up the roller map of the United States. She had a suspicion that the janitor, Mr. Ferguson, might be letting some of his pets among her students sneak a peek at the board ahead of time, and this was her solution to that problem.

She had just finished putting the spelling list on the board and taken the roller map from the supply cabinet when she heard a sound behind her and turned around, assuming it was Jamie coming in to see if she needed any help. Instead, she saw Seth Timmons standing at the back of the room, black Stetson in hand.

He nodded politely. "Miss Dawson, you asked to see me?"

She hadn't expected to see him in person this soon, hadn't really planned out what she wanted to say, so she just said, "Yes, thank you for coming."

Then, aware that she was still holding the map, she decided to take advantage of his height, and she asked, "Would you mind unrolling this map and putting it up on those hooks so it hides the spelling list?"

He put down his hat and gloves on one of the desks and walked in an easy stride towards the front of the room. When he came over to take the map from her, their hands touched, and she noticed her fingers were all covered in chalk dust. She resisted the impulse to go over to the mirror at the back of the supply cabinet to see if she had transferred any chalk to her hair or face during the afternoon. It was an occupational hazard he would be familiar with, but she didn't want him to think her untidy.

As he finished hanging the map, she said, "You mentioned that you were teaching at Pine and Larkin Primary. What grade?" *How stupid, of course I know he is at that school since I sent the note there. He must think me an idiot.*

"Fourth."

Taking out the handkerchief she kept tucked in her sleeve, she swiped ineffectually at the chalk on her hands and started talking quickly to fill the ensuing silence. "And how do you find your class? Pretty lively I might expect, at least from my limited experience. I must say I like teaching seventh-grade students much more than I did the younger students at Cupertino Creek. I was surprised that they hired you...I mean not you personally...it just was my understanding that schools generally hired women for the primary grades. I really think that is a mistake, but then what man would want to accept the low salaries that the school board is now offering primary teachers?" Laura stopped, aghast at where her nerves had taken her conversation.

Seth didn't respond but simply looked at her, raising one eyebrow in the irritating way he had. She tried to rescue herself, saying, "I expect that teaching young boys and girls is an interesting alternative to herding cattle, which I gather you did this summer."

"Yes, Miss Dawson, it is. But I don't expect you asked to meet with me to discuss the relative merits of teaching and cattle ranching." A slight smile deepened the indentations in his cheeks that echoed the curves of his mustache.

After reading his letters to Hattie, she'd realized that in all their rides together this fall she'd never thought to ask him how he had spent the previous summer. He must have thought her very rude and self-involved. But then, his one-syllable answers to the questions she did ask hadn't encouraged her to press any further into his personal life. *But positivism and Comte, if I'd only known, what interesting discussions we could have had.*

Taking a deep breath, Laura tried again to find her conversational footing. "I'm sorry, Mr. Timmons; I don't mean to waste your time. First of all, I do want to apologize for my reaction to seeing you at the Gardens. I confess that the death of Hattie, Miss Wilks, has seriously upset me."

Seth made a dismissive motion with his right hand. "Miss Dawson, no need to apologize. Being with Miss Wilks when she died must have been unsettling."

"Yes, and I want to clarify. I didn't really think you had followed me or attacked me. It is just that…well, I never quite understood why you were being so attentive to me this fall. Now, having read Hattie's correspondence from you, I realize you were simply responding to a request from her and that she had given you my address."

Seth stiffened and said, "You read my letters?"

"Yes, Hattie's parents asked me to go through her things, decide what needed to be kept." Laura felt on the defensive at the accusatory tone in his deep voice. "I...well...I needed to know if she had confided in you about...I'm sorry...I am not explaining myself well."

Laura had been so determined to find out what Hattie'd told Seth in her letters to him that she hadn't thought about how he might respond to this invasion of his privacy. Looking at how his grey eyes darkened under his frowning brows, she scrambled to make him understand her motivation. "You see, I wouldn't have read them except that I am desperate to find out more about why Hattie decided to give up all her plans and marry Mr. Russell. There are some very suspicious circumstances around her death. I am afraid..."

"What do you mean, suspicious?" Seth asked, his voice rising as he took a quick step towards her.

"She was being persecuted by someone who made vicious accusations and may have hounded her to death. We found these notes...they said awful things, and it isn't clear how she fell. In her last words to me, Hattie said something that makes me suspect that it might not have been an accident...so you can see..." Laura faltered, now afraid she may have said too much. Just because Hattie had trusted him didn't mean that he was trustworthy. Oh, why hadn't she taken the time to check with Annie or Nate about the wisdom of meeting with Seth? Or at least have planned out how to approach this conversation.

"You said she was hounded to death? How exactly did she die, Miss Dawson?"

"I told you, she fell down the stairs at her boarding house. I was notified, but when I got to the hospital...there was internal bleeding. They couldn't stop it." Laura turned away, afraid she was going to start to cry.

"Are you saying it wasn't an accident?" Seth asked.

"I can't really...say right now," Laura said, turning to face him again. "Not until I get a better understanding of what happened this fall and the exact reasons for Hattie's decision to quit teaching. Did you know that she was planning on marrying Mr. Russell in just a few weeks?"

Seth smoothed his mustache, a mannerism she had learned meant he was thinking of what to say next. He then said slowly, "Well, I did know that she had met someone she was quite fond of named Russell. She did tell me she had resigned her position but not why."

Laura, hurt once again to discover Hattie had confided in Seth but not her, said, "I don't understand. She didn't say a word to me in any of her letters. And you never mentioned this to me, either."

Now Seth looked uncomfortable. He said, "It didn't seem to be any of my business."

Laura had the urge to snap that it certainly wasn't his business, but since she was trying to find out what Hattie had confided in him, she refrained. Instead, she tried again to ask for details. "In her letters, did she give you the impression she felt pressured to quit teaching and marry Russell?"

"No, but she didn't write much about herself. Mostly, she wanted to know how you were doing, how my classes were going. And she didn't give me any specifics in her first few letters. Just that she had joined this study group to prepare for entrance into the University. Then she hinted she had met someone in this group she respected a good deal."

"When did she tell you about quitting her job?"

"Several weeks before the end of fall term, when she wrote to me about the opening at Pine and Larkin. She knew that I had run out of funds and was looking for work."

Laura thought about the timing. Would Hattie have even known she was pregnant by then? Perhaps not. Once she found out, however, she would have had to scrap any plans to teach in the spring, and marriage would be the only respectable option. But was this a mutual decision between Hattie and Russell? She really wished she knew if Russell had known about Hattie's condition. One thing she knew for sure, she wasn't going to tell Seth Timmons about the pregnancy or about the real reason Hattie had bled to death.

Seth interrupted these thoughts. "I still don't understand. How is this related to some man attacking you? That's what you said, didn't you, that you thought I had attacked you?"

Laura thought he looked angry and wondered if he could ever forgive her for her stupid accusations. "I'm not saying it is related...I don't know. You see, two weeks ago, on my way home, a man grabbed me in the alley behind the boarding house where I live. I thought he was someone I knew by the way he spoke. And I know I wasn't very nice to you after your fight with Buck because you'd frightened me so. And then I was worried that you might have blamed me if Buck's father made trouble for you. Please, Mr. Timmons, I am sorry I ever entertained the idea it might have been you. I have apologized...can you let it be?"

As Seth looked down at her, she could feel the flush of embarrassment on her cheeks.

He then said, "Miss Dawson, I don't blame you. I am just sorry to have given the impression that I would ever do you harm. I should have kept my temper more under control that day...when I...when I found that lily-livered cur pressing his attentions on you. I know I frightened you. But I can promise you, I mean to find out just exactly where Buck Morrison was two weeks ago, and if he is responsible...then all I can say is he will wish he were dead."

Chapter Twenty-one
Saturday afternoon, January 24, 1880
"The old Ocean House road requires macadamizing from the Industrial School to Mission Street. The rock is being quarried with prison labor." —*San Francisco Chronicle*, 1879

For his drive with Annie today, Nate had chosen the new Ocean Road that wound through the sand dunes north of Twin Peaks. He wanted to avoid the traffic that would be clogging up both the former Point Lobos toll road and the newly completed road that went through Golden Gate Park to the beach. He also wanted to avoid ending up at the Cliff House, with its still-painful memories for both of them. But now he doubted the wisdom of his choice as they left the protection of the hills and began to encounter a stiff western breeze, filling the air with fine grit. Even though the carriage roof was up, Annie had been forced to cover her nose and mouth with her scarf. Nate's hat sat down low over his forehead, but he still had to squint to shield his eyes.

Although he hated cutting their excursion short, Nate said, "Look, shall we turn around and head home? The wind would at least be at our backs." It had been nearly a week since he had seen Annie, and there was much to talk about that required more privacy than they would find if they stayed at her house.

"No, if I remember the one time you took me this way last summer, we should be hitting the old Ocean Beach toll road soon. Isn't that macadamized? Kathleen told me she and Patrick were at the Ocean Side House a few months ago and that they had a nice snug fire."

"Annie, I…"

"Oh shush. What is respectable enough for Kathleen and Patrick is fine for me. It's the Cliff House that has become notorious, not the Ocean

Side House. Besides, Kathleen would never suggest I go somewhere that wasn't proper. You know she and Beatrice are as careful of my reputation as you are. But do hurry, I am freezing." She turned and buried her face in his shoulder.

He could see the House of Corrections and the old Industrial School ahead, which meant they were about to join the better road, so he continued on, urging the two horses to a faster trot. The team would be equally glad to reach their stalls in the stables next to the restaurant.

Once sitting at a table with a view of the ocean in front of them and the fireplace at their back, Nate felt himself relax. For some reason, every time he took Annie out for a ride, he became anxious. It was not just the memory of their first trip to the ocean together and its disastrous conclusion but some deep-seated fear that something would go wrong that would undermine her respect for him. The hostlers would fob off a carriage on him whose cushions were badly sprung or an axle would break or the waiter would give them a table located near the kitchen— something that other men would know instinctively how to handle. That her father, or her former husband, would have known how to handle. It was an idiotic insecurity, but there it was.

If only she would tell him more about her husband, maybe he wouldn't worry as much. He knew she'd been unhappy, that her husband was responsible for the loss of her inheritance and that he eventually committed suicide. But that was the fate of many a good and honorable man during the terrible financial panic of 1873. He also knew from experience that men born to New York City wealth, like her father, like her husband, had an ease about them that he'd never mastered. They commanded respect without even trying. And she must have loved John Fuller at one time. She married him, after all. What if the underlying sadness he'd sensed coming from her recently was because he just didn't measure up to her father or to her husband and that was why she didn't want to marry him?

Annie, who had stopped by the ladies' cloak room to freshen up, walked over to the table, and Nate leaped to his feet. There was something different about the outfit she wore today that emphasized her slender waist, and it was all he could do not to sweep her into his arms. Instead, he calmly pulled back her chair. As he slid the chair forward, he breathed deeply, noting that her usual scent today included the tang of salt. When he sat down across from her and noticed the high color in her cheeks and the redness of her lips, he wondered if her kisses would taste salty as well.

"Nate, why are you looking at me like that? I know I must look a fright. I tried to tidy up, but I am afraid that Kathleen is going to have to sweep extra carefully in my room after I undress tonight to get up all the sand. What did I say?" she added, and Nate began to choke on the sip of water he had been drinking.

Lord, doesn't she realize what the very idea of watching her undress for the night does to me? The waiter appeared, and Nate was saved from having to explain himself by the need to consult the menu and order tea and cakes enough to fortify them for the ride back. Then, when the waiter departed, he got right down to business.

"You've finished reading through Russell's letters? Did you learn anything that would prove or disprove Laura's theory that he was somehow pressuring Miss Wilks into marriage?"

"Well, there was nothing to suggest that he was anything other than what he appears to be, a man who fell violently, and unexpectedly, in love. The early notes are brave attempts to keep their relationship on a professional basis, full of scholarly quotations that he is asking her to translate. But his admiration for her shines through. Then something must have happened in late September because the next letter contains an open declaration of his feelings and his joy in discovering that they were reciprocated."

Nate said, "That sounds innocent enough. Anything else? Any mention of the notes we found?"

"Throughout the first two weeks in October, you can see they are trying to be very discreet. While they must have seen each other daily at Clement Grammar, his letters mention how difficult it is for him to see

her and not speak to her. There were some mentions of arranged meetings outside of school. Mostly, however, these letters are filled with
poetry and declarations of his love. Then a letter the third week of
October refers to some sort of crisis. He wrote several letters in a row
that she evidently did not answer, and he begged her to let him come see
her."

"That does sound a lot like he was pushing her to take a step she
didn't want to take. Has Laura read the letters yet?"

"Yes, I handed them over to her Wednesday evening, and we
talked about them last night when you couldn't stop by. She plans on
handing them back to Russell this week. I must say, Nate, I am beginning
to resent Able Cranston and how much he is monopolizing your time!"

Pleased that she missed him, Nate leaned over and took her hand,
saying, "The Purdy trial isn't the only thing that is keeping me busy. I
also had several meetings with Emory this week, but let's finish with
Russell and his letters. What did Laura say after she read them?"

"She reacted the way you might think, angry that he would put
such emotional pressure on Hattie. But she did admit that he seemed
sincere about his affection for her."

Nate held up his hand, and they were silent as the waiter poured
their tea and offered them a plate piled high with tasty cakes and pastries.
When the waiter left, Nate said tentatively, "Do you think that the crisis
you mentioned was her discovery that she was…that she had discovered
her condition and that is why she decided to resign at that time?"

Annie shook her head. "Oh, I don't think so. That series of letters
came right after the crisis, in mid-October, and they had only declared
their love for each other a few weeks earlier. There is no way she would
know. Let's just say it is much more likely that it was the first note,
accusing her of immorality, that probably spurred the decision to resign.
Someone must have seen them together."

"Does Russell mention the notes outright? Or speculate on who
might have written them?" Nate asked, getting excited by the idea that
there might be something in Russell's letters that would help determine

who had been making accusations about Mrs. Anderson.

"No, never directly. He does mention that he will make sure that the Clement Grammar principal, DuBois, gives her a good recommendation, so it seems she was still planning on teaching elsewhere in the spring, another indication that pregnancy wasn't motivating her at that point. Then the addresses on the envelopes change. Hattie had been living in a boarding house on Hyde, but in the middle of November, she moved to the Mission Street boarding house. Laura thought Hattie had to move because she didn't have any income, but that wouldn't explain why she moved before the term was over." Annie stopped, waiting for the waiter to refill their teapot and leave.

She continued. "I wondered if Hattie was worried that someone in her former boarding house was behind the letters. Or it could be that they decided it would be easier for the two of them to meet on the weekends if she moved south of Market, further away from work. Once she made the move, the letters are less frequent, but they sound happy as they start to plan the wedding."

"Still no mention at any time that they *have* to get married?"

"No, if Biddy's mother hadn't told me about the miscarriage, I would never have guessed her condition from the letters. I think it is possible that Russell didn't know. I suppose it is even possible that Hattie herself didn't know."

"Heavens above, how awful," Nate said. Then he noticed the tears welling up in Annie's eyes. It seemed every time the circumstances of Hattie's death came up, Annie was overcome with grief. There had to be more to it than she was admitting. Why couldn't she trust him enough to tell him what was wrong?

Before he could say anything, she took a sharp breath and said, "I wish we could ask Russell directly, but if there is the slightest chance he was behind the notes or behind the attack on Laura or at all implicated in Hattie's fall, I don't think we can risk it."

"Did Laura say anything more about her other candidate for the attack, Seth Timmons, that fellow who tracked her down at Woodward

Gardens?"

Annie sat up straighter, her eyes brightening the way they did when she was excited, and she said, "You won't believe this. She has completely exonerated him, at least in her own mind. She found some letters of his to Hattie, and it turns out Timmons was visiting her at Hattie's request. I do think Laura was rather put out by this, but it convinced her that he didn't have some awful obsession with her and that he couldn't have been the man who attacked her."

"Wait, what about the fact that he knew where she was living? And followed her to the Gardens?" Nate exclaimed.

"Well, she says that after having read the letters it makes perfect sense that Hattie would have given him Laura's address as soon as she learned he was moving up to San Francisco. Timmons told Laura that it was Hattie who told him about the job he got, just as she did for Laura. I wonder if Hattie wasn't a bit of a match-maker…"

Nate held up his hand to stop her and said, "Timmons told her? She's seen him since Sunday?"

"Yes, she wrote him after reading the letters. She told me she wanted to quiz him about what Hattie wrote to him about Russell and her decision to quit teaching. In response, he showed up at Clement Grammar on Wednesday after school was out. Laura says he said Hattie didn't mention the anonymous notes or say anything that indicated she was being pressured into marrying Russell."

Nate felt a surge of anger and said, "Annie, she told him about the notes! We can't have that information bandied about. Who knows who he might tell? Damn it, Annie, how could she be so foolhardy?" He took a deep breath and muttered an apology for having sworn. Thank goodness, Annie never seemed to get upset when he forgot to mind his tongue in front of her.

Annie patted his hand and said, "Calm down, Nate. If it is any consolation, she seemed ashamed that she had written him without checking with us first. I gather she didn't expect him to show up that way, either, but she felt she needed to tell him about the notes in order to justify all her questions. I did warn her that she needs to be more circum-spect in the future. Made me feel quite ancient, advising her to be more careful."

She smiled at him, and he felt the anger drain away.

She continued. "She assures me that she didn't give him any details. In any event, between the letters and her conversation, she seems very confident that Seth Timmons wasn't the one who attacked her. Something about the philosopher Comte, which I confess didn't make much sense to me."

"So do you agree with her?" Nate asked. "Do you think we can rule Timmons out as her attacker?"

"I don't think we can rule anyone out, and I do think it might be a good idea for you to go talk to him yourself. You know, I have felt from the beginning that her former student, Buck, the one who was harassing her, is a more likely candidate for the attacker. Evidently, that was Timmons' reaction, and now she is all in a dither about him going after Buck. She is worried he will get in trouble with the law or at the very least lose his job."

"What!"

"Yes, she asked me if you would be able to represent Timmons if he thrashed Buck again and Buck or his father pressed charges. She said she didn't know if it would be considered a 'conflict of interest.'"

Nate stared at her, hoping to discover she was teasing him. But when she shrugged and smiled, he knew she wasn't. Sighing, he shook his head and said, "Do you think we can send her back home to the ranch? When I promised Mother and Father we would look after her, I never, ever, imagined what that would entail."

Annie just laughed at him.

Chapter Twenty-two
Tuesday evening, January 27, 1880

"Thomas H. Reynolds had examined a note-book which contained the acknowledged handwriting of defendant, and after comparisons with the anonymous letters, concludes form his experience as an expert that the chirography of the note-book and letters was identically the same."—*San Francisco Chronicle*, 1879

Annie had been to Nate's law offices on Sansome Street in the financial district once before, and that had been the day after she met him for the first time. Sitting in the dark in the hansom cab that took her swiftly up Market, she remembered how confused she'd felt on that visit. Grieving over the death of Matthew Voss, frightened for her economic future, and puzzled by the strange attraction she'd felt for this young man who could be so infuriating and so kind in the time it took for her heart to beat.

Tonight she was confused again but not about her feelings for Nate Dawson. She was confused because of the letter he'd sent her asking her to come to his office this evening to attend a meeting with Mr. Emory and Mrs. Anderson. This was odd enough, since she had no idea what explanation he would give these two people for her presence at the meeting. Even more puzzling, however, was his request that she come to the meeting early because he had something of a "delicate nature" he wanted to ask her. As she'd read the letter she'd gotten the absurd notion that he was planning on renewing his marriage proposal. Then she'd immediately thought, *At a business meeting? Surely not.* But she couldn't get the idea out of her mind.

The cab slowed to a stop, and Annie handed the fare to the cabbie through the hatch before alighting. Kathleen had wanted to accompany her. But it was Tuesday, ironing day, and even with the help of the washerwoman and the part-time maid, Tilly, Annie knew that Kathleen would be completely done in by the evening. She had insisted she was perfectly safe taking a cab by herself. She even kept her irritation to herself when her motherly boarder, Mrs. Stein, tut-tutted about how unsafe the streets could be at night. She recognized this was the price she was paying for having frightened them all when she went off on her own a few months earlier. And there was Nate, as promised, waiting outside the building to escort her up to the second-story offices. She would have to be sure to report his gallantry to her friends when she got back home.

As they climbed the stairs, Nate told her that the new Superintendent of Schools had gotten another anonymous letter, again accusing the vice principal of Girls' High, Thomas Hoffmann, of colluding with Emory to hire Mrs. Anderson. However, this time the letter went on to suggest that Hoffmann was guilty of having "immoral relations" with a student.

Annie said that she thought this certainly suggested that the anonymous notes to Hattie were part of a broader smear campaign, and she asked if Nate had told Emory about the notes they had found among Hattie's correspondence.

"I told him I had evidence that another teacher had been targeted but that I couldn't reveal the details. Emory reiterated that he hasn't gotten anything directly, but I did want to ask Mrs. Anderson tonight, see how she reacts."

Annie paused as they reached the second floor landing and said, "Nate, we need to see the letter that was sent to the Superintendent of Schools, see if it bears any resemblance to the hand-writing of the notes sent to Hattie. What do you know about this Vice Principal?"

"Only that Emory says Hoffmann is well-respected, and he's held the position at Girls' High under Swett for five years."

They were now at the law offices, and Annie pointed to the name of the firm in the center of the door. "Oh look, *Hobbes, Cranston, and Dawson.* I don't remember you having your name up here when I came the first time. I guess your Uncle Frank has actually started to treat you as an equal partner."

Nate chuckled, and as he unlocked the door he said, "I wouldn't go that far." The reception room was as tiny as she remembered but neater. According to Nate, the business that Cranston brought into the firm meant they now had enough income for an additional clerk. They also had expanded into the adjoining offices, which provided rooms for the clerks and Cranston, while Nate inherited the deceased partner's office for himself.

As he turned up the gaslights, he mumbled something about leaving the outer door open for the others. She sighed. *Once again he is trying to protect my reputation. Maybe it would have been easier to just bring Kathleen with me.* Nate brought out extra chairs and put them around the table on one side of the room. Obviously, they were not going to go into his office. She was rather disappointed, having hoped to see what it looked like.

She broke the silence, saying, "How did Emory find out about this newest letter?"

"He's pretty friendly with one of the Republican board members, and Vanderling, that's the friend's name, was able to persuade Superintendent Taylor to hand the letter over to him for investigation. I am hoping Emory will be able to bring it with him, and that's why I asked you to bring Hattie's notes with you. But before they get here, I have to ask a favor of you, and you must promise me you will say no if you don't want to do this. I don't want you to feel any pressure to agree at all."

Annie's heart began to beat faster, and she could feel her cheeks get hot.

Nate continued, "Turns out my uncle took it upon himself to tell Emory about the work you did investigating Voss's death and the Framptons. As a result, Emory asked me to invite you to this meeting so he could ask you to help us in trying to figure out who is behind these anonymous accusations. He has some scheme he wants to lay out for you tonight, but I didn't want you to feel ambushed when he asks. I am really sorry, Annie. I tried to explain to Uncle Frank how unhappy you would be to know he had spoken to Emory without asking your permission."

Later, Annie would have to examine more closely her sharp disappointment that the proposition of a *delicate nature* was not a proposal of marriage. But right now, her overwhelming emotion was glee that she was going to get a chance to work on another investigation with Nate. She didn't want to appear too eager, however, or Nate might rescind the offer, so she kept her voice as moderated as possible when she responded, saying, "I am sure your uncle meant well, and I am honored by the faith he has in me. Of course I would like to help out in any way I can, although I reserve judgment until I have heard exactly what Emory's 'scheme' is. But thank you, Nate, for giving me a chance to think about it all ahead of time. And, by the noise I am hearing, I think that the rest of the members of this meeting have arrived."

Annie couldn't help but notice the look on Nate's face, like she had turned into a coiled rattlesnake, and she thought, *Oh, how well he knows me. I suspect he will rue the day he asked me to get formally involved in this little enterprise.*

"It was actually Tom Hoffmann's idea," Irving Emory said. "Naturally, when I told him about the letters and the accusations against him, he was very concerned. I assumed that this was all part of a political attack against me, but now, with both Dottie Anderson and Tom Hoffmann being implicated, it looks more like the source of the trouble might be found at Girls' High itself. We were trying to figure out how Dawson here could come to the school and nose around without causing too much suspicion. Hoffmann mentioned it was too bad that Dawson couldn't pretend to be a teacher when it occurred to me that, if Frank Hobbes is correct, Mrs. Fuller would be perfect for the job."

When Nate had introduced Emory to Annie, she wasn't surprised to see an older, well-tailored, well-barbered man of wealth who'd probably moved with ease from running his business to running the city. The fact that he owned the City of Hills Distillery would have helped because saloon keepers tended to run the ward elections for both parties.

Emory continued. "So, young lady, do you by any chance know the basics of bookkeeping?"

Annie, taken aback by the question, was curious about how much Frank Hobbes had shared about her history, including her unorthodox education in the fine points of finance and her current work as Madam Sibyl. She said, "Actually, I'm very familiar. My father used *Mayhew's Practical Book of Book-Keeping* to instruct me, and, while I have never run a large company, I do use the double entry system for keeping track of my boarding house business."

Mr. Emory beamed at her, saying, "Splendid! Splendid! Deerhurst, one of the new board members, has a 'bee in his bonnet' about the need for all young men and women to be instructed in the basics of accounting. As a result, Tom had already volunteered to include a series of lessons on the subject as part of his math classes, and I do believe he is using *Mayhew's* text. The principal, Swett, is going out of town for several weeks, and Tom will taking over some of Swett's senior classes in philosophy, so he was already looking for someone to substitute in some of his math classes. You can be that substitute, and while you are there, you can do a little detecting for us without anyone being the wiser."

Annie got a better appreciation for Mr. Emory's talents as a politician as he effectively swept away any problems she or Nate brought up with this little "scheme." She would have to teach only two classes a week, from 2-3 p.m. on Wednesday and Friday afternoons, although she could come as early in the afternoon as she wanted and stay until five when the school was locked up. She would be able to use Hoffmann's office to meet with students, and, since his office contained the personnel files, she would also be able to look through those files for possible motives among unhappy staff members. She would get paid, not just for the teaching but also for any investigating she did, and, finally, she could stop whenever she felt she had collected all the information she possibly could at the high school.

Since late afternoon was Madam Sibyl's least busy time—the

women had to get home to prepare for dinner and the men weren't yet
ready to leave their offices—she wouldn't lose much revenue and might
actually come out ahead, depending on how much she made in the
investigation. One positive outcome would be that they would no longer
need to ask Barbara to gossip about her colleagues. Annie had never tried
to teach anyone anything, and that was the most frightening part of the
whole plan, but she knew Laura and Barbara would help her design her
lessons.

"Oh, Mr. Dawson, you shouldn't let the boy pester you so," the
musical tones of Mrs. Anderson broke into her thoughts. While Annie
and Emory had been talking, Nate had gone into his office to compare
the letters Emory had been able to bring with him to the notes that Hattie
had received. But now he had returned and was sitting at the end of the
table with Mrs. Dorthea Anderson, whom Emory called affectionately
Dot. Nate had placed her four-year-old son, Jack, on his knee and was
doing a bit of "This is the way the ladies ride" with him.

Mrs. Anderson looked exactly the way Annie had imagined she
would from Nate's description. She was what was commonly called a
"fine figure of a woman." She'd blushed very prettily when Nate introduced her, and she was batting her wide-set cornflower blue eyes quite
charmingly at him now. She also had gotten very teary when Nate
questioned her about getting any nasty letters, inanely repeating that she
couldn't imagine who would be so mean as to impugn her good name or
to suggest that Mr. Emory or Mr. Hoffmann had behaved improperly.
What Annie couldn't determine was if Dot Anderson was really as dim
as she appeared or if she was just a very good actress.

Her son, on the other hand, was adorable, and as Annie watched
Nate send the child giggling back to his mother, she couldn't but think
about how devastating it would be if she couldn't give him children of
his own.

"Well, you and Emory got along just fine," Nate commented to
Annie as the cab took off down Market.

As promised, he was escorting her home, and she was enjoying the chance to lean close to him in the dark shadows of the cab. The storm that had blown in Saturday night had passed, but the sky remained overcast, with the full moon just a hazy orb.

"Yes," she replied. "He was certainly not what I expected. Having met him, I am less inclined to think that there is anything improper about his relationship with Mrs. Anderson."

"Yes, I suppose. He does act more fatherly towards her than anything else."

"And if there was something untoward going on, I doubt she would have flirted so shamelessly with you in front of him." Annie looked over at him to see how he would take this. The lamps along Market cast just enough glow for her to see him frown.

"Annie, I assure you, she was just being polite…oh, you're teasing me," he said, putting his arm around her.

Annie laughed but thought to herself that she needed to keep her eye out for some Girls' High teacher, or student for that matter, who might not like Dottie Anderson batting her blue eyes at the men in their lives.

Thinking of possible motives, Annie said, "Nate, I know you told Emory that the letters the school board received and the notes to Hattie were very different, but do you think this means they were written by different people?"

"On the surface they were different. The notes to Hattie, as you know, were written in block letters with very black ink, and the lined composition paper gave the impression they were written by a child, although the content was very adult. And, as you saw, the letters Emory brought were written in blue ink, on ordinary white letter paper, and the hand-writing was cursive but very shaky and slanted backwards."

"I see." Annie wished she had been able to spend more time studying the letters Emory had brought. "But I hear some hesitation in your voice."

"It's just that I think there may have been an attempt to disguise the hand-writing in both cases, pretending to be a child in the case of Hattie's notes, and writing with the left hand in the case of the other letters," Nate said. He continued, "My brother is left-handed, and I used to try to write the way he did to get him in trouble, but my parents could always tell when a note was legitimately written by him. These letters looked the same way mine did."

Annie saw that they were passing the Palace Hotel and would soon be turning onto O'Farrell. The ride was going too quickly for her. She said, "What could you learn from the actual content of the letters?"

"I don't know, but I would like your opinion before I say anything. Here, I made copies of them, and of Hattie's notes." Nate slid several sheets of paper out of his inside jacket pocket and gave them to her. "Tell me what you think after comparing them."

As she folded the papers to fit them into her purse, he continued. "I do hope your job teaching bookkeeping will shed some light on the accusations against Mrs. Anderson and Thomas Hoffmann. I gather Hoffmann will be expecting you tomorrow."

"Yes. Fortunately, on Wednesdays I don't have any clients after two, so I can meet with him at three. My first class, I gather, would be Friday. Not much time to study up on my *Mayhew*. But Nate, look, we will be at the boarding house soon. Can't we take advantage of the fact that we are all alone and you aren't the one driving the horses?"

Nate responded with alacrity, much to her satisfaction.

Chapter Twenty-three
Wednesday afternoon, January 28, 1880

"...Board of Education Special Investigating Committee, met in the Supervisors' Room at the new City Hall and heard testimony in the matter of the anonymous letter heretofore received by the Committee insinuating that Miss Susie Jacobs, a teacher in the public schools, had obtained her certificate by means of having had previous access to the question being asked at the examination."—*San Francisco Chronicle*, 1880

"Mrs. Fuller, I am pleased to meet you." Thomas Hoffmann stood up and came around his desk to greet Annie. "I apologize for how crowded the office is, but when John, Principal Swett, took over Girls' High in '76 and hired me as his vice principal, he offered me the larger of the two offices. He said he would be traveling so much, looking after our interests in Sacramento, it would be better for me to have the larger one. What I didn't know is that the man with the larger office also got all the student and personnel records. As you can see, any extra square footage has been more than taken up with those filing cabinets."

Annie smiled and shook his hand warmly, saying, "Well, for my purposes, this is just perfect. Thank you for agreeing to have me here. I know it is quite unorthodox, but whatever does come of my investigation, I promise you, your students will at least get my expertise in double-entry bookkeeping."

Annie had arrived at Girls' High, an imposing four-story building located near Hyde Street on the north side of Bush, just after classes were dismissed for the day. She felt quite transported back to her days at the New York Female Academy when a stream of young women pushed past her as she entered the vestibule. Barbara had told her how to find the vice principal's office on the first floor, across from the assembly room. She'd promised to come find her when the Literature and Debate Society meeting was over. They could walk together to Clement Grammar and walk the rest of the way home with Laura and Jamie. Meanwhile, Annie had at least an hour to get acquainted with Mr. Hoffmann and learn everything she could about what her class would expect of her on Friday.

After telling her where the students were in the text and discussing with her the topics he'd planned on covering in the next few weeks, Mr. Hoffmann said, "I am sure you will do an excellent job. I just wish I could help out in your investigation as well. I am at a loss to explain why anyone would attack either Emory or myself for the hiring of Mrs. Anderson. Before her marriage, she taught the art classes at the Bush Street Primary School for over five years. She is also a very accomplished pianist and was active in her normal school drama society back in Ohio. We were delighted she would be able to teach our music classes and take our theatre group in hand as well as teach art."

Annie responded, "I am sure she is qualified; the question is, were there any other persons who applied for her job who might have seen themselves as more qualified? Particularly if they had the highest level teaching certificate that is usually needed to teach high school, a disappointed candidate might see this as a way to strike back."

Hoffmann nodded and walked over to a file drawer, saying, "I understand that is the most logical explanation, and I have found the correspondence related to that position. You might as well start there," he said, handing a file folder to her. "I suppose you will want to go back some years, in case there is an applicant for another Girls' High position who chose to use Mrs. Anderson's appointment to express their dissatisfaction. You will also want to speak to Miss Della Thorndike, currently our Normal Class teacher; she was the person who reviewed all the files and selected the candidates I should interview."

Annie was impressed. He was being extremely helpful and not at all defensive. She wasn't sure she would be as cooperative if she were the focus of a malicious letter to her employer. All Emory had shared with her about Hoffmann was that the Vice Principal was in his mid-forties, had a wife and three children, and that he had written a well-received master's thesis on something called the prime number theorem. He was also a handsome man with a full head of glossy brown hair and a neatly trimmed mustache and goatee, and he wore his expensively tailored suit with ease. There was money somewhere in his life; she wondered if it was his or his wife's. He also seemed to have a very slight accent and she wondered if he had earned his master's degree at a German university.

She hated bringing up the delicate matter of the accusations of impropriety, but she needed to know what his response would be. She said, "Thank you, I will take this file home with me, if that is acceptable, then start to look at the other files on Friday. However, I did want to get your reaction to the other part of the letter…the part that…"

"Suggested I was having an improper relationship with one of my students?" Hoffmann finished her sentence. "Of course I completely deny the accusation, but, then again, even if it were true I would say that. What I can say is that I try very hard not to do anything that might lead to a whiff of scandal. However, talk to any man who teaches young women over the age of twelve, and you will find that at some point there have been rumors. Young girls get crushes on male teachers, often the only men in their lives that have time for them. They also get jealous of other girls who might get a better grade or more attention from a male teacher."

"I would imagine that female teachers also have to deal with this phenomenon," Annie responded, thinking of her all-female academy.

Hoffmann chuckled dryly. "And it isn't just female students who cause problems. Yes, Mrs. Fuller, you are quite right. Yet I have found that the rumors generated about male teachers and female students are more likely to be taken seriously by parents and school boards. That's one of the reasons I welcomed your offer to help discover who is behind this particular rumor. I know it isn't true, but I am very aware that if it is not disproved or the person behind it isn't found and discredited, it could still ruin my career."

*****

"What did you think of Mr. Hoffmann?" Barbara Hewitt asked Annie as they crossed Bush at Leavenworth.

"Very personable and straightforward. It can't be easy to face accusations of wrong doing and have some strange woman poking around in your business, but he was very helpful."

They turned onto Leavenworth, which swooped down steeply all the way to Market. Annie could see Potrero Hill and Bernal Heights framed by the higher peaks of the San Bruno Mountains further south down the peninsula. The low-lying winter sun threw out a few shafts from the grey clouds that had filled the sky all day.

She turned up the collar of her coat and said, "More importantly, Barbara, you work with him. What do you think of him?"

For a moment, her companion was silent. Annie knew Barbara had been very glad to learn that Annie's investigation meant she was off the hook as the primary source of information about Girls' High. What Annie didn't know was if this meant she wouldn't help out at all. She studied Barbara's face while she waited for her to respond. She was taller than Annie by several inches, a handsome, not beautiful, brunette, with a long oval face framed by a fringe of tight curls. Her eyes were hazel. Jamie must have gotten his brown eyes from his father, the never-mentioned Mr. Hewitt, although she and her son both had long dark lashes that Annie envied. Barbara often looked very tired, and the ink that seemed permanently to stain her fingers testified to the stacks of essays she had to grade as the teacher of English literature and composition. Her mouth was of a generous size, but she seldom smiled. When she did, Annie felt she had earned something of value.

A smile now caused two dimples to appear on her face, and Barbara looked over at her and said, "Don't fear, I will cooperate. You know it makes me uncomfortable to talk about my fellow colleagues, but I can see how such accusations can create a poisonous atmosphere, and I don't know of anyone else I would trust more than you to get to the bottom of everything. Vice Principal Hoffmann appears to me to be a very talented teacher of mathematics and an able administrator. I believe he was a Union officer in the war, so he has a natural authority. But he does have a temper. It is my impression he doesn't suffer fools gladly, perhaps as a result of his Germanic heritage. He is also one of the last men I would expect to be taken in by a pretty face, whether on a fellow teacher or a student."

Annie laughed. "My, my. You will need to expand just a bit on that, if you don't mind. Let's take the pretty face first. So you don't think it likely that he would have shown favoritism in hiring Mrs. Anderson?"

"Well not for her pretty face. I am sorry, that was a bit spiteful. I feel sympathy, of course, for any widowed woman who has to make their way in the world with a small child, but I find her constant...I don't know how to describe it...her constant attempts to captivate everyone she meets, male or female, rather distasteful. "

Annie was impressed with Barbara's acuity and said, "Exactly. I guess it might be a kind of insecurity, as if she has to make everyone love her. But I confess I was left with the feeling she was being insincere when I met her last night."

They stopped at Sutter Street and waited until a horse and wagon lumbered past before crossing. Annie then went on, "But you think that Mr. Hoffmann is too astute to be taken in? Do you think he would hire her for Mr. Emory's sake, as a favor for a friend?"

"I don't know. From what I have heard about Hoffmann's relationship with Principal Swett, however, I would say that he is a very loyal person. If Swett mentioned that Emory was a good friend to teachers and that Mrs. Anderson was highly recommended by him, I could see this swaying him in his decision. I am even newer to the city than you are, but it's obvious that politics have a lot to do with the hiring choices that are made in this school district."

"So you think that the motives for these notes are political rather than personal?" Annie asked.

"Not necessarily." Barbara hesitated. "You said that Laura's friend Hattie also received anonymous accusations as well. Do you think those notes are connected to the letters about Mr. Emory and Mr. Hoffmann?"

Annie hadn't given Barbara any details about the notes they had found among Hattie's letters, and she hoped that the content would never come out, but she did feel it was important that Barbara understand the personal dimension of her investigation. Choosing her words carefully, she replied, "We don't know for sure. But I have compared the letters the school board received to the notes directed at Hattie, and I can tell you that there were some similarities in phrasing and word choice that made me think they might have been written by the same person."

Barbara remained silent, and Annie got the distinct impression she was upset. They were now at Post Street, so she waited until they had crossed and were continuing down Leavenworth to resume their conversation. Annie continued, "If they were written by the same person, then it does seem more likely it was a personal grievance by someone who was passed over for a job. Hattie was hired at the last minute, and Mrs. Anderson didn't have the appropriate level teaching certificate. I can understand why a primary teacher, for example, who has seen his or her salary slashed this year, might feel resentful."

"Yes, yes, that might be it," Barbara replied. "Would it be helpful if you found someone else who got a similar letter?"

"Well we were hoping that Mrs. Anderson had received one, but she says she didn't, although I am not sure I believe her. Do you think there is someone else?"

"I can't really say at this point," Barbara responded, beginning to walk more quickly. After a block of silence, she said, "Just in case there was someone, if they spoke to Mr. Dawson about…anything, it would be confidential, wouldn't it? He couldn't reveal their name if they didn't want him to?"

Annie assured her that anything that a person said to Nate, if they retained his legal services, would remain confidential. She refrained from asking any other details because Barbara seemed nervous, but she would tell Nate that if Barbara didn't come to him, he might want to seek her out.

She thought, however, it might be good to change the subject. As they turned onto Geary she said, "You mentioned Mr. Hoffmann having a temper. Were you thinking of someone he had lost his temper with who might have written the letter?"

"Well, there is the janitoress, Mrs. Washburn. It is my understanding she has worked at Girls' High ever since it opened in '71, and I have heard her complaining to the other teachers that Hoffmann doesn't 'treat her right.' I actually heard him once being quite sharp with her about some breakage in the chemistry classroom. And while I haven't heard anything from the students about him raising his voice in the classroom, there was one incident last spring in the teachers' room. It was after school, and I overheard an argument between him and Mr. Stoddard, the other math teacher at the time. I believe Hoffmann was calling him lazy or a lazy thinker. In any event, Mr. Stoddard didn't return this fall, and I understand that Mrs. Rickle, who replaced him, is considered a very competent teacher."

There was silence for a few moments as they turned into the front steps leading up to Clement Grammar where they were to meet Jamie and Laura. Barbara said hurriedly, "Annie, before we meet up with Laura and Jamie, I do want to ask you something. Talking about men with tempers reminded me. Last Wednesday, I got here a little early, so I went on up to the third floor to find Jamie and Laura, and I ran into a man who was leaving her classroom. Laura seemed quite upset, and the man looked rather menacing. I don't mean to pry, but considering what happened a few weeks ago, I wanted make sure you knew about this incident."

"Oh, thank you, you were right to mention it, but Laura did tell me about it. The man is Seth Timmons, a former classmate from San Jose Normal who is now teaching, I believe, at Pine and Larkin Primary. He was also a very close friend of Hattie Wilks. Laura briefly thought it might have been him in the alley but has now decided he wasn't the man. Instead, it seems there is a young hooligan she taught last fall named Buck who is a more likely candidate."

"My goodness. I thought she had no idea who the man was."

"I know. I wish she had been more forthcoming at the start. But she barely knew me three weeks ago when this all started, hard as that is for me to imagine now. I think she was embarrassed. But I am glad you have seen Timmons. Do let me know if you see him hanging about. From her description, he sounds like just the kind of brooding, heroic man that a young woman like Laura might find fascinating. Nate is planning to go and have a chat with him, and then we may be able to assess better if he is a threat to her physical well-being or to her heart."

Chapter Twenty-four
Wednesday evening, January 28, 1880
"Wuld that I was an artist & had the material to paint this camp & all its horors or the tounge of some eloquent Statesman and had the prileage of expresing my mind to our hon. rulers at Washington, I should gloery to describe this hell on earth were it takes 7 of its ocupiants to make a shadow." Sgt. David Kennedy, *Andersonville Prison diary*, July 9, 1864 *(Original spelling preserved.)*

Nate walked steadily up Union Street toward Russian Hill. The incline was gradual most of the way, and he had only about eight more blocks until he reached his destination. He could use the exercise after eating one of his boarding house cook's heavy and unappetizing dinners. The clouds, having broken up and dissipated during the day, left the night clear and cold, and street lamps created welcome pools of light at each corner. He'd gotten Seth Timmons' address today from the Board of Education offices on the third floor of the new City Hall. He hoped he would catch Timmons at home, although Lord only knew exactly what he was going to say to him. *Did you attack my sister?* What about the old familiar adage? *What are your intentions in regards to my sister?*

He was going to feel like a fool whatever he said, but he didn't know what else to do other than meet the man in person and let him know that Laura wasn't without her protectors in town. So far, he'd abided by Laura's plea that he not tell his parents anything about the attack or any of the details surrounding Hattie Wilks' death, but he wanted to be able to give a good accounting of himself if they ever did find out. Laura promised she would write their mother and tell her about Hattie, so he figured he would soon receive a letter from his mother asking for a report on how Laura was holding up.

Nate paused at the corner where the North Beach and Mission

Street Railroad turned north up Mason, waiting for one of the cars to rumble past before crossing the street. He used the light from the gas lamp to check the time on his pocket watch. It was already seven, the sun long set. He turned up his overcoat collar since the next stretch of Union was steeper and the wind from the west was biting. A few minutes later, as he got to Taylor, he looked up to his left, where the house lights marched up to the rim of Russian Hill, and then to the right, where the hill plunged down to North Beach. He loved the views from this part of the city.

He took a deep breath and thought he could smell salt water. Angel Island looked like it had a few beacons lit on the headlands, but it was more likely to be the lamps on a steamer coming down the Bay. When he moved from the ranch to live with his uncle and go to Boys' High, he spent every Saturday on the docks, dreaming of sailing to the Sandwich Islands or exploring the North Pole with Charles Francis Hall. One of the reasons he continued to stay in his cramped attic rooms in the Vallejo boarding house was for the short walk up Telegraph Hill where he could see every section of the peninsula laid out before him.

Reaching Leavenworth Street, the highest point of his route, he looked around, taking in the extraordinarily beautiful sight of the moon rising up over Mt. Diablo across the Bay. He wished Annie was next to him, viewing the night sky. He thought about their cab ride home last evening. The memory of the long, intense embrace just as they arrived at the boarding house warmed him. Yet he wondered how she would react if he wasn't so careful about limiting the time they spent alone.

He thought about Miss Wilks and Andrew Russell. Had their need to keep their relationship secret caused them to break the bounds of propriety? Had a buggy ride into the empty by-ways of Golden Gate Park one late night led to a passion that swept away all reason, all sense of responsibility? For the first time, he wished he'd paid more attention to the braggarts at college when they detailed their sexual conquests. Maybe then he wouldn't worry as much about some invisible line he mustn't cross. Did Annie know where that line was? She'd been married, so presumably she was more experienced in these matters than he was, but that thought didn't comfort him at all. Neither did the realization that his own little sister might be facing some of the same questions he was facing. *Maybe it is a very good thing she has such a negative view of marriage and men. I will feel a darn sight more comfortable if she just concentrates on getting a law degree!*

Nate turned right when he got to Larkin and began to search for Timmons' address. Where it should have been, all he could see was a small shoemaker's shop squeezed between a greengrocers and a bakery. All three establishments were shuttered for the night. Then he noticed a narrow passageway between the shoemaker's shop and the bakery. The set of wooden stairs leading up to a second story landing would have been invisible without the light shining out of a window above the bakery. When he got to the top of the steps, he saw a pale strip of light around the badly hung door and could hear movement within. He knocked and waited nervously, still not knowing what he would say.

"I'm sorry, Jenkins doesn't live here, the shop will reopen at seven tomorrow," said the man who opened the door.

"Are you Mr. Timmons?"

"Yes I am. Just who are you?" Timmons asked, giving Nate a long stare and not budging.

"I'm Nate Dawson, Laura Dawson's brother. We need to have a talk."

Timmons' grey eyes narrowed and traveled down to where Nate's open coat revealed a holstered gun at his hip. He then shrugged and turned away, moving back into the center of the room with unspoken confidence.

Nate looked swiftly around, noted a bedroll and a bare mattress on an old iron bedstead, a small, pot-bellied stove with a coffee pot and what smelled like a can of beans sitting on top. There was a stack of wooden crates that held clothing, eating and cooking utensils, and a good number of books. A chair and small table, with more books and a kerosene lamp, stood next to the one bare window at the back of the room. A hook on the wall next to him held a black Stetson, a belt and holster with a standard Army-issue Colt. Timmons was in stockinged feet, and his well-worn boots were on the floor under the hat and gun.

Nate had assumed the strong smell of leather was coming from the shoemaker's shop below until he noticed that a full saddle and tack sat next to the chair at the back of the room. A tin of saddle soap lay open on the table. Immediately transported to the bunkhouse of his father's ranch, he relaxed. This was a man he could deal with.

"Well, I guess I shouldn't be surprised by this visit," Timmons said, pulling the chair around and nodding a clear invitation for Nate to sit.

Nate hesitated, then sat down as Timmons picked up the saddle soap and a cinch and sat on the bed to continue working on the leather.

"Laura didn't ask me to come. Probably going to give me a tongue-lashing if she hears of it but then, from what I hear, you aren't a stranger to that side of her," Nate said, bringing forth a quick grin from the man across from him.

He went on, "Seems like whatever happened this fall when she was teaching at Cupertino Creek might have followed her to San Francisco, and I wanted to hear your thoughts on that before I made any decisions about what I should do."

Timmons head stayed bowed over the cinch for a few moments, and Nate speculated about how old he was. His face was lined and weathered, and there was definite grey in his hair and mustache. Yet, he'd moved easily, and his hands, while showing the effects of hard work, didn't exhibit any of the telltale swollen joints most cowboys had by their forties.

When the silence continued, he said, "Laura says you fought with a Pennsylvania regiment. My older brothers were with the Department of Ohio troops. When did you sign up?"

"Sixty-three. I was sixteen. I lied and said I was eighteen. By that time, they would've taken me if I was twelve, but you know how it was," Timmons responded, then went silent again.

Nate was startled. The math said this man was only three years older than he was. Of course, that three-year difference was the reason Nate's father had tracked him down and dragged him home when Nate tried to sign up after his older brothers died at Shiloh and Chickamauga. That three-year difference meant Nate didn't end up dead or in the dreaded Confederate Andersonville Prison as this man had. It also meant Timmons was thirteen years older than Laura.

Cranston, the new law partner to the firm, kept telling Nate that well-placed silence was one of the best tools for interrogating a witness, but he suspected the man in front of him had more patience with this game than he did, so he said, "Tell me about Buck Morrison."

"Stupid, arrogant son-of-a-bitch. But don't you worry. I'll take care of him," Timmons spat out.

Nate felt the temperature in the room drop. Keeping his voice calm and matter-of-fact, he said, "Mr. Timmons, you will not take care of him, not if it means you ending up in jail and my sister's name in the papers. Now, once again, tell me about him, so *I* know what *I* need to do next."

Timmons glared at him for a moment, his jaw clenched, then he visibly slowed his breathing and went back to working the leather. He said, "I could tell he was trouble the first day I stopped by to check on… your sister. Miss Hattie Wilks had asked me to look in on her since it was on the way up Cupertino Creek where I go camping. She said a boy in Laura's class was being disrespectful. First day I showed up, I could see this Morrison was crowding her as she came out the door to the school house. She wouldn't tell me anything but his name, but I could tell she was upset."

After a moment, Nate prompted him, saying, "So you decided to lend my sister your protection."

"I asked around at the local store after I dropped her off where she was boarding. Didn't like what I heard. Father is a big fish in a small pond. Son a bully. Thought I ought to keep an eye on her."

"Did you ever speak to him…before you…"

"Beat the living daylights out of him? Only once. Second time I stopped by, I ran into the worthless bastard skulking in the trees outside where she was staying that week. I told him what I would do if he didn't leave her alone. I thought he'd gotten the message fair and square. She seemed more at ease the next weekend, so I thought that was that."

"Until…"

"Until it wasn't." Timmons leaned forward, looking Nate in the eye. "I don't need to apologize to you for what I did. I suspect you would have done the same. I am sorry I frightened her. Should have waited until she was gone."

"And you think Buck might be the man who attacked her?"

"Could be. Just like the little coward." Timmons paused, put down the cinch, and stood up, saying, "Look, last week, after your sister told me what happened, I wrote to a friend of mine in San Jose. Asked him to ride up to Cupertino Creek, find out where Buck was earlier in the month. Get his address if he's here in the city."

"And you'll let me know what he finds out and promise to stay out of it," Nate replied, standing up in turn.

Timmons paused, shrugged, then held out his hand towards Nate, saying, "No promises. But I will let you know what I find out, before I do anything. If, in return, you let me know if anything else happens to your sister."

"You say he survived Andersonville Prison?" asked Mitchell, the medical student who lived in Nate's boarding house as he lounged against the door to Nate's attic room.

"Yes, one of my sister's professors mentioned he was a 'Plymouth Pilgrim," Nate replied, pouring out a finger of whiskey into a tumbler and handing it over. "You remember, that group of Union soldiers who got captured at the Battle of Plymouth in '64. From what he told me, he would have been no more than sixteen or seventeen when the Rebels tossed him into Andersonville Prison."

"God, what a hell-hole it must have been," Mitchell said. "I had an older cousin who spent a few weeks there before being shipped out.

Would scare the dickens out of us telling stories about some gang of prisoners who terrorized the rest of them. Said if the trots or starvation didn't get you, the Raiders would." Mitchell fingered his ginger mustache, then threw back the shot of whiskey.

Nate sipped his drink more slowly. When he'd gotten back home from visiting Timmons, he ran into Mitchell on the stairs. Between his studies at the University medical school and his job as an orderly at St. Mary's, Mitchell was seldom around, so Nate invited him up for a nightcap.

Mitchell shook his head. "He wasn't ever quite right after that, you know. My cousin. Drank, got into fights, never could settle down. Sort of disappeared around '74, family's not heard from him since."

"Sounds a lot like Seth Timmons," Nate said. "Don't know about the drinking, didn't see any sign of it, but he looks like he has moved around a lot and lived hard. While he seems to be trying to keep it under control, there's a nasty temper there that I wouldn't want to rouse."

"And you think this Timmons is courting your sister?" Mitchell snorted and held out his glass.

"I don't know. He certainly seems to have taken on the mantle of her protector. Needless to say, that it makes me uneasy. But if he can find out about this Buck Morrison, who was harassing Laura, I'll be in his debt." Nate poured another inch of whiskey into Mitchell's glass.

"Well, Nate my boy, I would keep an eye on him. Half our charity beds at St. Mary's are filled with down-on-their-luck soldiers, from both the North and the South. Banged up in barroom brawls, dying of liver disease, some of them just plain out of their heads. That war left a lot of good men permanently damaged. One of the ward doctors says they have something called 'soldiers heart.' Seems to me, a fellow broken like that isn't such a good marriage prospect for any young woman."

Chapter Twenty-five
Friday afternoon, January 30, 1880

"The Books of the Debtor should likewise specify both the quantity and the value of every article bought by him, unless *bills* are received of goods purchased, *which is always preferable.*" —*Mayhew's Practical Book-Keeping: Embracing Single and Double Entry, Commercial Calculations, and the Philosophy and Morals of Business,* 1866

"Please read the pages in *Mayhew* that cover 'Cash Accounts,' 'Rules for Debtor and Creditor Entries,' and 'Bills of Parcels' for next Wednesday's class," Annie said, noting with satisfaction that everyone seemed to be taking down her words on their slates. She continued, "Since I have been informed by Mr. Hoffmann that you have already read the material up to page forty, you shouldn't have any difficulties with the terminology."

"Yes, Mrs. Fuller," was the group's response, which made Annie feel like giggling. It was disconcerting to have thirty-eight senior-class girls give this response, in unison, to her every statement. She'd been extremely nervous when she and Hoffmann walked into his late afternoon math class, but he'd done a wonderful job of paving the way for her in his introduction. He emphasized how fortunate they were to have someone with practical experience in bookkeeping as his substitute, and she could tell from the girls' response that they were inclined to treat her well for his sake. That alone was a good recommendation of his character, but she knew she needed to remain impartial. It wasn't just her job to find out who sent the accusatory letters about Emory, Dottie Anderson, and Hoffmann but to find out if there was any truth to the allegations.

The clanging of the school bell told her it was time to dismiss the class, and she watched with relief as the girls gathered up their books and left the room. Now the real work began. She had two hours before the school was locked up to begin going through the personnel files in Hoffmann's office. She was starting with the supposition that the anonymous letters, at least about Mrs. Anderson, were from disappointed job applicants. She'd already read through the correspondence relating to her hiring and found it very thin. There were six letters from candidates, each expressing interest in the position, each listing their qualifications. There was a note from Della Thorndike recommending that Hoffmann interview Mrs. Anderson and a Mr. Frazier, but that was all. Fortunately, Hoffmann had asked Miss Thorndike to stop by and visit her in his office this afternoon.

Understanding that Annie wanted to keep the real reason she was at Girls' High a secret, he'd told Miss Thorndike that Annie had friends who were looking for a private arts instructor for their child. This was a very clever ruse, since it gave her a reason to ask Della Thorndike to expand on her impressions of the rejected candidates.

When she got to Hoffmann's office, Annie found it empty. He'd given her a key and told her he had moved into Swett's office that morning since the Principal was already on his way back east for the annual National Education Association meeting in Boston. She put down her copy of *Mayhew* and notes and was just sitting down at the desk when there was a knock on the door. A handsome middle-aged woman peeked in, saying, "Mrs. Fuller, I presume? I hope I'm not interrupting you, but Mr. Hoffmann told me about you agreeing to help out with the bookkeeping classes, and I wanted to welcome you. Oh, how silly, I didn't tell you who I am, I'm Della Thorndike."

By this time, Annie had gotten up and come around to shake Miss Thorndike's hand and ask if she would like to sit down for a minute, an invitation that was promptly accepted. What ensued was a lively conversation in which Annie discovered a great deal about Miss Thorndike...or rather, Della. She had insisted that Annie call her Della, which of course required that she give Della full use of her own Christian name. She learned that Della had been born in a small town in Ohio, lost her fiancé at the battle of Bull Run, and come out west to dedicate her life to the profession of teaching. She had first taught in a number of rural schools in Nevada and California, then moved to San Francisco in 1869. She had been teaching at Girls' High as one of the English and Composition teachers ever since. Her pale blue eyes flashed, and she smoothed back her neat-as-a-pin blonde hair when she talked about how much she enjoyed working with the students in the Normal class. Annie could see why both Hattie Wilks and Laura had taken a liking to the friendly Miss Della Thorndike.

Della also proved a skillful interrogator, drawing out of Annie an abbreviated version of how the loss of her husband, like the loss of Della's fiancé, had forced Annie to make her own living running a boarding house. Madam Sibyl stayed safely unmentioned.

"And Mr. Hoffmann tells me you are also interested in getting my advice on someone to tutor a friend's child in the arts?" Della asked.

Annie, glad that her work as Madam Sibyl taught her to improvise, went on to embroider the storyline Hoffmann had started. She described how one of Mrs. Stein's grand-daughters was proving to be unusually artistic and that she'd been commissioned to find someone to give the child personal lessons. Annie assuaged her conscience by telling herself that surely one of Esther's numerous grandchildren was actually talented in music or drawing.

Finally, Annie said, "Vice Principal Hoffmann mentioned that you had recently interviewed some promising candidates for the arts position here, so I was wondering if you could tell me about them. Perhaps one of them would be a good fit."

"Well, three of the candidates were young ladies without an iota of real teaching experience," Della replied. "They seemed to think that singing in their church choir and cultivating a taste for water colors were sufficient qualifications to teach here at Girls' High. One of them had gone to a Normal school in the Midwest, but as far as I could tell, she had never actually been in a classroom. We insist that our Normal class students have practical teaching experience before they graduate."

Annie murmured, "Yes, I can see how important that might be," which seemed all the encouragement Della required to continue.

"There was a young man with excellent references. He came from a very prominent family in Philadelphia, studied art abroad in Paris for a year, and then made his way to California to make his fortune. When I asked him if he would be able to take over the music as well as the art classes, he admitted he had no experience in that realm at all. Such a shame. But I do think that Mr. Weld, that was his name, might be just the person your friend is looking for. So refined. He is currently engaged in teaching art at one of our local private female academies, and I imagine he would welcome the additional income."

Annie dutifully wrote down the name of the refined Mr. Weld and then asked Della if she could think of anyone else, just in case her friend, Mrs. Stein, wanted someone who could teach both music and art.

"Well, I forwarded two names on to Mr. Hoffmann. Mr. Jonathan Frazier and Mrs. Dorthea Anderson, whom he subsequently hired. I'm not sure why Mr. Hoffmann chose Mrs. Anderson, given her lack of the appropriate level teaching certificate, although she certainly did have adequate teaching experience. It is just that…"

Here, Della Thorndike's voice lowered. "You see, Mr. Frazier has the right level certificate, and he has worked with older students like our girls here. I would have thought…well, but then I wasn't there at the interview, was I? Mr. Hoffmann *said* that the deciding factor was that Mr. Frazier had no background in teaching theater, but I had already volunteered to teach the dramatic arts class. I always assisted the former teacher, Miss Rochester. Perhaps it was just as well, given how busy the Normal class has kept me. And Mrs. Anderson *is* very charming, a favorite with her students. I expect that Mr. Hoffmann may have taken into consideration her situation."

"Her situation?" Annie asked.

"Her little boy. Children can be such a worry financially when you are a widow. We have several other women who are trying to juggle the demands of teaching with motherhood," Della said, a slight frown appearing. "Some of the single teachers feel they may take advantage…

you did say you don't have children, didn't you?"

Annie said, "Yes, I did, but Mrs. Hewitt, Barbara Hewitt, your English Literature colleague, is one of my boarders, so I know how difficult it can be to work and raise a child."

Della looked surprised. "Oh my, I didn't know. Then young Miss Laura Dawson must also be one of your boarders. Such a lovely, competent young lady. I am quite in her debt, since she has taken in hand one of my students who needed to get her practice teaching done this term."

Annie, aware that time was passing quickly, wanted to get back to the failed candidates. She said, "Yes, I have become quite fond of Laura, and she speaks very highly of you. But this Mr. Frazier you spoke of, do you think he would be interested in tutoring my friend's granddaughter?"

Della responded with enthusiasm. "Oh, he would be a splendid choice. Do ask Mr. Hoffmann for his address. You see, I did wonder if Mr. Hoffmann took into consideration that Mr. Frazier also has family responsibilities. I know for a fact he has four children to support, and the salary he is currently making as part of the California Theater orchestra isn't nearly sufficient."

"Do you think he was very upset at not getting the job?" Annie asked.

"Oh, I really couldn't say," Della replied hastily. "It was really Mr. Hoffmann's decision; I just tried to help out." Standing up, she said, "Well, this was pleasant, but I really must go. Do let me know, however, if there is anything I can do to help make your time with us at Girls' High more pleasant. I would be glad to bring you around the teachers' study and introduce you next Wednesday."

Annie, feeling she had gotten a good deal of information to work with, thanked Miss Thorndike warmly and then casually added, "There is one thing. Could you tell me the best way of finding Mrs. Washburn? Mr. Hoffmann said that I should ask her about getting into the supply cabinet. He seemed to indicate that she might be difficult to track down."

Annie crossed her fingers under the table, Mr. Hoffmann having said no such thing. But she did want to get someone else's impression of the relationship between Hoffmann and the janitoress since Barbara had mentioned some strain between the two. Having worked as a domestic for a few weeks, Annie was well aware of how invisible women could be who did menial work of any sort. She wondered what Mrs. Washburn saw as she cleaned the classrooms and offices of Girls' High and whether she would have any reason to use that knowledge to redress a personal grievance.

Della bristled. "Oh, Mrs. Washburn, the dear, of course she is hard to find. She is run ragged taking care of this huge building. As little as six years ago, there were only about four hundred students attending Girls' High, and now the number of students has doubled, which means double the workload for that poor woman. If she is hard to find, that is Vice Principal Hoffmann's own fault. Such inconsideration! You would think a *good* administrator would figure out that one person can't take care of this whole building, all by her lonesome."

Chapter Twenty-six
Friday afternoon, January 30, 1880

"No good reason can be given why the Principals of the Boys' and Girls' High Schools should be paid $333.33 a month...when it is thought more than sufficient to allow an educated teacher of ten years experience $70 per month..."—*San Francisco Chronicle*, 1879

Laura decided that this would be the day she would confront Andrew Russell. She needed to return the letters he had written Hattie since both she and Annie had read them. Her plan was to bring up the anonymous notes they'd found among Hattie's correspondence and see what he had to say. She had left a note in his box in the teachers' room first thing this morning asking him to come see her in her classroom between three and four-thirty. Normally she would have gone home with Barbara and Jamie at three on a Friday, but Annie was working late at Girls' High and had said she would stop by on her way home.

As soon as classes were over, Kitty Blaine left, but two of the girls in her class asked to stay after to clean the boards. They then hung around for a few minutes chatting with her. Hoping this friendliness wasn't just an attempt at buttering her up, she repressed her irritation at their obvious attempt to find out if the "tall man" who had been seen talking to her the previous week after school was her beau. Laura finally sent them on their giggling way, noticing that the janitor, Mr. Ferguson, was mopping outside her door as the girls left. She had found that it took very little encouragement for him to move on into her room after classes to "have a wee chat," so she busied herself putting up the next day's assignments on the board, hoping he would take the hint and go on with his work.

She hadn't heard from Seth Timmons, and she rather wished she'd never told Annie about his visit. Annie, of course, had to tell Nate. Too embarrassing. The events of the past few months certainly confirmed her belief that nothing good came from having any sort of relationship with any man. Hattie's pregnancy was a stark reminder of the consequences of romantic entanglements. Once she was satisfied that she knew exactly what had happened to Hattie and had held to account whoever was responsible, she would move forward on her career path, depending on no one but herself.

"Miss Dawson. You asked to see me?"

Laura turned around swiftly, her heart pounding. Over two weeks had passed since Hattie's death, and she was shocked at the change in Andrew Russell's physical appearance. He'd lost an appreciable amount of weight; his hair, never very neat, was long and untidy; and there were dark circles showing below the bottom rims of his glasses. She pushed away the brief spurt of compassion she felt, reminding herself that he was alive and Hattie wasn't.

She took a breath, then said, "Yes, I did. As you requested, I am returning the letters you sent to Miss Wilks."

Russell made a small noise in his throat and stepped forward precipitously, bumping into one of the school desks, but he stopped when she held up her hand.

"I will return them to you, under one condition. You must tell me what you know of the anonymous letters Hattie received."

"She saved them?" Russell whispered and then hid his head in his hands.

"Yes. And I need to know when they came and who you think sent them." Laura stared at him, wishing she could tell whether or not his distress was real. *And what caused it? A guilty conscience?*

Russell looked up at her and said, "Why? Why do you want to know? What does it matter? You must know that they were all lies. Just malicious gossip."

"Gossip that forced Hattie to quit teaching and give up her dreams of the University." Laura felt her bitterness rise in her throat.

"That wasn't what I wanted. I would have done anything to make sure she continued on with her plans." Russell shook his head slowly from side to side. "I even offered to find another position in another school so she could continue teaching at Clement. You have the letters I wrote; you know I offered. But Hattie insisted that she be the one to quit. She'd turned in her resignation letter before I even knew about the anonymous notes."

"And do you know who sent them?"

"No. She showed me the first one, and I didn't recognize the handwriting. She never would show me the others." Russell shrugged. "She said that they were all written on lined composition paper, which you know we use in the schools, but she had compared the hand-writing to all of her students' work, and she didn't believe the notes came from any of them."

Laura hadn't thought of this possibility. Thank goodness Hattie had already eliminated the students, or she would have found it difficult to go into class on Monday without looking at all them in a suspicious light. Poor Hattie, what she must have suffered. And she hadn't written one word of all this to Laura, or Seth for that matter. It sounded as if she hadn't even fully shared all she had been going through with Russell. *If he was telling the truth. He could be playing a double game.*

"Did Hattie say who she thought might have sent them?" Laura asked. "Was there another teacher, for example, who could have resented her getting the job at Clement? Or anyone who saw the two of you together outside of work?"

"I don't know!" Russell stood up straighter. "There were the Girls' High students who attended the small group I tutor in Greek and Latin, but once Hattie and I...well, she stopped coming. Otherwise we didn't do anything in public that would invite criticism. However, even if someone suspected, I can't understand why they would write an anonymous letter in that fashion. Slipped under the door to her room..."

"The letters were delivered to her boarding house," Laura interrupted, "not at the school?" Russell nodded in assent.

She thought quickly, *This means that they could have come from anyone, might even be politically motivated as Nate has suggested. But to what purpose?* Laura asked Russell, "You didn't get anything similar, did you? Or hear that Mrs. Dubois, the principal, had gotten any sort of communication concerning your relationship to Hattie?"

"No, no, nothing. And the letters stopped as soon as Hattie's resignation became public. But I still don't see why you are pursuing this. She wouldn't want you to. We determined that we would not let someone's disordered mind destroy our happiness. And it didn't. When she agreed to marry me, well...the next few months were the most wonderful months of my life."

Laura watched impatiently as Russell took off his glasses to wipe the tears from his eyes. He didn't deserve her sympathy. It was his fault, whether directly or indirectly, that Hattie had died. *Bled to death.* She walked away and went to her desk, taking out a small key from her pocket and unlocking the desk drawer where she kept her purse. She pulled out Russell's letters and other memorabilia that Hattie had tied together.

When she was back standing in front of Russell, she held the ribbon-tied bundle to her chest and said, "If the love for Hattie that you professed in these letters was real, then you would want to know who was responsible for the notes. You would want to hold them accountable for what they did."

"It's been my impression you think I am responsible in some fashion," Russell replied, putting his glasses back on and staring unwaveringly at her. "And I take full responsibility for the fact that my love for her made her the object of those anonymous letters. But don't you see, if you pursue this, you will be the one who ruins her reputation. Imagine what it would do to her parents if they found out that there had been the slightest hint of impropriety in their daughter's behavior. For what purpose? The letters don't have anything to do with her accident."

"How do you know that? Do you know why she fell?" Laura could feel herself losing control, and she stopped.

"What are you saying?" Russell stepped forward, clearly agitated. "Are you saying that those letters are connected to her death? Based on what? Did she say something to you about them? Had she gotten some more that I didn't know about? Tell me."

"She didn't have time to say anything to me about the notes. You interrupted the one conversation we had together. Until the night she fell. Then, as she lay dying, she said that her fall was no accident. How would you interpret that?"

"You can't be saying she took her own life?" Russell shook his head in a sharp negative. "That is ridiculous. She had done as the notes asked. She had resigned. We were getting married. And if the letters had continued, even if they were made public, I had already promised that at the slightest breath of scandal, I was willing to move out of the city. She didn't want to move away…because of you. She was so looking forward to the two of you being together again, pursuing your degrees." Again, emotion overcame him.

Laura walked over and held out the letters. "I would like to believe that, but I don't have the luxury of believing that her death was an accident. You should ask your friend Thomas Hoffmann. Maybe you will believe *him* when he tells you that whoever was behind the notes to Hattie hasn't stopped this filthy campaign, and Hattie may not be the last victim if the person responsible isn't stopped."

It was slightly past five in the evening when Annie reached Clement Grammar from Girls' High, and Laura was waiting for her on the front steps. The evening had turned chilly and damp. Laura's wool scarf was pulled up around her ears, and she seemed to be shivering.

Annie said, "I am sorry I am so late. I hope you haven't been waiting long."

"No, I just didn't want to stay inside," Laura said.

"Well, a brisk walk will warm you up nicely. We do want to make it home before the sun sets completely, or Beatrice will worry."

Annie noticed Laura stiffen and wanted to kick herself for even alluding to the topic of the assault in the alley. Her focus on investigating the anonymous letters had driven that incident temporarily out of her mind, but she was sure it was never far from Laura's thoughts, particularly on these walks home. Annie had been struck by how uneasy she felt when she left Girls' High this evening. She realized that she hadn't been out on her own in the evening since the dangerous events of this past fall, and she was glad that Laura had Barbara and Jamie to walk home with her every day.

Casting around for a different topic of conversation, she went on to say, "I met your Miss Thorndike today. Very personable. I would say even charismatic. I'm not surprised that they chose her to take over the Normal class. I would expect she's quite inspiring to young women interested in teaching. Within a few minutes, she had me feeling like I was her closest friend. She also praised you, so of course I liked her!"

Laura smiled. "Well I don't know what she would be praising me for. She hasn't been in to observe me, or Kitty, for that matter, yet."

"Well, perhaps Kitty has been praising you to her?"

"I think that is highly unlikely. That girl is such an enigma; I don't have a clue what she is really thinking. However, she did ask if she could come to the boarding house tomorrow for some help preparing for the section of class she is teaching for me on Monday. Maybe she will open up more with me then. But, tell me, did you learn anything today about who might have sent the letters about Mrs. Anderson? And how was your first class?"

As they crossed Jones and turned south towards O'Farrell, Annie briefly recounted how her first bookkeeping class had gone and what she had learned from Della. She concluded by saying, "I think the man who Hoffmann interviewed, and who Miss Thorndike obviously thought was better qualified, is someone worth checking into. I'll ask Nate to find out if Emory or Mrs. Anderson knows him. If this Jonathan Frazier is still working at the California Theater, and Russell and Hattie attended a performance, then it is possible that he might...Laura, what have I said? What is wrong?"

Laura had stopped walking, and Annie could see by her face she was very upset.

"Oh Annie, I saw Russell today. It was awful." Laura started forward again, and Annie worked to keep up with the younger woman's long strides.

"Did you give him his letters back?" Annie asked. "What did he say?"

"I did give them back to him, but it wasn't what he said so much as how he looked and behaved. I am so confused. He appears to have aged ten years in the last few weeks, but I can't decide if that is because of grief or a guilty conscience."

"Did you tell him about the anonymous notes?"

"Yes, and he admitted he knew about them, but he says he only saw the first one. He professed to have no idea who had sent them. The one thing I would swear to is that he doesn't know a thing about Hattie being pregnant. She must not have told him. I couldn't bring myself to tell him, either."

Annie gave Laura's arm a squeeze and said, "I know meeting with him was hard, but it's done now, and there really isn't any reason you need to talk to him again."

"I know. It's just…I lost my temper when he kept saying there was no reason to try and figure out who sent the notes, that it wouldn't do anyone any good. I told him Hattie wasn't the only person to receive notes and he should ask Mr. Hoffmann if he didn't believe me. I know I shouldn't have said anything. Nate will be so angry. What if Russell tells Hoffmann details about the notes to Hattie and rumors spread? Russell said Hattie wouldn't want me to pursue the notes. That I could end up being the one to ruin her reputation. What if he is right?"

Chapter Twenty-seven
Saturday afternoon, January 31, 1880

"VILLE de PARIS HOLIDAY PRESENTS! In addition to our Large, Fresh and Complete Assortment of LADIES' KID GLOVES, VIENNA AND PARIS LEATHER GOODS, PLUSH TRIMMED CLOAKS & DOLMANS, ENGLISH WRAPS AND SHAWLS, FANCY HOSIERY FOR LADIES AND CHILDREN, A Beautiful Line of Lace Goods, Fichus, Long Scarfs, Handkerchiefs, Barbes, etc, of the very latest designs."—*San Francisco Chronicle*, 1880

Laura watched impatiently as Kitty Blaine flicked through the pages of the *Third Reader*, deciding what essay she should use on Monday to demonstrate the rules regarding commas. This would be the first time Kitty had taught the seventh-grade class on her own, and she was obviously nervous. Laura had surprised herself when she agreed to let Kitty come to visit her on a Saturday. Sitting next to her on the settee in the boarding house's formal parlor, watching Kitty dither between two different essay choices, she was beginning to regret the impulse.

Laura poured herself another cup of tea and looked around the room, wondering what Kitty thought of her surroundings. The old parlor had beautiful, dark-oak paneling and furniture that Kathleen kept polished to a high gloss. To Laura, who had grown up in a house on a working ranch and previously lived in threadbare rooming houses, this parlor, with its thick oriental carpet of dark blue and red and its matching velvet curtains, was the height of elegance. But she knew from reading the illustrated magazines that a young woman as wealthy as Kitty, living in a Nob Hill mansion filled with marble, grand paintings, and cut-glass chandeliers, would find this room unimpressive. Della Thorndike had told her that Kitty's mother had died in her daughter's infancy and indicated that her father was very traditional and perhaps over-protective of Kitty. Laura wondered what Mr. Blaine thought of his daughter's desire to become a teacher. Perhaps he was like many parents who assumed that going to school or being a teacher was just something for a woman to do until she married. *Which, at this rate, might happen before Kitty ever makes up her mind about which essay to use.*

Laura was just about to say something to hurry the process along when Kitty leaned back and said, "Tarnation," her eyes filling with tears.

"Whatever is the matter?" Laura asked, surprised at the oath and the emotion behind it.

"I'm so *stupid*. This always happens to me. I'm so afraid of making a mistake, I can't think." Kitty swiped at her tears. "I keep hearing my old governess, Mrs. Stone, reciting, 'The pursuit of perfection, then, is the pursuit of sweetness and light.' She was English and a great admirer of Matthew Arnold. But under her tutelage, learning never felt very sweet. That's why I admire you so much, Miss Dawson. You make learning fun for your students."

Laura reached over and patted Kitty's hand. "Well, I was fortunate that it was my mother who was in charge of my early schooling, and she had a very different philosophy. She'd read some lectures by Cardinal John Henry Newman, who she often quoted, and she would say, 'A man would do nothing if he waited until he could do it so well that no one could find fault.' My mother was adamant that I enjoy my education."

"Oh my, I don't think my *Protestant* governess would be happy with me taking my inspiration from a Catholic," Kitty said, laughing. "But my *Irish Catholic* father would be delighted!" She took out her handkerchief and mopped up the remaining traces of tears.

Laura said, "I will also tell you a secret; I am terrified half the time I step in front of the class. But it gets easier. There is a reason it is called practice teaching, and surely Miss Thorndike has talked to you in your pedagogy classes about telling students that making mistakes is often the best way to learn."

"Well...I am not sure that Miss Thorndike ever makes a mistake, but Mr. Russell has said that if I ever want to be comfortable in conversational German, I need to be able to make errors. I am learning so much from him."

Laura drew back, disturbed by how Kitty's words echoed Hattie's when she'd spoke about Russell. *Could Kitty be his newest conquest?* Trying to keep her voice neutral, she said, "Miss Thorndike mentioned that you were very good with languages. Are you also a member of the Greek study group he leads?"

"Yes, we meet most Thursdays after school in a classroom at Girls' High," Kitty replied.

"Yes, my friend mentioned these meetings. I assume you met her, Miss Wilks."

"Oh, yes. Miss Thorndike told me about...she said that Miss Wilks and Mr. Russell had been engaged...and that we shouldn't mention Miss Wilks to him...because he is too cut up by his loss. Was Miss Wilks a very good friend of yours?"

"Yes. We attended San Jose Normal School together. She was my closest friend."

"Oh Miss Dawson, I am sorry. I only met her briefly at the Greek study club. I was very impressed. She was picking up Greek very rapidly for a beginning student. Clearly, she was brilliant. She once told me that she intended to become a doctor. Such a tragic loss."

"Thank you," Laura said warmly. "It is good to hear you speak about her. None of my friends here knew her, and, well...it is comforting to know that there is someone else who understands what a fine mind she had."

Kitty said softly, "I am sure that Mr. Russell shares your sentiment. Despite what Miss Thorndike said, I think it would do him good to speak of her with someone such as yourself..."

"No," Laura said harshly, then tried to moderate her tone. "I am afraid I am not quite the admirer of Mr. Russell that you are. But then I don't know him that well." Laura picked up the *Third Reader* and said, "Either of the essays you have chosen will work equally well; why don't you just pick the first so we can move on to discussing the rest of the lesson?"

Laura wasn't sure how it came about, but an hour later Kitty and she were walking into the elegant City of Paris department store that filled most of the first floor of the Occidental Hotel. Kitty had responded to Laura's urging that they get back to planning the grammar lesson by suddenly becoming decisive. Over the next half-hour, she sketched out the rest of her plans for Monday and secured Laura's approval. She then looked at the clock on the mantel over the parlor fireplace and said her father's carriage would be waiting for her, so she must go. As she stood up, she'd hesitatingly asked Laura if she would like to accompany her to do some errands.

"You would be doing me such a favor," Kitty explained. "Otherwise, I will need to return home and fetch my maid. My father won't let me go anywhere alone. I know it is an imposition, but I would so enjoy your company. The coachman will take us right to the City of Paris, and he will take you home whenever you wish."

Laura had immediately agreed, running up to her room to get her cloak, her purse, and, more importantly, the instructions Miss Minnie had given her regarding the material she needed for the new outfit the elderly seamstresses had promised to make for her.

So here they now were, walking in the Sutter Street entrance to the store, and Laura felt overwhelmed. She knew the history of the City of Paris, named for the ship from France the Verdier brothers brought to San Francisco in 1850. A ship loaded with the casks of wines, brandy, and champagne, along with boxes of silks, laces, fashionable bonnets, stockings, and petticoats that formed the basis for their mercantile business. But knowing the history didn't prepare her for how intimidating it was to stand in a cavernous space of polished-wood floors and filigreed plaster columns nearly a block long and half a block wide. The innumerable wooden counters and glass-fronted display cases were arranged in rows resembling city streets. At least she'd had the good sense to put on her one good suit today, the royal-blue cashmere. As a result, she didn't feel too dowdy compared to the other fashionably dressed women walking up and down the store aisles or sitting at the counters in front of her. Not wanting to feel too much like a country bumpkin, she told Kitty to get her errands done first, hoping that as they made their way around the store she would figure out where she needed to go to make her own purchases.

Kitty took her arm and said, "I have just a few things, but I am afraid they are scattered around in different departments. This is why I like shopping here, though. You don't need to go up and down the street looking for different stores. But I do need some new gloves, and that will bring us right next to where they sell fabrics."

Laura, pleased that her plan had worked, said, "That would be splendid. Lead the way."

Kitty went down a row of counters holding men's ties and hand-kerchiefs, then turned to the right and walked rapidly to a section holding books and a variety of other objects. She said, over her shoulder, "I need some plain notepaper and envelopes, and Miss Thorndike suggested that I get some blank books to keep a record of my class preparations. She said that the stationary and book department here had some of different sizes. Oh look, there they are."

Laura was stunned by the choices in notepaper, pens, pencils, ink bottles, ink blotters, scrap books, albums, and calendars. She barely knew where to look. She saw a leather-bound diary with 1880 embossed in gold on the front that she instantly coveted, picking it up to see the price, *a dollar!* Then she noticed a pad of lined paper that she thought looked exactly like the kind on which Hattie's anonymous letters had been written. The pads were probably sold in every stationary shop in the city, but they were only fifteen cents, so while Kitty was deciding over notepaper, she paid for the diary and the pad of paper.

As they moved on with their brown-paper packages dangling from strings, Kitty led Laura back through what she called the men's furnish-ing section and on to the millinery and handbag department. Hats of all shapes and sizes sat on pedestals around them, some of plain straw that one could decorate oneself, others with elaborate bows, feathers, and artificial flowers, like so many over-decorated cakes. Laura thought to herself that she might return here another day, if she had any money left over after buying the material for her dress, to see if there was a hat that would go with her new outfit.

Kitty was looking at the handbags and said, "I am afraid I am hard on my purses. My pens tend to leak, so cloth or embroidery just won't work. What do you think of this black alligator one? It seems well-made, and it has this outside pocket where you can keep your change."

Laura dutifully admired the bag's stitching and the leather-covered handle, trying not to feel too jealous when she compared this to her plain brown velvet purse.

Kitty suddenly turned to her and gave her a warm smile. "Oh Miss Dawson, this is much more fun than shopping with Marie. She is French and thinks that we Americans have no sense of style. She disparages everything I look at and takes all of the enjoyment out of it for me."

Laura smiled in return, glad she had decided to come with Kitty. She said, "This has been a treat for me as well. And I must say, your own taste is impeccable. I am going to depend on you to guide me in my fabric choice. I have a limited amount to spend, and I want to make sure the outfit is something that is versatile and fashionable."

Almost an hour later, having finished all the rest of Kitty's errands and handed over their purchases to one of the clerks for safe-keeping, they got down to the serious business of finding just the right materials for Laura's new suit. She'd already established with the Misses Moffet that she wanted an outfit with the new long and tightly fitted silhouette that was just coming into vogue, similar to the style that Kitty favored.

Millie Moffet, the silent one of the seamstress sisters, had sketched out a lovely cuirass bodice that would hug her hips, and Miss Millie had suggested that Laura get a light wool material for the bodice and satin for the rest of the skirt, including enough satin to construct large lapels and cuffs to lend some interest to the wool top. The most daring aspect of the outfit was to be the lack of any real bustle beyond a slight fullness created by the horizontal satin pleats in the panel that would fall down the back of the skirt. Kitty announced that the design was charming when Laura showed her the sketch and that she was sure they would find something to fit both her budget and her taste.

Laura eventually settled on a deep bronze satin and an ivory shade of wool that went well with the bronze and had the advantage of matching the skirt of her serviceable dark brown wool dress. The Misses Moffets had insisted that once Laura purchased the material, they would make the garment for free. She had been reluctant to agree until Annie suggested that she offer to read to them in the evenings while they worked. She was so glad when they acquiesced. Otherwise, she never would have been able to afford such an elaborate outfit. She was carefully figuring the cost of the dark brown lace she had chosen for the trimming, not wanting to spend so much she wouldn't have enough left over for thread and buttons, when Kitty interrupted her.

"Look Miss Dawson," she said, pointing discreetly toward the front of the store. "I think you have an admirer. That young man in the brown tweed suit and brown derby has been staring at you the past few minutes, and I think I saw him several times earlier at different parts of the store."

Laura, surprised, turned around to see where Kitty was pointing. She gasped, seeing a man who resembled Buck Morrison loitering in the men's furnishing department. He was the right height and general build, but he had a small mustache that Buck hadn't had six weeks ago, and he kept ducking behind one of the store's columns so she couldn't get a good look at him.

Kitty moved closer to her and lowered her voice so the clerk who was standing across the counter from them couldn't overhear. "Who is he?"

"I think he might be one of my former students. He isn't at all a nice person, and I don't like the idea of him being in town, much less following me. But I need a clearer view to be sure. Would you try to keep an eye on him while I finish this transaction? Then we can move closer."

Kitty nodded vigorously and picked up a piece of ribbon, pretending to hold it up to the light in order to keep staring over towards the man.

Laura paid for the brown lace, hoping she hadn't gotten more than she needed in her haste. She asked the clerk to put it with the rest of their packages. Then she looped her arm through Kitty's, and they walked towards the front of the store. Kitty kept up a running dialogue, describing the man's actions, while Laura studiously looked elsewhere, not wanting to alarm him if he were Buck.

"He's moving away, towards the front door. There, look quickly, he has turned around so you can see his face clearly."

Laura looked up and for a second found herself staring directly into a pair of blue eyes she knew she would never forget. Buck then spun around and wove his way through the crowd and out the front door.

"Oh dear, he's gone. Do you want to try and follow him?" Kitty was clearly getting caught up in the spirit of the chase.

Laura paused, then she shook her head. "No, he'll be long gone. But if you don't mind, I think that I should return home."

They retrieved their packages and left the store. Kitty's carriage was waiting, as promised, at the corner of Montgomery and Sutter. Laura thought briefly about asking to be dropped off at Nate's law office rather than the boarding house. She'd only been there once, but she knew it was just a few blocks east and north on Sansome Street. But it was nearly four, and she had no idea whether he would still be working. Perhaps it would be better to tell Annie first, anyway, give herself time to figure out what she wanted Nate to do about this sighting.

She just wished she was sure that Buck was the man in the alley. He'd looked so different today, all citified, with the mustache, derby, tweed suit and all. It was her impression that the man who accosted her was rougher or, at the very least, that he had been wearing the broader-brimmed hat she associated with working men. *But even if he wasn't the man who attacked me, what is he doing in the city, and why is he following me?*

Chapter Twenty-eight
Saturday afternoon, January 31, 1880

"School Director Sullivan is in receipt of an anonymous letter, in which the author threatens that in the event he or she be injured, to expose the sisters of Mr. Sullivan, who are charged with having obtained fraudulent certificates."—
San Francisco Chronicle, 1879

Nate ushered Barbara Hewitt into his office and asked her to please sit down. She had written to him on Thursday saying that she needed some legal advice and had information that might be related to the case he was investigating. He could tell she was nervous, sitting on the edge of her seat, clutching her purse tightly in her hands. He didn't know her well, but she'd always struck him as a reserved person, so he decided a very business-like approach might work best.

"Mrs. Hewitt, how I can help you? We can have a very informal conversation first, if you wish. Or, if you would feel more comfortable, you can sign a retainer that makes anything you say confidential."

She sat up even straighter, smoothed the skirt of her somber grey ensemble, and said, "Mr. Dawson, I hope you realize how much this means to me. I do think that since I will be asking your legal advice, I should sign the retainer. I wasn't sure of the fee." She started to open her purse.

"Please, Mrs. Hewitt. There is no need for that now," Nate said quickly. "And if you have information that might shed some light on my investigation into the anonymous letters that have surfaced, I should think that would be more than enough compensation for any help I can give you."

He pulled out their standard printed legal form, filled out the top section, and asked her to read and sign her name, with the date. As she did, he tried not to speculate on what she was going to say, what it was that she hadn't felt she could tell Annie. He'd assumed Mrs. Hewitt was older than Annie because of her son Jamie, whose ninth birthday party he had attended last September. But today, having the occasion to examine her more closely, he realized that she could well be under the age of thirty, depending on how young she was when she married. If Annie'd had a child with her husband, the child would be...

"There, Mr. Dawson." Mrs. Hewitt handed the signed paper back to him. "And now, I expect you would like to know why I am here." She opened up her purse again and took out a piece of paper that had been folded several times and held it out to him. "Please look at this, and I think you will understand why I have come to you for advice."

What Nate saw was a folded page from the *San Francisco Morning Call*, dated January 17th of this year. It appeared to be one of the inside pages of the paper that contained general news on one side and advertisements on the other. It was dirty, and one side was ragged as if the page had been hastily ripped from the accompanying sheet. Skimming through the headlines and seeing nothing that looked like it would have anything to do with Barbara Hewitt or the anonymous letters, he looked up at her in puzzlement. "Mrs. Hewitt, I don't understand. Is it one of the ads I am supposed to look at?"

She leaned towards the desk and pointed. "See the letters that are circled throughout the page? Here is what they spell out if you write each one of them in turn." She handed him a plain piece of paper, on which was written, "*I know who you are. You will pay for taking what is mine.*"

"Good heavens," Nate exclaimed. He took out a loose piece of paper and his pen and went through the newspaper page, writing down the circled letters in turn as she suggested. *Damned if they don't spell out those two sentences.* He looked at her and said, "However did you figure this out?"

"I nearly didn't. In fact, I almost threw the newspaper page away when I received it, thinking it some sort of joke. But the way it was given to me seemed to indicate otherwise. Wednesday before last, Jamie had some class work to do, so I offered to take Dandy for his last walk. We had just gotten to the corner of O'Farrell and Taylor when a young boy came running up and thrust an envelope into my hand, then ran off down Jones."

"And in the envelope was this piece of newspaper, nothing else?"

"Yes. I was thoroughly confused. When I got home, I read the articles, but there was nothing that seemed relevant. Then, having noticed a few of the circled letters, I turned the sheet over and looked through all the advertisements, wondering if this was some odd new marketing ploy. But none of the ads were circled, which made me go back and look at the circled letters on the other side again. Took me a while, but once I hit on the pattern, it was easy to see."

"And was there anything on the envelope? Was it addressed to you specifically?" Nate tried to remain calm, but it was hard, given the inescapable implication that here was another example of an anonymous threat, once again directed at a teacher.

"No, nothing on the envelope. I did ask Jamie about whether any of his schoolmates might be playing a joke on him. I didn't show him the actual paper or tell him what it said. I didn't want to upset him. I just asked if it was a new fashion to pass messages between friends by circling letters in a newspaper." Barbara Hewitt smiled briefly. "He seemed very surprised, but he told me it was a 'jolly good idea' and that he was going to try it with Ian, Kathleen's younger brother."

Nate leaned back, looking again at the two sentences. "Well this 'You will pay for taking what is mine' surely looks like it could be from the same person who has accused Mrs. Anderson of getting her job through favoritism. I suppose it could be someone who feels they deserved your job or any job at Girls' High for that matter. The animus towards teachers with the better paying positions could be general, not specific. But why didn't you tell Annie about this right away?"

"It wasn't until this Wednesday, when Annie told me about the notes sent to Hattie Wilks and the new letter accusing Mr. Hoffmann, that I realized this message could be connected."

Nate looked at her, her head bowed as she fiddled with the clasp, and he asked gently, "Mrs. Hewitt. What do you think the sentence, 'I know who you are' means?"

After a long pause, she looked back up at him, her face pale and her eyes brimming with tears. She said quietly, "I think it means that whoever sent the message knows that I am not Barbara Hewitt."

Chapter Twenty-nine
Saturday late evening, January 31, 1880

"THE CALIFORNIA DETECTIVE BUREAU attends to detective work in all its branches; in the city or country; office 331 Kearny street, room 4; strictly confidential, terms moderate." —*San Francisco Chronicle*, 1880

The clock on her mantel chimed eleven as Annie sat at the small table in her bedroom, reading the Saturday evening edition of the *Daily Bulletin*. She was gathering information she might use next week as Madam Sibyl, trying to make up for the time she'd lost this week working at Girls' High. With any luck, she would need only two more weeks to complete her investigative work there. She knew from past experience how wearing it was to juggle Madam Sibyl's work, run the boarding house, and investigate a possible crime. She did have to admit, however, that she enjoyed getting a chance to solve a puzzle again, this time with Nate's blessing. It was ironic that Nate was the one who'd asked for her help, given all their past arguments about her penchant for sticking her nose into other people's business. *Detecting, that's what professionals call what I'm doing. Here, right in the Daily Bulletin is a large advertisement for the "Pacific Detective Bureau, 632 Market St. San Francisco."*

Evidently, when Emory first brought up the subject of hiring someone, Nate had recommended they consult one of these local private detectives. But his Uncle Frank argued that Annie would be able to do something that none of the former treasury agents or Pinkertons who advertised their services would be able to do: pass herself off as a teacher. And she'd already discovered at least one person who was a possible suspect. Mr. Frazier, the job applicant who'd lost out to Mrs. Anderson. Frazier might very well blame his own economic difficulties on any teachers who got one of the coveted teaching jobs or the administrators who hired them. In other words, he could be behind the accusations aimed at Dottie Anderson and Hoffmann, as well as those accusing Hattie and, perhaps indirectly, Russell.

This thought led to Laura's description of her meeting with Russell. The dear girl obviously couldn't decide whether he was the villain or another victim in what happened to Hattie. And Buck Morrison's appearance at the store today seemed to have added to her confusion. She was tying herself up in knots over whether Buck was the man who attacked her. The events of the past few months were undermining Laura's confidence in herself. As Annie had intimated to Nate, she believed that the root of all of Laura's distress was her disillusionment with her beloved Hattie. If she could be wrong about Hattie, then she could be wrong about everybody and everything. From her own painful experiences, Annie knew only time and a willingness on Laura's part to accept Hattie for who she was, flaws and all, would heal that wound.

"Mrs. Fuller? Annie?"

Annie heard a faint knocking and her name being called, so she got up and opened the door a crack to see Barbara Hewitt standing in the hallway with Jamie's dog, Dandy, clutched in her arms. Opening up the door wider, she put out her hand to have it eagerly licked by Dandy and asked Barbara what she could do for her.

"I hate to bother you," Barbara said very quietly, "but I could see light coming out from under your door and hoped this meant you were still up. I wonder if you would mind coming up to the landing that leads to the top floor and look out with me. I think that I saw someone lurking in the back alley."

"Just a minute," said Annie, and she went and got the candle she kept by her bed. Lit candle in hand, she joined Barbara and Dandy in the hallway. As they walked to the back stairs, Barbara again apologized for disturbing her, whispering so as not to wake Laura or the Steins, whose darkened doorways they were passing. There wasn't any light coming from the small back room David Chapman and Spencer Harvey shared or the water closet, either.

When they made it to the landing that led up to the attic where Barbara, her son Jamie, the elderly Moffets, and Beatrice O'Rourke all had their rooms, Annie stopped and blew out the candle. She said, "Please, don't apologize. I am glad you came and got me. I need to let my eyes adjust, so tell me exactly what you saw."

"I was up grading. Jamie was asleep in the curtained alcove. Dandy got off the bed and came to stand by me, barking softly. I thought he just needed to be let out, so I picked him up and started down the stairs. But when we got to the landing, he started to growl. Just like he is doing now."

Dandy was straining towards the window, emitting a low gurgling sound. Barbara tried to calm him, saying, "Dandy, hush. You'll wake everyone. There's a good boy."

She then said to Annie, "When I looked out toward the back of the lot, I thought I saw someone moving down the alley. At first I thought I would just need to wait until the person passed by before letting Dandy out into the yard. Then I saw a flare of light and realized that someone was standing near the gate, probably smoking a cigarette."

Annie, whose eyes had now adjusted to the dark, leaned close to the window and looked to the back of the yard. Her house was taller than those on either side, and the houses across the back alley were on Ellis, which was further down the gentle slope leading to Market. This meant they had a good view of the surrounding neighborhood. The moon was rising on the left, and while it was definitely waning, it still provided a good deal of light. She looked at the back gate and saw nothing.

Since Dandy was now quiet, his erect ears at attention, she said, "I don't see anything. But if you don't mind, let's just stand here and look out for a moment, see if there is any movement. Then we can go to the kitchen and let Dandy out. He will tell us if there is someone still in the alley, and we can get Mr. Chapman or Mr. Harvey to come down and check things out."

Barbara agreed, and they stood in companionable silence. The moonlight made the shadows of the apricot tree dance on the white paving stones, and the wood in the fence and gate were a bleached grey, interrupted here and there by dark black shadows that Annie tried to identify. A rake, a bushel basket, the trash barrel, and what looked like an old sweater hanging on one of the post of the clothesline. No shadow, however, that corresponded to a person loitering in the alley or yard. Perhaps Barbara's imagination had played a trick on her. Not surprising given the terrible events of this past fall when Dandy had alerted his owner to a very real crime in the neighborhood. Well, the small dog was calm now, so they could probably assume if anyone had been out back, they were now gone. Annie was about to suggest they go down to let the dog out when Barbara broke the silence.

"Annie, I saw Mr. Dawson today. I wondered if he told you about our meeting." Barbara shifted slightly next to her.

"No, I haven't spoken with him today. He is planning on coming by tomorrow evening." Annie paused, hoping that Barbara would continue.

"I...I showed him a note I got that I thought might be from the same anonymous person who wrote to Miss Wilks and has been spreading rumors about Mr. Hoffmann and others." Barbara went on to tell Annie about how she had received the note and what it said.

"Oh my goodness," Annie said when she was finished with her story. "I am so sorry this happened to you. How awful." She wanted to give Barbara a quick hug, but she didn't know if that degree of intimacy would be welcomed by such a self-contained woman.

"There is more, and I promise you I will understand if...if you feel that what I have to tell you next changes irrevocably our...position here. I just ask that you consider Jamie..."

Barbara stopped speaking for a moment. She went on in a rush. "You see, what the note said, that they knew who I was, must have meant that they knew I had taken another woman's identity. The real Barbara Hewitt died six years ago, and her sister-in-law gave me her birth certificate and teaching credentials, so I could get a job and support Jamie."

Annie didn't know what to say. *Barbara...no...that isn't her real name...but then who is she?*

Before she could respond, Barbara continued. "You see, I had attended Kansas Normal School a few years after Barbara Hewitt did, but when my mother died I had to return to our ranch, never getting my certificate. A year later my father died, and I married. Bobby had been our ranch hand. He tried to make a go of the ranch, and I got taught for a few terms in a nearby town to help out, but in '74 we were wiped out by locusts."

"Then what happened?" Annie prompted, after a brief pause.

Barbara sighed. "We lost everything, and Bobby...he didn't take it well. It was better that we go our separate ways. Jamie and I traveled west with the Hewitts, who offered me a position helping out on the trail taking care of their six children. We all wintered in Nevada. Nan Hewitt's husband thought maybe there'd be work in mining, but the silver boom was pretty much over."

"That was in '75?" Annie asked.

"Yes, and when a position opened up in a local school...well... money was scarce for all of us, and we were becoming pretty desperate. Nan suggested I use her sister-in-law's teaching credentials to get the job. The real Barbra Hewitt had died the year before, and Nan had her birth certificate and Kansas Teaching Certificate and letters of recommendation. Everything I would need. So I became Barbara Hewitt."

"And you think that this is what the anonymous note was about?"

"It must be," Barbara declared. "Someone who knew me, maybe back in Kansas, or knew the real Barbara. Knew that I wasn't who I said I was and thought that I didn't deserve the job I have. I was so worried when I got the note. What if they wrote the school board or Principal Swett? I don't know what I would do if I lost my teaching position."

"What did Nate say? I assume that one of the reasons you spoke to him was to get his legal advice."

"Oh Annie, he was so kind and reassuring. He got some law books out while I was there and showed me where it said under California law that you have the right to use a different name. As long as you don't do it to defraud anyone. And you see, when I got to California, I didn't use any of the documents that Nan had given me. I had my own recommendations from the three years I taught in Nevada and Colorado, and I took the California examination and got the highest level Certificate on my own merits."

Annie felt the anxiety that had been building up as Barbara told her story ease a bit, but she said, "What about that first job?"

"He said I had probably broken the law that first time, but he doubted whether anyone would care. But that is what still worries me. I may not have broken any California law, but would a school administrator see it that way? And what if it came out, what would I tell Jamie?"

"He doesn't know about the name change?"

"He was only three when we left Kansas. When the Hewitts moved on the next spring, I stayed behind to continue to teach, and from that point on everyone we knew simply called me Barbara Hewitt. So he has never known himself by any other name than Jamie Hewitt. I don't talk about our past much or his father. I told him his father died. It seemed kinder…but now I don't know if that was right. And what will he think of me if he learns that I changed our names and why? What must you think of me?"

Annie reached out, putting a hand on Barbara's shoulder, and said, "I think that you did what you had to do to take care of yourself and your son. And who am I to judge, when every day I use a false name in order to make money as Madam Sibyl? We do what we have to do to support ourselves in a world with very few options for women. But do you mind if I ask? What is your real name?"

"Linda…Linda Norman. But Linda Norman is another woman, from another time and place. A not very happy woman and not someone I ever want to become again."

Chapter Thirty
Wednesday afternoon, February 4, 1880
"RADICAL REDUCTION DECIDED UPON LAST EVENING...All janitors receiving more than $50 per month were subjected to a cut of ten percent." — *San Francisco Chronicle*, 1879

As Annie sat at Mr. Hoffmann's desk, taking notes on the files of past hires, she thought about what she had learned from Barbara Saturday night. *Linda, no, Barbara, that's what she wants to be called. No wonder she is so reserved.* And the husband? Bobby Norman? Annie could only guess what it must have been like, married to her father's ranch hand, a man who was probably much less educated than Barbara. She'd said little about him, beyond the fact that he was, like many men who drifted into Kansas working on cattle drives, a Civil War veteran. But Annie didn't have to guess at what economic ruin could do to a man or to a marriage, because she had her own experiences to draw on. She also understood the desire to put the humiliations and pain of the past forever in the past. But someone knew about that past and had threatened to reveal it. *Who?*

Today, as she looked through the files for teachers who had failed to secure a position, she noted down those who had ever lived in Kansas. She also found the employment records for Barbara and saw that Mr. Hoffmann had hired her. Yet there was no indication that Mr. Frazier sought Barbara's position. That didn't mean that Frazier, or some other disappointed applicant, wouldn't target any recently hired teacher they felt didn't deserve their position. What she needed to find out, however, was if Frazier had lived in Kansas or knew someone who had lived in Kansas and might have mentioned knowing Barbara by another name. She thought the best way to get this information was to contact Frazier with the manufactured story she had given Della Thorndike. Tell him she was looking for a tutor for Mrs. Stein's granddaughter, then interview him. She even got Esther Stein's permission to do so, but when she told Nate about her plans on Sunday, he completely opposed the idea.

In fact, Nate's visit on Sunday evening was an unmitigated disaster. First of all, he was late. He didn't arrive at the boarding house until after eight, and by then she had given up on seeing him and had joined the rest of the boarders in the formal parlor. David Chapman was teaching Jamie how to play a card game called California Jack, with Jamie's mother looking on. Esther Stein, her husband once again up in Portland on business, sat in a corner knitting and talking to the Misses Moffet. Mr. Harvey was supposedly reading a book, but he was watching Jamie with fondness, no doubt longing for his ailing wife and his own children who lived with his in-laws in Sacramento. When Kathleen ushered Nate into the parlor, he spent some time chatting with everyone out of politeness, so it was nearly eight-thirty before she could come up with an excuse to draw him back over to the small parlor. He insisted that they leave the door open for propriety's sake, irritating her more than usual because she really had wanted the privacy to discuss Barbara's surprising revelation. Then Laura, seeing the open door as an invitation, waltzed in and interrupted them before she had been able to even go through what she had learned on Friday at Girls' High.

To make matters worse, when Laura told her brother about seeing Buck at the City of Paris department store, he told her about his visit to Seth Timmons. Laura was furious, saying he'd humiliated her and bringing up a number of childhood incidents when he interfered unnecessarily in her affairs. Nate then lost his temper and said that if he'd known how much trouble she was going to get into, he would never have supported her decision to take the job at Clement Grammar, adding a few childhood tales of his own to illustrate his point that she was headstrong and took dangerous risks. When he said that maybe he should write their parents and advise that she go back to the ranch until everything had settled down, Laura told him she would never forgive him if he did that and stormed out of the parlor.

Nate had instantly felt remorseful, one of his more admirable qualities, so Annie told him that she would reassure Laura that he didn't mean it when he said he was going to write their parents. But when she brought up her plan to interview Frazier, he got right back on his high horse and told her he would handle this aspect of the investigation, saying she should stick to the safe job of looking around at Girls' High.

Later, Annie congratulated herself on not responding to this overt provocation, understanding that Nate was still upset about his fight with Laura. But a few minutes later, when he mentioned that he'd attended a dinner meeting Friday with Mr. Emory at Mrs. Anderson's, despite having told her that he couldn't make it to the boarding house because he had too much work, Annie could no longer hold back her anger. She told him she was surprised he preferred to spend his time with a woman who wielded her widowhood and her own child like weapons to get men to take care of her. He snapped back that if she would occasionally invite him to dine with her at the boarding house, he wouldn't have to look elsewhere for a decent meal.

She had said…well, she hadn't really said anything, knowing that he was speaking the truth. She didn't invite him to dine with her because she only ate with her boarders on Sundays, preferring the solitude of meals in her own room after a long day talking to clients as Madam Sibyl. And she didn't want to share him with anyone else when she got to see him so infrequently.

Annie had tried to change the subject, telling him what happened the night before when she and Barbara finally took Dandy down to the kitchen. The small terrier had rushed out to the back fence to sniff vigorously with his snub nose along the bottom of the gate. He then gave a short bark as if to say, "whoever you are, stay away," and calmly trotted to the back of the garden to do his business.

She'd hoped the image of Dandy as the minuscule guard dog would amuse him. Unfortunately, Nate's response had been to reprimand her for not rousing one of her male boarders to check for an intruder.

She'd kept her mouth firmly shut, knowing that whatever she said next she would probably regret. After a few chilly, silent minutes, Nate said he had an early meeting with Cranston and left. She hadn't heard from him since, not even a note.

The small clock in Hoffmann's office chimed, and Annie realized there were only forty-five minutes left until her class started. She put the files away and spent a few minutes looking over her notes, then she decided she would go to the women's washroom before class to make sure she didn't have any smudges on her nose. Since this was a relatively new building, the washroom, holding several toilets and standing sinks, was part of the original construction, unlike the water closet in her own home that her aunt had paid to have constructed in the back hall. When Annie pulled open the heavy wooden door with the discreet word *Ladies* carved into it, she found it occupied by an older woman. Annie identified her as the janitoress, Mrs. Washburn, since she was standing next to a bucket and leaning on a mop.

"Oh, excuse me, I don't want to get in your way," Annie said. "I will just nip over here and wash my hands. I am afraid I have gotten some ink on them."

"Nae problem m'dear. Go right along, but mind yer steps. The floor might be a wee bit wet."

Mrs. Washburn smiled brightly at her, leaning the mop handle against the wall. She was a tall, broad-shouldered, square-faced woman, whose white hair had the faint orange cast that hinted she had been a redhead in the distant past. A past that probably included a birthplace in Scotland, if her accent was any indication. While she moved easily, the wrinkles, white hair, and the washed-out blue of her widely spaced eyes suggested she was on the far side of fifty.

She walked over to Annie and sketched a curtsy, saying, "Pleased t'meet yer. I'm Mrs. Washburn."

Annie, drying her hands on the towel next to the wash basin, said, "Glad to meet you as well. I am Mrs. Fuller. I'm temporarily lecturing on bookkeeping for Mr. Hoffmann's senior math class."

"My, what an *unusual* subject for a lassie." Mrs. Washburn took a rag that she had tucked in her apron and walked over to wipe out the sink Annie had just used.

Annie laughed. "I believe one of the new school board members felt it was a practical subject that every young girl should learn."

"Practical?" Mrs. Washburn cocked her head, a small frown appearing. "Well, mebby it could help a lass make her household sums come out straight. A sight more practical than the strange foreign languages those young girls are lairning on Thursday nights with that Clement Grammar Vice Principal."

"Oh yes, I believe I heard that Mr. Russell is tutoring some of the girls in Greek and Latin."

"Greek?" The older woman shrugged, eloquently expressing her skepticism.

Annie cast around for some other subject that would keep the janitoress talking. "I was wondering if you were the person I should ask about getting into the supply cabinet. Miss Thorndike spoke very highly of you the other day, and she said that if I needed any help that you were the person to ask. I need some graph paper for an assignment I am giving the girls next week."

"Humph." The older woman snorted, two angry spots of red appearing on her wrinkled cheeks. "Don't expect Mr. Hoffmann to give me a copy of his precious cabinet key. No, you will have to ask him. If you can find him."

"Oh dear, that is too bad. Well, with Principal Swett away, he does have a lot to manage. But it is strange that a long-term employee such as yourself wouldn't be trusted." Annie paused, then added, "Particularly with all the work that having these extra-curricular activities must create. Greek study groups, drama classes, the Literature and Debate Society and such. I saw the list on the board in the front hall. Seems there is something every night. However do you get the rooms cleaned?"

Mrs. Washburn went back to her mop and stabbed it into the bucket, slopping water over the sides, then she began to swish it around on the floor under the window. Over her shoulder, she said, "Ah, you dinnae ken the half of it. And there's that Mrs. Anderson's room, all covered in paint and clay and such. Her screeching at a body when they're just trying to do their job. But here I am blethering on, keeping yer from yer duties."

Annie looked at her pocket watch and said, "Goodness me. How right you are, and I need to go gather my notes. Wouldn't do for me to be late to class. It was lovely chatting with you, Mrs. Washburn." *And you, my dear, have just gotten yourself on my list of possible suspects.*

Several hours later, after a successful class and five more years of files gone through and refiled, Annie leaned back in her chair and stretched. She now had a list of people she wanted to investigate further. Mr. Frazier had been joined on the list by a Miss Agnes Easton, one of the young women who Della had dismissed due to lack of experience. Miss Easton had attended Kansas Normal School just a year ago, so she wouldn't have attended when either the fake Barbara or the real Barbara were there. She did apply for the job Barbara now held, however, as well as for the arts position, which did seem suspicious to Annie. There were a few others she put on the list because they had applied and failed to get positions at Girls' High multiple times. None of these applicants, however, seemed to have any Kansas connections. Then there was the janitoress, Mrs. Washburn, who had managed to say something negative about Russell, Hoffmann, and Mrs. Anderson. Annie had rather enjoyed the image of Dottie Anderson dropping her mask of a refined lady to scream at Mrs. Washburn.

A knock interrupted this thought, and when Annie got up to open the door she had left locked for privacy while going through the files, Miss Thorndike stood there smiling warmly.

"Mrs. Fuller. May I bother you for a moment?"

"Of course, come on in and sit down. What can I do for you?" Annie quickly put the list she'd compiled in the folder that held her bookkeeping notes.

"I ran into Mrs. Washburn after classes were over, and she mentioned she had met you today."

"Oh yes, in the ladies' washroom. It was delightful to hear that Scottish accent again. When she learned I was teaching bookkeeping, she very reluctantly admitted that this might be practical for a young woman. This reminded me of my father's housekeeper in New York when I was growing up. Mrs. McGregor was very proud of how well she managed the household accounts, and she would say, 'Mony a mickle maks a muckle' and my father would nod and say to me, 'You pay attention to Mrs. McGregor and you will end up a rich young lady.'"

Della laughed and said, "How droll. I understand your father was Edward Stewart? Laura Dawson mentioned that he had been a famous stock broker in San Francisco in the sixties. You later moved to New York?"

"Yes. I only moved back to San Francisco two years ago. Did you ever live in New York City?"

"Oh no, but my family lived only about two hours away by train, near Poughkeepsie, so we often went into the city for the weekend to attend lectures and visit the Opera House or the art galleries. I can tell you that one of the real regrets I have about moving west is the lack of cultural stimulation."

"Yes, I suppose. Although I didn't have much leisure time to enjoy that side of city life after I left school and married." Annie wondered where this conversation was going.

"Yes, yes, I know what you mean. As I mentioned to you the other day, between my father's financial reversals in the panic of 1857 and his subsequent death, and then the death of my fiancé, well, I have, like you, suffered the 'slings and arrows of outrageous fortune.' Which is why I do believe that it is important for us as working women to stick together."

Annie nodded, remaining confused about Della's point but wondering just exactly what Laura had told Della about her. She might have to warn her to be careful. Della obviously liked to gossip, and Annie didn't want anyone to learn the real reason she was at Girls' High.

Della continued. "You see, Mrs. Washburn, dear soul, was a tiny bit concerned that she had overstepped her bounds; she was so enjoying her conversation with you."

Ah, that's it. "Oh, dear, do tell Mrs. Washburn not to worry in the least. I quite agree with you that she is clearly overworked. It's natural she would express some dissatisfaction. I'm sure having to wait to clean the classrooms until all the clubs and societies and study groups break up must be inconvenient. I wonder if some other accommodation could be found for such activities as Mr. Russell's Greek study group."

"Oh, Vice Principal Russell is no problem. He holds his study club in the school library. Quite unexceptional. It is Mr. Hoffmann that I worry about. Just this year, he took over the job of sponsoring the science club, when it seems to me that Mrs. Rickle would be a more appropriate choice. He holds his meetings in a classroom with the door closed! I am not sure this is quite proper without an older female chaperone present. It is just that I worry that young women like Kitty Blaine, my student who is practice teaching with Laura, might be taken advantage of under the circumstances."

Annie's pulse sped up; here was new information. She wondered what Della meant by "circumstances," so she probed further. "'Taken advantage?' Oh Della, you aren't suggesting anything untoward is happening?"

Della leaned closer and lowered her voice, even though the door to the hallway was closed. "Kitty's father may be wealthy, but he got his start as an ordinary saloon keeper, and he is now an important man in the Democratic Party. I can't help but fear that, despite hiring some English governess for her, he has not been a suitable moral guardian for his daughter. She has confided in me that she acts as hostess for his formal dinners, no doubt filled with his party cronies. Not a desirable upbringing for a young girl."

"And you think that Mr. Hoffmann may have designs on her?"

"Well, I do know that he has spoken out quite sharply about the dominance of Republicans on the Board. I can't help but wonder if he isn't favoring Kitty because he wants to garner influence with her father and the Democrats."

"Have you tried to warn her?" Annie asked.

"I have hinted that she might want to be careful, not let her enthusiasm for her studies lead her to overstep the boundaries of propriety. But she is a proud and stubborn young woman, and I must say I fear for her."

Chapter Thirty-one
Wednesday evening, February 4, 1880
"$10 REWARD - LOST ON MONDAY night...a small black-and-tan Terrier Dog, with clipped ears, answering to the name of Dandy." —*San Francisco Chronicle*, 1879

Annie was drawn down to the kitchen by a burst of laughter. She needed a good laugh. She was tired and disgruntled. Because she'd wanted to get to Girls' High by noon today, she'd scheduled her first Madam Sibyl appointment an hour early, thereby losing an hour of sleep. Several of her clients were unusually resistant to her advice, and it didn't take any clairvoyance to foresee a rather disastrous financial failure for Mr. Harper, the notions merchant, if he persisted in speculating in South Dakota "gold finds." It was Annie's belief the Homestake mine was the only profitable enterprise in that region and that Harper would do better, if he insisted on speculating in metals, by investing in one of the newly opened Leadville, Colorado, silver mines. She wondered if he would have been more willing to take her advice if he knew her as Mrs. Fuller, Edward Stewart's daughter, rather than Madam Sibyl, pretend clairvoyant. *Probably not.*

She worried that if she couldn't figure out a way to "retire" Madam Sibyl and begin to make the income she needed as plain Mrs. Annie Fuller, financial consultant, that this would be a insurmountable barrier to ever marrying Nate. She couldn't ask him to jeopardize his own career, which was just taking off, by linking his future with a fortuneteller, pretend or not. And what about the possibility she might never be able to have children? How would he react if she told him?

Last fall when she asked Nate to slow everything down and give them both time to get to know each other better, she'd been delighted that he agreed. Now she worried that the limited time he spent with her and his scrupulous attention to the proprieties meant he was falling out of love with her. When he'd asked her to help out in the investigation of the anonymous letters, she'd hoped this would bring back the old closeness. However, except for the short ride home from his office nearly a week ago and their argument on Sunday, he'd made no effort to spend any time alone with her since their trip to Ocean Beach.

Tonight had proved no exception. A letter from him was waiting for her when she got home, canceling his plans to come over, citing the demands of the trial. Nate did apologize in the letter for his behavior Sunday and asked, by way of amends, if she and Laura would like to attend the theater with him this coming Saturday. But even that didn't make her feel any better, since it meant that once again they'd have no time alone and nothing of importance would be discussed.

She paused at the top of the last flight of stairs leading down to the kitchen and leaned against the wall, listening to the voices coming up from below. She could hear that Barbara Hewitt was there, with Jamie and Dandy, whose yips added to the conversation at intervals. The voices of Kathleen and Beatrice intertwined in counterpoint, and the rich chuckle was undoubtedly from Esther Stein. Why couldn't she be content with this group of people as her chosen family? Did she really need a husband and children to be happy?

A skittering sound caught her attention, and Dandy appeared at her feet, with his wide doggy smile, his curled pink tongue, and brown bulging eyes, alight with triumph in nosing out her presence. She leaned over and scooped him up, letting him lick her face as she went the rest of the way down the stairs and into the kitchen.

"Oh Mrs. Fuller, it's you! I wondered why Dandy started going up the stairs. He must've heard you coming." Jamie took Dandy from her and went to the back door. "Come on, Dandy, time for you to go out. Be a good dog and be quick about it."

Barbara Hewitt moved up behind her son, putting her hand on his shoulder. Dandy sprinted out into the darkness, growling. In a moment, they could hear the growls give way to barking and the thumping sound of Dandy leaping up against the back fence.

"You stay here, Jamie, until we can see what is going on," Barbara commanded.

Kathleen ran over with matches and quickly lit the lantern that sat by the back door, handing it to Annie.

Annie hushed Beatrice and Esther, whose exclamations of concern were making it hard for her to hear, and then she went up the few steps into the back yard, holding up the lantern. She shouted, "Who's there?"

There was no moon visible, and a thin mist obscured the stars, but she could see the flash of white from Dandy's front paws and forehead near the back gate. When no one responded to her shout, she moved slowly forward. Dandy ran over to her and then quickly back to the gate, where he stood and started growling again. The light from the lantern revealed that his head and ears were stretched forward, his fur was standing up in a ridge along his back, and his small crooked tail stuck straight out. As she got closer, she could see that the growls, deep in his chest, shook his whole small body. Abruptly, his body relaxed, as if a string had been cut. Then he began to sniff loudly at the gate as he had Saturday night, but this time he continued to sniff along the whole back fence.

"What is it boy? Who was there? Are they gone?" Annie whispered, following along behind him.

"Annie, is everything all right? Should I get Mr. Chapman or Mr. Harvey?" Barbara called.

"Dandy seems to think they're gone. Don't you, boy?" She said this more loudly, hoping it was true.

After Dandy completed his inspection of the fence, he did his business, and Annie and he returned to the kitchen.

Barbara told Jamie to take his dog upstairs and start to get ready for bed. Once he was out of hearing, she said, "I don't know what has gotten into Dandy, Annie. I am sorry. He has started spooking at every-thing, even on walks. Last weekend, Jamie said he almost got away from him, barking and lunging at some man who was walking past him on Ellis. Earlier this evening, when I took him out for a walk by myself, I practically had to drag him down the street; he kept turning around and trying to go home. I finally gave up at Leavenworth."

Kathleen, who had returned to drying the dishes, turned around with a plate in her hand and said, "I think he is being a good guard dog, and we need to listen to him. There's something fishy going on. Last few weeks, every time we let him out during the day, he goes right to that back gate to sniff. Didn't use to do that. Most times, he seems satisfied there's nothing wrong, and he trots back to us, happy as you please. But some mornings, he sniffs and sniffs like something, or *somebody*, has been standing there."

"It's that man, the one who attacked our Miss Laura. I just know it." Beatrice added, her usually cheerful face looking strained. "I want to know what you're doing to find out who he is and put a stop to it." Beatrice's gray bun at the top of her head bobbed emphatically as she nodded at Annie.

"Now, Mrs. O'Rourke, you know our Annie's done all she can, making sure that Laura doesn't go anywhere by herself, asking the patrolman to walk the alley a couple of times a night on his beat," Esther Stein said, putting down her knitting.

"Do you think it's the man who met Miss Laura at Woodward's Gardens the afternoon she went with us?" Kathleen asked. "A tall fella who seemed to upset her so."

"Do you mean Mr. Timmons, the older student who was with her at San Jose Normal school?" Barbara frowned. "I thought she'd decided he couldn't be the one."

"Mr. Timmons? Was that his name, Ma'am?" Kathleen put down the plate and began to wring her hands.

Annie, puzzled at this sign of distress, said sharply, "Yes, Seth Timmons. Kathleen, what's the matter?"

"Oh dear, I thought there was something odd," said Kathleen. "But it didn't seem my place. Monday morning when I brought Miss Laura her tea and toast, she gave me a letter. Asked if I could mail it later in the day when I went to do the shopping. Not just put it in the front basket with the rest of the mail like she usually does."

"And the letter was addressed to Mr. Timmons?"

"Yes. The address was the school on Pine and Larkin. That's what eased my mind. I thought it must be important school business. But then this afternoon, she got a letter in return from him. When I mentioned this to her, she seemed all excited like, as if she wanted to get the letter before anyone else saw it. He knows where she lives. What if he's the man what's been hanging out in the alley upsetting Dandy?"

Annie had to raise her voice to be heard above the general commotion that Kathleen's statement caused. "If it will make any of you feel better, Nate already went to see Mr. Timmons, and he agrees with Laura that he probably isn't the man who attacked her. But I have been meaning to tell you all that there is another young man we need to be on the lookout for. He was one of Laura's older students this fall. His name is Buck Morrison, and he gave Laura a good deal of trouble. She got a glimpse of him this Saturday, so she knows he is now in town."

She shared the description Laura had given her of Buck: seventeen, tall, straw-blonde hair, blue eyes, a small mustache. "Laura said that he has the build of a farm-boy and usually is dressed in jeans but that when she saw him this Saturday, he was all decked out in a flashy, royal-blue waist-coat and tight-fitting black wool pants and coat."

"I'll be sure to tell Patrolman Stanley tomorrow about him. And about Mr. Timmons. Just in case," Kathleen announced.

"And I will tell Jamie that we both need to be on the lookout for these men when we are walking to and from school. Especially in the evenings when we walk Dandy. But now I need to go up and make sure that Jamie is studying and not bothering the Misses Moffet." Barbara chuckled, "They always have a treat for both him and Dandy when he goes by their room."

As Barbara went over to the stairs, she paused and said, "Kathleen, would you like to have Dandy sleep down here with you for a few nights? I'm sure if I explained why, Jamie wouldn't mind. I know he couldn't really protect you, but he would certainly wake up the house trying."

Kathleen's dark curls bobbed as she shook her head no. "That's so kind of you, Mrs. Hewitt. But I will be just fine. I will make sure the doors and windows are locked up tight at night."

Mrs. O'Rourke spoke up and said, "Don't you worry none. She's a smart girl. Sleeps with the dinner bell beside her bed, case of fire, so's I'm sure she'll ring out if she thinks there's any danger." Then she turned to Kathleen and admonished, "And you just put off taking the ashes out back until the sun's up and Dandy's been out to check out the yard, you hear me!"

"Indeed I do, Mrs. O'Rourke." With that, the young maid gave a saucy curtsy. "If you will all excuse me, I'll just go and start getting the fireplaces cleaned out and set for morning."

After saying good night to Barbara Hewitt, Annie crossed over and took a chair next to Mrs. Stein, whom she hadn't had a chance to talk to in some days. She loved sitting in the kitchen at this time of night, surrounded by the smell of sourdough as Beatrice worked the starter into the flour for tomorrow's bread; the click, click, click of Mrs. Stein's knitting needles, creating, as if by magic, a new sweater for one of her grandchildren; and the calming sight of Kathleen going about her tasks.

"Well, my dear. Just what do you think of our Miss Laura, writing to this young man?" Mrs. Stein looked at Annie over the small silver wire-framed glasses she had taken to wearing in the evening. "I could see it wasn't a complete surprise to you."

Annie sighed and said, "From what she's told me, Seth Timmons was rather a knight in shining armor for her this fall. While she *says* she is determined to forgo any romantic entanglements and concentrate on furthering her education, I imagine it would be hard not to be flattered."

"But why did she write him?" Beatrice asked, demonstrating that she was closely following Annie's conversation with Esther.

"She probably wanted to apologize to him for her brother arriving on his doorstep to check up on him. I am sure it is no secret to any of you that Laura had a terrible fight with Nate on Sunday when she found out about his visit to Timmons' place. I'm sure their fight could be heard throughout the house."

Esther smiled. "Well, we did gather that there was some disagreement. But I think that your Mr. Dawson was quite right to go see this young man, and I don't suspect he'll be happy to know they are corresponding."

"No, and I will need to speak to Laura about this, make sure she hasn't arranged another meeting with Timmons. She must understand that she needs to be very careful until we are absolutely sure we have found out who attacked her."

"You will tell Mr. Dawson about the letter," Esther stated flatly, again giving Annie one of her admonishing looks.

"Of course, or get her to tell him herself." Annie sighed. "I hate getting in the middle of their disagreements. He has every reason to worry about her, given the events of the last month. But he does have to remember when he talks to her that she isn't a small child."

"Does Mr. Dawson know about this young fellow? Did you say his name is Buck?" Esther asked, taking up her knitting again.

Annie went on to tell them briefly of Laura's troubles with Buck during the fall term and how Seth, at Hattie Wilks' request, looked out for her. This brought up the question of Hattie's death, and they asked what progress she was making with her investigations at Girls' High.

"Actually, there are a few interesting avenues to follow-up," Annie said. Her dissatisfaction with Nate's decision not to come this evening returned. She said rather bitterly, "There is a lot I would like to look into further if Nate would bother to find the time to consult with me or let me act on my own. After all, he is the one who asked for my help. But now he is too busy to come and discuss what I have learned."

Esther frowned and said to Annie, "Not able to come tonight as planned? Well, Herman says the case he is working on with Cranston could be the making of him. Some important state constitutional issues.

You don't fault him for taking his career seriously, do you?"

"No, I don't. That would be hypocritical on my part," Annie replied, unable to keep her irritation out of her voice. She stood up and went over to the sink and fiddled with the geraniums on the sill of the window. "But isn't it his responsibility to find out who the anonymous letter writer is as well? There are things he needs to know."

"Can't you just write to him?" asked Esther.

"Yes, but it's not the same. I need the time and privacy to really discuss the case with him. At one time, he would have been glad of the excuse to…but…now, I just don't know what he wants." Annie stopped, appalled at how much she had revealed of her fears, fighting back tears.

Beatrice came up behind her, put her arm around her waist, and said softly, "Oh, dearie. It seems to me he's already said what he wants, dear man. You're the one who said no."

Esther, who had come up to stand on the other side of her, gently wiped her cheeks with a handkerchief and said, "Annie, Beatrice is right. You told me that you asked him to withdraw his suit, agree to go forward slowly. Seems to me, it's not what Nate Dawson wants that's the issue but what you want. Maybe it is time for you to figure that out."

Chapter Thirty-two
Saturday evening, February 7, 1880
"As in the case of nearly all the burlesques, the original story serves only as the motive for introducing as absurd relations, a number of shapely people in handsome costumes..." —*San Francisco Chronicle*, 1880

Annie looked over at Laura, who stood on a stool in front of the mirror in the corner of Annie's bedroom, having some last minute alterations made on a dress Annie had given her. *She is so beautiful. I wish her mother was here to see her*, Annie thought suddenly.

Laura smiled at her and said, "I can't thank you enough for giving me this lovely outfit. My brother is so *stupid*. Asking us to the theater without a thought of what I would have to wear." She blew Annie a kiss while Miss Millie Moffet sewed a ruffle of light rose satin at the hem to accommodate Laura's greater height. "Miss Minnie and Miss Millie are truly angels to make it over to fit me in two days. I am such an Amazon next to you, Annie."

Annie, who was drying her hair by the fire, saw Miss Millie smile but knew she wouldn't say a word. It was her sister, Miss Minnie, who was the talkative one, and she was still upstairs in their attic room making some last minute changes to the gown Annie was going to wear.

"I am glad to see the way Miss Millie has been able to alter it," Annie replied, "adding the satin to the bodice and the flounce of the underskirt. It looks an entirely different dress and very becoming on you. I rather think the rose works better with your darker coloring."

Thank heavens the Moffets weren't working on a deadline for one of their usual clients, who were among the wealthiest San Francisco women. The two sisters were already being incredibly generous in making a day-time suit for Laura, asking only that she read aloud to them in exchange. Laura would be chagrined if she had any idea the amount these two elderly ladies from Natchez usually got for their tailoring. In fact, it had taken some effort on Annie's part to persuade them to take any money at all from her for these last-minute alterations on both of their outfits.

Annie wondered what Nate would think when he saw his little sister all dressed up. The sight of Laura looking so happy was certainly helping to lift her own spirits. The Misses Moffet had cut the front of the bodice, revealing a discreet amount of Laura's chest, just enough to make the dress appropriate for evening wear. With her dark hair pinned up and threaded with a dusky pink ribbon that echoed the excited blush on her cheeks, she looked stunning.

A soft knock on the door was followed by Kathleen's entrance. When she saw Laura, she threw up her hands and said, "Oh my, don't you look grand."

"Indeed she does, Kathleen," said Esther Stein, who'd followed Kathleen into the increasingly crowded room. "You will turn some heads this evening, young lady."

Coming over to where Annie stood by the fireplace, Esther gave her a swift kiss. "Here, I brought you both some gloves. They've always been too tight for me. Goodness knows why I held on to them. But I thought they would be just the thing for tonight."

"Oh, Esther, silk. How elegant. Thank you," said Annie. "Do check to see which pair fits Laura best. She was just saying that her brother didn't understand exactly what going to the theater entails for a woman. All he has to do is add a silk tie to his usual formal wear, and he'll be ready to go."

When Esther raised her eyebrows at this comment, Annie laughed. "I know, I know. I shouldn't complain. This is rather a treat. But if you will remember, last summer when Nate invited me to the theater, he cancelled at the last minute. I just hope he shows up, or everyone's work to get us ready will be for naught!" Annie deliberately kept her tone light, not wanting to reintroduce the subject she had been thinking about constantly since Esther and Beatrice had their "heart-to-heart" with her—whether or not she was ready to move forward in her relationship with Nate.

Esther smiled and patted her on her cheek, then went over to Laura and Miss Millie. Kathleen came up to Annie and held out her dressing gown, which she put on over her corset and petticoat, and directed her to a chair, saying, "And you, ma'am, sit, so I can do up your hair. Miss Minnie says she will be down with your dress in about ten minutes."

As Kathleen began deftly to arrange Annie's red-gold curls, she said very quietly, "Please, ma'am, I need to tell you something. I was hoping I would get a chance to speak to you when you were alone, but I don't think it should wait."

"Good heavens, Kathleen," Annie responded in a whisper. "What's wrong? Go ahead, Esther and Laura aren't listening."

"Right before dinner, my brother Ian stopped by the kitchen on his way home. He'd been off with David Chapman and Jamie trying to fly a kite up on Lone Mountain."

"That was nice of Mr. Chapman."

"Yes, although I think he hoped Mrs. Hewitt would accompany them."

Oh poor Mr. Chapman. No wonder he's made no headway with Barbara. Not when there's the possibility that her legal husband is alive somewhere. Annie shook off this melancholy thought and told Kathleen to get to the point.

"Well, Ma'am, he told me that he and Jamie have a plan to catch the man who attacked Laura. When Jamie's ma told him about keeping an eye out for that Buck or any man who seemed to be hanging around the house, he got it into his head that someone's been following them home from Clement Grammar. They think it must be the same person who's been hanging out in the alley, disturbing Dandy so."

"Oh dear, did Ian say why Jamie thought someone was following them?"

"He says Jamie can feel someone's eyes on the back of his head as he walks down the street. You know boys. They've got themselves all worked up to be heroes."

Annie smiled. "So what is their plan?"

"Ian said next Wednesday he's going to run up from his school, you know he goes to Eighth Street Grammar, and get up to Clement in time to hide out at Foster's store where he could see out the window if any man seemed to be following all of you. He figures if he saw someone that he'd follow and see where the man goes, maybe figure out where he lives."

Annie turned to look at Kathleen, who sharply told her to sit still. Staring forward again she said, "That's actually a clever idea. Someone could be loitering up Leavenworth a block, and we'd never notice them. But Ian shouldn't do it. What if Buck, or whoever, caught him at it?"

"That's what I told him. I said that this was something for Mr. Dawson to take care of and under no circumstances should he carry out the plan."

"Do you think he will listen to you?"

"I don't know. And what if Jamie tries to catch the man himself? I thought Mrs. Hewitt should know. Will you tell her?" Kathleen then said, "There, your hair is done."

Annie stood up and turned to Kathleen. "Thanks so much for letting me know. I'll tell Mrs. Hewitt tomorrow, and I will bring it up to Nate tonight if I get a chance. But here's Miss Minnie. I need to get dressed if I don't want to be late. You go on down to answer the door; Mr. Dawson should be here any minute."

Sitting in the first balcony of the California Theater and looking around, Laura's senses were overwhelmed. The heady aroma of perfume and flowers overlaid the distinct smell of gas emanating from the lights mounted on the walls and the gigantic chandelier that hung down from the ornate ceiling nearly four stories above her. The voices of the two thousand people in attendance rose to a deafening roar above the discordant sounds of the orchestra musicians tuning their instruments. Every wall was heavily decorated with gilded plaster frescos that framed murals portraying familiar San Francisco landmarks. The limelights at the edge of the stage were so bright it was if the San Francisco Bay panorama painted on the curtain was in full sunlight. Yet all the beauty of the building's interior couldn't out-shine the visual splendor of the crowd itself. Like enormous flowers, the women's dresses were of every color and hue imaginable; the plain black formal dress of the gentlemen who were present only enhanced the vibrancy of the women's outfits.

"Laura, does this meet with your expectations?" Annie leaned across Nate to touch her arm.

"Oh, my, it exceeds my expectations." Laura tucked her arm through Nate's and said, "Thank you so much for bringing us. I have never seen so many people, so beautifully dressed, in one place in my life. However did you get the tickets? I feel like I could lean over the railing and practically touch the stage."

"My new law partner, Cranston, has season tickets. But he is too caught up in the trial, so he offered them to me. I didn't realize it was a Burlesque, though. I'm not sure how Mother would feel about me taking you to see something this…"

"Unrefined? Scandalous?" Laura laughed. "Seems to me that after centuries of civilized people going to see plays by Shakespeare where the female roles were played by men, no one should complain about women playing men's roles. Turnabout is fair play, I say!"

Annie laughed and said, "Bravo, Laura. I did read that Miss Roseau is excellent in the role of Manrico, the wandering minstrel. Since both Laura and I are quite familiar with what a woman's nether regions look like when encased in bloomers and hose, I would think that it is you, Nate, who might find this opera too risqué."

Laura felt her brother stiffen.

Then he took a deep breath, laughed weakly, and said, "In that case, I beg both of you to keep the information that I attended such a play from my parents. I wouldn't want them to lose respect for me."

Laura gave his arm another squeeze then looked at the large playbill Nate had bought for her when they entered the building. Amused by what she read, she said, "This should be fun. Listen to this. The playbill says that the 'Ill Treated Il Trovatore or The Mother, The Maiden, and The Musicianer' is 'an Original Burlesque…founded on a famous though somewhat confused Opera.'"

Laura continued to read the synopsis of the play silently, looking to see if she recognized any of the songs but mostly trying not to eavesdrop on what Nate and Annie were saying to each other. She'd gathered from Annie that last Sunday, after she had left them alone in the small parlor, they'd disagreed about the next step to take in their pursuit of the anonymous letter writer. She hoped they were working that out.

At Annie's urging, she'd apologized to Nate this evening for her own loss of temper on Sunday. She came down to the parlor first and found him looking very stiff and handsome. He'd obviously remembered, for once, to go to the barber's. His collar and cuffs were starched to perfection, and he'd even put in the heavy gold studs their father gave him as a graduation present from college. Because he was quick to compliment her on her dress and didn't say a word about the neckline, she got up the nerve to tell him about writing Seth Timmons. She explained that she thought Seth should know right away about her seeing Buck and that he had written back a short note. He'd reported that he hadn't found out yet if Buck was in the city when she was attacked, but he planned to travel to Cupertino Creek this weekend to see what he could learn. Nate frowned but didn't say anything. Thankfully, Annie had come into the room right then, which seemed to have rendered him speechless.

Annie certainly looked beautiful tonight. Miss Minnie had told Laura she was wearing a dress the Steins commissioned as a Christmas present for her, but they had altered it for evening wear by making it sleeveless, changing the neckline, and putting on a train. The material for the bodice was a dark royal-blue velvet, with a slightly lighter shade of satin for the skirt. The neck was square and cut quite low, but it and the straps that fit over her shoulders were trimmed with blue lace. The train was also satin, edged in embroidered velvet. As Laura had watched Nate's first reaction to Annie's appearance, she remembered reading once that the hero "devoured" the object of his love with his eyes. She'd never quite understood what that meant before.

"But Nate, Frazier is our best lead."

Laura's attention was caught by the frustration in Annie's voice.

"I said I would interview him, and I will," Nate replied, sounding equally frustrated.

"Della Thorndike mentioned that he played in this theater's orchestra. Maybe at intermission, we could find him and talk to him together." Annie picked up the playbill, and Laura could see her point at it. "See, there is an intermission between the two acts."

She missed Nate's answer when there was a brief spurt of applause. She noticed that the orchestra had gone quiet and that there was a man in formal dress standing to the side of the stage next to the curtain. The noise of conversation began to sputter out, and a few stragglers moved hurriedly towards their seats. Laura leaned forward, scanning the house to take it all in once more before the curtain went up. Then she noticed a face that looked familiar across from her on the second balcony. Della Thorndike, her blonde hair nearly white in the gaslight, was standing near the end of an aisle, apparently waiting to take her seat.

Laura turned to Nate and whispered, "Look, there's Miss Thorndike. The teacher I am working with who leads the Normal class at Girls High. Isn't she elegant?" Reaching over Nate to touch Annie's arm and get her attention, Laura whispered, "Annie, Miss Thorndike. She looks wonderful in that grey-blue silk. I wonder who she's with? Oh, there, that must be her escort."

Laura froze. All the gaiety of the evening evaporated for a moment as she watched Andrew Russell bow politely and help Della Thorndike into her seat.

Chapter Thirty-three
Late Saturday evening, February 7, 1880

"The character of 'Arlene' is taken by Miss Eme Roseau, and affords us another opportunity of noting what rapid process this gy-rating gy-url is making in the walks and talks of burlesque." —*San Francisco* Chronicle, 1880

We always try to be Quite Good, sang Laura in a surprisingly strong alto. "I loved that song by the chorus, although the performers were a little old to be playing girls at a finishing school. You went to a ladies' academy, didn't you, Annie? Tell me, did you ever spontaneously break out into song and dance?" She then squealed as the hansom cab made the turn onto O'Farrell, and she started to slide off the cab's small pull-down seat.

She had insisted in taking this seat across from them, apparently finding the precariousness of her position all part of the fun. Nate was pleased that his sister had regained her high spirits after the shock of seeing Andrew Russell at the theater. He wasn't sure what upset her the most, that Russell was out with another woman so soon after Hattie's death or that the woman was Della Thorndike, someone she'd previously quite liked. Laura flickered in and out of his vision like a magic lantern show as they passed the gas lamps evenly spaced along their route, and he mused on how grown up she looked in her fashionable gown. At the same time, watching her treat the carriage as some sort of carousel ride, he was reminded of what she was like at age ten when he took her to the county fair.

As they arrived at the boarding house, Nate turned to Annie and said quietly, "Would you be willing to stay behind for a few moments, after Laura has gone in? You were correct; we do need some time to talk about what you have learned at Girls' High and what we should investigate next."

After he had ushered Laura into the waiting arms of a sleepy Kathleen, who had obviously waited up to hear all about the evening, Nate told the hansom driver to wait and climbed back into the carriage. He brought back a shawl Kathleen had handed him, and he now wrapped this around Annie's shoulders. The night was clear and very cold, and she was wearing a light lace wrap, which, while very pretty, did nothing to keep her warm.

It also did nothing to keep Nate from the fantasy he had been obsessed with all evening. He kept imagining placing his fingers on that exposed place at the base of her neck, where her pulse beat, and slowly caressing her exposed skin, down, down, until he could slip his hand under the lace and velvet and cup her breast. *Damn it. Can't I even control myself in a public carriage?*

"Thank you, Nate. I was getting a little chilly," she said quietly, pulling the shawl more tightly around her shoulders. "I do want to tell you how much I enjoyed this evening. The program was unbelievably silly, but I think we all needed something to lift our spirits. The music was the best part; I'm not surprised that Laura has some of the lyrics memorized already. I had no idea that she could sing so well. I wonder if I could talk her into joining the choir at a local church. It would be a good way for her to meet some new friends, maybe take her mind off of…well, you know."

Nate nodded. "Yes, I know. Thank goodness the play started right after she saw Russell and she could get caught up in the production. I thought at first that she was going to drag me across the theater to call him out, right then and there."

Annie put her hand on his arm. "At least she'd calmed down a bit by intermission, although I don't think it was particularly diplomatic of you to point out that she, like Russell, was having a night out."

"I can't believe I said that. I thought she was going to insist we leave, she was so overcome with guilt. I swear she was never this volatile before. I mean, certainly when she was little she could be full of high jinx one minute and in flat despair the next, but I thought she had grown out of that. I don't know what to do."

Annie took his hands in hers. "Just give her time. Between the attack in the alley, Hattie's apparent betrayal of their plans for the future, and her questions about Hattie's death, it's natural she is having trouble regaining her equilibrium."

Nate's heart swelled. Annie could always make him feel better, calmer, more optimistic. *She is the source of my equanimity,* he thought. He said, "Annie, I can't thank you enough for taking Laura under your wing. I'm not sure I could sleep at night if I didn't know she was in your protection."

"Don't thank me. I have quite fallen in love with your little sister, so even if…" Annie stopped and brought out her handkerchief.

Nate felt an unexpected sense of dread. "What, Annie? What is the matter? What do you mean? 'Even if.'"

Annie looked away from him, then she continued, her voice artificially cheerful. "Why, Nate, even if she has your temper. Now, let's discuss the case. Principal Swett is returning to town next Thursday, and Hoffmann is going to need his office back. I have scheduled a meeting with him on Wednesday, and I need to know if there is anything you want me to ask him."

There it was again, Annie's sadness and her unwillingness to tell him why. *I promised not to push her, but damn it, why doesn't she trust me enough to speak her mind?*

"Nate, what's wrong?"

Now it was time for Nate to pretend nothing was amiss. He knew enough not to open up this topic sitting in a hansom cab, with the driver listening in. So he replied, "I guess I am just having trouble understanding the motives of the letter writer. The notes don't actually ask for anything."

"Like they would if it were a straight case of blackmail? You're right. None of the letters have actually demanded, 'Give me a job or I will make this charge public.' If Hattie was the victim of the same anonymous letter writer, they did get the satisfaction of seeing her resign, but then it was Laura who got her job. Could this explain why Laura was attacked?"

Nate thought about this a moment. Then he said, "Yes, I suppose that is possible. Didn't she say that the man who grabbed her said something about 'ruining my life?' He could have been referring to losing Hattie's job to Laura. Seems rather far-fetched to me. Did you find anyone who applied for both Hattie's position and Mrs. Anderson's this fall?"

"No, I haven't, but I would need access to Clement Grammar records to be sure. Another thing to track down." Annie paused and then said with hesitation, "There is the theory that Laura came up with tonight."

"That Russell is after Hoffmann's job, perhaps with Della Thorndike's assistance?" Nate shook his head. "Do you think there could be any truth to that? I thought it was just her searching for another reason to blame him for everything." Nate remembered how emotion had temporarily distorted his little sister's face as she pointed across at Russell and whispered her accusations in Nate's ear. It was troubling to see how angry she got whenever Russell was involved.

Annie sighed. "I don't know. I suppose it makes some sense. If Hoffmann were dismissed from his position as Vice Principal, Russell would be a prime candidate for the job, and I imagine that the Girls' High position pays better. Della could be the source of the gossip about Hoffmann and Mrs. Anderson. It is even possible that someone else sent the letters to Hattie last fall and that gave Russell the idea."

"Emory came up with a new theory this week," Nate said. "He's decided that a corrupt political boss, Chris Buckley, might be behind all this. According to him, Buckley, who owns the Alhambra Saloon, is starting to make a move to control the local Democratic Party machinery. Oddly, he's blind. Makes me wonder if he drank too much of his own product. Anyway, according to Emory, since Buckley has boasted that he will take back the school board from the Republicans, he might be using some disaffected teacher to cause a scandal, hoping to use that in the next election. Emory has opposed him within the Democratic Party. He figures that might be why he was targeted by one of the anonymous letters."

"That's very interesting," Annie said, leaning closer, and Nate put his arm snugly around her waist. She continued. "Della Thorndike told me Kitty Blaine's father owns a saloon and is also a powerful man in Democratic politics."

Nate loved watching Annie trying to figure things out. She was so quick. He asked, "Have you run across anyone else with political connections who might be working with Buckley if Emory is right? I am having trouble seeing Miss Thorndike or Russell in that role."

"I don't know. Wait a minute. Do you remember what I wrote to you about Mrs. Washburn, the Scottish janitoress at Girls' High? How vindictive she was about Hoffmann? What if one of her relatives is active in the Democratic Party, maybe works for this blind boss Buckley. My, my, 'Blind Boss Buckley,' that's a name you wouldn't forget."

Nate laughed. Then he felt Annie shiver beside him. He tucked the shawl more tightly around her and said, "Much as I want to, I can't keep you here any longer. Look, I can at least ask Emory if he knows of any connections between Kitty Blaine's father and Buckley."

"And I will see if I can learn anything more about Mrs. Washburn," Annie added. "But don't forget you promised to track down Frazier. I still think he is the most likely candidate if we are dealing with a vengeful teacher, even if he turns out to be the pawn of some politician."

Nate nodded but didn't know how he was going to comply given how busy Cranston was keeping him. Hoping to change the subject, he said, "By the way, make sure you let me know right away if Seth Timmons contacts Laura again and has any news about Buck Morrison."

"Oh Nate, I didn't tell you. There are signs that whoever did attack Laura might still be hanging around the boarding house. Dandy is acting oddly. And we know how effective that little nose of his can be in

ferreting out wrong-doing. In addition, Jamie thinks someone is following him and his mother and Laura when they walk home. He and Ian,
Kathleen's brother, got up some scheme to try and figure out who it is."

"I hope you've put a stop to that!"

"Well, Kathleen told Ian not to do it, and I will tell Barbara Hewitt
about the plan tomorrow. But I think the faster we can figure out who is
writing the anonymous letters and learn for certain that there is no
connection between those letters and the attack on Laura, the better. It's
one thing to see all this as part of the usual political shenanigans or even
the petty jealousy of a single individual, but…"

"But what?" Nate again felt her shiver and pulled her closer.

Annie turned a very troubled face toward him. "I keep thinking
about Hattie's last words. Laura is still convinced Hattie was trying to
tell her that she felt coerced into resigning her teaching position and
marrying Russell. But if her exact words were 'no accident' and 'pushed
me, pushed me,' then it *is* possible she was physically pushed down the
stairs by someone. Someone who let her lie there, bleeding to death. We
could be talking about someone whose mind is so disordered that they
would be willing to commit murder, and that someone could still be a
threat to Laura."

Chapter Thirty-four
Sunday evening, February 8, 1880

"Valentines! Just Received, Direct From London...Also, Full Lines of AMERICAN VALENTINES Sentimental and Comic." —*San Francisco Chronicle*, 1879

"Mr. Dawson isn't going to stop by this evening?" Kathleen asked, drying her hands on her apron after putting the table linens into the metal washtub that stood next to the kitchen sink. Monday was always wash day, which meant she needed to put the whites in the tub to soak the night before.

"No. It's that dratted trial," Annie said. "It seems to be taking up all his time. I know this could be Nate's big opportunity, helping Cranston with the defense in such a well-publicized case. But since he is in court most days, he has to spend nights and weekends trying to keep up with all his other responsibilities for the firm, wills and such, plus doing any legal research Cranston needs."

Beatrice, who was putting wood chunks into the fire box, stood up and frowned at her, saying, "Well, at least he was able to take you to the theater. I hope you were properly appreciative."

Beatrice was doing all the baking for the next day because the kitchen would smell strongly of blueing once the washwoman started scrubbing away in the morning. As Annie rocked slowly in the kitchen rocking chair, her muscles twitched in sympathetic memory of the rigors of that dreaded chore. Her brief experience as a domestic servant was one of the reasons she was willing to lighten Kathleen's workload by paying for a laundress, as well as for Tilly's part-time help, even though it strained the boarding house budget.

She had spent much of the day reading newspapers and financial reports, and she now had a slight headache, partly the result of not getting enough sleep last night. She'd lain awake for hours, anxiously going over her conversation in the carriage with Nate, trying to convince herself that no one, not some political boss or disappointed teacher, could possibly have a reason to kill Hattie or pose a threat to Laura. But she was haunted by the echo of Hattie's last words and the image of Laura sitting forlornly in this very rocking chair after the assault.

"Well dearie, off in a dream world, are you?" Beatrice's fists were on her waist, and her head was cocked. "Kathleen says you stayed out in the carriage for ever so long with Mr. Dawson. You wouldn't mind telling us just what was going on, would you?"

"Oh, Beatrice, you can be sure Mr. Dawson was the perfect gentleman. All we did was talk." Annie chided herself for never being satisfied. She'd wanted to speak with Nate about the investigation, which they did. She just wished that they'd had longer together. And more privacy. Maybe then she would have gotten up the courage to tell him what she had meant by "even if." That even if she couldn't have children, having Laura as her sister-in-law would help ease her heartache. But that would mean telling him about her miscarriage and bringing up the subject of their future together. *And I can't be expected to bring that sort of subject up sitting in a carriage or in the parlor with the door open, can I? I just want some time completely alone with him. Is that so much to ask?*

She glanced up and saw that Beatrice was still looking sharply at her. Embarrassed, she bent down and picked up the old black cat, Queenie, who had been rubbing up against her foot, saying, "It was very nice of Nate to invite us, and Laura and I had a lovely time. The singing and dancing were very professional."

Kathleen chimed in. "Miss Laura said the leading lady was all dressed up as a man, wearing pantaloons and stockings so's you could see her calves, plain as day! I'd feel mighty uncomfortable going with my Patrick to such a spectacle."

Annie laughed, her mood lightening as it always did in Kathleen's presence. "Well, Mr. Dawson was a trifle embarrassed when he realized he had brought us to a burlesque. But having been to a number of similar productions in New York, I can testify it was really quite tame."

Annie went on to provide Beatrice and Kathleen with details about the play. She described the costumes and had them chuckling at the convoluted plot. She then told them about Laura's reaction when she saw Hattie Wilks' fiancé, Russell, at the theater.

"Besides being angry at him, she decided she was being heartless because she was out enjoying herself less than a month after her friend's death. I took a chance and asked her what Hattie thought about deep mourning and if she would want Laura to dress all in black and lock herself away from society. She thought for a moment and then said Hattie got quite cross at people who made a big show of their grief. But I am afraid she wasn't as easily persuaded to forgive Mr. Russell or his companion, Miss Thorndike."

Beatrice, who'd just put two loaves of bread and a pan of rolls into the bake oven, snapped the door shut and said, "Well, dearie, I have always thought you Protestants have a difficult time of it. Your aunt, God rest her soul, spent all that money fitting herself up in black after your uncle died, and she didn't even allow herself the little cheer that playing whist with her friends would have provided."

Annie, forced by poverty and her in-law's expectations to wear nothing but black for five years, tended to agree with Beatrice. She said, "Well, men have always had it easier. A dark arm-band, which I think Russell was wearing last night, is considered perfectly respectable for anyone but a recently departed wife. I do think that having a large party to celebrate a loved one's death, the way the Irish do, is a sensible alternative to spending the next year reminding everyone of your loss."

"Celebrate? Drink themselves silly's more like it," exclaimed Kathleen. "The last wake I went to, my uncles lost several days' wages from 'celebrating' the death of some good-for-nothing they barely knew. But I am glad that Miss Laura was able to enjoy herself at the theater. She practically sang her way up to bed last night."

"Hush now, I think I hear someone coming down the stairs,"

Beatrice interjected.

The three of them looked over at the opening to the back stairs in time to see Dandy tumble into view and then race twice around the kitchen, his small white feet scrabbling on the linoleum flooring. He finally skidded to a halt in front of Annie, his brown eyes widening when Queenie arched up in her lap and hissed. This was a well-practiced ritual, however, the two animals having come to an understanding six months ago. Dandy simply sat down, his white chest thrust forward, and watched as the cat circled twice and resumed her position, purring contentedly. The terrier then trotted to the back door and waited to be let out by Barbara Hewitt, who appeared through the doorway alongside Laura.

"Mmm. I could smell the bread baking all the way upstairs," Laura said, going over to the kitchen table and putting down a large brown package. "Annie, Kathleen said I could borrow this pair of scissors from your study. Is that all right?"

"Of course. I use them for cutting out newspapers, so you might want to wipe them off first." Annie then addressed Barbara, saying, "Wednesday is my last day teaching at Girls' High since I don't really think there is anything more I can find out looking through the personnel records. Do you happen to know anything more about the janitoress, Mrs. Washburn, or her family? She is clearly Scottish, but I wondered if there is a Mr. Washburn, or a brother, she is close to."

Barbara stood back as the black and white terrier pranced in and sat down to scratch his ear with his back paw, looking like he was going to fall over in the process. She replied, "I believe one of the other teachers suggested that there wasn't a Mr. Washburn, nor had there ever been. I don't know about any family or even if Washburn is her maiden name."

"That's interesting," Annie said. Aware that discussing a woman's decision to take on a name not her own was probably a little too close to home for Barbara, she hurried on, "I just wondered because it occurred to me that she might have male relatives active in politics."

"Are you talking about the janitoress from Girls' High?" asked Laura. "Barbara, do you remember last Wednesday when we were leaving Clement and you mentioned how odd it was she was over at my school?"

"That's right. I'd forgotten. Who was she talking to?"

"Our janitor, Mr. Ferguson."

Annie said, "Would Mr. Ferguson be Scottish, by any chance?"

Laura chuckled. "Since he calls me a 'bonny lass,' I always assumed he was. He's very chatty, will talk your ear off. But I have trouble imagining him writing some anonymous letter or threatening Hattie, for that matter. He was quite nice to me when the news about Hattie's death made the rounds at Clement. Someone must have told him she was a good friend because he came up and gave his condolences."

Annie wondered how close he was to Mrs. Washburn, but she decided not to pursue the question any further, hearing the sadness that had crept into Laura's voice as she told them about the janitor's condolences. Instead, she said, "What's in the package?"

Laura cut the string that tied the parcel, saying, "Kitty, my practice teacher, had a wonderful idea last week. Saturday is Valentine's Day, and we are going to make valentines for all the students and hand them out on Friday. She and I went down the street to the stationers on the corner of Geary and Larkin during lunch time and got the supplies. I thought I would practice tonight and make a few to be sure we have enough material."

Beatrice came up to the table to watch as Laura peeled back the brown paper, revealing large stacks of white card stock, red colored paper, and white perforated paper that looked like lace. There were also several bottles of glue, red and white yarn, and rolls of pale pink and red ribbons. Finally, at the bottom, there were at least ten copies of *Godey's Lady's Book* and *Harper's Bazar* magazines.

"Miss Laura, how beautiful. But all this must have cost you a fortune," Beatrice said, leaning over and touching the ribbons delicately with her index finger.

"Oh, Mrs. O'Rourke, I know. I feel like a child on Christmas morning." Laura held one of the sheets of embossed lace paper up to the oil lamp in the center of the table. "Kitty's father gives her a simply enormous weekly allowance, and she insisted we buy all this. She *said* we were economizing because all of this cost much less than if we had bought the ready-made valentines at the stationers. This way we can make cards that are special for each child."

Annie gently put Queenie onto the floor and went over to the table to see better. Exchanging valentines had been all the rage in the late sixties when she was at school, but she had never made one before. Nor had she ever gotten one from a sweetheart. She had a sudden desire to make one for Nate, to see how he would respond.

Barbara and Laura both went up to their rooms, leaving Annie alone in the kitchen with Beatrice, almost too tired to walk up the two flights of stairs. Beatrice was waiting for the last of the baking to come out of the oven, but she had shooed Kathleen off to bed. She would need to get up even earlier than usual to get the breakfast going before the washerwoman arrived. The kitchen was nice and warm, and the yeasty smell of rolls was tantalizing. Annie was content to rock slowly back and forth, not thinking about anything and letting Beatrice's idle chatter flow over her. Suddenly, she noticed that Beatrice had stopped talking. She looked over to where the older woman sat at the scarred wooden table in the center of the room and saw that Beatrice was again frowning at her.

"Annie, have you taken the advice Mrs. Stein gave you t'other evening to heart?" Beatrice pushed a strand of her grey hair up and tucked it back into her bun at the top of her head.

Annie came abruptly wide awake. For a second, she contemplated pretending she didn't know what her dearest friend was talking about. But Beatrice deserved better from her.

She sighed and said, "Yes, of course I have, and maybe she is right. If I love him, and oh I do, Beatrice, I do love him, there shouldn't be any obstacle to us being together, but...I don't know..." Annie stopped.

Beatrice shook her head. "You don't know what, dearie? If loving him is enough?"

Annie looked down and stroked Queenie, who was once again in her lap.

When she didn't say anything, Beatrice continued. "You're frightened to trust a man again, aren't you? What a talking-to I'd give your father if I had the chance. He should never have let you marry that Mr. Fuller. Your sainted mother would've seen through him."

Annie imagined Beatrice shaking her finger at her father and wondered if she were right. If her mother had still been alive, would she have rushed into marriage with a man who turned out to be a weak, foolish drunkard? She was only now beginning to forgive her father for not recognizing how miserable she'd become in her marriage and for leaving her financially dependent on John. Maybe, if she had been honest with her father and hadn't tried so hard to hide the fact that John was downright cruel at times, he would have changed his will before he died. Maybe, if he'd been honest with her about his own ill health, she'd have been better prepared to handle his unexpected death. Pride, her own and her father's, had kept both of them from confessing the truth to each other.

"Bea, I'm not going to tell you that the problems in my marriage to John haven't made me reluctant to marry again. But, as I keep reminding myself, Nate isn't John. I believe that with all my heart. He *is* the man I want to spend my life with. But Beatrice, what I am afraid of is… what if it turns out…what if…"

Queenie, showing her disgust at Annie's sudden tears, leaped down to the floor and stalked silently over to her basket next to the stove.

Beatrice handed her a soft, clean kitchen rag and pulled a chair up next to her, patting her on the back as Annie wiped her eyes. She said very quietly, "Annie, my dearest, what is really wrong?"

Closing her eyes tightly as she did when she was small and needed to confess her deepest fears to her mother, Annie said, "Bea, what if it turns out I can't have children?"

"Why ever would you be worried about that?" Beatrice sounded surprised. "Just because you didn't get pregnant with your first husband?"

"But I did," Annie burst out, her eyes flying open to see the concerned warmth in her friend's clear blue eyes. She then haltingly told Beatrice about her panic when she discovered her pregnancy and how she'd waited to tell her husband until she could talk to her father. How she'd hoped he would know how to protect her and her unborn child from John, who was spiraling out of control. "You see, my father had gone up to Maine on business. I was going to tell him when he got back to New York. But he never came home."

Beatrice whispered, "And what happened to the babe?"

Annie, gathering her strength to get through this last part of her story, said slowly, "I know I've told you that John hid my father's illness from me, so that I would have no chance to see him before he died. What I never told you was that when I got the terrible telegram from John telling me that my father was dead and buried, I miscarried. No one ever knew. No one but my young servant."

"Oh Annie, and the way that Miss Laura's friend's died has brought it all back again, hasn't it? My poor child. But surely you don't think losing a baby, the way you did, means you'll never have another?" She patted Annie on the shoulder and said, "At least you know you can get pregnant."

Annie, remembering Beatrice's own childlessness, felt awful. She said, "Beatrice, please, I didn't mean to cause you any pain. Let's not talk about any of this anymore. I was being silly."

"Don't be daft, Annie. I made my peace long ago with never being able to have a child of my own. And what would I have done, trying to raise young ones alone after my husband died? But I still don't understand why you would think that young Mr. Dawson wouldn't want to marry you if he knew about your miscarriage."

Annie sat for a moment. "It's not the miscarriage so much, although I always feel awkward when I mention anything about my past with John, as if it were in bad taste to bring him up to Nate."

"Then what is it?" Beatrice asked.

Annie didn't answer for several moments, then she said, "Bea, if you had known that you couldn't have children before you married, would you have told your husband-to-be?"

It was Beatrice's turn to pause. "I suppose I would. Secrets of any kind aren't a good way to go into marriage."

"That's what I think as well. I know Nate wants children. He's said as much, and he was so charming with Mrs. Anderson's little boy the other day. But I am afraid that he will think differently about me, about marrying me."

"And are you saying you aren't sure you want children?" Beatrice leaned in as if she were trying to read into Annie's heart.

"Oh Bea, no. I long for children. For Nate's children." Heat rose to her cheeks as she experienced the strong wave of mingled desire and longing that came every time she thought of Nate and bearing his child.

"Well, my dear, I am having trouble understanding just what the problem is, then. The women I know who had children after a miscarriage could fill a church hall!"

"But you haven't thought about my mother. Beatrice, I'm the only child she had. My father always said how much I physically resembled her. What if that's true and the poor mite I lost was my only chance? I have to tell Nate. And I'm afraid that…that he won't want me then."

Beatrice reared back and just shook her head at her.

Annie sat and thought a minute, then smiled. "I know what you are going to say. If I were playing Madam Sibyl and a female client said what I just said, I would say that if she really thought that the man she loved wouldn't want to marry her under those conditions, maybe she needs to re-examine whether that is the man she wants to marry."

"And, if you were that woman, what would you tell Madam Sibyl?"

"That I do trust Nate. That he's proven over and over he is willing to accept me just the way I am, Madam Sibyl and all. And this shouldn't be any different. And if it is, well, better to learn that now than later."

Beatrice smiled warmly at her, and Annie felt suddenly lighter.

"And there is one more thing you need to know, my dear," Beatrice said. "I was still working for your aunt and uncle when your parents lived with them and helped deliver you right in this very house. The doctor at your birth told your dear mother that having any more children would 'be the death of her' because of her bad heart and all. That's why she didn't have any more children. There's nothing wrong with your heart, so you've been worrying your poor self over nothing."

Chapter Thirty-five
Monday afternoon, February 9, 1880

"NO NAME SERIES - 'Is the Gentleman Anonymous? Is He A Great Unknown' --Daniel Deronda. A Masque of Poets including Guy Vernon, a Novelette in Verse, 1878

Classes had gone well today, and Laura was feeling pleased with the success of Kitty's first forays into solo teaching this week. Ever since their shopping trip together, Kitty's shyness with her had eased, and Laura enjoyed the talks she had with her every day at noon as they dissected the students' progress and planned the next day's lessons. Such a difference from the loneliness and frustration she'd felt teaching by herself in the one-room school at Cupertino Creek. She also looked forward to her walks home with Barbara and Jamie, hearing the young boy talk about his day, sharing stories with his mother about the funny things their students said and did.

Laura's good mood was punctured by a feeling of irritation when she saw the janitor, Mr. Ferguson, hovering near the door to the teachers' room, mop in hand. She'd already decided to seek him out after classes on Wednesday, when she had more time to try teasing out information on his relationship with the janitoress at Girls' High. But this afternoon, she didn't have time. It was nearly twenty past three, and she needed to check her mailbox before she went out to meet Barbara and Jamie, who were probably already waiting for her in front of the school.

Consequently, she gave him only the slightest smile as she passed, saying, "Good day Mr. Ferguson. I would love to talk, but I'm running late."

"Aye, little lassie. All you young ladies are always in such a hurry. Be careful you don't slip." He winked and turned away from her, pushing the mop on down the hall.

For once, there wasn't anyone in the teachers' room, and Laura walked quickly over to her box, which seemed empty except for a book. She assumed it was the *Elementary Geography* that Jamie's teacher had promised to loan her, but when she saw the title of the book, she gasped.

It was the *Masque of Poets,* and its black cover with the delicate flowers etched in red brought back such sharp memories of Hattie that she was momentarily stunned. The slender volume, which featured anonymous poems by prominent authors, had been published her last year at San Jose, and she and Hattie had bought copies for each other for Christmas. She'd spent long pleasant hours arguing with Hattie over what authors might have written which poem, although they both had agreed that the one entitled *Pilgrim* was probably by Thoreau. But how had the book come to be in her mailbox? She knew her copy was right beside her bed, since she had read "Carpe Diem," one of her favorite poems, just last night. *Was it possible this is Hattie's copy?*

She quickly opened the book to see if the inscription she had written to Hattie on the title page was there, but she was disappointed to discover that this page had been torn out, only a ragged edge of paper sticking out of the binding. *Surely Hattie would have taken better care of her copy.* The book looked well worn, and she could see that something was tucked into its center. *Maybe it's a note from whoever put the book in my mailbox.*

Opening to the page, she saw the object was a pressed rose, its formerly scarlet petals blackened by age. Then with horror, she saw that the rose was marking Hattie's favorite poem, "Husband and Wife," a haunting verse about a loveless marriage and a woman who died at childbirth. Now the words were nearly obliterated by splashes of dark red ink, dripping down the page like blood.

Later that evening, Laura came down to the kitchen to work on her students' valentines. The room was crowded, with Beatrice supervising Tilly, the young Irish girl who helped out, in the correct way to clean the iron skillets and Kathleen standing at the ironing board pressing the newly washed table linens. In addition, Barbara Hewitt sat in the rocking chair with Dandy in her lap, and Annie welcomed Laura to join her at the kitchen table.

Laura was glad of the company, still feeling shaken by her discovery of the book of poems. She hadn't wanted to talk about it with Barbara in front of Jamie on the way home, and now that she'd had time to reflect, she wasn't sure she should bring it up at all to anyone.

The explanation could be very innocent. Maybe Hattie had loaned it to another teacher who thought Laura would appreciate having it as a remembrance of her friend. But then, why the torn-out inscription and no note saying who it was from? And why pick the poem about a mother's death to deface?

What if the person who had been behind the anonymous notes to Hattie knew Laura was looking into the causes of Hattie's death? Russell knew; she had foolishly told him. Could this then be a sort of warning to let well enough alone? And if not Russell, who else might be behind it? One of the teachers at Clement Grammar? Or a girl from the Greek study group? Surely not the janitor, Mr. Ferguson? Suddenly, the way he hovered outside her classroom and showed up when she visited the teachers' room felt sinister. What if he were the anonymous letter writer? Maybe Hattie had brought the book to school with her and he'd stolen it. Maybe he'd already used its blood-like defacement to frighten Hattie and was now doing the same thing to Laura?

She shivered but then chided herself for using such a small incident to turn the janitor into some dreadful villain. In truth, anyone could have come in during the day and put the book in her box, even Buck. She'd read out loud from the *Masque of Poems* numerous times to her students at Cupertino Creek. He could have bought a copy, thinking that he would give her a nasty shock by putting the defaced book in her box. Just the sort of infantile joke he'd play.

Whether the book's appearance was innocent, threatening, or simply a mean joke, it still unsettled her, and it felt good to be surrounded by friends in the boarding house kitchen, doing normal things, with the comforting smell of pies baking in the oven. She would concentrate on the task of making valentines.

Laura carefully cut out a heart from a piece of red paper and placed it on the front of the rectangle of white card stock. She then picked up an illustration of a small boy on his knees playing marbles, which she'd cut out of one of the *Harper's Baazar* magazines. When she put it on top of the heart, she saw that she would have to trim the picture a little in order to make it fit. This would be perfect for her student Frank Spencer. She was pleased he hadn't tried the trick with the marbles again, figuring this meant she had passed muster with him. Kitty had promised to come up with a brief message for each of the students that they would write on the back of the cards. Annie admired the finished product, and Laura began to feel her frazzled nerves relax.

The bell attached to the front door jangled, causing Dandy to bark, and Laura instinctively jerked. As Kathleen left the kitchen to go see who was there, she turned to Annie and said anxiously, "It's 8:30. Was Mr. Dawson planning on coming by this evening?"

"No, he told me on Saturday he probably wouldn't have time to see me all week."

Beatrice chimed in. "It can't be Mr. Harvey, forgettin' his key again, because Kathleen already had to let him in right before supper. I don't know what is wrong with the man. He can't remember a simple thing like putting the door key in his pocket when he goes out of the house."

When Kathleen reappeared, Laura was shocked to see Seth Timmons coming into the room behind her. He stopped abruptly, his grey eyes blinking as they adjusted to the well-lighted kitchen. He stroked his dark mustache and looked slowly around the room. His height and broad shoulders were accentuated by the low kitchen ceiling, and Laura was struck by how very masculine and dangerous he seemed in this domestic setting.

"Ma'am, this is Mr. Timmons, come to see Miss Dawson," said Kathleen to Annie. "I thought you might think it better, late as it is, if he spoke to her down here. I hope I did right."

Annie rose and walked over to him, holding out her hand. "Mr. Timmons, I am pleased to make your acquaintance. I am Mrs. Fuller, and I own this boarding house." She then introduced him to the rest of the women in the kitchen and said, "Would you like to take a seat? Kathleen would be glad to fix you a cup of tea."

As Seth began to move towards the kitchen table, Laura felt a strong inclination not to have her interaction with him the object of scrutiny by her well-meaning friends. She quickly stood up and said, "Mr. Timmons, I expect you have come to tell me about what you found out on your visit down the peninsula. Would you like to take a short stroll around the back yard while you tell me what you learned? The kitchen can be awfully hot when there is baking going on."

With irritation, Laura saw him glance over at Annie as if for her approval, then silently blessed her friend when she said, "What a good idea, Laura. Why don't you take Dandy with you? Here, take this shawl. It should keep you warm enough."

The terrier seemed to understand he had become the designated chaperone. With his short crooked tail whirling, he trotted to the back door, which Kathleen unlocked. Laura put a match to the lantern that hung by the door and carried it out into the chill dark of the yard. She turned and saw Seth speaking quietly to Annie before following her out.

Laura placed the lantern on the bench underneath the apricot tree and sat down. Seth came over and stood in front of her until, uncomfortable having to look up at him, she patted the seat beside her and asked him to please sit. "I will get a crick in my neck otherwise, Mr. Timmons."

When he sat down, leaving a decorous space between them, she got right to the point. "Did you learn something about Buck that proves whether or not he could have been the man who attacked me?" *Or put that book of poems in my mailbox?*

Seth cleared his throat. "He could have been, since he came up to San Francisco the first week in January. I talked to Mr. and Mrs. Spears. They sent their regards, by the way, and said to tell you their twin boys miss you. According to them, there were rumors that Buck's father was so angry at him for being on the losing end of a fight that he sent him up to San Francisco, 'to make a man of him.' The Cupertino Creek postmistress told me that Buck is working for his uncle in a North Beach warehouse. I have the uncle's name, and I'll track him and Buck down. I came by because I promised your brother to let you all know as soon as I had any information. Wouldn't like him to think I was holding anything back."

Laura, again feeling guilty that she had ever suspected him, pointed to Dandy, who was now sitting on Seth's lap and being scratched around the ears. She said, "You do realize, don't you, that Dandy's approval of you completely clears you of any suspicion that you were the man who attacked me."

When Seth looked startled, she explained. "I expect the only reason Kathleen brought you down to the kitchen was to see how Dandy reacted. I can assure you that if he had taken exception to you, there is no way you would have been permitted to sit out here alone with me. Dandy is the one who rescued me from the attacker."

She leaned over and patted the terrier on his round head. "Didn't you, boy? Ran right up and launched yourself at the big, bad man. Made him run away. Everyone in that kitchen is convinced that the attacker is still hanging around the house, because some mornings Dandy has a fit, growling and sniffing along the back gate."

She then told him about Jamie's theory that Dandy was unwilling to go on walks because he felt the need to guard the house and Jamie and Ian's scheme to see if anyone was following them on the walk home from school. "Jamie's mother and Kathleen, Ian's sister, quickly squashed that idea."

"Is there any particular pattern to when Dandy gets upset?" Seth asked.

Laura was surprised she hadn't thought of that. "I don't know. That's a good question. I'll ask. Anyway, it might not even be Buck who attacked me."

Silencing the voice in her head that said Nate would disapprove, Laura then told Seth about the anonymous letter writer. She explained that there was a possibility that the same person who sent the letters to Hattie, threatening to expose her relationship to Russell, could have been Laura's attacker.

Seth, who had been looking down at his Stetson held loosely in his hands between his knees, straightened to look directly at her. "Are you saying that Miss Wilks was the target of someone who wanted her job and that they attacked you when you got the job after she resigned?"

"That is one explanation. However, since other teachers have also been targeted, the letter writer could be someone expressing a general dissatisfaction, or, as my brother's client suspects, it might be someone with a political agenda."

"So that is what you meant when we last talked and you said you thought someone had hounded Miss Wilks to death. Didn't the threats stop when she quit teaching?"

"As far as we know. But what if they didn't stop? What if there were more letters, more threats? What if Russell was behind the letters? If he didn't really want to marry her? If he thought she was ruining his career, he could have taken up where the original anonymous letter writer left off. Pushed her until she felt the only option was to...to take her..."

"Take her own life? Damn it, Laura, I can't believe you would think Hattie Wilks would throw herself down a flight of stairs on the off chance she might die. She wasn't stupid, and she was no coward. You were her closest friend. How could you know her so little?"

Stung by his anger, she said bitterly, "I *thought* I knew her. But I guess I was wrong. She changed completely, her goals, her values, everything. I *thought* I was her closest friend, but maybe I was wrong about that as well since she didn't even tell me about Russell or the threats, much less that..." Laura stopped. She would not reveal Hattie's final secret, no matter how angry and betrayed she felt.

Seth abruptly stood up and said, "Don't be such a child, Laura. Seems she was right not to tell you, given the way you've reacted. Seems all you cared about is your future, your plans, not her happiness. Hattie Wilks was a wonderful, caring woman, and she was always a good friend to you."

If he said anything else, Laura didn't hear it as she buried her face in her hands, sobbing. She felt a fleeting pressure on her shoulder, but she just turned away, whispering "Please go," and in a moment, she felt rather than saw him leave her side. Eventually, she became conscious that Dandy, who'd jumped up beside her, was digging frantically at her arms, trying to reach her face.

"Dandy, no, leave her be." Annie's soft voice accompanied the removal of the dog's sharp nails.

Laura, still hiding her head in her arms, whispered, "Is he gone?"

"Yes, my dear." Annie stroked her hair.

Laura looked up. The night air chilled her hot, wet cheeks.

Annie handed her a handkerchief and said, "Mr. Timmons came running into the kitchen and said he'd lost his temper and that you were crying. He was quite upset. Wringing his poor hat in his hands. I tried to get him to stay in the kitchen, but he mumbled something about you asking him to leave, and he practically ran out the back gate."

Seth's words reverberating in her head, Laura confronted the reality she had been trying to deny for the past month. She had been a miserable friend to Hattie: selfish, jealous, petty. That last Saturday in Hattie's room, instead of supporting her friend, telling her how happy she was for her, all she'd done was whine. No wonder Hattie hadn't confided her troubles to her. Seth was right. She was nothing but a spoiled child, and she didn't deserve Hattie's friendship or his respect.

Annie broke into those thoughts. "Laura, dear. Tell me what happened; I am sure it isn't as bad as it seems right now."

Laura shook her head, not trusting her own voice. Then Dandy, who'd been wriggling in Annie's arms, lunged over to Laura's lap, put his paws on her chest, and triumphantly began to clean her tears with rapid, delicate licks of his tongue. Laura didn't know whether to laugh or cry, so she threw herself into Annie's arms and did both.

Chapter Thirty-six
Wednesday afternoon, February 11, 1880

"A primary teacher has extra expenses that a servant has not, such as car-fare (to many), $3 per month; extra clothing, to appear well-clad in and out doors, $5 per month; total $8; which, taken from the $46.50, leaves $38.50, which is $13 less than a good girl in the house gets." —*San Francisco Chronicle*, 1879

Annie put down her pen, finished recording the grades from the quiz she had given today in her last bookkeeping class. While she'd only substituted for Hoffmann four times, the students still clapped for her when she said her farewells. She now understood why people dedicated their lives to the teaching profession. Nothing had prepared her for the boost of energy she felt each time students excitedly thrust their hands into the air when she asked a question or laughed when she came up with an example that amused them. Then there was the gratification when the students' faces lit up once they finally grasped a concept that had eluded them.

"Mrs. Fuller, may I come in?" Thomas Hoffmann stood at the open door to the office.

"Of course you may. It's your office after all. Do sit down, although I feel I should get up and switch sides of the desk, a sort of a changing of the guard," Annie said.

"No, no. Swett will return on Friday. That's when I will come happily back to my domain among the file cabinets." Hoffmann sat down across from her. "I hear such good reports from the students about your lectures that I am afraid they will be sorely disappointed in my return."

Annie smiled and put the quizzes and her records in a folder, which she handed to Hoffmann. "I was just thinking how much I enjoyed the class. Here are the last assignments and my grades. Feel free to call on me in the future if you need a substitute. If I am not otherwise engaged, I would be very glad to help out. However, I do have a few follow up questions I would like to ask before I go."

"Certainly. I hope you feel you have made some progress." Hoffmann leaned forward and fiddled with the folder she'd given him. "I am glad to have the chance to speak with you. I wanted to mention something that rather disturbed me. Andrew Russell, the vice principal at Clement Grammar, stopped by to see me after class on Monday. He was agitated because he said one of Clement's teachers, a Miss Dawson, indicated there were anonymous notes directed at teachers floating around the district."

"Oh my. Did he say why he wanted to know about them?" Annie asked.

"Russell was vague. He made it sound like he was just curious. I passed it off as inconsequential and made some joke about the dangers of teaching in an all-female school. I assume that the teacher who told him must be some relation to Nate Dawson, the lawyer who is representing Emory."

"Yes, she is his sister. I am glad you didn't confirm the story. The fewer people who know, the better."

"I figured as much, and I didn't want to say anything that might compromise you and your investigation. I did wonder if maybe he, or someone he knew, was on the receiving end of similar letters and that is why he asked."

"That's possible. Let me ask Mr. Dawson what he thinks we should do." Annie mentally chastised Laura for having said anything to Russell. *Thank goodness he didn't mention Hattie's name to Hoffmann.*

"But you said you had some questions. I do want to help," Hoffmann said.

"Certainly, I wondered if you could tell me a little bit more about Mr. Frazier, the other applicant you interviewed for Mrs. Anderson's position. Anything that would give me an idea if he could have been angry enough about not getting the job to write a letter."

Hoffmann leaned back in his chair and put his hands behind his head. "Well...he was very personable, but it was my impression that he was looking for a full-time position, so I assumed he might not take the job if I did offer it to him. He did have very good credentials, but I could see Miss Thorndike's point that his lack of theater experience would be a problem, given that a third of the classes we are offering in the arts are drama-related and..."

"Miss Thorndike pointed that out?" Annie interrupted him. "That's odd. She implied this was your objection to him and that she felt he was the better person for the job."

Hoffmann looked startled. "Are you sure you heard her correctly? In fact, I remember she suggested that the girls' parents might be uncomfortable with a man in charge of the drama club."

Annie, wondering if this inconsistency meant she couldn't trust Della's other pronouncements, decided to see if her suggestion that Hoffmann was interested in Kitty Blaine held any truth. She said, "Miss Thorndike does seem particularly concerned about the issue of propriety regarding male professors and female students. Perhaps that is what she meant when she discussed Frazier with me. Have you had any problems with parental concern over your sponsorship of the science club?"

Hoffmann chuckled. "Beyond the fact that a couple of the parents can't understand why their daughters would have any use for this subject? I do send a letter home to the parents at the start of every year detailing the benefits of each of the clubs to young women who plan to go on to teach, which is what I found works best at quieting their fears. I don't mention that both the science club and the Greek study group are important for those girls wishing to attend the California University."

Thinking about Nate's lack of enthusiasm for his sister's plan to pursue a law degree, Annie asked, "Are there many girls who are interested in going on to the University? Miss Thorndike mentioned that one of her Normal class students, Kitty Blaine, was planning on doing so." Annie watched Hoffmann's face carefully, looking for any sign that he might find her line of questioning uncomfortable.

"Oh, I expect she might be interested in going on. She is definitely bright enough but awfully shy. She doesn't say much inside or outside of class, and she certainly hasn't confided in me what her future plans are or if her mother or father have any difficulty with her extra-curricular activities."

"So her parents haven't contacted you?" Annie asked, noting that he didn't seem aware that Kitty Blaine's mother was deceased.

"Heavens no. She did stop attending the science club this winter, but I think I remember her saying something about it interfering with her practice teaching. I'm not really sure I even know which school she was assigned to, but Miss Thorndike would, and I believe that Miss Blaine is still attending Russell's Greek and Latin study group."

Hoffmann frowned, and he said, his voice sharpening, "Has there been a complaint against me from Kitty Blaine, or any other student, beyond the vague intimation of impropriety in the letter the school board received?"

Annie shook her head and said, "No, Mr. Hoffmann. I didn't mean to give that impression. It just occurred to me that it would be fairly difficult to accuse any of the Girls' High teachers of wrong-doing within the classrooms themselves—too many witnesses—but that after school activities would be more likely to lead to gossip."

He appeared to relax and said, "That makes sense. It is one of the reasons I have the science club meet in the lab and keep the doors open. Of course, this upsets Mrs. Washburn, who thinks I am doing it on purpose to make it difficult for her to clean the room."

"Yes, Mrs. Washburn didn't seem too fond of any of the extra-curricular activities when I spoke to her," Annie said.

Hoffmann smiled. "No, not at all. And I did mean to mention to you the wrangle she and Mrs. Anderson got into over Mrs. Washburn 'tidying-up' some of the student art projects. I suspect she resents the fact that her brother, who I believe works at Clement, gets paid more for keeping up a slightly smaller building. I can't blame her. One of the unfair aspects of a pay scale that differs for men and women."

Annie nodded, for the first time feeling some real sympathy for the janitoress. But the familial connection between Washburn and the Clement janitor was worth pursuing to see if Ferguson had political ties. Maybe Nate's client, Mr. Emory, would know.

Later, as she started on the short walk to Clement Grammar, she admitted to herself that, except for discovering she rather liked teaching, she wasn't sure her two weeks at Girls' High had revealed much of importance, certainly nothing that led to the discovery of the letter writer. Beyond a number of vague suspicions, there was nothing concrete. *Some private investigator I turned out to be.* It was interesting that Della Thorndike was proving an unreliable source of information regarding Hoffmann. Annie wondered if this had any connection to her friendship with Russell and the possibility the letters were designed to remove Hoffmann as an obstacle to Russell's career path. She really wished Laura hadn't said anything to Russell. If there were any chance at all that Russell was involved in the anonymous letter-writing campaign, this could put Laura in danger. The image of Hattie, broken and bleeding on the floor, came unbidden to her mind.

Chapter Thirty-seven
Wednesday afternoon, February 11, 1880
"The progress of art education in this country is readily seen in the improved styles of Christmas, Easter and Valentine cards." —*San Francisco Chronicle*, 1881

There was a thump outside in the school hallway, and Laura looked up nervously from her desk where she was carefully pasting four small red hearts onto the front of a card. Yesterday evening when Barbara mentioned that the literature club wasn't meeting today, Laura told her that she and Jamie should go on home without her since Annie would be stopping by to accompany her after work. She'd expected to spend the time finishing up the valentines with Kitty. The plan had been to complete the decorating today, so all they would have to do before Friday was copy over the little poems that Kitty had been working on for each girl and boy. However, Kitty hadn't shown up at Clement this afternoon so Laura was all alone in her classroom. Consequently, as the school emptied of students and then other teachers, she felt more and more uneasy.

The westward setting sun was still bright against the houses across the street, but this left the classroom in deepening shadow, and Laura debated about turning up the gaslights. She assumed that Mr. Ferguson was still cleaning somewhere in the building. He had probably been the one to produce the thump. Given the suspicions she had been entertaining about the janitor and the defaced book of poems, this wasn't a pleasing thought at all.

Laura checked her watch again. It would be an hour before Annie was due to arrive. She now wished she'd gone home with Barbara and Jamie. She realized that since the attack on her in the alley, she had never been completely alone, except when she was in her own room. Even then, she had the comfort of knowing that there were numerous other people in the boarding house, just a shout away. She was now reminded unhappily of the months working in the one-room schoolhouse, dreading the afternoons she would have to walk by herself to whichever home she was currently boarding at, dreading the appearance of Buck at the schoolroom door. Another thump, this time next door, made her jump. What if Buck *had* found out where she lived and where she worked? What if he had left the book in her mail box? Attacked her in the alley? Furious at her for rejecting him. Furious at the humiliation of being beaten up by Seth.

And would Seth even bother to track Buck down? She hadn't heard from him since Sunday, and she probably never would. Everyone had been extraordinarily kind, not asking questions about what had gone on in the back yard, why he'd left so precipitously. Barbara did mention the next morning that, in her experience, former Civil War soldiers like Seth, who'd never settled down and who couldn't control their tempers, should be avoided at all costs.

Yet, no matter how Laura thought about what happened, she couldn't bring herself to blame Seth. She'd written and torn up letter after letter trying to explain, trying to justify, and finally trying to apologize to him. Seth, while obviously in love with Hattie, had still been able to put his personal feelings aside and wish her the best in her engagement to Russell. Why hadn't Laura been able to do the same? She'd pretended to be pleased when Hattie asked her to be maid of honor, but Hattie would have seen right through her. It was Hattie she really needed to apologize to, and she would never get that chance.

Laura got up, opened her door, and looked down the hallway. All the rooms were dark but her own. She turned the key that increased the gas output in the overhead chandelier, brightening the room considerably, and returned to her desk. Since it was only four in the afternoon and Annie might not be here for another hour, she should be able to get all the cards decorated if she just concentrated. Picking up the valentine she was working on, she used the black pen to draw four lines from the red hearts to come together at the hand of a small child, turning them into four heart-shaped balloons. This made her smile. Kitty would like this. Working on this project was bringing her closer to the younger woman, and Kitty's absence today worried her. She must be quite ill not to have even sent a note.

Della Thorndike, who'd stopped by right after classes to tell her that Kitty was missing from her Normal classes this morning, snidely commented that she'd never missed a day of class during her entire teaching career. Laura expressed the hope that this meant Miss Thorndike had the good fortune of excellent health, rather than the willingness to expose her students to illness in order to come to work. Della had smiled icily, stating that she was indeed fortunate to come from good Anglo-Saxon stock. She then swept away, no doubt to console her *dear friend*, Vice-principal Russell. Laura wasn't sure whether the remark about her heritage was directed at Kitty Blaine, with her Irish beauty, or Laura's own Shawnee ancestor. In either case, it cemented Laura's feeling that Della Thorndike wasn't nearly as nice as she'd appeared at first.

A noise from the hallway again startled her, and when she looked up, there stood Kitty Blaine, hesitating in the doorway.

"Oh, Miss Dawson, I am so glad you are still here. I…I didn't want you to think I was abandoning you. I…" Kitty's voice faltered.

Laura got up and ran to her, shocked at the young woman's appearance. She was hatless, her hair was windblown, and she didn't appear to have a coat with her. Her cheeks were bright red, and when Laura took her bare hands into her own, she found them freezing.

"Kitty, good heavens, where's your coat and gloves? You've never come out without them, not on a cold day like today, not even in a carriage."

Kitty shook her head and whispered, "I walked. I sneaked out of the house. I just had to see you. Oh Miss Dawson, my father…my father has pulled me from school. *My life is ruined.*"

Seeing that the poor girl was barely holding back tears, Laura drew her into the classroom, shut the door, and sat her down on a student desk in the back row. She went and got her own cloak, putting it around Kitty's shoulders. Sitting down next to her, she took up the girl's hands again to rub some warmth into them. "Now, tell me exactly what has happened," she said.

What poured forth was a jumbled and tearful story of an anonymous letter that Kitty's father had received the previous evening, his towering anger and bewildering questions about her relationship to the vice-principal of Girls' High, and her fear he was going to marry her off to someone she called "that ghastly Patterson boy."

Just as Laura was about to ask Kitty for details on the letter, which seemed to have started everything, they both jerked around at the sound of a knock at the classroom door. The door swung open into the hallway, and there stood Annie. Laura had never been so relieved to see anyone in her entire life.

As she alighted from the hansom cab she had squeezed into with Laura and Kitty, Annie noted how the neighborhood adroitly straddled the edge of Nob Hill, with its mining and railroad barons, and the Western Addition, home to the prosperous middle class of the city. Located on the corner of Gough and California, Kitty Blaine's home was a Queen Ann-styled mansion with a plethora of bay windows, pitched gables, and elaborately carved trimming, all done in a tasteful soft grey. The most striking part of the residence, however, was a three-story tower, topped by a conical roof that should have sported a pennant and a fair maiden waving from the highest balcony.

"Kitty, I can't believe this is where you live," Laura exclaimed as they started up the long flight of marble stairs leading to the front door. "It's like a fairy castle. I've never seen a more beautiful house."

Annie saw Kitty blush and tried to ease the girl's embarrassment by asking how long they had lived there.

She replied that they'd moved in only a year earlier. "It took two years to finish, and Father let me sit in on the planning sessions with the architect. It was fascinating. I would have preferred something simpler, but my father was determined to out-do his rival, 'Nobby Clarke,' who is building a grand house in Eureka Valley."

At the top of the stairs were a wide portico and a set of double wooden doors with insets of beveled glass. Kitty, clearly apprehensive about coming home, hesitated when they reached the doors. Annie finally reached out and pulled the bell cord. After only a few minutes, the doors opened to reveal a black-suited butler, whose austere countenance broke into a warm smile when he saw his young mistress.

In a cultured English accent, he said, "Miss, would you and your friends please come in? Shall I inform your father that he has visitors?"

"Yes, Jenkins. We will be in the front parlor."

Kitty led Annie and Laura into an elegant room on their left. The setting sun streamed into the west-facing windows, bouncing off the rose-patterned carpet, the highly polished oak wall panels, and the red-marble fireplace and turning the room into a glowing jewel. Annie thought that Kitty should be commended for so successfully transform-ing her father's wealth into a home of exquisite taste.

Annie knew from the research she had done on Nate's client that Peter Blaine, Kitty's father, was a well-to-do saloon keeper with a financial stake in Irving Emory's City of Hills Distillery. Blaine was one of the many Irish immigrants who had come to San Francisco and made their fortune. In addition to owning several saloons and shares in the distillery, he also owned the construction company that had won the prize contract to build San Francisco's new City Hall.

This afternoon, when Annie heard about the anonymous letter Kitty's father had received accusing his daughter of having been seduced by Thomas Hoffmann, she explained to Kitty that it was very possible that her father, like Emory, was the target of some sort of smear campaign. Annie knew this letter represented a significant break-through in the investigation, and she readily agreed when Kitty insisted that they come home with her immediately to tell her father about the other letters.

Kitty explained, "My mother died at my birth, and I am all he has, so he's over-protective. It's not that he isn't proud of his humble origins, but he wants more for me. He worries constantly that without a mother to guide me, I will be led astray in some fashion. The sooner you assure him there isn't the slightest bit of truth to that letter, the better, for both of us."

As Annie listened to Kitty calmly show Laura around the parlor, exhibiting the pride of a woman who had helped choose every piece of furniture, every color, every tasteful ornament, she marveled at the maturity the young girl had demonstrated so far in this crisis. Her father had nothing to be ashamed of, at all. He'd done an excellent job of raising her.

The door to the room flew open, and a man barked, "Katherine Therese Blaine, what do you mean by giving your maid the slip? The woman has been in hysterics for the past hour. I know you said she was a silly fool, but I had no idea, blathering on about you eloping. Where in tarnation have you been?"

Annie completely revised her preconceived notions about Peter Blaine. She'd been picturing him as a tall, polished man of wealth, along the lines of one of the Irish Silver Kings. She'd imagined pomaded hair, slicked back, a luxuriant mustache and beard, a gold watch chain straining across a padded stomach, and hands all soft and manicured. Instead, the man who stood before her was short and clean-shaven, with thick red curls that stood out wildly about his head and traveled down into narrow side-burns. These wild curls framed a broad, reddish-hued face, high forehead, and bright blue eyes. There was a gold chain across his chest, but his hands were rough and the size of a stevedore's, and his shoulders and chest gave the impression he was someone who could still do a solid day's work of physical labor.

At last, those bright blue eyes turned on Annie and Laura, and Peter Blaine said, "And who might you two ladies be?"

In the practiced voice of a hostess, Kitty said, "Father, this is Miss Laura Dawson and Mrs. Fuller. Miss Dawson is the woman I have spoken to you about who kindly permitted me to do my practice teaching with her at Clement Grammar. Mrs. Fuller is her boarding house keeper and friend and has accompanied me home at my request. I went to Clement Grammar this afternoon because I had promised to help Miss Dawson make valentines for the children in her class today, and I felt I must explain to her why I wasn't able to honor my promise."

Her father frowned. "And what of your promise to me that you wouldn't go out unescorted, young miss?"

Kitty stood up straighter, her chin rising, and she said, "Father, that is for us to discuss later. It is important that you hear what Mrs. Fuller has to say. She is a busy woman, and you shouldn't be wasting her time."

Blaine raised his own chin, there was a brief stand-off as they both glared at each other, and then he shrugged and turned to Annie. "Mrs. Fuller, Miss Dawson, please, won't you both sit down and tell me how I can help you?"

Annie smiled and took a seat in a well-upholstered armchair, part of a pair next to the room's tall windows, while Laura and Kitty sat close together on a settee against the inside wall. She said, "Mr. Blaine, I understand that you have been the recipient of an anonymous letter, and I thought that you should know that there have been a number of similar letters that have targeted San Francisco teachers and school officials, including the Vice Principal of Girls High, Mr. Hoffmann, and one of the school board members, Mr. Irving Emory."

While she probably shouldn't have revealed Emory's name without asking his permission, she knew she'd have to do so to keep Blaine from dismissing her out of hand.

Blaine leaned forward and said, "Just exactly how did you come by this information, Mrs. Fuller?"

Annie ignored the implicit challenge in Blaine's tone and replied quietly, "Mr. Emory has engaged Miss Dawson's brother, Mr. Nathaniel Dawson, of Hobbes, Cranston and Dawson, to get to the bottom of these letters. Mr. Emory asked me to help out when he learned that I have some experience in discreet investigations of crimes. I have just completed a temporary position at Girls' High because several of the personnel at that school have been singled out by these letters. I would suggest that you contact Mr. Emory if you need verification that what I am telling you is the truth."

Blaine nodded. "Yes, you may be sure I will do so. But I still fail to see why *you* came to see me today. Are you suggesting that I engage you in a similar fashion?"

Annie felt a spurt of anger that her motivation was being questioned, but she reminded herself that a self-made man like Blaine would be used to being approached by people primarily interested in taking some of his wealth.

In a steady voice, she said, "Mr. Blaine, I am here because I thought you would be relieved to learn there is an explanation for why your daughter, who I am sure you know is blameless of any wrong-doing, was the subject of such a letter. Mr. Emory feels that there might be a political motivation behind the letters…"

"Buckley, by God!" Blaine said, his face reddening alarmingly. "I'll kill the bastard!"

"Father!" Kitty got up and went over to him, putting her hand on his shoulder. "Please, calm yourself."

Annie ignored the outburst and said, "That is certainly one possible explanation, although we don't have any proof. In fact, there is the also possibility the letters could be from a disgruntled teacher and that there is no political motive whatsoever."

"But then why would my daughter be involved? No, it's that underhanded Buckley, I'm sure of it. He can't stand it that men like myself and Emory aren't willing to go along with his schemes."

"Your daughter may have been picked by the writer because the writer wanted to harm Mr. Hoffmann, not you," Annie replied. "When the earlier letters didn't result in Mr. Hoffmann's dismissal, the letter writer may have hoped this accusation would result in you using your political influence to get him fired."

Kitty, having returned to her seat next to Laura, said, "See, Father, this is what I told you. Mr. Hoffmann has behaved with perfect propriety towards me. But you were going to march over to the school tomorrow, weren't you, and demand Hoffmann be dismissed."

Annie added, "This is why we need to be very careful. Turning this into a public scandal is the last thing we want for your daughter and the other innocent victims."

"But what can I do? How do I ensure that my daughter's reputation is protected?"

Blaine's fear rang in his words, and Annie reflected on how difficult it must be for a parent not to be in a constant state of anxiety, worried that something or someone was going to hurt their beloved child. She suspected it was doubly upsetting for a powerful man like Blaine to feel powerless to protect his own child from harm.

Keeping this in mind, she said, "Mr. Blaine, you can help us find out who is behind these letters and stop them. I would like to give you a couple of names to see if you recognize them. If you don't, I would ask that you do some discreet investigation into whether they have any political connections. Then I would like you to meet with Mr. Emory and his lawyer, Mr. Dawson, to share information and perhaps formulate a plan on how to unmask this person or persons."

Blaine nodded. "Mrs. Fuller, I will be glad to help. I'll contact Emory tonight; I know what club I will find him in." Turning to the two girls on the sofa, he continued, "Kitty, my dear, get a bit of that fancy letter paper you keep in the desk over there and jot down the names Mrs. Fuller wants me to check out."

As Kitty went across the room, Blaine leaned closer to Annie and said in a whisper, "I know my girl, and she is going to pester me something awful to let her return to her classes tomorrow. But what if I'm not the only one who got such a letter and rumors are spreading about her as we speak? I would do anything to spare her the humiliation that would follow."

Annie, remembering Della Thorndike's hints about Kitty and Hoffmann, thought that Blaine's fears were well-placed. She said, "Let me suggest to Kitty that she not go to her morning classes at Girls' High for the next few days but come directly to Clement Grammar. Working with the students and getting the fun of distributing the valentines will take her mind off of everything. I will write to Mr. Hoffmann and explain why she isn't attending her morning classes. I am confident that he will ensure that her grades won't be affected. But all the more reason to work swiftly to find out who is behind this and end it, *peacefully,* and without any scandal."

Annie looked squarely at Blaine, whose polite smile said he understood her point but whose hard blue eyes said he would use any means necessary to protect his daughter, including violence.

Chapter Thirty-eight
Wednesday evening, February 11, 1880
"During the afternoon a person who had been actively at work in the interests of the Republican ticket...was assaulted by Jake Lido and one 'Shorty' Simpson, two Democratic ward politicians..." —*San Francisco Chronicle*, 1880

Nate sat in a chair in the small parlor awaiting Annie, the formal parlor again occupied by a number of the boarders. He rubbed his temples, trying to relieve the headache that had plagued him all day. Tomorrow, Cranston would start his examination of the defense witnesses, and for the past few weeks, Nate had gotten little more than three or four hours of sleep doing the additional research Cranston kept demanding. He'd never known a lawyer who came to court as well-prepared as the firm's new partner, even though Nate seemed to be doing most of the work. It was all worth it to see how Cranston turned the dry legal precedents Nate had found into an effective legal defense. He really should be home working right now, but he wasn't sure when he would be able to visit again once this stage in the trial started, and he didn't want Annie to feel neglected. Besides, a visit with her, especially the few stolen kisses at the doorstep when he left, infused him with a sense of well-being that beat a shot of whiskey and a full night's sleep.

"Annie sent me to tell you she'll be here in a few minutes." Laura entered the room and pulled a chair around to face him. "We got home after six, which sent Mrs. O'Rourke into a bit of a conniption, so Annie is down in the kitchen placating her."

Nate sat up, his fuzzy mind sharpening. "And why did it take the two of you so long to get home? You know neither of you should be out after dark!"

Laura waved her hand dismissively, like he was some old hen, and said, "Oh Nate, we were properly carried home in a carriage, if you must know. But wait until you hear what happened!"

Laura proceeded to tell him about Kitty's appearance at Clement, the story of the anonymous letter her father got, and their visit to Kitty's home. From Nate's perspective, she dwelt over-long in her description of the house, but when he pressed her to tell her how the conversation with Blaine went, she said that Annie would tell him the details when she came down. Instead, she pulled her chair closer to his and said, in a much more serious tone, that she had something she wanted to ask him. This sent up alarm bells.

"I had a rather disturbing experience this weekend. One of the essayists I studied last year, De Quincey, would call it an epiphany. I came to the realization that I don't think I have ever truly loved anyone. I thought I had. But could it have been love if I wasn't willing to sacrifice for that other person? I mean really sacrifice, put their happiness before my own and do it gladly?"

Nate, not sure what Laura wanted from him, said, "Of course you have loved someone. Mother and Father, for instance."

"But if Mother and Father asked me to stop teaching and come home, would I be willing to do it? Even if that would make them happy? I'm not sure I would. I'm not even sure that I believe sacrificing your own needs and desires for someone else is a good thing. When I think of the couples I lived with last fall, I can't help but wonder how many of the women gave up their dreams in order to marry and if that was why most of them were unhappy."

"Perhaps they were unhappy because they didn't really love their husbands or didn't feel loved by them," Nate said, feeling his way through this alarming subject. "You must admit that Mother is happy, don't you?"

"Yes, but maybe being a wife and mother wasn't a sacrifice for her, and I have trouble picturing Billy's wife, Violet, doing anything else. But I can't imagine settling down, settling for that as *my* future. Which brings me back to the question, maybe I simply haven't ever truly loved anyone else." Laura turned her head away and said quietly, "Maybe I don't have that capacity."

Nate's heart ached for his sister; she seemed so forlorn. He was searching for something to say to lighten her spirits when she startled him with another question.

"Would you give up your career for Annie? Do you love her enough to do that if she asked it of you?" Laura leaned closer and stared into his eyes.

"Yes," he said, surprised at his lack of hesitation. "But I think one of the reasons I love her is that I don't believe she would ever ask me to do so. She might ask me to move and practice the law somewhere else or cut down on my hours or even to take different clients, but I just can't see her asking me to give up my profession."

"Would you ask her to give up something she loved, like her work as Madam Sibyl or an investigation she had embarked upon?"

The scenes of last fall flashing before his eyes, Nate said, "There was a time when I would have, when I did. Then I decided that wasn't the kind of man I wanted to be. I realized if I truly loved her, I wouldn't want her to give up anything to marry me. Thank goodness she's given me a second chance to prove to her she can trust me."

"Then why haven't you asked her to marry you again?"

"Because I'm afraid she will say no and there will be no third chance." The words came out without thinking. Before he could examine their import, he saw Laura turn towards the doorway, where Annie was just entering the room. He went over to her and gave her a warm hug, whispering in her ear, "Thank goodness you've come. I was getting in very deep waters."

Annie pulled away and wrinkled her brow in a puzzled fashion.

Laura passed them as she headed to the doorway, saying, "I will leave you two alone; I have some class preparation to finish. Annie, I told him you would fill in the details of our meeting with Mr. Blaine." And then she was gone, leaving the door ajar only a few inches.

Nate, about to open the door wider, thought, *Hang it all. Everyone knows we are in here, and we can't be getting up to any trouble.* Instead, he arranged the two chairs in the room side-by-side, and as they sat down together, he slid his arm around Annie's shoulder and pulled her in close for a swift kiss.

Annie laughed softly when the embrace ended. Putting her hand up against his cheek, she said, "Was that for rescuing you? Whatever were you two talking about?"

"She said she wasn't sure she'd ever really loved anyone. I didn't know what to say. Do you know what happened to cause this, I think she called it an 'epiphany?'"

"Oh, you poor dear. What happened was a distressing conversation with Seth Timmons on Sunday night, and I believe she's still feeling guilty that she didn't support Hattie enough before she died."

"Timmons came by on Sunday? Did he have any news about Buck?" Nate was surprised that Laura hadn't mentioned this.

"Yes. He found out that Buck was in San Francisco at the time Laura was attacked, working for an uncle. He told Laura he would find out if Buck has been following Laura home from work or hanging out behind the house at night and upsetting Dandy."

Annie paused. "Dandy was very friendly to Seth on Sunday. It made me wonder if someone could take Dandy to where Buck works to see how Dandy responds. It wouldn't prove anything definitively, but it would give us an indication if our suspicions are correct."

Nate nearly laughed out loud at the image of the diminutive dog leaping and snapping at some lumbering youth. But, not sure he wanted to encourage this plan, he changed the subject. "Tell me how Peter Blaine responded when you told him he wasn't the only one to receive an anonymous letter."

"He initially thought I was there to squeeze some money out of him. I hope I didn't cause any trouble by letting him know that Emory was one of the other people who had been targeted. I was afraid that, otherwise, Blaine wouldn't have been willing to talk to me. He said he was going to track down Emory tonight, check on my story. Do you think

Emory will be upset?"

"I don't think so; but Blaine must have been furious to think someone would be trying to ruin his daughter."

"Yes, he immediately named Buckley, that corrupt political boss you mentioned, when I brought up the possibility of a political motive behind the letters. I asked for his help to see if there were any connections he could find between Buckley and any disaffected teachers. I gave him Frazier's name, the one who lost the job to Mrs. Anderson. I also gave him Mrs. Washburn's name, the janitoress at Girl's High who dislikes Hoffmann so much, and the name of her brother.

"Her brother, why? Who is he?"

"His name is Ferguson, and he's the janitor at Laura's school. Both he and his sister are Scottish immigrants, and there is always the possibility Ferguson is part of Buckley's political organization. I know this is far-fetched, but it occurred to me that it was an odd coincidence that Hattie Wilks ended up in that run-down boarding house owned by another Scotsman. And Laura confessed to me last night that she had been getting a 'bad feeling' about Ferguson. She wouldn't tell me why."

Nate didn't see the connection, but he trusted Annie's instincts. He just said, "Did Blaine say he'd help you?"

"Yes. I'm just hoping Emory will be able to restrain him. He was so sure Buckley was behind everything that I feared he was going to go right out and strangle the man."

"Surely he understands that he shouldn't do anything that would lead to public scandal. That really would threaten his daughter's reputation."

"Yes, but Nate, what if it is too late? It was last week that Della Thorndike hinted that there was some sort of relationship between Kitty and Hoffmann, which suggests rumors have already started."

"Is there any possibility that the rumors about Miss Blaine and Hoffmann are true?" Nate couldn't help but think about the thread of truth behind the notes to Hattie. What if Kitty was another young woman who had been seduced?

Annie shook her head. "I saw no evidence that Hoffmann had any interest in Kitty. From everything I've heard, the teacher Kitty is closest to is Andrew Russell. She is evidently a brilliant linguist and his prized student, and it is possible she has developed a school girl's infatuation with him. In fact, if I hadn't met her in person, I would have said that she might have the strongest motive for sending the notes to Hattie: jealousy at losing Russell's attention. But now I would swear she is innocent of any wrong-doing, and, of course, there is no reason she would have sent the anonymous letter to her own father."

"But where did Miss Thorndike get the idea about a relationship between Hoffmann and Kitty Blaine?"

"She is such a gossip, she could have heard something from anyone. For example, one of the other Normal class students might be jealous of Kitty. To my mind, Mrs. Washburn, the janitoress, is the most likely candidate since she seems to have an ongoing feud with Hoffman. But what if Della Thorndike made the story up herself? What if she were the letter writer?"

"You have mentioned this idea before. But why would she do that? What political motivation would she have?" Nate had trouble picturing the elegant woman he saw last week at the theater sneaking around putting poisonous notes in people's mailboxes.

"Remember, Laura's theory is that Miss Thorndike might be trying to get Hoffmann fired so Russell would get his position. But that doesn't make sense if the notes to Hattie were by the same person who is targeting Hoffmann. Russell's reputation would have suffered as well if the accusations had become public. Well in any event, I also gave Blaine both Thomas Hoffmann's and Andrew Russell's names. I thought, why not? What could it hurt to see if there was any connection between them and either political party?"

Nate sighed and said, "None of this quite fits. Do you think we are being led astray by our assumption that the anonymous letters are all from the same person? We need another meeting. Get Blaine, Emory, maybe Hoffmann all in the same room, share information. Why are you smiling?" asked Nate.

"Because I told Blaine the same thing," Annie replied. "Right now I could believe almost anything. Buckley might be behind these most recent letters, or it could be a disaffected teacher like Frazier or an unhappy school employee like Mrs. Washburn who wrote them."

Annie then made a small strangled sound in her throat, and she looked at him with fear, saying "Oh, Nate, if it were *Russell*, writing the letters as part of a twisted attempt to bring Hoffmann down and move into his job. What if he saw Hattie as an obstacle to that plan, giving him a reason to push her down a flight of stairs and leave her there to die? What if Laura has been right about him all along?"

Chapter Thirty-nine
Thursday evening, February 12, 1880

"FALSE REGISTRATION: A Bold Attempt to Commit Wholesale Fraud. The landlady informed him that the room had been rented by Chris Buckley, who had furnished her with a list of the names of the alleged lodgers that were to crowd themselves into the single bed." —*San Francisco Chronicle*, 1880

At Nate's insistence, Annie took a cab to his law firm's offices. As she walked up the stairs, she felt grateful she'd done so. She was very tired. By the time Nate and she had thoroughly discussed what they wanted to accomplish at the meeting with Blaine, Emory, and Hoffmann, it was later than either had expected, and both of them still had work to do before they retired. She'd hoped to have the time, and the courage, to bring up the topic of their relationship. But she'd taken one look at the dark circles under his eyes and determined this was not the moment for a deep personal conversation. Surely, when the investigation was over and the trial he was working on was completed, there would be time.

When she reached the firm's office, the entry door stood open. She took a minute to appraise the men who were gathered in the outer room. Emory and Blaine, similar in age and status, were so different in appearance. Emory was tall and elegant, displaying his wealth prominently on his person. Blaine was short and plain and could have passed unnoticed among the men working at his construction sites. Yet they shared a distinct air of power and confidence as they chatted animatedly with each other.

In contrast, Nate and Thomas Hoffmann, both young men making their way up the professional ladder, stood talking more quietly to the side. Nate, who must have gone to the barber early this morning, looked well-groomed and polished for once, as befitted a lawyer. Hoffmann, on the other hand, looked for the first time as if the strain of the accusations were getting to him, with his shirt collar slightly wilted and chalk dust sprinkled over his coat.

Just as everyone finished offering their polite greetings to Annie, the door to one of the inner offices swung open, and the man who came into the room instantly eclipsed every other male there. Able Cranston, the new law partner, wasn't physically imposing, but when he came up to her to be introduced, she experienced the full force of his personal magnetism. He told Annie that he'd greatly admired her father when he was a young man. He then gracefully complimented her for using her business acumen to help in the current investigation and praised Nate for his contributions to the on-going trial. No wonder he was known as one of the best defense lawyers in the state. She would be hard-pressed as a jury member (if women were ever allowed to serve on juries) not to believe every word he said no matter how guilty his client.

When Cranston left, the meeting began with everyone sitting around the conference table. Blaine was the first to speak, and he reported that he wasn't able to find any evidence of political connections for Frazier, the applicant for Mrs. Anderson's job, or Stoddard, the math teacher who Hoffmann had dismissed. Ferguson, the Clement Grammar janitor, was a different matter.

"I learned he is well-known among saloon keepers south of Market for getting out the vote for the Democrats," said Blaine. "I don't know if he is working directly for Buckley, but I'm looking into that."

Nate asked, "What about Andrew Russell?"

When Blaine simply shook his head in the negative, Emory spoke up. "After Blaine tracked me down last night and told me about the latest letter, I spent some of today dropping in on three of my fellow school board members, all Republicans. I said I was looking for an educated man to offer a position in my company, floated the name of Andrew Russell."

Emory continued. "Frankly, I wanted to see if anyone had gotten a letter similar to the ones that had accused Hoffmann of impropriety.

Nothing like that was mentioned, but one board member did say he'd met Russell at a couple of Republican fund raisers. Didn't remember anything else but that he was a school administrator and that Russell mentioned an older brother who'd been a New York state senator during the war."

Hoffmann spoke up and said, "Look, I've known Russell for at least five years. If you are saying he wrote the letters about Emory and myself in order to curry political favor, I just don't buy it. The man's only ambition is academic. He's got his head in the clouds half the time, parsing out some poem he's translating."

"But could he be manipulated by someone?" Nate asked. "A Republican who wanted to weaken Principal Swett's position at Girls' High or Buckley who wanted someone who'd undermine Swett's influence with the legislature in Sacramento?"

A fierce debate erupted between Blaine and Emory over whether the anonymous letters were more likely to have been written to advance a Democratic or a Republican agenda. Annie finally stood up, forcing all the men at the table to stop talking and rise out of politeness.

She smiled and said, "I have a suggestion. We need to flush out the letter-writer, force them to reveal themselves. Even if this person is working for someone else, knowing the writer's identity is key to figuring out the motive."

Emory looked interested and said, "And just how do you suggest we do that?"

"There are risks, but I would write a letter to all of our suspects, an *anonymous* letter, that states that we know what they are up to and are prepared to expose them unless they meet with us and agree to terms."

Blaine guffawed and said, "By gum, blackmail them! Aren't you a smart little lady?"

Annie, seeing Nate stiffen at Blaine's tone, said quickly, "Exactly. While it is possible that someone who is innocent might show up, I think we could probably deduce they aren't involved pretty easily."

"So we write to Ferguson, since he has the political connections,"

Emory said, "and hope that if he shows up, we can determine if he is working on his own or for Buckley?"

"Well, I doubt whether Ferguson, or his sister, is clever enough to write the letters on their own," Annie replied. "But even if Ferguson goes to Buckley and asks him what to do, wouldn't Buckley send him to the meeting, if only to find out who's on to him?"

"That's what I would do," Blaine said. "But I might send someone with a bit more authority, as well, just to make sure this Ferguson has the guts to keep quiet."

"That's why I think I should be the one who shows up to the meeting," Annie replied quietly.

When the uproar ignited by that statement finally died down, she continued. "I would want several of you nearby. Perhaps hidden in an adjoining room. I'm not foolish."

Nate said something under his breath, and Annie decided to ignore him. She said, "If Ferguson comes on his own, I can tell him I am investigating for the school board and that I can get him fired if he doesn't confess. If he is working for someone, he might push the blame on them."

"What if he brings one of Buckley's henchmen?" Blaine said.

Annie replied, "In that case, I suspect they wouldn't see me as much of a threat, so there would be less chance of anything violent happening. And if you or Emory recognizes someone who works for Buckley, this would actually help us. Anyway, if you felt I was getting into trouble, you could step forward."

Blaine nodded, and Emory said, "And we do the same with these other names you've give me, Frazier and Russell? Assume that they will either say something that will implicate themselves or reveal someone they are working for."

"Yes, but I would suggest we also send a letter to Della Thorndike."

Emory exclaimed, "Who's Della Thorndike?"

Hoffmann, who had been quiet during this last conversation, turned to Emory and said, "She teaches at Girls' High and is temporarily teaching the Normal class. But I must say, I think she would be even less likely than Russell to be our letter-writer."

"She knows everyone involved," Annie replied. "She seems close friends with Ferguson's sister, who works at Girls' High; she knows all the teachers who have been maligned; and she wasn't completely truthful with me when she reported her role in getting Mrs. Anderson hired. In addition, she is a very close friend of Andrew Russell's."

Hoffmann shook his head. "Well, she does like to be in the thick of things, so I could see her inadvertently playing a role. Maybe giving Ferguson some information or being used by Russell."

"But you just described Russell as a dreamer, while Miss Thorndike strikes me as being very practical," replied Annie. "She's intelligent and wields a good deal of power and influence among the teachers and administrators in the school district. What if it was Della Thorndike who is using Russell and Ferguson to serve her own ends?"

"But what ends?" Hoffmann said. "What possible motivation would she have?"

"Is this Thorndike the teacher my Kitty dislikes?" Blaine blurted out. "The one Kitty says always tries to make her feel stupid?"

He looked at Annie, who nodded, and he said, "Seems if she wanted to damage my girl's reputation, a girl who never did her any harm, maybe she's writing these letters just because she's one of those people who likes to hurt others."

Nate stood nervously at the front door to Annie's boarding house, waiting for Kathleen to let him in. He'd told the cab driver to wait since he only had a few minutes to spare, but he knew he must see Annie before she went off to Girls' High.

The door opened, and the young maid smiled warmly as she ushered him in. "Sir, what beautiful flowers. Mrs. Fuller will be pleased, but you need to be a little more careful with them. Shall I get a vase for you?"

Nate looked down at the nosegay of violets he'd bought from a corner flower seller and saw that he was crushing the short stems. He'd spent a good half hour yesterday at the stationers near his office picking out a valentine card. The simple card he ended up buying showed a small boy giving his teacher an apple, with the caption, "Be Mine." *Be Mine.* This morning, when he reread the card before signing it, all he could think of was how possessive that sounded and that Annie would hate it. And the illustration? When he got it, he was thinking of her stint teaching at Girls' High, but for a valentine? Was he supposed to be a little boy? Was she supposed to be teaching him something? The last-minute decision to buy flowers came from his panicked doubt about giving her the card, which was in his coat's inner pocket and would probably stay there.

He followed Kathleen into the formal parlor, empty of boarders for a change. Annie was sitting at the small writing desk near the front bay window, and she looked up at his entrance and smiled. He said, "I can't stay but a minute, the cab is waiting, but I wanted to see you before…are you sure you are all right with me not being there with you?"

Annie put aside whatever she had been working on and came over to stand next to him. She took the violets from his hand, brought them up to her nose, and breathed deeply. Then she said firmly, "Yes Nate, I am sure. Do I wish you were going to be standing beside me the whole time? Of course I do. But I quite understand why Blaine and Emory don't want a lawyer there when I confront whoever shows up today. If anyone shows up. That is really my greatest fear. That this will all be for naught and they will think me a fool for even suggesting this plan."

"They jumped on your idea fast enough."

"I know; I was rather surprised by that. I am sorry I sprung the idea without telling you, but it came to me in the cab on the way over to the meeting."

Nate shrugged. He'd been upset at first, but how could he complain when he was the one who got her into this investigation in the first place? Did he really expect Annie to play a passive role, content to rummage around in file cabinets? He said, "I just worry that if Buckley is the one behind the letters, one of his hoodlums will show up."

"That's why Hoffmann chose the Chemistry lab as the meeting place," explained Annie. "There is a small pass-through room between the lab and the classroom where the chemicals are kept locked away. It's big enough for Emory, Blaine, and Hoffmann to stand in and overhear what is going on, and they can be in the room with me in an instant if they feel I am in danger."

Nate knew she was right. Emory and Hoffmann were both tall, strong men, and Blaine looked like he could take care of anything, bare-handed, so they would be able to protect her as well as he could. But he wished it wasn't going to be Annie taking the greatest risk. Laura's question to him reverberated in his mind. *Would he ever ask her to give up her career or an investigation?* He'd said no, without hesitating. Now was the time to prove to himself that he was telling the truth.

Thinking of Laura, Nate said, "You didn't tell her about this afternoon's plan to trap the anonymous letter writer, did you?"

Annie laughed. "No. I didn't want her worrying. One Dawson's furrowed brow is enough for me!" She reached over and ran her hand over his forehead. She then continued, "If this works today and we find that the persons involved had nothing to do with the attack on Laura, we must concentrate on figuring out if Buck was responsible."

"I know. I promise I will seek out Seth Timmons tomorrow, see what he's learned," Nate said. "Where is Laura?"

"She's out for the afternoon with Barbara, Jamie, and Ian. They went up to North Beach to Meiggs Wharf to watch the Italian fishermen bring in their catch. They promised to bring back some fresh fish for supper. Would you be able to get back here by seven and join us?"

"I don't know if I can get back by then. When do you expect to get home, given that you've staggered the times you asked each person to come to the school?"

"Blaine insisted that I invite Russell to come first at three o'clock, then Della at three-thirty. So we could 'get them out of the way.' I invited Ferguson for four o'clock, and then Frazier a half an hour later, so I can't imagine I won't be home by seven."

"What are you going to do if someone shows up but seems to be innocent?" This had bothered Nate about the plan from the beginning, worrying about the legal ramifications of making a false accusation. Even worse, someone could accuse Annie of blackmail.

"Well, I decided to address the note to 'the anonymous letter writer' and to say that they needed to come to ensure their 'actions do not result in being prosecuted for libel.' I figured that a person who wasn't in-volved at all would either ignore the note or check with someone in authority about what to do. I doubt they would just show up."

"And you think the threat of libel will cause the guilty party to show up?"

"Yes. If only to find out who sent the note and what information they had. I didn't want to say anything about exposing them because that sounded too much like blackmail."

"Smart woman." Nate's attention was arrested by the quarter chime on the mantel clock. "Look, I have to go. I'll get back here as soon as I can, hopefully be here before you get back. But let me take you out to dinner. Something special for Valentine's Day. Something more than these sad flowers."

Annie put the nosegay up to her cheek again and said, "Don't you speak ill of my violets. I love them. Now go. Don't keep Cranston waiting."

Nate pulled her into his arms and hugged her tightly, then he said, "Be safe," and left before he changed his mind and stayed.

Chapter Forty-one
Saturday afternoon, February 14, 1880

"ADELPHI THEATER—"Uninterrupted success of the Great Local Drama: *Female Detective,* Miss Mollie Williams in Five Different Characters." —*San Francisco Chronicle*, 1880

At slightly after two in the afternoon, the winter sun had already begun its downward slide toward the Pacific, casting dark shadows along the southern side of Bush Street. Yet the day had been warm enough that Annie decided to wear just her light shawl over her brown wool polonaise. She assumed that one of the gentlemen would escort her home in a cab, so even if the fog rolled in she should be fine. Maybe she would get to ride home again in Blaine's comfortable carriage as she had on Wednesday.

She desperately hoped everything would be resolved satisfactorily today. There were too many people who could be hurt if all this didn't go well. Barbara had been wonderful about not asking any questions, but she must be worried about what would happen if her qualifications to teach came under question. And none of this could be pleasant for Mr. Hoffmann. Even if he were blameless, would the parents of his students, or his wife for that matter, believe him if the rumors about him became public? She wasn't as worried about Mrs. Anderson, who she suspected would be shielded by Mr. Emory from any negative financial consequences. Yet if scandal did erupt, the flirtatious widow might find it more difficult to find male sponsors in the future. And Kitty Blaine? Annie would do almost anything to try to protect that lovely young woman, and she hated to think what it would do to Laura if her newest friend had to leave town because her reputation was ruined.

Going up the steps to the school, Annie saw Hoffmann waiting for her in the open doorway. He ushered her in, saying, "I am going to keep the doors locked until two-thirty when Blaine and Emory are to arrive. We don't want some student or teacher wandering in by mistake."

"Quite right," Annie replied. As they walked up the stairs to the third floor, she said, "Are you as nervous as I am?"

Hoffmann paused and said, "I don't know whether I am more nervous that no one will show up and this whole thing will drag on or that some tough of Buckley's will turn up to say that his boss has taken all the accusations to the papers."

"Oh, don't even think that," Annie said. "I do believe that our best chance of success lies in my appearing confident that we have proof that this is a coordinated smear campaign and that all the targeted people are cooperating. That's why I asked Mr. Blaine to give me a copy of the letter he received about his daughter. That, along with the copies of the letters we already had from Mr. Emory and a couple of other notes that have come into my possession, should make our letter writer think twice about acting once they see the evidence we have."

"Well, I must say you are a brave young woman, and I am very grateful to you for doing this." Hoffmann continued to lead the way up the stairs.

When they got to the second floor landing, Annie stopped and said, "Do you mind if we take a look at Della Thorndike's room, see if there is anything in her desk that might implicate her? And does Mr. Russell have any sort of file cabinet or anything at Girls' High that he uses for his classes?"

"Russell just brings his materials with him in his satchel. But I happen to know he has been using Della's classroom for his language classes and his Greek study group since she is teaching in the Normal classroom most of the time."

Annie knew that the most likely candidate was Ferguson, working alongside his sister to curry favor with the Democrats. This is certainly what Blaine and Emory expected. But she just couldn't get rid of the thought that Della was involved in some fashion, even if just as the conduit of information to Ferguson through his sister or to Russell. She was getting as bad as Laura, letting a personal bias against someone cloud her judgment. Maybe there would finally be some concrete evidence in the classroom.

Hoffmann used his keys to open up Della's classroom. Located on the south side of the building, the room had enough sunlight coming in from the tall windows that they didn't need to turn up the gaslights. When they got to the desk at the front of the room, they found it was locked.

Hoffmann swore under his breath, revealing to Annie just how anxious he was. She wondered if he'd told his wife anything about the trouble he was in.

"Wait a minute," he said. "These desks all work on a few common keys. Our biggest concern is keeping the students from rifling them, not other teachers. I have several extra keys in my office. I'll get them."

"Splendid," Annie replied. "While you do, I'm going to look in the cabinet over there. We do have time for this, don't we?" She looked at her pocket watch and saw it was only five after two, twenty-five minutes until Emory and Blaine were scheduled to arrive.

Hoffmann nodded and sprinted out the door. In the classroom where she'd been teaching, the cabinet was filled with graph paper, protractors, some extra math texts, and odd wooden geometrical shapes that she assumed Hoffmann used for his geometry classes. The cabinet in Della's room held a shelf of English Literature textbooks, extra pens, a rolled up map of England, a plaster bust of Shakespeare, and some reams of composition paper. She remembered that Laura had brought home some paper she found at the City of Paris store to check against the paper used for Hattie's notes. While they'd been disappointed to discover the lines were spaced differently, Annie had noted that the paper for Hattie's anonymous notes all contained a dark black spot near the right hand corner, as if someone had carelessly let a ink pen rest on the paper long enough for the ink to bleed through.

Pulling the top ream of paper out into the light, she felt a spurt of triumph when she saw a similar dark spot. She opened the folder of anonymous letters she had brought with her and removed Hattie's notes. When placed side by side, it was obvious they had come from this same ream of paper. Proof that someone who had access to this room had written the notes to Hattie.

When Hoffmann returned and Annie showed him what she found, she cautioned him, saying, "You know, Mrs. Washburn, Andrew Russell, and Della all could have taken the paper from this cabinet, so this doesn't prove which one was the anonymous letter writer. But it does indicate we are on the right track."

Looking for additional evidence, they turned to the desk. After several tries, Hoffmann hit upon the key that opened up the drawers. In the middle drawer, they found nothing but pens and pencils, erasers, chalk, and bookmarks that looked like gifts from students, and the side drawer held old student papers and a stack of grade books. Hoffmann showed her some heavier bond paper, which did look similar to the paper that had been used for the letter to Blaine, but it didn't have the same water mark, so it wasn't a match.

"Well, it really would have been too good to be true to find additional proof, and I still have difficulty believing that Miss Thorndike is directly involved," said Hoffmann.

"Conversely, if she is the letter writer, it might mean she is clever enough not to keep any incriminating materials at work. At least we have the composition paper. For a person with a guilty conscience, that might be all it will take to get a confession."

Hoffmann locked the desk, and they went on up to the third floor. As he opened the door to the Chemistry lab, he noted, "It's nearly two-thirty. Go on and check out the room, and I will go down to wait for Blaine and Emory. I hope they will be on time."

Annie walked into the laboratory. The room was large and filled with four rows of tall tables, their centers crowded with glass beakers in stands, various metal implements she didn't know the names of, and scales and weights. A sharp tang of chemicals tickled her nose. She saw the door to the pass-through was open, so she went and looked in. There was a little light coming from the laboratory and the adjoining classroom, but most of the narrow room was nothing but shadows and the dark shapes of cabinets. The chemical smell was even stronger here, and she hoped that Blaine, Emory, and Hoffmann wouldn't have to stay closed up in the room too long. She also hoped they would be able to hear what was being said with the door just slightly ajar. She would test this with Hoffmann and the other men when they got here.

Walking back into the chemistry laboratory, Annie put the folder on the end of the center-most table. Her hands shook, her mouth felt dry, and the chemical smell began to make her feel slightly faint. Turning towards the windows, she worked to unlatch and open one of them a crack, and then she took several deep breaths of fresh air.

"I told you Mrs. Fuller was behind this. She's nothing but a black-mailer. And you saw Hoffmann leave the building. He's in it with her. I'm sure of it."

Annie swirled around to see Della Thorndike and Andrew Russell standing at the door to the laboratory.

Chapter Forty-two
Late Saturday afternoon, February 14, 1880
"William Zimmerman, teacher of German in the Boys' High School...was arrested yesterday on the charge of libel on the complaint of George Schwartz. The libel was alleged to have been committed in sending anonymous letters to the Investigating Committee of the Board of Education."—*San Francisco Chronicle* 1880

Annie repressed her sense of triumph in seeing Della Thorndike and Andrew Russell in the doorway. She'd been right in her suspicions! Now the hard work began, getting them to confess to writing the letters and agree to stop. *And where in Heaven's name is Hoffmann, and why did Della say he left the building?* Annie needed to guide the conversation carefully, hoping Hoffmann had seen Della and Russell arrive early and was out intercepting Blaine and Emory so they wouldn't give themselves away as they made their way upstairs.

Taking a deliberate breath to steady herself, she said, "Please, Miss Thorndike, Mr. Russell, do come in. What can I do for you?"

Della walked determinedly into the room and announced in a stern school-teacher voice, "Mrs. Fuller, don't play games with us. You know very well why we are here. We are here to make it clear to you that you and Hoffmann and your other confederates will not get away with your threats."

Della was dressed as usual in an exquisitely tailored suit, the shades of sky-blue in her tweed wool jacket and satin underskirt highlighting the odd pale-blue color of her eyes. Her dyed kid gloves, the small, fancifully decorated hat, and her sleek blonde hair added to the general impression of competent femininity. The blotches of pink staining her cheeks were the only sign she wasn't in complete command of herself.

Russell, on the other hand, with ink on his shirt front, a book stretching out the pocket of his wrinkled jacket, and his badly cut hair, looked wind-blown and thoroughly confused. He muttered, "Now Della, please, I don't understand why you keep insisting that Tom Hoffmann is involved in…whatever this is, and I am barely acquainted with this Mrs. Fuller, so why would she be threatening me?"

Annie decided to ignore him and addressed Della, saying, "Miss Thorndike, please enlighten me. In what fashion have *I* threatened either you or Mr. Russell?"

The pink on her cheeks fading, Della smiled as if Annie had handed her a present. "Don't pretend ignorance, Mrs. Fuller. Dorthea Anderson told me you were hired to teach at Girls' High as a pretense to spy on us. I assume when you found nothing, you decided to send both Andrew and me letters, threatening us with libel. Did you think you would make a little money on the side? Do the people who hired you even know you and Hoffmann are doing this?"

What a fool Mrs. Anderson is. Annie prayed she hadn't ruined everything, but she knew she needed to tread even more carefully since Della had been forewarned. Producing a smile of her own, she said, "Miss Thorndike, what I don't understand is, why are *you* here? Did you receive a letter addressed to *you*?"

Della pulled a piece of paper out of her purse and walked towards Annie, waving it. "Here it is, Mrs. Fuller. Shall I read it to you? It says, 'Please come to the Chemistry Room at Girls' High at 3 p.m to ensure your actions do not result in being prosecuted for libel.' Now tell me you didn't write this and it wasn't meant as a threat."

Annie reached out and took the letter from Della, purposely knocking the rack of glass beakers beside her as she did, trying to cover up the slight noise she'd heard to her left. A noise she desperately hoped was the sound of Hoffmann and the other two men moving into the room next door.

"Actually, neither I nor Mr. Hoffmann wrote it," Annie replied, while internally congratulating herself for having the foresight to ask Kathleen pen the short note for her, although why it was important not to lie to this woman, she couldn't say. Pretending to look at the letter, she asked, "Why do you insist the letter was addressed to you? It says, 'Dear Anonymous Letter Writer.' *Did* you write any anonymous letters?"

"No, I did not! I…"

"Then I don't see that there is any reason for you to be here," Annie interrupted.

Della was momentarily flustered. Leaving the note in Annie's hand, she walked back towards Russell, who'd been following their conversation with a puzzled look on his face.

"However, before you go," Annie said, "I do have a question. Why did you tell me that it was Mr. Hoffmann who thought Mrs. Anderson was the best candidate for her job when it was actually you who objected to the other candidate, Frazier?"

Della whipped back around to face her. "That is not true. Mr. Hoffmann would have hired Mrs. Anderson no matter what I said because all he is interested in is currying favor with members of the school board."

"And how would the hiring of Dorthea Anderson curry favor? Isn't she qualified for the position?"

"No, she is not. Everyone knows that Irving Emory is her special friend." Della shot back.

"Really? Mr. Russell, did you know of this special relationship between Mr. Emory and the Girls' High art teacher? Or is it possible that you heard this piece of gossip from your friend Miss Thorndike and decided to use it in a letter to the other school board members?"

Russell just shook his head and said, "Art teacher? Mrs. Anderson? I barely know her. I don't know what you are talking about."

Annie took up the folder from the bench and pulled out the copy of the first letter to the head of the school board, saying, "I couldn't help but notice that this letter states that Mrs. Anderson shouldn't have the position because she didn't have the appropriate level Certificate, which is one of the reasons Miss Thorndike gave me for why she didn't think her qualified for the job. And you say she never told you this or urged you to write a letter to the school board?"

Della became agitated, shaking a slender finger at Annie. "Andrew Russell has nothing to do with any of this. How dare you try to implicate him. See Andrew, I told you, this is a conspiracy on the part of Mr. Hoffmann and this...this...I don't even know what to call her, dare I say Hoffmann's mistress, to ruin your good name."

Annie found it telling that Della felt the need to convince Russell that there was a conspiracy against him. It confirmed her instinct that Della was behind the letters and that Russell was, at the very most, being used by her. What Annie wasn't sure of was Della's motive.

She decided to use Della's jibe about Annie being Hoffmann's mistress to see how Russell would react to the news that she'd made similar statements about Kitty Blaine, by all reports one of Russell's favorite students. She tucked the letter Della had so conveniently given back to her into the folder. As she took out the letter that had been sent to Kitty's father, which had been written on a small piece of flimsy notepaper, she saw Della's eyes widen. It looked like Dorthea Anderson hadn't told Della that Peter Blaine was now part of the group trying to expose her.

Annie said, "Miss Thorndike, you can say whatever you want about me, but I do think it was irresponsible of you to suggest that Mr. Hoffmann has behaved improperly with a student. Don't you agree, Mr. Russell?"

He suddenly looked alert and said to Annie, "What are you saying about Tom Hoffmann and a student?"

"I wasn't the person spreading this rumor; it was Miss Thorndike who said something to me," she replied.

Della tugged at Russell's arm, trying to turn him towards the door. "We don't need to listen to her any more. Obviously she has no proof of her accusations. Please, let's go."

Russell resisted her and turned back to Annie. "Please, Mrs. Fuller. I confess I am very confused. I know I've met you once...at the hospital, and I know you are Miss Dawson's friend. But I don't understand what is going on and what your role is in all of this."

"I have been asked by a member of the school board to discover who has been trying to create a scandal within the school district by sending anonymous letters. I'd hoped that you and Miss Thorndike, if you were not directly involved, would want to help uncover the identity of the person who is trying to ruin the reputation of teachers like Mr. Hoffmann."

"Of course, I see." Nodding at Della, Russell continued, "I am sure Miss Thorndike would be glad to help discover who is out to ruin poor Tom's reputation."

"Oh Andrew, what do you mean *poor Tom*?" Della snapped, giving his arm a little shake and looking like she would like to box his ears. "He's not the one stuck working at Clement Grammar under that incompetent DuBois woman. Why won't you ever speak up for yourself? Hoffmann should have never gotten the job at Girls' High. That should have been your position. He doesn't need it, with that wealthy German wife of his and all her father's political connections. If you'd just made the slightest push to bring yourself forward, then I'd…"

Della stopped speaking as Russell brushed her hand off of his arm and backed away from her. Della's words confirmed Annie's earlier speculations. The letters about Emory, Mrs. Anderson, and probably even Barbara Hewitt, were all designed to get Hoffmann fired so Russell could take his position. But why? Did Della think this would further her own career? That a grateful Russell, once in Hoffmann's position, would give her the Normal class permanently? Or was his gratitude supposed to result in an entirely different kind of offer?

Russell's air of distracted confusion was now gone, and he said, "Mrs. Fuller, please go on. Just what is Hoffmann being accused of?"

"Kitty Blaine's father received this letter saying that Mr. Hoffmann had seduced his daughter." Annie waved the letter, watching Della blanch. "You can imagine how upset he is. I wanted to ask Miss Thorndike about this because she had mentioned something similar to me."

Della reached out to Russell and pleaded, "You mustn't believe her.

All I did was express my concern that I had heard rumors that Hoffmann was trying to take advantage of Kitty. Miss Blaine is one of my students, and I was looking out for her."

"But Miss Thorndike, surely you must realize that even repeating such a rumor could damage the reputations of both the teacher and the student," Annie replied. "And, as far as I can tell, you're the only one who has expressed such a concern. Miss Blaine isn't even in any of his classes this semester, nor in the science club."

Annie looked directly at Andrew Russell and said, "You see, Mr. Russell, I thought if Miss Thorndike isn't the person who wrote this letter, she would be willing to tell me where she got the information or to whom she might have passed it on. That might help me track down the source of these nasty rumors."

Russell took Della's hand and said, "Do tell her what she wants to know. I know you've always disliked Tom, but can't you see how important this is? Just think of what damage a rumor of this sort could do to Miss Blaine and her future. She shows such great academic promise. I believe Miss Blaine could go on to the University, have a career in languages. She really is one of the finest linguists I have encountered in my years of teaching, and…"

Della cut him off, spitting out, "Rubbish. Once again you have been misled by a pretty face. Don't you see Miss Blaine is nothing but the tricked-out daughter of a common Irish barkeep, giving herself airs? Do you think that some over-paid English governess can undo what centuries of in-breeding and pig-farming have done to creatures like her?"

Annie was shocked by the venom in Della's voice and by the overt nativism of her sentiments. This certainly seemed to rule out the possibility she was working for Buckley or any of the Democrats. She realized that now was the time to find out if any Republican political elements were part of Della's schemes.

Raising her voice, she said, "So is that why you picked on Kitty, because you thought that her father would use his Democratic Party connections to get Hoffmann fired? You must have been frustrated when none of your letters to the Republicans on the school board produced any action."

"The Republicans are no better than the Democrats in this city, up for the highest bidder," Della said, disgustedly. "*Frau* Hoffmann and her husband got to dine with President Grant when he came to visit, but we had to buy a ticket to stand among the unwashed to see him from afar. It just wasn't right, and..."

"Della, what are you saying?" Russell said urgently, moving in front of her to block her off from Annie's sight. "Are you saying you *did* write to these men and make accusations about Tom? Is Mrs. Fuller correct? You wrote an anonymous letter about Miss Blaine to her father. Why ever would you do that?"

"I did it for you, and it worked. I finally got their attention. Don't you see that now they'd better do what is right and promote you, or I will make sure everyone hears about..."

"Della, don't say another thing. Libel is a serious offense. You know what happened last fall when Cleary made unfounded accusations against the superintendent and some board members. It ruined his career. We need to straighten this out. I am sure if you apologize and explain you were misguided..."

Annie moved closer, worried that she wouldn't be able to hear what Della said next.

Della's voice sounded calm and confident as she said, "Andrew, you poor man, don't worry. They have no proof. Some anonymous letters, which could have been written by anyone. Do you really think that Mr. Emory or Peter Blaine would ever let this come to a public investigation or trial? Cleary was a fool to make a public accusation."

Annie wished she knew for sure that someone else besides herself was hearing all of this. Della was right. They wouldn't want to make this a public scandal. Yet, if she could convince Della that there *was* proof and get Russell to agree to testify that he'd heard her confess to writing the letters, then Della might be persuaded to stop the letter-writing campaign.

She reached out and tapped Russell on the shoulder. As he turned around, he stepped to the side, revealing Della, whose pink cheeks were still the only sign of how upset she was.

Annie said, "Actually, Mr. Russell, there is proof. If you will come over and examine this ream of composition paper I discovered in Miss Thorndike's classroom, you will see what I mean."

Annie drew Russell over and pointed to the pile of paper she'd pulled out of her folder. "Can you see this spot of ink that has bled through this stack of composition paper? If you look closely at these notes to Miss Hattie Wilks, which I believe you have already seen, you will notice the same ink spot. That, plus the fact that these notes, and this note to Mr. Blaine, close with the same statement, 'A Concerned Citizen,' make a pretty convincing case that they were both sent by Miss Thorndike, who had access to the composition paper and a motive for attacking both young women."

Annie stopped and waited as Russell looked at the material in front of him. He pushed irritably at the shock of hair that fell into his eyes, and he suddenly looked quite ill. She had gotten so caught up in the struggle to get Della Thorndike to expose herself, she'd ignored how personally devastating this all was going to be for Russell. She was asking him to accept that a close friend and trusted colleague had been the one to cause him and the woman he loved so much pain. She started to tell him how sorry she was to be the one to break this news to him, when she felt a hand grip her shoulder and wrench her away from the table.

"Andrew, give me those papers!" Della shrieked. She let Annie go and pushed towards the table, reaching out for the documents on it. Russell turned and grabbed Della by the upper arms, holding her off as Annie darted forward and scooped up the folder and the notes and held them to her chest.

Della struggled, trying to break away from Russell. "Andrew, let me go. You don't understand; I must have those papers. It would be the ruin of both of us. Get them from her." A strand of Della's hair slipped down into her face, and her mouth distorted in anger.

Russell continued to hold her at arm's-length, giving her a little shake. "Why did you write those notes to Hattie? How could you do that to her?"

"How could I do that to *her*? What about *me*? I've done everything for *you*, sacrificed everything for *you*. You were the one who said that people such as ourselves were married to our professions, to our callings. I was content to watch you progress in your career, basking in the knowledge that I had done my part to smooth your way. Then that Hattie Wilks waltzed in, and all your principles went out the window, leaving me with nothing."

Della's eyes filled with tears, and after a moment Russell let his hands drop. With sadness, he replied, "Oh, Della. I know what a good friend you have been to me. I did mean it when I told you I didn't expect to marry. But I fell in love with Hattie. I didn't plan it. It just happened."

"Oh, my dear, Andrew. I know you didn't plan it." Della wiped her tears and rested her hands gently on his chest. "You're such an innocent. As soon as I heard you had agreed to marry her, I went to plead with her not to ruin your career. But then I saw she had seduced you, and I understood how clever she'd been."

Russell stiffened and in a tight voice said, "What do you mean, seduced me?"

"Well, I suppose the child might not have been yours. When I suggested as much, she got quite indignant. *Little whore.* She became so upset that I almost believed her. But no matter; it all worked out all right in the end."

Annie's skin crawled as she watched Della throw her head back with an arrogant little smile. *This must be what Hattie meant when she told Laura that her fall was 'no accident' and that she was 'pushed,'* she thought. And here was Della, practically admitting she was the one who had pushed her.

Russell looked like he had been hit with a sledgehammer. When Della tried to tuck her arm through his, he pushed her away violently and said, "Don't you touch me. What do you mean, everything 'worked out'?

Hattie died. And you are telling me now that she died carrying my child? Did you kill her?"

"Oh Andrew, don't be so dramatic. It was an accident; she slipped. It wasn't my fault. Besides, I don't think that anyone is going to want to reveal that little 'Miss Perfect' was pregnant when she died. Even that obnoxious friend of Miss Wilks, Laura Dawson, wouldn't want that."

Putting her hand out to pat his arm, Della said, "So now, we just need to convince Mrs. Fuller to hand over the documents, and we can go about our business."

Russell looked at her with horror, plucking Della's hand from his arm as if it were a noxious insect. "'Go about our business.' You must be mad! There is no 'we.' There never was, and there never will be. You killed the only woman I will ever love. I never want to see you again as long as I live. "

As Russell started to walk away, Della's eyes widened, and another one of those chillingly arrogant smiles appeared. Before Annie could register what was happening, Della had reached out and grabbed one of the glass beakers on the table beside her and swung it in an arc towards Russell's head. Annie's cry gave him an instant's warning, and the glass shattered over the hand he put up in defense. Annie started towards Russell, but Della launched herself at her back, bringing the two of them toppling to the ground. Annie felt a sharp pain in her left hand when she landed on the glass-covered floor. She tried to scramble to her knees, but the weight of Della sprawled on her back kept her from rising.

In moments, the weight was lifted. As she struggled to rise, Thomas Hoffmann appeared beside her and helped her to her feet. She saw that Emory was trying to staunch the blood coming from multiple cuts on Russell's hand, while Peter Blaine held a weakly struggling Della in a crushing embrace.

Blaine gave her a wide smile and said, "Gracious me, Mrs. Fuller, that was well done. I'm not sure I could have handled it better myself. But do let Hoffmann take you home. I think Emory and I can take care of things from here on."

Chapter Forty-three
Early Saturday evening, February 14, 1880
"It has been a few years since nothing was to be had in Valentines but the vulgar, comic, or tawdry tinsel and lace-paper affairs of foreign manufacture."
—*San Francisco Chronicle*, 1881

"That should do it," Mrs. O'Rourke said, putting the last strip of sticking plaster on the gauze bandage that covered the two small cuts on Annie's left hand. "And now my dear, let Kathleen fix your hair. I have to go down and see if Mrs. Hewitt and Miss Laura have returned with the promised fish for supper."

As the bedroom door closed behind Beatrice, Annie gave Kathleen a broad smile and said, "I can't believe that she didn't scold me more."

Kathleen laughed. "Yes, ma'am. But if she ever gets a chance to meet that Mr. Blaine, he's in for a tongue lashing for sure. She was that upset to learn a tough Irishman let a lady do his dirty work for him."

"I'm just glad it is all over and that I could help. I don't relish telling Laura what I learned about her friend's death. Or how wrong she was about Andrew Russell." Annie sighed and closed her eyes, letting Kathleen brush out her hair and re-pin it. She hoped that Nate would get here soon so they could tell Laura together.

After finishing with Annie's hair, Kathleen took the brown polonaise down to the kitchen to clean, deploring the spots of blood she found on the skirt. Finally alone, Annie stood and checked herself in the mirror over the mantel. She'd put on her good navy, which, apart from the new dress she wore to the theater, was still her best dress. She smoothed down the Basque-styled bodice that fit snugly over her hips and turned around to make sure the heavily draped silk folds of the overskirt were secured tightly to the back of the bodice. She saw that Kathleen had newly starched the lace at her collar so that it stood up to frame her face, which looked very pale and tired. She pinched her cheeks a little, but that simply reminded her of Della, and she turned away, pulling the lace at her wrists down to see if it would cover the bandage. It didn't.

Looking impatiently at the clock that said it was only fifteen minutes after five o'clock, she sighed. The time between Della's and Russell's entrance to the Chemistry lab and Della's vicious attack had been less than a half hour, but Annie felt as if she had been engaged in a form of mental combat for hours. At the time, she'd been carried along by sheer nerves. Now, several hours later, she was exhausted. She wanted Nate to be here. She wanted to tell him everything that had happened, even the things she had withheld from Beatrice and Kathleen. She wanted him to take her in his arms and reassure her that what she had done this afternoon was necessary, even if it meant adding to Andrew Russell's already considerable pain.

She took the small vase of Nate's violets off the mantel and smelled their sweetness. Then she wandered over to the table and picked up the valentine she had made for him. She'd worked on it off and over the past few days, enjoying fashioning the hearts out of red paper and arranging them with bits of ribbon on top of the white card stock. On the blank side, she had copied out a poem by Charlotte Richardson, a writer unknown to Annie but good enough to have been included in one of Laura's literature text books:

> Custom, whose laws we all allow,
> And bow before his shrine,
> Has so ordained, my friend, that you
> Are now my Valentine.

Annie felt the verse, while certainly conveying her affection, was safe. Something she could send a very good friend without embarrassing either the recipient or herself.

Safe, but do I want safe? Annie put the valentine down in irritation.

Listening to Della talk about sacrificing herself for Russell had started up the fearful old refrain she had been playing in her head since her husband's death—the one that said she would never sacrifice her happiness or her independence for another man ever again. But she was tired of that tune.

And Nate wasn't John, as he demonstrated over and over. She remembered the look on his face this afternoon as he said good-bye. She could tell he wanted with every fiber of his being to demand that he go with her to Girls' High in order to ensure her safety. But he hadn't. He'd let her go, not knowing what kind of danger she was going into. Although she doubted any of them had really imagined the level of Della Thorndike's insanity, which had apparently already contributed to the death of one woman.

She shivered, thinking about Andrew Russell. His initial grief would now be compounded by the knowledge he had lost both Hattie *and* his unborn child. Yet she kept thinking about the sentiment expressed by Tennyson, "'Tis better to have loved and lost than never to have loved at all." And wasn't that true? Wasn't that why, after her talk with Beatrice, that she had finally decided that she was willing to risk future miscarriages in order to have a chance of producing a child of her own?

And who else did she want that child with but Nate? If so, why was she hesitating? She picked up the valentine and added a line under the verse before she could change her mind, and she went downstairs to wait.

"She sounds completely insane!" Nate said, when Annie completed her recitation of the afternoon's events. They were sitting in the small parlor where she'd been waiting for him. Cranston had finally let him leave around five, telling him with some disgust that he might as well go since his mind wasn't on the work. Sprinting down to Market, he'd caught a cab, not caring about the expense, and was at Annie's door in under fifteen minutes.

"I have never seen the like," she replied. "And at the end, Della showed no remorse. She seemed to have no comprehension that her actions were criminal and no real fear of the consequences."

"But you said she cried."

"Yes, but in some ways that was even worse. She turned the tears on and off like a faucet. One minute she was arrogantly sparring with me, apparently confident that no one could prove her wrong-doing; the next minute she was trying to win Russell's sympathy through tears. Then, without warning, she turned into some feral animal."

Nate took Annie's bandaged left hand in his and brought it up to his lips, kissing it gently. "And you are sure the cuts aren't too deep, and I shouldn't take you to Mitchell to stitch you up?"

She smiled at him. "No, I am fine, and you can be sure that Beatrice would have insisted I get medical attention if she thought I needed it."

"What is going to happen next, do you think?" Nate wondered if he needed to schedule an appointment with Emory for Monday, trying to figure out how to fit this in with the trial.

"I'm not entirely sure. Mr. Blaine hustled Hoffmann and me out of there pretty quickly. I don't think he or Emory wanted witnesses to what happened next."

"Annie, you don't think they were going to do violence to her?"

"Oh my, no. Blaine was being quite gentle with her, once she calmed down. No, from what he and Emory were saying to Russell, I think they are going to try to have this treated as a medical problem. There was mention of Dr. George Shurtleff, who's the director of the recently opened Napa Asylum for the Insane."

"Ah," Nate said, his mind searching for what he knew about the legal process of commitment. "They will need to get a judge's order and two witnesses. That should be easy for such well-connected men to arrange. Does she have any relatives that you know of who might object?"

"I don't think so, at least not in the West. I keep telling myself she is, in fact, insane. She probably pushed Hattie down the stairs or, if it really was an accident, it appears she was there and left poor Hattie alone to bleed to death. And something she said made me wonder if she hadn't planned on targeting Laura next with her slander. Yet I am still uneasy with the idea that she won't get a trial."

Annie's voice quavered, and Nate once again regretted ever getting her involved in this investigation. He said, "Consider this, Annie. If her case came to trial, she would get what she wanted, the ruination of everyone she saw as standing in her way." Nate paused, then continued, "And, if she can be as charming as you describe her, without a speck of moral conscience, a jury might find her not guilty, and she would go on ruining other people's lives."

Annie nodded, but he could see she was still bothered. He added, "I will talk to Emory. Make sure that they get a legitimate medical evaluation for her."

Her smile was a gift, and he leaned in and kissed her.

He heard some voices coming up the back stairs from the kitchen and said, "I wonder if that is Laura. I am surprised they stayed out so late. Maybe we can postpone telling her what happened until after she's eaten."

Annie stood up, and so he rose, noticing for the first time that she'd been holding something in her lap. Oddly, he could see that the card, which was clearly a valentine, trembled as she handed it over to him.

She whispered, "It's home-made. I don't know that I ever made one before, so you should feel honored. I just wanted you to have it before…"

"Ma'am, sir, something terrible's happened." Kathleen burst into the parlor, trailed by Patrick McGee and her youngest brother, Ian. Pushing the young boy in front of her, she said, "Ian, tell 'em what you told me."

Then, not giving the out-of-breath boy a chance to start, she went on. "He says some rough sailor grabbed Jamie and dragged him on board a ship at Meiggs Wharf. When Ian tried to follow them, some other man threatened him with a knife, so he went and got Mrs. Hewitt and Miss Laura. They were just down the dock. Mrs. Hewitt told him to run get a copper and then come get you. Ian says he told the first patrolman he saw but that they didn't believe him. So he ran right here. Oh, ma'am, why ever would anyone try to kidnap our Jamie!"

Chapter Forty-four
Saturday evening, February 14, 1880

"I asked a policeman to get me back my child. But he said he was my husband, and that child was his. The policeman asked me was he my husband, and was the child his? and I answered yes. The policeman shook his head and walked away."—Her Child's Cry, *San Francisco Chronicle* 1879

Laura groaned. The crushing panic that always accompanied her nightmare about Buck's attack began to recede. Then fear came flooding back when she realized she wasn't in her own bed. Instead of a smooth pillow, a hard wooden surface bruised her face. Her hands and arms weren't caught in bedclothes but were tied in some fashion behind her back. Her mouth was stuffed with some vile tasting cloth, and for a moment the returning panic kept her from breathing. She painfully turned her aching head to the side, making it easier to get air, and worked to take in slow, calming breaths. All she could see were a few square inches of rough wood that kept brightening and darkening from a wavering light source. She wanted badly to sit up, but the memories that trickled back suggested caution.

First, there was the memory of taking the North Beach horse car to Meiggs Wharf this afternoon with Barbara Hewitt, Jamie, and Ian. Then she remembered Barbara negotiating for some salmon with an Italian fisherman who'd just tied up his single-masted felucca at the dock. That was when Kathleen's brother Ian came running up and yelled that some man had grabbed Jamie. "Some sailor," Ian had said. There were tears running down through a cut on his cheek.

She next remembered that Ian had dragged them to the *Pacific Consort,* a three-masted ship docked at the wharf, and said that was where Jamie had been taken. During the afternoon, there had been a constant stream of men boarding the ship, carrying bags, barrels, and crates into the hold. But the ship now looked deserted. They had sent Ian to get help, and then she and Barbara had crept on board in the failing light of sunset, desperate to find Jamie. And then someone had hit her over the head. *How long have I been unconscious?*

She must still be onboard the ship since she could hear the sounds of creaking boards and feel the up and down motion of waves. She only hoped to heaven the ship was still tied to the dock rather than heading out to the ocean through the Golden Gate. *If only I could see more,* she thought.

Then there was a sound of wood scraping against wood. She heard Jamie shouting from somewhere close by, "Stop hurting her! Stop it!"

A man replied angrily, "God-damn it, boy, I'll kill her if you don't shut your trap."

It sounded like the man who'd assaulted her in the alley. *Buck?*

Laura frantically rolled herself onto her left side. Using her shoulder, she pushed herself into a sitting position, feeling one of the seams in her bodice rip. What she saw was worse than any nightmare. Towering all around her were pyramids of barrels and crates badly illuminated by a swinging lantern. At the center of these pyramids stood a tall, roughly dressed stranger who was struggling with Jamie. Although the man was only a few feet from her, she could barely make out his face. He wore a cap pulled down to his eyes, and a dark brown beard and mustache surrounded a snarling mouth. But he was definitely *not* Buck.

Jamie came staggering in her direction, cuffed aside by the man, and he stumbled down beside her. She tried to say his name, and Jamie started to take the gag out of her mouth.

This caused the man to brandish a long knife as he said, "Leave the bitch be. I'll slice her, boy, and your mother, if you don't sit down and behave yourself."

Jamie kneeled close, putting his arm around her, and Laura could feel his slight frame tremble. They watched together as the man turned back to where Barbara was sitting, huddled next to one of the tall stacks of barrels. Jamie's mother also had her hands tied behind her back, but there was no gag. Her hat was gone, and her dark hair hung in loops, the pins having given way. Blood trickled down one side of her face.

The man crouched down, pulled Barbara Hewitt's head back, and hissed at her. "The lovely Linda, did you think I wouldn't find you? Don't look so lovely now. You know, I didn't much care that you left. I was tired of you anyway. But you took my boy, my Robbie. You took what's mine. And that I'll never forgive."

Jamie stirred beside Laura and said, "Look, mister. I think you've gotten mixed up. That's my mother and she's Barbara, Barbara Hewitt. And my name's Jamie, not Robbie. I'm awful sorry you lost your little boy, but I'm not him."

The man cursed and put the point of the knife up against Barbara's neck, saying, "You tell him or I'll cut you. Maybe slice off that pretty little ear. Tell him the truth. Tell him I'm his pa. And his real name is Robert James Norman, and your name is Linda, Mrs. Bobby Norman. Will be until the day you die."

Laura felt she'd gone down the rabbit hole like Alice in Wonderland.

"Bobby, stop it, you're scaring him," Barbara whispered. "Just tell me what you want."

"I want you to tell him! Tell him how you stole him away from me when he was just a tyke. Just three. He was the only good thing that ever happened to me after the war. My little good luck charm. And you stole him. Never had a day's luck since. *You tell him.*"

Laura saw Barbara lock eyes with Jamie and give the tiniest of nods as tears ran down her face. Jamie sobbed.

The man, Bobby, looked satisfied and sat back on his heels, taking the knife away from Barbara's neck. He remarked in a conversational tone that was oddly chilling, "So, now we have that settled, this is what's going to happen. I'd sort of hoped that Robbie here would've recognized me and been willing to come along without setting up a squawk. And I didn't plan on the two of you creeping on board. But turns out this might be for the best."

Another man stepped into the light, sending Laura's pulse racing even faster. This was the man Barbara and she had encountered as they crept through the darkness of the top deck. They'd just finished peeking into the empty kitchen at the center of the boat and were looking down a ladder that led below when the man showed up beside them. The smell of liquor poured off of him, and he'd seemed to be swaying more than the gentle rocking of the waves warranted. He held up a lantern and said, "If you wanna see the boy, he's down there," pointing into the hold. They'd climbed down as directed, but Laura had only taken two steps towards a narrow passageway when the blow to her head came and she lost consciousness.

"All ship-shape above board?" Bobby asked.

The man simply nodded, then he said, "Look mate, there's no telling when the captain's gonna come back. Gotta get this squared away soon."

Bobby frowned. "Don't you worry. You just do what you're paid to do. Go on up and keep watch."

When the man left, disappearing into the darkness past the lantern light, Bobby stood up and dragged Barbara to her feet. "Now here's the plan. Robbie, son, you are going to come with me. We're going to go on a trip. I got my eye on a nice little cattle ranch over in Wyoming."

He turned to Barbara and said, "Funny thing. Two years ago when I was there, ran into Jack Hewitt, the *real* Barbara Hewitt's little brother. Told me this story about how his younger sister's family moved out from Kansas to Nevada the year after their older sister died and how this schoolmarm who traveled with them took the dead sister's name. Told me about it because he'd remembered that the woman's name was Norman, same as mine. Wondered if I might know her. I've been searching ever since, looking for you and Robbie. Took awhile, but I always knew I'd find you."

Jamie spoke up, his fists clenched. "Mister, I'm not going anywhere without my mother."

"God-damn it, boy, don't you talk back." Bobby's eyes narrowed, and he pointed the knife at Jamie. "You will come with me, because I'm going to leave your mother and her friend tied up in the hold under Lenny's sweet attentions. Ship's taking off in the morning, that's why everyone is on shore tonight, and first port of call is San Diego. If Lenny finds a letter there from me saying you were a good boy and we got away nice and clean, he'll let them go. If not, he'll slit their throats and drop them overboard. So, unless you want that to happen, you'll come with me quiet and respectful-like."

Nate instructed Annie, "You and Ian go back up the dock to that tall building at the end where there should be some sort of wharf master, night watchman, or something. Let them know what's happening." He looked up towards the deck of the ship, the *Pacific Consort*. "Patrick and I will try to figure out how to get on board."

He had tried to get Annie to stay at home since she'd already been through so much today, but she'd insisted on coming. The two of them, plus Ian, took the first hansom cab they found on Taylor. Patrick followed behind in a separate cab so he could detour past the northern district police station to report in. He'd come running up behind them as they stood looking up at the ship, trying to figure what to do. The whole ride here, Annie'd held Ian tightly, quieting his fears while eliciting as much information as she could. She was clearly trying to figure out if the man was Buck, maybe snatching Jamie in order to lure Laura to some secluded place, but Ian hadn't been able to describe the man in enough detail for them to be sure of anything.

Nate had hoped that when they got to the wharf they would find all three safely back on shore. But the long pier that ran straight out into the Bay was dark and empty, except for a few lanterns scattered along the short dock that jutted out from the pier and paralleled the shore. They could see there were a few fishermen still securing their boats on the shore side of that dock but no sign of Barbara, Jamie, or Laura. Even though the sun had just set, there was enough ambient light to help them pick their way to the apparently deserted three-masted ship that was up on the outer Bay side. Nate saw there was a lantern near the *Pacific*

Consort gangway, providing enough light so that they could see the gangplank was pulled in. But that was all he could see. There wasn't a glimmer of light from any of the port holes along the upper deck. If anyone was on the ship, they must be below. The hairs along the back of his neck rose at an image of Laura being assaulted in some dark hold at the bottom of the ship.

"Annie, please go. There's nothing you or Ian can do here, and it may be that some dock official can help," Nate said. "See if you can get a lantern. Soon there won't be any light to see by."

Once she and Ian were on their way back to shore, Nate turned to Patrick and said, "Any idea of how we get on board?" The *Pacific Consort* was at least six feet from the dock, and while there were ropes between the dock and the ship, they led to small port holes that weren't big enough for either of them to squeeze through. Besides, he would need to be a tight-rope walker to use the ropes to board. Ian might have been able to manage it, but the boy had carried too heavy a load this day already.

Patrick said, "Sir, let me see what help I can get from one of the fishermen." He walked toward the small ring of lanterns that had sprung up as a knot of Italians had gathered to comment in their own language about the strangers on their dock. Still dressed in his blue police uniform with the seven-point star prominently displayed on his left breast, Patrick spoke softly with the assembled men who seemed to be nodding and gesticulating. When he rejoined Nate, he brought a small, wiry man with him. The man doffed his cap politely to Nate then leaped agilely onto one of the mooring ropes. Using both hands and feet, he swarmed up the rope to a porthole and stood on the lip of the hole to pull himself on board. A moment later, they heard a scrape and rattle as he pushed the gangplank forward and down to connect to the dock. Nate extracted a banknote from his wallet and gave it to the man as he came down to the dock. Another man appeared at their side and offered a lantern, whispering, "Buona fortuna."

*****

Laura watched helplessly as Jamie argued with the man. *His father.* If only she wasn't gagged and could say something that might calm the boy down and get him to see that this was not a man to be reasoned with. *But how would he know?* The men he knew, David Chapman who took him to fly kites, her brother who always had hard candy in his pockets to give him, and Patrick who took him and Ian on excursions, were all gentle men. *But Barbara knew.* Laura could tell by the terror in her eyes as she pleaded with Jamie to do as his father demanded. Barbara knew and had protected Jamie by changing their names and trying to put half a continent between her boy and his father.

"You little spoiled brat. I don't give a damn what you want. You're mine, and I'm going teach you how to obey your pa." Bobby Norman held Jamie by the scruff of the neck, his fury visible in the bulging veins on either side of his neck. He then shifted to a high, mincing voice, saying, "'Don't touch the baby. He's delicate. Don't give the boy a beating. He didn't mean to wake you.' Stupid woman, coddling you and turning you against me." He then jerked Jamie closer, slapped him hard, and pushed him towards Barbara.

Jamie ran to his mother and wrapped his arms around her. His father looked over at the two of them in disgust, then in two strides he was at Laura's side. She struggled to shift away from him as she heard him say, "God damn it, boy. If you don't believe me, how about I just slit this bitch's throat and throw her overboard now? She wasn't part of my plan anyway. Then you might believe me when I say that if you don't do what I want, I'll kill your mother."

As he pulled Laura upright, she heard Barbara scream, but the knife in Bobby's hand was all she could see. He moved the knife towards her neck, and she tried to twist away. Then she heard someone shout her name, and Bobby let go of his grip on her. She slid back down into a sitting position. When she looked up, she saw that Seth Timmons had appeared out of nowhere and was struggling with Bobby, trying to get his knife. The two men were so alike in size, and so ferocious was their battle for control, that she couldn't follow whose fist punched whose face as they ricocheted around the small confined space.

Finally, when their bodies slammed into a column of crates that tumbled on top of them, they separated, panting. Seth pulled his gun out of his holster and pointed it at Bobby, saying, "It's over. Put down the knife."

Bobby cursed, leaned over, and grabbed Jamie from where he cowered with his mother, putting his knife to the boy's throat. He snarled out, "If I can't have my boy here on earth, I'll take him to hell with me. Go ahead and shoot, and I'll slit his throat before the bullet leaves your gun."

Time froze, and Laura watched Seth calculate the risks. Bobby, his eyes dead calm, held Jamie square in front of him with the knife pointed a hair's breath away from the boy's jugular. As the seconds ticked by, Bobby smiled and said, "I didn't think so. I could tell you're not the kind to chance killing the boy to save yourself. Put the gun down and slide it towards me."

Seth slowly crouched down, put the gun on the floor, and slid it across, never taking his eyes off of Bobby and Jamie. Laura tried to scream, the noise coming out around the gag as a moan. Seth glanced over at her just long enough for Bobby to push Jamie aside, swoop down and grab the gun, and come up shooting. Seth clutched at his side as he stumbled back and then fell. Laura tried to get up so she could go to him, but Bobby knocked her aside and casually walked over to where Seth lay, pointing the gun at his head. With horror, Laura saw him start to cock the hammer when from somewhere in the dark came the sound of a second gunshot. Bobby Norman jerked back and then slowly toppled to the ground. Out of that darkness came her brother and Patrick McGee, his revolver still smoking.

Chapter Forty-five
Late Saturday evening, February 14, 1880

"Wry Fate denies me joy,
But Venus' boy
Still strings my heart-strings to his bow:
The thrill whene'er his arrows go,
O Fate, how can I view thee?
O Love, how still pursue thee?"
—*Love and Fate*, by anonymous, *A Masque of Poets*, 1878

Laura sat alongside Seth's hospital bed and waited for him to open his eyes. His skin was pale, his dark curved mustache providing a stark contrast. She couldn't help but remember Hattie lying in this same hospital just a month ago with, as far as she could tell, the same black-robed Sister of Mercy sitting quietly in the corner. The sister had assured her that Seth would be fine, that the bullet had only nicked a rib and exited cleanly, and that he would be released in the morning. But when Nate tried to get her to leave, she'd insisted on staying until Seth woke. She wanted him to know she hadn't abandoned him.

Annie, who'd followed them to St. Mary's after safely depositing Barbara and the two boys at home, had brought a shawl for her. She'd had the foresight to predict that Laura wouldn't want to keep her brown coat on, soaked as it was in Seth's blood. Such a clever, thoughtful friend. Laura wrapped the shawl more tightly around herself, wincing from the pain in her shoulders caused by having had her hands tied behind her back for so long. She looked down at her wrists, thankful that there didn't seem to be anything but bruises, and they could be hidden under the decorative ruffles on her cuffs.

"Miss Dawson?" The words were hesitant, slightly slurred, but Seth looked alert as he used his right arm to push himself up to a sitting position. He also grimaced, so she knew he was in pain.

"I believe that you called me Laura earlier tonight, a familiarity that seems warranted, given that you saved my life, Mr. Timmons." Laura smiled and pulled her chair closer.

He reached over and gently touched the side of her mouth. "You're all right? He...who was he? What did he want with you?"

Laura told him briefly about Bobby Norman, Barbara's abusive husband, and his determination to take his son away, and his threats to kill both of them if Jamie didn't cooperate. She said, "He was the man who attacked me in the alley. I recognized his voice, so it wasn't Buck."

Seth nodded. "No chance of running into Buck any time soon, in any event. I tracked down his uncle this afternoon. That's why I was in North Beach. His uncle sent Buck home two days ago in disgrace for stealing from his uncle's cash box."

Laura thought how strange that Buck now seemed like such a harmless boy in comparison to Bobby Norman. She then asked, "How did you know we were on the ship? Nate said you weren't with him and Patrick."

Seth looked away. Then he smoothed his mustache and looked steadily into her eyes. "I was passing by Meiggs Wharf on the way home from seeing Buck's uncle and noticed the boys...recognized them from Woodward's Gardens. Thought you would want to know about Buck, so I just hung out near the entrance, waiting for a chance to speak to you."

Laura, remembering their last encounter, could understand his reluctance to approach her. She said, "And you saw Jamie get pulled onto the ship?"

"No, I missed that. I did see the other boy running off towards town and you and the other woman going on board the ship, which seemed odd. So I waited. I could see there was a sailor hanging about on the gangway. That would be normal if most of the crew were on shore leave, but when he pulled up the gangplank and disappeared from sight, I got worried. I spent a year on a China clipper, so I knew how to get aboard. When I ran into the sailor I'd seen and he wouldn't tell me where you were, I put him out of commission. But it took some time to search the decks and find you. I'm truly sorry I took so long."

"Better late than never," Laura said, then felt enormously stupid. *What do you say to a man who saved you from having your throat slit?*

"That man, that policeman, was the real hero. He's a good friend of yours?" Seth asked her. "I thought I saw him with you at Woodward's Gardens."

"I wouldn't really call Patrick McGee a good friend," Laura said, not sure why that was important to establish. She continued. "I mean, he is Mrs. O'Rourke's nephew. You met her the other evening. She's Mrs. Fuller's cook and housekeeper. He's also courting Kathleen, who you met as well."

"He certainly saved my bacon. When you see him, tell him I owe him."

Laura thought of how much she owed Patrick as well.

Silence ensued. Seeing the lines on Seth's face deepen, Laura knew she shouldn't stay any longer. But there was one more task she needed to accomplish, since she didn't know when she would see him again. She repeated to him what Nate and Annie had told her earlier while Seth was in surgery, about Della Thorndike and the anonymous letters and the role the insane woman had played in Hattie's death.

The distress in Seth's grey eyes echoed her own feelings, so she said, "I know that this doesn't lessen the pain of losing Hattie…for either of us. But I thought it might help to know that Hattie's faith in Andrew Russell wasn't unwarranted. You were right, she *was* happy. I was selfish to question that happiness."

Laura took the edge of the shawl and blotted the tears that were falling despite her best intentions. *No wonder he thinks of me as a child. I'm either crying or having a temper tantrum.* She took a deep breath and said, "And I want you to know I appreciate that you felt bound by your promise to Hattie to look after me…although I'm sure she never thought you'd end up being shot in that service. I think that you've more than fulfilled your promise to her, so you are no longer under any obligation to…" She stopped, not really knowing what to say next.

Seth gently touched her bruised wrist, and she noticed how the back of his hand was criss-crossed by faint scar lines. She wondered if she would ever hear the stories about those scars, or his year on a China clipper ship, or what it was like to be a soldier in the war and survive Andersonville Prison.

Seth interrupted those thoughts with a chuckle. "I must say Miss Dawson...Laura, your first year of teaching has turned out a darn sight more eventful than our pedagogy teachers at San Jose predicted."

Laura laughed. "Well, thank you for helping me survive it all."

"Miss...Laura," Seth hesitated and withdrew his hand from hers. "I may have started out visiting you at Cupertino Creek school because of a promise to Miss Wilks, but in a short time it became my pleasure. I was hoping we might be able to take another buggy ride in the future."

Laura smiled and wondered what Hattie would have said about that.

"Laura took the news that Della Thorndike probably had a hand in Hattie's death better than I thought she would," Nate said to Annie as they walked down the hospital corridor to the alcove they'd found the last time they visited St. Mary's Hospital.

Annie leaned on his arm, her fatigue starting to overwhelm her. "Almost getting killed herself today may have put it all in a different perspective."

"I thought that would make it worse. But she was amazingly calm on the carriage ride over here, concentrating on trying to stop Timmons from bleeding. No hysteria, no tears. Then we tell her about Miss Thorndike, and she says, 'Well, that explains a good deal, doesn't it?'" Nate's voice was incredulous.

Annie sighed as she sat down on the alcove bench. "For good or ill, your little sister has had to do a lot of growing up these past few weeks. I think that what Laura feared the most was the idea that Hattie may have killed herself or deliberately tried to end her pregnancy. She's probably relieved to learn that Hattie was killed by someone else, whether deliberately or not. Most likely, though, she is just feeling numb. I would not be surprised if later on there isn't some sort of delayed emotional reaction to everything that has happened today."

"I just hope she doesn't do a complete turn-around and decide to fall in love with Timmons," Nate commented. "As is, I don't know what to tell my parents."

That made Annie laugh. Putting her hand on Nate's cheek, she said, "If she does, it won't be surprising. I can testify to how appealing a man can be who rescues you from a nasty ruffian with a knife."

Nate looked uncomfortable and then chuckled. "I certainly wasn't the hero today; that was Patrick."

"You should have seen the look on Kathleen's face when I told her about it." Annie smiled. "Proud doesn't begin to describe it. He's certainly going to get a hero's welcome when he returns to the boarding house. There aren't going to be any repercussions to him for killing Barbara's husband, are there?"

"Can't imagine there will be. First of all, he did report the kidnapping on the way to the wharf. And I will make it clear to the police when I give my testimony tomorrow that if Patrick hadn't fired when he did, Seth Timmons would be dead."

Annie shook her head. "Oh Nate, it must have been awful."

"The worst thing was not knowing who the man fighting with Seth was. You said his name was Bobby Norman? When we first came on the scene, Timmons and this Norman were fighting over a knife. Far as I knew, Seth could have been Laura's attacker and this other fellow was defending her."

"How did Patrick know to shoot Barbara's husband?"

"When Norman put the knife to Jamie's throat and then shot Timmons, it became pretty obvious that Norman was the aggressor. Then, when Laura tried to get to Timmons, and Norman kicked her aside and stood over Seth with the gun, I shouted, 'stop him' at Patrick, who already had his gun out, and he did."

Annie shivered, having trouble picturing Patrick, who always looked about twelve to her, killing someone. Thank goodness his Aunt Beatrice would know how to help him get his bearings.

Nate looked over at her and said, "How is Mrs. Hewitt? You couldn't get her to come to the hospital?"

"No. She insisted that she and Jamie were just bruised. She did have a cut on her scalp, but it seemed shallow. Beatrice and Kathleen will make sure that both of them get baths and hot milk and will tuck them up in bed. But they, like Laura, may need a lot of care over the coming months. Jamie in particular. Poor brave boy."

Nate took up Annie's hand and traced the lines on her palms. "Don't you wish you could really tell the future by looking at these lines? I was thinking about Barbara Hewitt. We were all so busy worrying about Laura's safety when it was she and Jamie who were really in danger. Laura told me as we rode to the hospital that Norman was definitely the man who attacked her in the alley. He must have thought she was Mrs. Hewitt, since Jamie was with her. They are of a similar height and build."

"The threatening letter that Barbara received might very well have come from her husband. That would explain why it was such a different style from the other anonymous notes." Annie shook her head sadly. "She must have spent all these years fearful that if the truth about her name came out that he would find her. And then her fears came true." Annie paused. "For her sake, I'm glad he's dead. Imagine the nightmare of trying to get a divorce from him and living in terror that he would get custody of Jamie."

"How could she have married such a man?" Nate said.

Annie shook her head again, the memories of her own bad choices flooding in. "She was young. Her parents had just died, and she was desperate. He might not have shown his violent side until after they married. I certainly didn't see that side to John until afterwards."

"Your husband hit you?" Nate's voice was tight with anger.

"Yes, but only once, and only after my father died. But he could be cruel in so many other ways that the physical pain was actually a relief," Annie said quietly, knowing Nate deserved to hear the truth. Somehow, just saying this made all the other secrets she'd been keeping, pointless.

She went on, saying quietly, "One of the worst things he did was hide from me the knowledge that my father was dying, so that I couldn't be with him at the end. I now think John was afraid I would convince my father to change the terms of his will so he wouldn't have control over my fortune. But, you see, what neither John nor my father knew is that I was pregnant, and when I got the terrible telegram telling me of my father's death, the shock was so great that I lost the child."

Annie felt Nate's arms surround her, and she sobbed for the poor young woman she'd been and for her lost child. After some time, as her crying abated, she heard him whisper, "I'm so very sorry, Annie. No wonder you are reluctant to put your trust in any man."

Annie pulled back in order to see his face clearly. He looked so sad that she couldn't bear it. "Oh Nate, that's not true any longer. What I have learned is that I just need to do a better job of choosing the right man to trust." She gave him a swift hug, noticing a crackling sound when she did so.

"Nate, the valentine I made you! Is it in your pocket?"

He looked surprised, putting his hand in his inner coat pocket and pulling out the rather crumpled card. "I guess I stuffed it there when Ian and Kathleen came to tell us about Jamie. And I never got to take you out to eat."

"Well you should read the card now. I worked awfully hard on it." She tried to make light of her request, but her heart began to thump painfully.

Nate complimented her on the hearts on the front of the card with an admirably straight face. Then he turned the card over and began to read the poem out loud in a self-conscious voice, until he got to the last line she had written, just this afternoon.

He looked at her, then back down, and finally he said the line out-loud, haltingly. "Dear Nate, if you ask me again, I will say yes."

So he did, and she did.

The End

Acknowledgements

I would like to express my appreciation to all the family and friends who gave their support during the writing of this book. As always, my beta readers have made this a better book than I could have achieved on my own, so thanks to my writer's group, Ann Elwood, Abigail Padgett, and Janice Steinberg; my Historical Fiction Authors Cooperative friends, V. R. Christensen, Iva Polansky, and Elisabeth Storrs; my fans, Pat Mc-Clintick, and Kilian Metcalf, and my friends Jim and Victoria Brown, Sally Hawkins, and Kathy Austin. I want to give special thanks to Misty Walker who found the images that went into the cover, and to Michelle Huffaker who continues to produce such wonderful covers, and to my editor, Jessica Meigs who has the eye for detail I lack.

Finally, this book, as always, wouldn't have been possible without the support of my loving husband Jim, my daughter Ashley, and her family, and my sister Alice Clark.

About the Author

M. Louisa Locke, a retired professor of U.S. and Women's History, has embarked on a second career as the author of novels and short stories set in Victorian San Francisco that are based on Dr. Locke's doctoral research on late 19th century working women. *Maids of Misfortune* and the sequel, *Uneasy Spirits,* are best-selling historical mysteries, and her short stories, *Dandy Detects* and *The Misses Moffet Mend a Marriage,* offer a glimpse into the lives of minor characters from the novels. This third book in the series, *Bloody Lessons*, features the teaching profession in 1880 San Francisco.

Locke is an active member of the Historical Fiction Authors Cooperative, and you can find more about her journey as an indie author and gain a deeper glimpse into the world of Victorian San Francisco, if you check out her website at http://mlouisalocke.com/ If you enjoyed *Bloody Lessons*, please let the author know at mlouisalocke@gmail.com and post a review.

Made in the USA
Lexington, KY
25 April 2014